# OLD M

---
❊
---

WOMEN'S HISTORY IN SHORT STORIES

Two companion volumes:

**OLD MAIDS**
*Short Stories by Nineteenth-Century US Women Writers*
Compiled and with an Introduction by Susan Koppelman

**DARING TO DREAM**
*Utopian Stories by United States Women: 1836-1919*
Compiled, edited and introduced with annotated bibliography
by Carol Farley Kessler

Editorial consultant: Annette Kolodny

**Old Maids**

**Susan Koppelman** grew up in Cleveland, Ohio, where she was educated in the public schools of Cleveland Heights by, among others, a number of dedicated, demanding, old-fashioned Old Maid schoolteachers; and in the religious school of Park Synagogue. She went to Barnard College, and returned to Cleveland after her father's death to graduate from Cleveland College of Western Reserve University. She has an MA from Ohio State and a PhD from Bowling Green State University. Memories of her high school English teachers Nettie Morris and Edith B. Malin got her through graduate school.

**Cover illustration and design** Marion Dalley.

P A N D O R A   P R E S S

# OLD MAIDS

*

## SHORT STORIES BY NINETEENTH CENTURY US WOMEN WRITERS

*Compiled and with an introduction by*
### SUSAN KOPPELMAN

# PANDORA PRESS

Boston, London, Melbourne and Henley

First published in 1984
by Pandora Press (Routledge & Kegan Paul plc)
9 Park Street, Boston, Mass. 02108, USA
39 Store Street, London WC1E 7DD, England
464 St Kilda Road, Melbourne,
Victoria 3004, Australia and
Broadway House, Newtown Road,
Henley-on-Thames, Oxon RG9 1EN, England

Set in Sabon by Columns of Reading
and printed in Great Britain
by Cox & Wyman Ltd, Reading

Library of Congress Cataloging in Publication Data

Old maids.
Bibliography: p.
1. Single women – Fiction. 2. Short stories,
American – Women authors. 3. American fiction –
19th century. I. Koppelman, Susan.
PS648.S5304   1984   813'.01'08352042      83-24631

British Library CIP available

ISBN 0 86358 014 9

# CONTENTS

———— ✳ ————

# THIS WORK IS FOR:

Annette Kolodny, who fights my demons and encourages me to defeat them, and who asked for this book.

Joanna Russ, whose love and conversation sustain me, and who said, 'Today, not perfect!'

Emily Toth, whose wry wisdom, wild humor, and practical advice have kept me 'up' for more than a decade.

Dennis Mills, who has made this book possible in all the practical ways, and who takes me for rides in his Studebakers.

Edward Nathan Koppelman Cornillon, who quotes Chekhov, *The Seagull*, Act II, when I complain that it is hard to write, and who says that these stories are okay even if they are old.

Frances Bollotin Koppelman, my mother, my teacher, my friend. *Sine qua non.*

Helen Eisen, who has been my beloved companion in the reading and thinking about and loving women's stories.

Florence Luscomb, citizen extraordinaire, sister, inspiration to a new generation of women's rights activists, and friend.

This Consciousness that is aware
Of Neighbors and the Sun
Will be the one aware of Death
And that itself alone

Is traversing the interval
Experience between
And most profound experiment
Appointed unto Men –

How adequate unto itself
Its properties shall be
Itself unto itself and none
Shall make discovery

Adventure most unto itself
The Soul condemned to be –
Attended by a single Hound
Its own identity.

*Emily Dickinson*

# PREFACE

———————————— * ————————————

This book is the product of ten years of research on short stories written by women in the continental United States or territories that later became states. Late in 1972 I became a member of the English department committee at Bowling Green State University which had as its purpose the decision of whether all sophomore introduction to literature courses should use the same textbook(s) and, if so, which one(s). We were supplied eagerly by publishers' representatives with many many books for our consideration, both multi-generic and single genre, both thematic and historical, both national and international. I was responsible for examining, analyzing, and reporting on all the short story anthologies. Amazed by the unending sameness of the books – the same authors, the same stories over and over – I was appalled by the results of an analysis of the tables of contents. The anthologies, all of which had been published or reissued in new editions within the last five years, contained a preponderance of stories by writers who were white and male. Not only were women and non-whites *under*represented (there was an average of less than one woman for every seven men), but *mis*represented. Flannery O'Connor, Eudora Welty and Katherine Ann Porter formed a kind of holy trinity, usually to the exclusion of all other women writers. When women writers were represented in volumes that pretended to be historically representative there would be one women writer from the nineteenth century (either Sarah Orne Jewett or Mary Wilkins Freeman, but never both), one from the early twentieth century (either Edith Wharton or Willa Cather, or, if the collection was international, Katherine Mansfield), and between one and three from the late 1960s – most often Joyce Carol Oates. The only black woman included in any of these collections was Diane Oliver, already dead at a tragically early age.

I began to wonder what had happened to the women included in the anthologies I had used in high school and college in the 1950s. I re-examined those texts, rereading Mary McCarthy, Jean Stafford, Dorothy Canfield Fisher, Shirley Jackson and Caroline Gordon. They were as good as I remembered; they had not diminished in their power to move me; they had just disappeared from contemporary publications. Then I looked in the books that had belonged to my mother and her five sisters, all avid readers, in the 1920s and 1930s. There were Dorothy Parker, Katharine Brush, Ruth Suckow, Edna Ferber, Zona Gale, Fannie Hurst – still as powerful as they had been when my mother had read them to me when I was a little girl. Next I began to haunt used bookstores in Bowling Green, Toledo and Cleveland – especially Kay's Book and Magazine Supermarket where I had been buying books since my first solo trips after school to my daddy's office in the late 1940s – looking for old short story anthologies. I spent hours in the History of Education libraries at Bowling Green University and the University of Missouri, St Louis, after I moved in 1974. Clear back to the 1880s when the patterns that still prevail seem to have been established, women and non-white writers have been underrepresented and misrepresented. Women and non-white writers, when they have been included at all, have been consistently presented as among the most recent writers, except for a very few antiquated curiosities. And yet a careful study of the history of the short story genre makes it clear that women writers predominated in the early years of its development, creating the bulk of the stories written from the 1830s to the 1880s.

However, because each decade's women writers were replaced rather than supplemented by the women writers of the next decade, readers have been denied an historical perspective on women's fiction and, by extension, on United States fiction. Only the very earliest anthologies of stories from the *Atlantic Monthly* and *Lippincott's Magazine* in the late 1860s included equal numbers of male and female authors. I decided then to compile a collection of short stories that would recapture the historical reality.

I soon realized, none the less, that reading only short stories included in anthologies, almost all of which had been edited by and therefore reflected the preferences and predispositions of men, was insufficient to accomplish the work of recovery that I had embarked upon. I began to read in depth the individual women whose work I encountered in anthologies. As I began to use specialized bibliographies and literary histories to track down the women whose work hadn't been included in anthologies, I was excited to find how many other women had been writing; women of color, immigrant women, women whose politics were radical, whose religious ideas were unconventional, and women who weren't interested enough in men to make male characters central to the lives of the women in their stories. I was struck by the fact that the stories included in collections compiled by male editors dealt with themes and issues and types of characters not typical of women's writing.

One meets again and again in the work of women writers certain themes that are explored and embellished, analyzed, debated, celebrated and agonized over. Two scholars who have been particularly helpful in identifying and exploring these themes are Nina Baym in her *Woman's Fiction; A Guide to Novels By and About Women in America, 1820-1870* (Cornell University Press, Ithaca and London, 1978) and Annis Pratt in her *Archetypal Patterns in Women's Fiction* (Indiana University Press, Bloomington, 1981).

Some of these themes explore the dynamics of relationships between and among women, such as the emotionally laden ones between mothers and daughters, the sometimes supportive, sometimes competitive ones between sisters, the intense and often transforming ones between friends, and the painful and often self-reflecting ones between women who are both involved with the same man, whether at a different or the same time. The theme explored in this collection, the theme of the Old Maid, relates to and incorporates the other themes portraying significant relationships between and among women. In some stories, it seems as if once the issue of heterosexual romance and marriage is dealt with in some final way, the central female characters are ready to turn to the real business of life — whatever that turns out to be: earning a living, building a community, working for social change, teaching, creating art or literature, raising children — and to each other.

# ACKNOWLEDGMENTS

———————————— ✳ ————————————

Had it not been for the encouragement, enthusiasm, and emotional coddling by Annette Kolodny and Joanna Russ, none of the results of my research during the past decade would ever have been shared, as it begins with this book to be shared, except in letters to friends. Emily Toth, as always, provided brilliant insights into the material and great jokes about life. My correspondence with sister scholars, sister feminists, women engaged in the work of recovery, rediscovery, and redefinition has been a source of life for me during the last five years. I want to thank the following people for sharing ideas and materials that relate to the stories and the writers included in this book: Dr Carol Farley Kessler on Elizabeth Stuart Phelps; Dr Frances Foster on Frances Ellen Watkins Harper; Dr Nancy Walker on Mary E. Wilkins; and Dr Josephine Donovan on Rose Terry. In addition, I want to thank Dr Susan Sutton Smith for introducing me to Marion Harland's collection of stories *Handicapped* and Dr Mary Anne Ferguson for directing my attention to Alice Carey. For practical help, imaginative suggestions, and unfailing kindness, my debt to Barbara Lehocky, Head, Reference Services Division, the Thomas Jefferson Library, the University of Missouri, St Louis, is immeasurable. I also want to express my gratitude to Barbara Haber, Karen Morgan, and the staff of the Arthur and Elizabeth Schlesinger Library of Radcliffe College. Special thanks go to the historians Dr Susan Hartmann, Dr Nancy Cott, Dr Lee Chambers-Schiller and Dr Evelyn Hu-Dehart for sharing insights and information on the subject of unmarried nineteenth-century American women. I am appreciative of the help of Mary Ellen Movshin whose editorial skill was graciously offered and eagerly accepted and Professor Lois

Neville for emergency research assistance. Dr David Elliott's help on this project was indispensable.

Thank you to David Alpers, MD, and Ray Clouse, MD, for keeping me going these last seven years. And my gratitude to Philippa Brewster and Dale Spender of Routledge & Kegan Paul, new friends and editors extraordinaires.

And I want to thank my husband, Dennis Mills, and my son, Edward Nathan Koppelman Cornillon, for the patience with which they tolerated the invasion of every aspect of our family life by my work. Thank you, Dennis and Nathan, for your interest in and respect for this project, and for your kindness to me.

In April of 1972, Miss Florence H. Luscomb spoke in the basement of a small church in Bowling Green, Ohio to a group of about thirty people who had come to hear her lecture on 'Women: Serf to Citizen – or How Women Became Members of the Human Race.' Born in 1887, she was only 5 when her mother took her to hear Susan B. Anthony speak at a women's suffrage convention. Her career as an activist dedicated to the realization of the ideals of democracy began. A list of her involvements from women's suffrage, the American Civil Liberties Union, the National Association for the Advancement of Colored People, the Women's International League for Peace and Freedom, to the Anti-War movement would take more space than I have here. During the question and answer period following her talk, a student at the university asked Miss Luscomb if she had ever regretted all that she had sacrificed for the various causes in whose service she had spent her life. Miss Luscomb, in a very kind voice, asked her questioner what sacrifices she was referring to; she, herself, could think of none. The young woman looked a bit embarrassed for a minute and then said, 'I meant a husband and children.' Just then, the storm that had been threatening all day broke and the room was lit up with the eerie cold light of nearby lightening. Miss Luscomb drew herself up even straighter than was her usual wont and said, with eyes flashing, 'I have sacrificed nothing. I consider myself privileged to have been able to spend my life in service of the greatest cause of all: human freedom.' And the thunder rolled.

I began to think about the lives of women who never married on that day.

Four years later Miss Luscomb came to St Louis and stayed

in my home for two weeks while she spoke at fourteen institutions of higher education and – to accommodate my almost 8-year-old son – one elementary school. Once again I listened as she spoke of the great struggles she had participated in during her long life and once again I heard over and over the words 'fortunate' and 'privileged' when she spoke of her life.

She conveyed to me a sense of life so full, so rich, so vital, so impassioned, and so deeply rooted in conviction, dedication, and a sense of responsible involvement in the world shared with all the brothers and sisters, all the children and grandchildren, all the people who, past and future, share in the life of this planet that I couldn't help remembering the question I'd heard put to her four years earlier and I understood its irrelevance in a new way. And the idea for this book began to grow. I want to acknowledge that Florence Luscomb and the life she has lived have been the real inspiration for this book.

# INTRODUCTION

———————— * ————————

I like each of these stories. Each moves me in its own way; the women portrayed seem real to me, my sisters in one way or another. These stories open outward, leading me to knowledge of experience not my own, and yet, having read the stories and thought about them, now my own.

These stories defend unmarried women from cruel, demeaning and limiting stereotypes that are still used to frighten and coerce women. They appeared first in a variety of popular periodicals, mostly directed to a middle-class, white, female audience over a period of many decades, in contexts that otherwise supported the roles of wife and mother as the proper and best destiny of the adult women. Read all together, they present a powerful argument in favor of autonomy for women.

Most of these stories are *very nice* stories and therefore could be criticized for glossing over some of the complexity – and some of the pain – which was associated with being a single woman. There are, for example, no free love advocates, no lesbians, no dedicated artists, no victims of sexual assault or physical coercion among these single women, although such women did exist and make known their ideas and experiences during the nineteenth century. Rather, in many of the stories, the old maid is presented as more pure, more pious, more modest than other women; she is even seen as more maternal than women who marry and have children. This presentation of old maidism as possessing the attributes of the cultural ideal of 'true womanhood'[1] provides some indication of the context in which these stories were written – and the model of women with which unmarried women had to contend.

These stories are about women who were not only unmarried during all of their adult lives – or who married at ages considered 'very late' – but women who lived in the United States during the nineteenth century. Each had to come to terms, in one way or another, with the opprobrious epithet 'old maid' and these stories depict those 'coming to terms' times in their lives. Other than this similarity, their lives were as different one from another as the lives of adult women living in the nineteenth century could be. They lived in different regions of the country. Some had to earn their own living, while others enjoyed inherited wealth. Some spent their lives at home, among people they had known and been known by all their lives; others travelled to distant cities where they made new lives for themselves. In some of the stories mention is made of the enormous social and technological changes of the nineteenth century; some seem almost timeless.

All the great reform movements of the nineteenth century, from temperance to abolition to trade unionism, from dress reform to religious reform, from health reform to legal reform, from religious evangelism to utopian communitarianism, all fueled the great engine of change. All fed into and were fed by the women's rights movement. Women learned to organize, to raise money, to control money, to speak publicly, to lobby, and to succeed, on local levels, on small issues, and on bigger and bigger issues and levels, to succeed in working for themselves.

The debates raged endlessly about what was right and wrong, what was intended by the 'Maker' or predestined by biology, what was fair, what was just, what was natural, what was profitable. United States periodicals were filled with endless debates and analyses of the meaning of these questions and these changes. Pulpits and public halls echoed with the arguments of all the sides in all the debates. And many of those debates continue into our own time.

The 'old maid' stories are part of the great debate referred to as The Woman Question, which might be stated as follows: Resolved – a woman's life shall belong to herself; her body, her time, her energy, her talents all belong to her; she is to consult first of all her own best interests – which she is to define – her own preferences, her own needs in making choices about the dispensation of these limited and personal commodities.

Many women have suffered and many women still suffer, great agony in trying to choose between a family and a career. Many women have felt that such a choice was necessary to 'do justice' to either. Many other women have suffered trying to have and 'do justice' to both. The deprivations inherent in any of the choices or absences of choice have been so obvious that one would hardly think it necessary for a great campaign to be mounted to persuade women to marry and raise children.

Nevertheless, such a campaign has been waged since the early nineteenth century. It often took the form of making the lot of the women who did not marry appear so loathsome, so ridiculous, so pathetic, so unnatural or unhealthy, so empty and cold, that no one would willingly choose such a life. The term 'old maid' came to represent an unattractive, malicious, prudish, petty, narrow, simpering, drab, gossipy, barren, shallow, trouble-making, envious, withered, characterless, bossy, snoopy, selfish, unsuccessful and impoverished woman. The unmarried woman was attacked and belittled in every aspect of her being: physical, emotional, intellectual, ethical. The pejorative quality of the stereotype was so taken for granted that spokesmen for the most liberal and enlightened causes and points of view felt no pressure to moderate their prejudices on this issue.

Writers confronted the stereotype and rejected it, as did this anonymous writer in *The Garland*, an 1830 gift book: 'The term "Old Maid" is, I know, by many considered synonymous with "envy, malice, and all uncharitableness," yet in the full consciousness of the odium of the title, I have deliberately assumed it. . . .'[2] In 'Single Sisters,' the English writer Mary Howitt, in the American literary annual *The Keepsake: A Christmas, New Year's and Birthday Present for 1845*, declared that 'It is among the most vulgar of errors to consider women useless because they are single. Only look round your acquaintance – who is the one universally useful, the one applied to it every time of difficulty and trial? The single sister of the family.'[3]

Early vindications of unmarried women most often took the form of declarations of their usefulness, claiming that these women made themselves valuable by their service to their extended families and did so in ways that were traditionally virtuous and womanly. The early writers ask that the virtue of single women be praised rather than that their persons be ridiculed or scorned.

These defenses make no distinction between the poor single woman and the wealthy woman. And, indeed, in the days before industrialization and other forces had succeeded in

3

putting an end to the self-sufficient rural family, the lives of unmarried women, wealthy or poor, were spent in pursuits relatively similar in that they were traditionally female and family-oriented.

However, as the century aged, the circumstances of life for poor single women changed, sometimes for the worse because they no longer even had homes more or less guaranteed by male relatives in exchange for endless work, whereas the world of the wealthy single woman had expanding opportunities for education, travel, and work chosen for its interest and satisfaction rather than out of grinding necessity. As Susan B. Anthony and Ida Husted Harper point out in their *History of Woman Suffrage*, 'The property rights of unmarried women always have been nearly the same as those of unmarried men.'[4] The life of a well-to-do and educated unmarried woman had an advantageous and desirable aspect with attractions that were increasingly noticeable. She was, indeed, autonomous. As if in recognition of the threat to the social order that such women represented, the popularizers of medical and religious theory proclaimed with increasing insistence that love − by which they meant marriage and motherhood − was necessary for a woman to be happy and, above all, healthy. A popular and highly acclaimed advice book for women declared that 'Love and marriage are the only normal conditions of life.'[5]

Reinforcing the pressure on women to marry was the increasingly sophisticated world of advertising. The whole world of commerce was oriented towards selling those goods that supported the advocated way of life, e.g., clothes sold in the new 'department stores,' clothing patterns included in ladies' magazines were for clothes that supported the philosophy of women's lives as feminine, ornamental and seductive, rather than clothes that supported a philosophy of living vigorous and independent lives (such as bloomers). (It has always been easier to buy clothes suited to and supportive of women's traditional roles than clothes appropriate for alternative life styles. The hems go up and down, but there are never enough big, usable pockets.)

The clothing worn during the nineteenth century by 'traditional' women encased the ribcage and upper abdomen painfully. Whalebone corsets were laced so tightly that women were often short of breath, faint, constricted and constrained in their movements. Women were made fragile, incapable and unhealthy by their clothes.

These stories are vindications of unmarried women. The earliest ones defend the single woman and place her in a respectable historical context. Later stories continue to defend and, in addition, make excuses for her condition. They also lay blame, if it is to be laid anywhere, elsewhere. They explain her life in ways which respond to the limiting preconceptions of others. They move to exploring the single woman's life from her own point of view, not as a defense against an attack, but as simple explication of what is there. These stories offer support to the woman whose life is lived outside the yoke of marriage; they provide sustenance. The final stories praise the single woman and her life of single blessedness.

The early stories present unmarried women who are so virtuous that the modern reader might find them almost without individuality or character. The primary thrust of the old-maid-as-exemplar stories is that if a woman is 'good' she will be a model of womanly goodness whether wife and mother or unmarried woman. The point is made repeatedly that it is not the circumstances of life, but the way in which the life is lived that renders a life worthy of praise or blame.

Women in either station, married or single, have equal opportunity to practice and to manifest successfully purity, piety, submissiveness, and domesticity – and equal opportunity to fail in their practice or manifestation of these virtues. And, incidentally, each woman is shown or reported as having had opportunities to marry which she rejected.

The single woman was vindicated in the early nineteenth-century stories in terms of her usefulness in the households of married women. But, while the writers of these old maid vindications were pointing out the usefulness of the unmarried woman and suggesting that the usefulness deserved recognition and respect, they were at the same time pointing out the need of the married couple for the services of the single woman. The typical marriage is presented in these stories as dependent on that competent and available single adult woman. These marriages, incapable of self-sufficiency, are presented as a type of parasite on the life of unmarried women – whether the single sisters who 'rescue' the family in a variety of crises, or succor and support the married woman after the loss of a husband through dissipation, defection or death which renders him unable to fulfill his husband's role.

The second group of stories — a smaller group — portrays single women in socially sanctioned female roles, but outside the home and not in the service of marriage.

The later stories clearly speak out against the social order in their protest against the personal, socially sanctioned and legal impositions that marriage makes on a woman. Sometimes the implication is that the right man would make marriage a heavenly state, but most men are clearly the wrong man. There is no suggestion that good sexual experience is desirable; rather, the imposition on a woman of an unloved or unloving, unrefined or impure man's sexual desires is something to be avoided. Such embraces are seen as deeply destructive of the woman forced to endure them. Even in the arms of a man she thought was deserving of her love, a woman is in danger. In these stories of old maids, married women frequently die in or become enfeebled by childbirth. In none of these stories does a sensually fulfilled woman appear. The point is made that old maids, unlike married women, belong to themselves: their bodies are their own.

Another way in which the lot of the single woman seems superior to that of the married woman is in the matter of satisfying human relationships. Single women have a wide variety of relationships available to them besides the marital one and they are freer than married women to cultivate those they choose. They may give priority to a relationship with a sister, a brother, a mother, orphan child, fellow boarder, or friend.

The writers of these stories do not overtly challenge that 'they' — the patriarchal hierarchy of religion, science and literature — have the right to establish the criteria by which women are to be judged. But they do demand that the criteria be applied strictly and equally, that all women be judged successful or failed, respectable or ridiculous, praiseworthy or blameworthy, admirable or pitiable, successful or not, in terms of the exact same standards. They want to be judged in terms of their demonstrations of virtues rather than by their relationships with men. Their submissiveness, of course, is their continued willingness to submit themselves to terms of judgment decreed by the patriarchy. If 'purity, piety, submissiveness and domesticity' are terms by which women are to be judged, then it is clear that a woman can be good, virtuous, useful, valuable, respectable, fulfilled, and valued without being married. Since a woman can choose to remain unmarried and still be 'good, etc.,' all women who find marriage, or those men available to marry, or the conditions of marriage, unacceptable may choose to remain single without social or spiritual sacrifice.

## NOTES

1 Barbara Welter, 'The Cult of True Womanhood: 1820-1860,' in *Dimity Convictions: The American Woman in the Nineteenth Century*, Athens, Ohio: Ohio University Press, 1976, p. 21.

2 Anonymous, 'Some Passages in the Life of an Old Maid,' in *The Garland for 1830*, New York: Josiah Drake, 1830, pp. 57-87.

3 Mary Howitt, 'Single Sisters,' in the *The Keepsake: A Christmas, New Year's and Birthday Present for 1845*, pp. 63-71 (p. 69).

4 Vol. IV, p. 455.

5 George H. Napheys, AM, MD, *The Physical Life of Woman: Advice to the Maiden, Wife, and Mother*, Philadelphia: George MacLean, 1870, pp. 39-40.

# OLD MAIDS

*

## Catharine Maria Sedgwick

'Old Maids' was originally published in the literary gift book The Offering, A Christmas and New Year's Present *published by Thomas T. Ash in 1834 in Philadelphia. Beginning with* The Atlantic Souvenir: A Christmas and New Year's Offering *for 1826, the literary gift book or annuals, so named because of their yearly publication, young American writers found a ready market for their stories, poems, and brief essays. These elaborately bound and lavishly illustrated volumes dominated the literary scene until the mid 1840s when periodical magazines began their rise to prominence.*

*Catharine Maria Sedgwick (1789-1867) is a significant figure in the history of American fiction. It was she, with her immensely respectable and impressive family connections, who legitimized the story that claimed no purpose other than to entertain. Nevertheless, when viewed from the perspective of feminist scholarship 150 years later, her stories seem to us more imbued with meaning than they did to contemporary critics.*

*In the first American literature textbook,* A Manual of American Literature, *John Seely Hart wrote about Miss Sedgwick five years after her death that she*

as a novelist, holds about the same rank among the writers of her own sex in the United States that Cooper holds among the writers of the other sex. She was the first of her class whose writings became generally known, and the eminence universally conceded to her on account of priority has been almost as generally granted on other grounds. The novels by which she is best known are Hope Leslie and Redwood. . . .

The quality of mind which is most apparent in Miss

Sedgwick's writings is that of strength. The reader feels at
every step that he [sic] has to do with a vigorous and active
intellect. . . .

Besides the 1835 volume of stories, Tales and Sketches, *in
which 'Old Maids' was reprinted, she wrote six novels, a
couple of volumes of stories for juvenile readers, a collection of
travel letters, a book of advice to young women, and a
biography of the poet Lucretia Davidson.*
*Herself never married, although she repeatedly lauded the
role of wife and mother in private and in public, this story is
not the only defense she wrote of the unmarried woman. In the
Preface to her last novel,* Married or Single? *(1857), she wrote:*

we raise our voice with all our might against the miserable
cant that matrimony is essential to the feebler sex – that a
woman's single life must be useless or undignified – that she
is but an adjunct of man – in her best estate a helm merely to
guide the nobler vessel . . . we believe she has an independent
power to shape her own course, and to force her separate
sovereign way. . . .

Our story will not have been in vain, if it has done any
thing towards raising the single woman of our country to the
comparatively honorable level they occupy in England –
anything to drive away the smile already fading from the lips
of all but the vulgar, at the name of 'old maid.'

This story sets the classic pattern for a story written in
defense of old maids. The elements of that pattern are these: (1)
the defense is spoken by a happily married woman who is
clearly respected and admired by (2) the unmarried young
woman who listens, is enlightened, is relieved of her own
prejudices and thereby granted expanded options for her own
life when she hears (3) the story contrasting the lives of two
sisters, one who marries and one who remains single. (4) The
married sister suffers much unhappiness and, by marrying, has
lost all power to remedy her own situation, while (5) the single
sister lives a useful and satisfying life. (6) Having confronted
the paralyzing stereotype and rid it of its power to coerce, (7)
the speaker sets up a new figure for pity and scorn – the
woman who marries for the wrong reasons, chief among which
is to escape being an old maid. (8) The sister who remained

9

single had ample opportunity to demonstrate her superior practice of the most traditional womanly virtues as she lived out her full life (9) devoted, with tenderness and loyalty, to another woman, her sister.

Sedgwick's recent biographers have commented at length about her apparent ambivalence towards the woman's role in Victorian America. Having turned down numerous proposals of marriage in order to remain independent, deriving all the traditional satisfactions of a married woman and mother from her intimate and devoted involvement in the lives and with the families of her brothers, the bulk of her fiction serves to reinforce the belief that a woman's greatest satisfaction and fulfilment comes from marriage and motherhood.

She was the sixth of seven surviving children born to Pamela Dwight, second wife of Theodore Sedgwick. Pamela was ill, despondent during most of Catharine's girlhood, and suffered two periods of insanity. Catharine assumed many of the duties her mother would have been expected to bear. Pamela died when Catharine was 17; Theodore married for the third time a year later. After that marriage Catharine was seldom home, spending most of her time travelling between the homes of her older, married brothers. Perhaps the reasons she chose to remain single might best be looked for in these circumstances.

The recovery of this story for modern readers is an exciting event. Old Maids is a truly germinal work, introducing all but one of the major themes characteristic of women's short fiction described in the Preface. With the presentation of each, Sedgwick sets the tone for strong, loving, nuturant and reciprocal relationships between women. But when this story was written, the short story was still new. The early stories retain vestiges of their roots in other genres, especially the personal ones, such as the letter, the diary and the memoir, but their taproot is the oral tradition. Like early writers of all cultural groups, the writers use many of the accoutrements of story telling. The oral and written traditions co-existed among women writers for longer than among other groups; hence the frequent use of the framing device of a story within a story, engendering a conversational style. The use of dialogue, drawing the reader's imagination into active participation (the goal of all story tellers), leads to telling about instead of showing in action the characters as they live their stories. These early stories relate to the later ones like radio and television.'

# OLD MAIDS*

———————————— ❋ ————————————

"To be the mistress of some honest man's house, and the means of making neighbours happy, the poor easy, and relieving strangers, is the most creditable lot a young woman can look to, and I heartily wish it to all here." (Pirate)

"Mrs. Seton, Emily Dayton is engaged to William Moreland!"

"To William Moreland. Well, why should she not be engaged to William Moreland?"

"Why should she, rather?"

"I know not Emily Dayton's 'why,' but ladies' reasons for marrying are as 'thick as blackberries.' A common motive with girls under twenty is the éclat of an engagement – the pleasure of being the heroine of bridal festivities – of receiving presents – of being called by that name so enchanting to the imagination of a miss in her teens – '*the bride.*' "

"But Emily Dayton, you know, is past twenty."

"There is one circumstance that takes place of all reason – perhaps she is in love."

"In love with William Moreland! No, no, Mrs. Seton – there are no 'merry wanderers of the night' in these times to do Cupid's errands, and make us dote on that which we should hate."

"Perhaps then, as she is at a *rational* age, three or four and twenty, she may be satisfied to get a kind sensible protestor."

"Kind and sensible, truly! He is the most testy, frumpish, stupid man you can imagine."

"Does she not marry for an establishment?"

"Oh no! She is perfectly independent, mistress of every thing at her father's. No, I believe her only motive is that which actuates half the girls – the fear of being an old maid. This may be her last chance. Despair, they say, makes men mad – and I believe it does women too.

*From *Tales and Sketches* by Catharine Maria Sedgwick, Carey, Lea, and Blanchard, Philadelphia, 1835. Dedicated to Harriet Martineau.

"It is a fearful fate."

"An old maid's? Yes, most horrible."

"Pardon me, Anne, I did not mean that; but such a fate as you anticipate for Emily Moreland – to be yoked in the most intimate relation of life, and *for life*, to a person to whom you have clung to save you from shipwreck, but whom you would not select to pass an evening with. To such a misery there can be no 'end, measure, limit, bound.'"

"But, my dear Mrs. Seton, what are we to do? – all women cannot be so fortunate as you are."

"Perhaps not. But so kind is the system of compensation in this life – such the thirst for happiness, and so great the power of adaptation in the human mind, that the conjugal state is far more tolerable than we should expect when we see the mismated parties cross its threshold. Still there can be no doubt that its possible happiness is often missed, and such is my respect for my sex, and so high my estimate of the capabilities of married life, that I cannot endure to see a woman, from the fear of being an old maid, driven into it, thereby forfeiting its highest blessings."

"You must nevertheless confess, Mrs. Seton, that there are terrors in the name."

"Yes, I know there are; and women are daily scared by them into unequal and wretched connexions. They have believed they could not retain their identity after five and twenty. That unless their individual existence was merged in that of the superior animal, every gift and grace with which God has endowed them would exhale and leave a 'spectral appearance' – a sort of slough of woman – an Aunt Grizzel, or Miss Lucretia McTab. I have lived, my dear Anne, to see many of the mists of old superstitions melting away in the light of a better day. Ghost is no longer a word to conjure with – witches have settled down into harmless and unharmed old women; and I do not despair of living to see the time when it shall be said of no woman breathing, as I have heard it said of such and such a lady, who escaped from the wreck at the eleventh hour, that she 'married to die a *Mrs.*' "

"I hate, too, to hear such things *said*, but tell me honestly, Mrs. Seton, now when no male ears are within hearing, whether you do not, in your secret soul think there is something particularly unlovely, repelling, and frightful, in the name of an old maid."

"In the name, certainly; but it is because it does not designate a condition but a species. It calls up the idea of a faded, bony, wrinkled, skinny, jaundiced personage, whose mind has dwindled to a point — who has outlived her natural affections — survived every love but love of self, and self-guarded by that Cerberus suspicion — in whom the follies of youth are fresh when all its charms are gone — who has retained, in all their force, the silliest passions of the silliest women — love of dress, of pleasure, of admiration; who, in short, is in the condition of the spirits in the ancients' Tartarus, an impalpable essence tormented with the desires of humanity. Now turn, my dear Anne, from this hideous picture to some of our acquaintance who certainly have missed the *happiest* destiny of woman, but who dwell in light, the emanation of their own goodness. I shall refer you to actual living examples — no fictions."

"No fictions, indeed, for then you must return to the McTabs and Grizzles. Whatever your philanthropy may hope for that most neglected portion of our sex, no author has ventured so far from nature as to portray an attractive old maid. Even Mackenzie, with a spirit as gentle as my Uncle Toby's, and as tender as that of his own 'Man of Feeling,' has written an essay in ridicule of 'old maids.'"

"And you are not perhaps aware, Anne, that he has written a poem called the 'Recantation,' and dedicated it to his single daughter, a most lovely woman, who was the staff and blessing of his old age. In your wide range of reading cannot you think of a single exception to the McTabs and Grizzles?"

"Miss Farrer's 'Becca Duguid,' but she is scarcely above contempt, trampled on by the children, and the tool of their selfish and lazy mammas."

"There is one author, Anne, the most beloved, and the most lamented of all authors, who has not ventured to depart from nature, but has escaped prejudice, and prejudice in some of its most prevailing forms. He has dared to exhibit the Paynim Saladin as superior to the Christian crusader. He has dispelled the thick clouds that enveloped the 'poor Israelite,' the most inveterate of all prejudices, transmitted from age to age, and authorised by the fancied sanctions of religion. I said the clouds were dispelled, but do they not rather hang around the glorious

Rebecca, the unsullied image of her Maker, as the clouds that have broken away from the full moon encircled her, and are converted by her radiance to a bright halo?"

"Mrs. Seton! Mrs. Seton! you are, or I am getting lost in all this mist and fog. What have Paynims and Jews to do with old maids? I do not remember an old maid in all Sir Walter's novels, excepting, indeed, Alison – Martha Trapbois – Meg Dods – one of Monkbarns' womankind, and Miss Yellowley, a true all-saving, fidgetting, pestering old maid, and the rest of them are entertaining but certainly not very exalting members of any sisterhood."

"But these are not my examples, Anne. I confess that they are fair examples of follies and virtues that, if not originated, are exaggerated and made conspicuous by single life. I confess too that for such foibles matrimony is often a kind and safe shelter. But to my examples. Sir Walter – and who is more poetically just than Sir Walter? – has abandoned to the desolate, tragic, and most abhorred fate of old maids, his three first female characters – first in all respects, in beauty, in mind, in goodness, first in our hearts. The accomplished Flora M'Ivor – the peerless Rebecca, and the tender, beautiful Minna."

"Bless me! I never thought of this."

"No, nor has one in a thousand of the young ladies who have admired these heroines laid the moral of their story to heart. Perhaps not one of the fair young creatures who has dropped a tear over the beautiful sentence that closes the history of Minna*, has been conscious that she was offering involuntary homage to the angelic virtues of an *old maid*. The very term would have wrought a disenchanting spell."

"I confess, Mrs. Seton, I am in what is vulgarly called a 'blue maze.' My perceptions are as imperfect as the man's in scripture who was suddenly cured of blindness. Besides I was never particularly skilful at puzzling out a moral; will you have the goodness to extract it for me?"

"Certainly, Anne, as I am the lecturer, this is my duty. First, I would have young ladies believe that all beautiful and

---

* "Thus passed her life, enjoying, from all who approached her, an affection enhanced by reverence, insomuch that when her friends sorrowed for her death, which arrived at *a late period of her existence*, they were comforted by the fond reflection, that the humanity which she then laid down, was the only circumstance which had placed her, in the words of scripture, 'A little lower than the angels.' "

loveable young women do not of course get married – that charms and virtues may exist, and find employment in single life – that a single woman, an old maid (I will not eschew the name), may love and be loved if she has not a husband, and children of her own. I would have her learn that if, like Flora M'Ivor, she has been surrounded by circumstances that have caused her thoughts and affections to flow in some other channel than love, she need not wed a chance Waverly to escape single life; that if, like Rebecca, she is separated by an impassable gulf from him she loves, she need not wed one whom she does not love, but like the high souled Jewess she may transmute 'young Cupid's fiery shafts,' to chains that shall link her to all her species; and if like poor Minna she has thrown away her affections on a worthless object, she may live on singly, and so well that she will be deemed but 'little lower than the angels.'

"After all it is not such high natures as these that need to be fortified by argument, or example. They are born equal to either fortune. But I would entreat all my sex – those even who have the fewest and smallest gifts – to reverence themselves, to remember that it is not so much the mode of their brief and precarious existence that is important, as the careful use of those faculties that make existence a blessing here, and above all hereafter, where there is certainly 'no marrying, nor giving in marriage;' but I am growing serious, and of course, I fear, tiresome to young ears."

"Oh, no, no, Mrs. Seton. These are subjects on which girls are never tired of talking nor listening; besides, you know you promised me some examples – such as Miss Hamilton and Miss Edgeworth, I suppose."

"No, Anne, these belong to the great exceptions I have mentioned, 'equal to either fortune,' who, in any condition, would have made their 'owne renowne, and happie days.'

"I could adduce a few in our own country, known to both of us, who are the ornament of the high circles in which they move, but for obvious reasons I select humble persons – those who, like some little rivulet unknown to fame, bless obscure and sequestered places. There is Violet Flint – I always wondered how she came by so appropriate a name. That little flower is a fit emblem for her – smiling in earliest spring, and in latest fall – requiring no culture, and yet rewarding it – neglected and forgotten when the gay tribes of summer are caressed, and yet always looking from its humble station with the same cheerful face – bright and constant through the sudden reverses of autumn, and the adversity of the roughest winter. Such is the flower, and such is Violet Flint. But as I am now in realities, I must call her by the old maidenish appellation that, spoiling her pretty name, they have given to her, 'Miss Vily.' She lives, and has for the last twenty years lived, with her brother Sam. He married young, a poor invalid, who, according to Napoleon's scale of merit, is a great woman, having given to the commonwealth nine or ten – more or less – goodly sons and daughters. After the children were born, all care of them, and of their suffering mother, devolved on Violet. Without the instincts, the claims, the rights, or the *honours* of a mother, she has not only done all the duties of a mother, but done them on the sure and broad basis of love. She has toiled and saved, and made others comfortable and enjoying, while she performed the usually thankless task of ordering the economy of a very frugal household. She has made the happy happier, tended the sick, and solaced the miserable. She sheltered the weak, and if one of the children strayed she was the apologist and intercessor. With all this energy of goodness the cause is lost in the blessed effects – she never appears to claim applause or notice. She is not only second best; but when indulgence or pleasure is to be distributed, her share is last and least – that is, according to the usual selfish reckoning. But according to a truer and nobler scale, her amount is greatest, for she has her share in whatever happiness she sees in any living thing.

"How many married dames are there who repeat every fifteen minutes, *my* husband, *my* children, *my* house, and glorify themselves in all these little personalities, who might lay down their crowns at the feet of Violet Flint! – Miss Vily, the *old maid*.

"The second example that occurs to me, is Sarah Lee. Sarah has not, like Violet, escaped all the peculiarities that are supposed to characterise the 'Singlesides.' With the chartered rights of a married lady to fret, to be *particular*, and to have a way of her own, her temper would pass without observation; but being an old maid, she is called, and I must confess is, rather *touchy*. But what are these sparks, when the same fire that throws them off keeps warm an overflowing stream of benevolence? – look into her room."

"Oh, Mrs. Seton! I have seen it, and you must confess it is a true 'Singleside' repository."

"Yes, I do confess it – nor will I shrink from the confession, for I wish to select for my examples, not any bright particular star, but persons of ordinary gifts, in the common walks of life. Had Sarah been married she would have been a thrifty wife, and painstaking mother, but she wore away her youth in devotion to the sick and old – and now her kindness, like the miraculous cruise, always imparting and never diminishing, is enjoyed by all within her little sphere. Experience has made her one of the best physicians I know. She keeps a variety of labelled medicines for the sick, plasters and salves of her own compounding, and materials with which she concocts food and beverages of every description, nutritious and diluent; in short, she has some remedy or solace for every ill that flesh is heir to. She has a marvellous knack of gathering up fragments, of most ingeniously turning to account what would be wasted in another's hands. She not only has *comfortables* for shivering old women, and well patched clothes for neglected children, but she has always some pretty favour for a bride – some kind token for a new-born baby. And then what a refuge is her apartment for the slip-shod members of the family who are in distress for scissors, penknife, thimble, needle, hook and eye, buttons, a needle-full of silk or worsted of any particular colour. How many broken hearts she has restored with her inexhaustible pot – mending tops, doll's broken legs, and all the luckless furniture of the baby-house – to say nothing of a similar ministry to the 'minds diseased' of the mammas. Sarah Lee's labours are not always in so humble a sphere – 'He who makes two blades of grass grow where one grew before,' says a political economist, 'is a benefactor to his race.' If so, Sarah Lee takes high rank.

"Two blades of grass! Her strawberry beds produce treble the quantity of any other in the village. Her potatoes are the 'greatest yield' – her corn the earliest – her peas the richest – her squashes the sweetest – her celery the tenderest – her raspberries and currants the greatest bearers in the country. There is not a thimble-full of unoccupied earth in her garden. There are flowers of all hues, seasons, and climes. None die – none languish in her hands.

"My dear Anne, I will not ask you if an existence so happy to herself, so profitable to others, should be dreaded by herself, neglected or derided by others. Yet Sarah Lee is an *old maid*."

"You are, I confess, very happy in your instances, Mrs Seton, but remember the old proverb, 'one swallow does not make a summer.'"

"I have not done yet – and you must remember that in our country, where the means of supporting a family are so easily attained, and when there are no entails to be kept up at the expense of half a dozen single sisters, the class of old maids is a very small one. Many enter the ranks, but they drop off in the natural way of matrimony. Few maintain the 'perseverance of saints.' Among those few is one, who, when she resigns the slight covering that invests her spirit, will lay down 'all she has of humanity' – our excellent friend, Lucy Ray.

"She is now gently drawing to the close of a long life, which I believe she will offer up without spot or blemish. She began life with the most fragile constitution. She has had to contend with that nervous susceptibility of temperament that so naturally engenders selfishness and irascibility, and all the miseries and weaknesses of invalidism. Not gifted with any personal beauty, or grace, she was liable to envy her more fortunate contemporaries. Without genius, talents or accomplishments to attract or delight, she has often been slighted – and what is far worse, must have been always liable to the suspicion of slights. But suspicion, that creator and purveyor of misery, never darkened her serene mind. She has lived in others and for others, with such an entire forgetfulness of self, that even the wants and weakness of her mortal part seem scarcely to have intruded on her thoughts. She has resided about in the families of her friends – a mode of life which certainly has a tendency to nourish jealousy, servility, and gossiping. But for what could Lucy Ray be jealous or servile? She craved nothing – she asked nothing, but, like an unseen, unmarked Providence, to do good; and as to gossiping, she had no turn for the ridiculous, no belief of evil against any human being – and as to speaking evil, 'on her lips was the law of kindness.' You would hardly think, Anne, that a feeble, shrinking creature, such as I have described, and truly, Lucy Ray, could have been desired, as an inmate with gay young people, and noisy, turbulent children. She was always welcome, for, like her Divine Master, she came to minister – not to be ministered unto.

"Lucy, like the Man of Ross, is deemed passing rich by the

children, and an unfailing resource to the poor in their exigencies, though her income amounts to rather less than one hundred dollars!!"

"We sometimes admire the art of the Creator more in the exquisite mechanism of an insect than in the formation of a planet, and I have been more struck with the power of religion in the effect and exaltation it gave to the humble endowments of this meek woman, than by its splendid results in such a life as Howard's. Lucy Ray, by a faithful imitation of her master, by always aiding and never obstructing the principle of growth in her soul, has, through every discouragement and disability, reached a height but 'little lower than the angels;' and when her now flickering light disappears, she will be lamented almost as tenderly (alas! for that almost) as if she were a mother; and yet, Anne, Lucy Ray is an *old maid*."

"You half persuade me to be one too, Mrs. Seton."

"No, Anne, I would by no means persuade you or any woman to *prefer* single life. It is not the 'primrose path.' Nothing less than a spirit of meekness, of self renunciation, and of benevolence, can make a woman, who has once been first, happy in a subordinate and *second best* position. And this under ordinary circumstances is the highest place of a single woman. Depend upon it, my dear young friend, it is safer for most of us to secure all the helps to our virtues that attend a favourable position; besides, married life is the destiny Heaven has allotted to us, and therefore best fitted to awaken all our powers, to exercise all our virtues, and call forth all our sympathies. I would persuade you that you may give dignity and interest to single life, that you may be the cause of happiness to others and of course happy yourself – for when was the fountain dry while the stream continued to flow? If single life, according to the worst view of it, is a moral desert, the faithful, in their passage through it, are refreshed with bread from Heaven and water from the rock.

"I shall conclude with a true story. The parties are not known to you. The incidents occurred long ago, and I shall take the liberty to assume names; for I would not, even at this late day, betray a secret once confided to me, though time may long since have outlawed it. My mother had a school-mate and friend whom I shall call Agnes Gray. Her father was a country clergyman with a small salary, and the blessing that usually attends it – a large family of children. Agnes was the eldest, and after her following a line of boys, as long as Banquo's. At last, some ten years after Agnes, long waited and prayed for, appeared a girl, who cost her mother her life.

"The entire care of the helpless little creature devolved on Agnes. She had craved the happiness of possessing a sister, and now, to a sister's love, she added the tenderness of a mother. Agnes' character was formed by the discipline of circumstances – the surest of all discipline. A host of turbulent boys, thoughtless and impetuous, but kind-hearted, bright, and loving, had called forth her exertions and affections, and no one can doubt, either as lures or goads, had helped her on the road to heaven. Nature had, happily, endowed her with a robust constitution, and its usual accompaniment, a sweet temper; so that what were mountains to others, were mole hills to Agnes. 'The baby,' of course, was the pet lamb of the fold. She was named, for her mother, Elizabeth; but, instead of that queenly appellation, she was always addressed by the endearing diminutive of Lizzy. Lizzy Gray was not only the pet of father, brothers, and sister at home – but the plaything of the village.

"The old women knit their brightest yarn into tippets and stockings for the 'minister's motherless little one' (oh, what an eloquent appeal was in those words!), the old men saved the 'red cheeked' apples for her, – the boys drew her, hour after hour, in her little wagon, and the girls made her rag babies. Still she was not in any disagreeable sense an *enfant gâtée*. She was like those flowers that thrive best in warm and continued sunshine. Her soft hazle eye, with its dark sentimental lashes, the clear brunette tint of her complexion, and her graceful flexible lips, truly expressed her tender, loving, and gentle spirit. She seemed formed to be sheltered and cherished – to love and be loved; and this destiny appeared to be secured to her by her devoted sister, who never counted any exertion or sacrifice that procured an advantage or pleasure for Lizzy. When Lizzy was about fourteen, a relative of the family, who kept a first rate boarding school in the city, offered to take her for two years, and give her all the advantages of her school, for the small consideration of fifty dollars per annum. Small as it was, it amounted to a tithe of the parson's income. It is well known, that, in certain parts of our country, every thing (not always discreetly) is sacrificed to the hobby – education. Still the prudent father, who had already two sons at college, hesitated – did not consent till Agnes ascertained that by keeping a little school in the village she might obtain half the required sum. Her father, brothers, and friends all remonstrated. The toils of a school, in addition to the care and labour of her father's family was, they urged, too much for her – but she laughed at them. 'What was labour to her if she could benefit Lizzy – dear Lizzy!' All ended, as might be expected, in Lizzy going to the grand boarding school. The parting was a great and trying event in the family. It was soon followed by a sadder. The father suddenly sickened and died – and nothing was left for his family but his house and well kept little garden. What now was to be done? – College and schools to be given up? – No such thing. In our country, if a youth is rich he ought to be educated; if he is poor he *must* be. The education is the capital whereby they are to live hereafter. It is obtained in that mysterious but unfailing way – 'by hook and by crook.'

"The elder Grays remained in college – Agnes enlarged her school – learned lessons in mathematics and Latin one day, and taught them the next; took a poor, accomplished young lady from some broken down family in town into partnership, and received a few young misses as boarders into her family. Thus, she not only was able to pay 'dear Lizzy's' bills regularly, but to aid her younger brothers. Her energy and success set all her other attractions in a strong light, and she was admired and talked about, and became quite the queen of the village.

"I think it was about a year after her father's death, that a Mr. Henry Orne, a native of the village, who was engaged in a profitable business at the south, returned to pass some months at his early home. His frequent visits to the parsonage, and his attentions, on all occasions, to Agnes, soon became matter of very agreeable speculation to the gossips of the village. 'What a fine match he would be for Agnes! – such an engaging, well-informed young man, and so well off!' Agnes' heart was not steel; but though it had been exposed to many a flame she had kindled, it had never yet melted."

"Pardon me, Mrs. Seton, for interrupting you – was Agnes pretty?"

"Pretty? The word did not exactly suit her. At the time of which I am now speaking, she was at the mature age of five and twenty; which is called the perfection of womanhood. Prettiness is rather appropriate to the bud than the ripened fruit. Agnes, I have been told, had a fine person – symmetrical features, and so charming an expression that she was not far from beautiful, in the eyes of strangers, and quite a beauty to her friends and lovers. Whether it were beauty, manners, mind, or heart, I know not – one and all probably – but Henry Orne soon became her assiduous and professed admirer. Till now Agnes had lived satisfied and happy with subordinate affections. She had never seen any one that she thought it possible she could love as well as she loved those to whom nature had allied her. But now the sun arose, and other lights became dim – not 'that she loved Caesar less, but she loved Rome more.' Their mutual faith was plighted, and both believed, as all real lovers do, that the world never contained so happy, so blessed a pair, as they were.

"Lizzy's second year at school was nearly ended, and one month after her return the marriage was to be solemnised. In the mean time Agnes was full of the cares of this world. The usual preparations for the greatest occasion in a woman's life are quite enough for any single pair of hands, but Agnes had to complete her school term, and the possibility of swerving from an engagement never occurred to her.

"Lizzy arrived, as lovely a creature as she had appeared in the dreams of her fond sister. In the freshness and untouched beauty of her young existence, just freed from the trammels of school, her round cheek glowing with health, and her heart overflowing with happiness. 'Here is my own dear Lizzy,' said Agnes, as she presented her to Henry Orne, 'and if you do not love me for any thing else, you must for giving you such a sister.'

"Henry Orne looked at Lizzy and thought, and said, 'the duty would be a very easy one.' 'For the next month,' continued Agnes, 'I shall be incessantly occupied, and you must entertain one another. Henry has bought a nice little pony for me, Lizzy, and he shall teach you to ride, and you shall go over all his scrambling walks with him – to Sky-cliff, Roseglen, and Beech-cove – the place he says nature made for lovers; but my poor lover has had to accommodate himself to my working day life and woo me in beaten paths.'

"The next month was the most joyous of Lizzy's life; every day was a festival. To the perfection of animal existence in the country, in the month of June, was added the keen sense of all that physical nature conveys to the susceptible mind.

"Wherever she was, her sweet voice was heard ringing in laughter, or swelling in music that seemed the voice of irrepressible joy – the spontaneous breathing of her soul. To the lover approaching his marriage day Time is apt to drag along with leaden foot, but to Henry Orne he seemed rather to fly with Mercury's wings at his heels; and when Agnes found herself compelled by the accumulation of her affairs, to defer her wedding for another month, he submitted with a better grace than could have been expected. Not many days of this second term had elapsed, when Agnes, amidst all her cares, as watchful of Lizzy as a mother of an only child, observed a change stealing over her. Her stock of spirits seemed suddenly expended, her colour faded – her motions were languid, and each successive day she became more and more dejected. 'She wants rest,' said Agnes to Henry Orne; 'she has been unnaturally excited, and there is now a reaction. She must remain quietly at home for a time, on the sofa, in a darkened room, and you, Henry, I am sure, will, for my sake, give up your riding and walking for a few days, and stay within doors, and play on your flute, and read to her.' Agnes' suggestions were promptly obeyed, but without the happy effect she anticipated. Lizzy, who had never before had a cloud on her brow, seemed to have passed under a total eclipse. She became each day more sad and nervous. A tender word from Agnes – a look, even, would make her burst into tears.

"'I am miserably, Henry,' said Agnes, 'at this unaccountable change in Lizzy – the doctor says she is perfectly free from disease – perhaps we have made too sudden a transition from excessive exercise to none at all. The evening is dry and fine, I wish you would induce her to take a walk with you. She is distressed at my anxiety, and I cannot propose any thing that does not move her to tears.'

"'It is very much the same with me,' replied Henry, sighing deeply, but if you wish it I will ask her.' He accordingly did so – she consented, and they went out together.

"Agnes retired to her own apartment, and there, throwing herself upon her knees, she entreated her Heavenly Father to withdraw this sudden infusion of bitterness from her brimming cup of happiness. 'Try me in any other way,' she cried, in the intensity of her feeling, and, for the first time in her life, forgetting that every petition should be in the spirit of 'Thy will be done,' 'try me in any other way, but show me the means of restoring my sister – my child to health and happiness!'

"She returned again to her little parlour. Lizzy had not come in, and she sat down on the sofa near an open window, and resigned herself to musings, the occupation, if occupation it may be called, of the idle, but rarely, and never of late, of Agnes!

"In a few moments Lizzy and Henry returned, and came into the porch adjoining the parlour. They perceived the candles were not lighted, and concluding Agnes was not there, they sat down in the porch.

"'Oh, I am too wretched!' said Lizzy. Her voice was low and broken, and she was evidently weeping. 'Is it possible,' thought Agnes, 'that she will express her feelings more freely to Henry than to me? I will listen. If she knows any cause for her dejection, I am sure I can remove it.'

"'Why, my beloved Lizzy,' replied Orne, in a scarcely audible voice, 'will you be so wretched – why will you make me so, and for ever, when there is a remedy?'

"'Henry Orne!' she exclaimed, and there was resolution and indignation in her voice. 'If you name that to me again, I will never, so help me God, permit you to come into my presence without witnesses. No, there is no remedy, but in death. Would that it had come before you told me you loved me – before my lips confessed my sinful love for you – no, no – the secret shall be buried in my grave.'

"'Oh, Lizzy, you are mad – Agnes does not, cannot love as we do. Why sacrifice two to one? Let me, before it is too late, tell her the whole, and cast myself on her generosity.'

"'Never, never – I now wish, when I am in her presence, that the earth at her feet would swallow me up; and how can you, for a moment, think I will ask to be made happy – that I could be made happy, at her expense? No, I am willing to expiate with my life, my baseness to her – that I shall soon do so is my only comfort – and you will soon forget me – men can *forget*, they say – '

"'Never – on my knees, I swear never!' –

"'Stop, for mercy's sake, stop. You must not speak another such word to me – I will not hear it.' She rose to enter the house. Agnes slipped through a private passage to her own apartment.

"She heard Lizzy ascending the stairs. She heard Henry call after her, 'One word, Lizzy – for mercy's sake, one *last* word.' But Lizzy did not turn. Agnes heard her feebly drag herself into the little dressing-room adjoining their apartment, and after, there was no sound but the poor girl's suppressed, but still audible sobs.

"None but He who created the elements that compose the human heart, and who can penetrate its mysterious depths, can know which of the sisters was most wretched at that moment. To Agnes who had loved deeply, confidingly without a shadow of fear or distrust, the reverse was total. To Lizzy who had enjoyed for a moment the bewildering fervours of a young love, only to feel its misery, that misery was embittered by a sense of wrong done to her sister. And yet it had not been a willing, but an involuntary and resisted, and most heartily repented wrong. She had recklessly rushed down a steep to a fearful precipice, and now felt that all access and passage to return was shut against her. Agnes without having had one dim fear – without any preparation, saw an abyss yawning at their feet – an abyss only to be closed by her self-immolation.

"She remained alone for many hours – she resolved – her spirit faltered – she re-resolved. She thought of all Lizzy had been to her, and of all she had been to Lizzy, and she wept as if her heart would break. She remembered the prayer that her impatient spirit had sent forth that evening. She prayed again, and a holy calm, never again to be disturbed, took possession of her soul.

"There is a power in goodness, pure self-renouncing goodness, that cannot be 'overcome, but overcometh all things.'

"Lizzy waited till all was quiet in her sister's room. She heard her get into bed, and then stole softly to her. Agnes, as she had done from Lizzy's infancy, opened her arms to receive her, and Lizzy pillowed her aching head on Agnes' bosom, softly breathing, – 'My sister – mother!'

"'My own Lizzy – *my child*,' answered Agnes. There was no tell-tale faltering of the voice. She felt a tear trickle from Lizzy's cold cheek on to her bosom, and not very long after both sisters were in a sleep that mortals might envy, and angels smile on.

"The rest you will anticipate, my dear Anne. The disclosure to the lovers of her discovery, was made by Agnes in the right way, and at the right time. Every thing was done as it should be by this most admirable woman. She seemed, indeed, to feel as a guardian angel might, who, by some remission of his vigilance, had suffered the frail mortal in his care to be beguiled into evil. She never, by word, or even look, reproached Lizzy. She shielded her, as far as possible, from self-reproach, nor do I believe she ever felt more unmixed tenderness and love for her, than when, at the end of a few months, she saw her married to Henry Orne.

"My story has yet a sad supplement. Madame Cotin, I believe it is, advises a story teller to close the tale when he comes to a happy day; for, she says, it is not probable another will succeed it. Poor Lizzy had experience of this sad mutability of human life. Hers was chequered with many sorrows.

"Lapses from virtue at eight and twenty, and at sixteen, afford very different indications of the character; you cannot expect much from a man, who, at eight and twenty, acted the part of Henry Orne. He was unfaithful in engagements with persons less merciful than Agnes Gray. He became inconstant in his pursuits – self-indulgent, and idle, and finally intemperate, in his habits. His wife – as wives will – loved him to the end.

"Agnes retained her school, which had become in her hands a profitable establishment. There she laboured, year after year, with a courageous heart, and serene countenance, and devoted the fruit of all her toils to Lizzy, and to the education of her children.

"I am telling no fiction, and I see you believe me, for the tears are trembling in your eyes – do not repress them, but permit them to embalm the memory of an *old maid*."

# THE FORTUNE HUNTER

*

## *Alice Ann Carter*

'The Fortune Hunter' was first published in The Lowell Offering *in June 1843, an irregularly published periodical when it was begun in 1840 under the editorship of a Unitarian minister in Lowell, Massachusetts. It became a regular monthly publication in 1841 under the editorship of Harriet F. Farley and Harriott Curtis, both regularly employed textile mill workers. The title page of this short-lived (it ceased publication after 1845) but important publication read 'A Repository of Original Articles, Written by "Factory Girls".' The* Offering *was written by young New England women who had left their home farms and villages to come to the rapidly industrializing towns along the Merrimack River to work in the factories. Although they lived in crowded, closely supervised, factory-owned boarding houses and worked long and exhausting hours, the experience of being away from home, earning negotiable currency that was theirs alone to spend, and enjoying opportunities for self-improvement through study groups and attendance at evening lecture courses created an environment that nurtured the development of warm, supportive friendships and a deep sense of community among the young operatives. The textile factory system started out as the embodiment of a capitalist utopian dream; it ended in bleak, alienating slums. But this period (1840-5) represented its finest hours.*

*In 1902, Harriet Hanson Robinson, who had spent her young girlhood working in the mills, and living in one of the company boarding houses which was managed by her widowed mother, compiled a list of names and noms de plume of women who had written for the* Offering. *The list, howver, was incomplete — she was working from memory — and not entirely trustworthy in terms of accuracy. It is from this list that we learn that the woman who signed herself 'Alice' was Alice Ann Carter and that she married a man whose last name was Currier.*

# THE FORTUNE HUNTER*

———————————— * ————————————

When I was a little girl I was quite a favorite with Aunt Miranda Putnam, a maiden lady of our town. Aunt Miranda was a perfect sample of a genteel village spinster; and she lived in just that neat, quiet, orderly way which is so apt to create the desire in married women, who have cross husbands and troublesome children, that they had always remained single.

Every thing about Aunt Putnam's house was always *just so*, and never seemed to admit of any possible variation. The cooper's wife went every Monday, rain or shine, to do her washing; and the baker brought her just so many loaves and seed-cakes every Saturday. She had a certain quantity of milk brought every morning, and no light was visible from her windows after a stated hour in the evening. Every thing seemed to go on according to square rule; and even her cat was trained to better manners than most of the children in the neighborhood. She always subscribed a certain sum for the maintenance of the minister, and was president of the "Female Charitable Society." The Sewing Circle met at her house every alternate month, and her name was regularly signed to every Temperance pledge, and Anti-Slavery petition. When cherries were ripe, she always invited the children of the district to spend an afternoon with her, and once a year she gave a large party, to which the doctor, lawyer, and minister, with their ladies, were sure of an invitation.

In short Aunt Miranda was one of the best and happiest single ladies with whom I have ever met; and fortunate was it for me that I was so early ingratiated in her favor, for her counsels were of great advantage to me. Having no mother to

*From *The Lowell Offering*, June 1843, Series II, Vol. 3.

watch over me, and both my deceased parents having been dear friends of Aunt Putman's, I was allowed a liberty of ingress and egress denied to all others. The few works of fiction which her little library contained, were early devoured by me, and I wept and smiled over *Paul and Virginia, Vicar of Wakefield, Sorrows of Werter, Religious Courtship*, and other *ci-devant* fashionable tales. I was perhaps more benefited by her volumes of the *Spectator, Guardian,* and *Rambler*; and I also had access to the few periodicals for which she was a subscriber.

Small as was her income she still contrived to do much good with it, and in her own still, quiet way she endeavored to be a benefactor to her race. Economical, though not parsimonious, her own personal expenses were regulated by the rules of a rigid self-denial. The same black bombazine gown was for years her nicest dress, and one of those green silk bellows-topped bonnets, called calashes, was worn by her long after they had been discarded by all others. But kind and charitable as Aunt Miranda was always allowed to be, yet it seemed to me that there was a want of real deep fervent feeling about her; she appeared as though the charities of her life were regulated by a sense of duty, rather than by sympathy for her fellow beings. I thought her too cold, too nice, and precise, to be capable of intense affection, and this was why I never made her a *confidante*. That she was interested in my welfare, that she wished to benefit me, I doubted not; but I could never open my heart to her; and when the most important event of my early life took place, when I had pledged my hand, and the fortune of which I should soon become mistress, to one of whom I then knew but little, I could not inform Aunt Miranda of what I had done. I knew that she would blame me, and I felt that she could never sympathize with the feelings which had led to that imprudence.

But she heard of it from others, she learned that I was to be married, – young, hastily, and imprudently, and I received an invitation to visit her immediately. I had been blamed by others, but she – the icy formal one – what would she say? My heart beat fast as I entered that little quiet parlor: it was always still there, and I had learned to lower my voice, and soften my step, whenever I approached it. She was sitting with her dark hair combed to Quaker smoothness over her high brow, and her dark eyes filled – not as I had expected, with all of anger that she was capable of feeling, but with an expression of deep sorrow.

"And so, Alice, you are to be married?" said she to me. I confessed that she was correct.

"And I was not to know it, I who had watched you closely, as I thought, I who had deemed that love and marriage were yet but names to you, I who thought that every feeling of that heart was to be confided to me. But I do not blame you so much as I do myself. I thought that these were themes for future days, and forgot how early the warm heart may throb to affection. But tell me Alice that he is not a fortune-hunter, that he does not seek the little gold which you may bestow. Oh, tell me that he does not want your money."

I was surprised, and almost overpowered, by this burst of feeling, but I quickly answered "No! I could not love one so base, so worthless, mean, and low, as a fortune-hunter. Edward is noble, high-minded, and disinterested. I have never heard him speak of wealth but as the means for doing good; a boon to be shared by others; an instrument for the accomplishment of high designs! My guardian is satisfied, and I do assure you that he is not all that is selfish and corrupt; for such a fortune-hunter must surely be."

"You may be deceived in him, Alice," was her earnest response, "and you would not be the first victim of such deception. I must tell you a tale; I ought to have told it before, but I did not wish to awaken feelings which I thought were slumbering now; sit by me Alice, and I will tell you a story of my own youthful days. You have always thought me cold, stoical and unfeeling, and that is the character in which I would wish to appear, but I was not always so. I was young once, and as merry as you are Alice, in your gayest hours, but all that passed quickly away, for I had early learned to love."

I started involuntarily, Aunt Miranda once in love — she whose very soul (at least all she possessed of soul) I had thought to be bound up in bright fire-irons, nice rug-work, and beautiful embroidery — she the very pink and pattern of discretion, the model of maiden propriety — she had once loved; ardently or she would not still remember it, and vainly for she was still unwedded. Never had I listened so intently to the gracious words which had been wont to proceed from her lips when she taught me how to make courtseys, plait ruffles, and write formal billets, as I now did, to this strange and unexpected declaration.

"Henry Formen," continued my aunt, "was a college friend of my brother: He was handsome, graceful, and accomplished; and I was young, imaginative, and ignorant of the world. He came into this quiet village that amidst its peaceful seclusion he might acquire that profession which was to be the stepping-stone to wealth and celebrity. He was ambitious, and placed his standard high; he aimed to be one of earth's proud and favored ones. There was something in his high aspirings which kindled my active imagination, which awakened my admiration, and which, with his fascinating manners, and gentle, constant, kind attentions, soon won my love. Yes, I soon knew that I loved him, and with that worshipping passion which enshrines the object of affection in a temple dedicated to all that is noble, pure and true.

Seldom is mortal endowed with so much of moral and mental superiority as that with which I had invested him. Every thing that he did was better done, and from purer motives, than were the actions of any one else. Yes, I loved him, I knew it by the throbs with which I listened to his slightest word, by the thrills which rushed through my frame at the slightest touch of his hand, or glance of his eye. I knew it by the dreams which came to me at night, and blushed at the first thought which came to me at morn, but still it was a love which ennobled me, I felt that I was a better being while my whole soul was filled with this absorbing fervent worship. But did he love me? I dared not in my inmost heart say yes! He was so far above me that I could not think myself worthy of his affection. Yet he was kind to me, aye, more than *kind*, but then he was my brother's friend, for his sake he would be even as a brother to me. But he sometimes dropped words which seemed to speak of another and warmer love. For a moment my heart would beat in raptures, and then, again, it sank within me, for surely that could never be. What was I that he should thus be interested in me? A being wholly unworthy of his interest, yet spite of all my fears, my self-abasement, my elevated opinion of him, the hope began to dawn upon me that I was the object of his love. To trifle with me, or with any one, was what I thought him incapable of doing: that low gratification of selfishness, or vanity, which prompts some men to win affection but to show how they can condemn and discard it, was not in his nature.

But there were looks and tones which I could not interpret otherwise than as the language of affection. Henry was poor, and I the expectant of more wealth than I have since possessed. Might not this influence his conduct? No; I utterly repudiated the thought. I was ashamed that it should once have entered my mind. Still there came no formal declaration, and I might have been the subject of self-delusion.

I had a friend, a lovely, dear and interesting friend, one who was gifted with far more brilliancy of mind, and beauty of person, than myself; and who was gentle and kind as she was fair and noble. Alicia had been the object of my brother's ardent admiration, and it was a cherished hope that she might one day be my sister. She had been absent from us long but was soon to return, and then, for the first time, she would see Henry. And Henry would see her, and to see either could be but to love and admire.

If Henry had been interested in me, how much more so must he be in Alicia? and my poor brother – if Alicia felt a friendship for him, she must surely feel something warmer for his companion. I had never before dreaded her arrival; I had never before felt aught but delight that she was to be with me, but now, though I schooled my heart to hide if it could not repress the unworthy feeling, I wished that she was not to come. But she did come, and they saw and admired each other. I had known it would be so, and my heart struggled in secrecy with its agony. I saw, day by day, the little attentions which had been devoted to me, shared with my beauteous friend, and at length they were wholly transferred to her, and I was a neglected one. I did not love him less for this – the spell was still strong upon me; for though I had never dared *believe* that I could awaken a permanent interest in Henry, I felt that Alicia was worthy of all, even his most ardent love. I was restless and miserable, but Alicia's soul was in one constant revel amidst sunshine, and song, and flowers. Henry was ever with us, and his fascinating powers were exerted to the utmost to make *her* happy. And she was happy; and blissful thoughts were ever pouring forth, like strains of gladsome music from her heart, and when, at morn, I rose from a sleepless couch, it was to behold her wrapped in smiling dreams. Far more pointed than the attentions which he had once bestowed upon me were those now constantly offered to my friend, and, in the eyes of the world, as well as of each other, they were lovers.

But the dreamer was to be awakened; the bubble to be broken; for Alicia was suddenly summoned to her father's death-bed. I have not told you that her father was rich; that she was the reputed heir of great wealth; for I did not like to speak of the bauble *riches*, while depicting feelings pure as her's. But it was so, and I thought the fear of opposition from the proud father was the reason why he had never formally declared his love. But when they were called upon to separate, it was no time for them to speak of it. Still it did speak in the expression of their eyes, in the faltering of their words, in the tremor of their hands, and his last words were,

"Alicia, we shall soon meet again."

They did *not* soon meet again. Days passed, and word came to us that Alicia was an orphan; and then was also brought the tidings that she was a *portionless one.* A sudden and irretrievable reverse of fortune had brought the old man to a bed of sickness and death; and his daughter was left penniless. But never had I envied Alicia as in that hour of trial and sorrow. There was one that would now be more than friend to that friendless one. One who would go, and wipe the tears from her eyes, or mingle with them the consolations of love and sympathy. He would now go, and be to that lonely girl all that affection could desire; and all that affection could suggest. Now was the time for Henry to show himself all that was kind, and true, and noble. But my faith in him began to grow dim — time passed by, and he went not; and when Alicia wrote to me, to know if he were still among the living, I was astounded. But even then I could not believe him base; there must be some mistake. I was to be undeceived. Ah, how totally had I been blinded. The mists of love had been around me, and how were they to be dispersed? Alicia still wept over a new-made grave, when Henry made a proposal of marriage to me. It was then the love of money which had prompted him to assume the garb of affection; it had been Alicia's expected fortune; and it was now my smaller but certain one which his ambitious spirit had desired, as the means of self-aggrandizement. I saw it all now, and I was roused from my long dream. It was a bitter stroke, and the wounded heart was henceforth to be a caliced one. I spurned him from me. I despised — nay, even detested him now, but that loving, trusting, idolizing faith could never more return. I had loved him, but I could never love again."

Aunt Miranda ceased, and for a few moments we sat in

silence. "But what," said I, "became of Alicia?"

"Alicia," continued she, "had loved with less of idolatry than myself, but with far more of hope and sympathy. Her mortification was greater also, for her affection had been more generally known, and openly acknowledged; but she called pride to her aid, and hid the wound which could not heal. There was one who had loved her in younger happier days, and whose affection continued, even through change of time, of fortune, and of her own feelings. That one knew not how earnest were her strivings for peace, for strength, and cheerfulness, and at length she seemed so happy that he deemed she had wholly overcome that ill-fated love. She yielded to his solicitations and became his wife, but her exertions to conquer, to forget, and to love again, had been too great. She died, ere one whole year had passed away, and begged of me to watch and love her infant child. I have endeavored to fulfil that trust; and when a few years since the father also died, leaving her the heir of much wealth, I determined that she should never become the victim of a fortune-hunter. Alice, I fear I have been too negligent, for it may even now be so."

"Then I am that orphan child."

"You are the offspring of my brother George, and my much-loved Alice," replied Aunt Miranda.

"But you called her Alicia."

"That was to prevent you from identifying her at first," and taking a lovely miniature from her bosom, she hung it around my neck. I looked upon the beauteous face, and burst into tears.

"Let her sorrows be warnings to you," continued my aunt, "and look long and closely before you take that last leap, which may consign you to a fortune-hunter."

"But what," said I, "became of Henry?"

"His ardent dreams of fame and wealth were afterwards realized. He married an heiress in a distant city, and revelled for a time in splendor. But this is the bright side of the picture. Many trials and disappointments have since been his, and he is now a broken-spirited prematurely aged man."

Aunt Miranda's warnings were not lost upon me. I thanked her for her counsels, and promised to guide my conduct by them. My marriage was deferred for several years, during which Edward was closely watched by the Argus eyes of my anxious aunt; and when at length the day arrived, which was to unite my fate with his, I had the pleasure of hearing her express her conviction that the only fortune which he had sought was the hand of                                                                    ALICE.

# MARY AND ELLEN GROSVENOR, OR THE TWO SISTERS

---------- * ----------

## *Mrs A.J. Graves*

'Mary and Ellen Grosvenor, or The Two Sisters' is the eighth
chapter in Girlhood and Womanhood: or, Sketches of my
Schoolmates, *a collection of stories about women who once
shared their schooldays with Ellen Maitland, the 60-year-old
narrator of this 1844 book by Mrs A.J. Graves who also wrote
Woman in America, as we are informed on the title page. The
entire book might be considered as a vindication of unmarried
women, since almost all of the marriages depicted are dreadful
either because the woman, a coquette, entered into the state of
matrimony too lightly, from impure or mercenary motives, or
because of the too-late revealed lowness of the character of the
husband, or because of some other equally banal reason. The
final chapter speaks of Miss Maitland's life and her philosophy
of marriage and single blessedness:*

> Like most other elderly maiden ladies, I have some
> 'confessions' to make, should I choose to do so, of the many
> suitors, who from time to time, sought to woo me from a
> state of single blessedness. . . . it will suffice to say, that I
> never met . . . 'a man after my own heart.' And as the
> cognomen of an 'old maid' was never enough of a scare-
> crow, to induce me to marry one who did not come up to
> my beau-ideal, I chose to remain as I was, knowing that it is
> character and not situation which procures the respect of all
> those whose respect is worth possessing. . . .
>     There is to me no sweeter picture in the world than a
> happy domestic hearth with its devoted father, its fond,
> thoughtful mother, and the little clustering band of lovely,
> affectionate children. It warms and stirs my heart to look on
> it, and I repulse with indignation the falsehood that belies

*my sisterhood, when it is said we are cold and heartless. . . .
the injustice with which old maids are treated by an ill-
judging world. Among my youthful companions I was
accustomed to hear them ridiculed and made a jest and by-
word by silly young men, and tittering girls. An old maid
was always associated with ill-nature, scandal, hatred of
children and a pet cat, but how rarely do we find the
original of this fancy's sketch. . . .*

*The fear of being called an 'old maid,' has been the cause
of more domestic misery than many are aware of, and many
a woman has thus thoughtlessly thrown herself away upon
the first one that offered, however unworthy, and has given
her hand to the man to whom she could not give her heart,
thereby sealing her own unhappiness for life. The reasons for
remaining unmarried are in many instances credible to the
head and heart of those who continue so. . . . In my own
pilgrimage through life, some of my happiest and most
delightful companions have been those of my own sisterhood. . . .*

*If I thought there was any probability that young ladies
would be tempted to declare against matrimony, I would not
have confessed so freely how happy and contented I have
always been in my single blessedness. But I know very well
that not one among them will be disposed to follow my
example, if she should happen to meet a man whom she
could love, particularly if* he *should happen to love* her.

Miss Maitland describes her own domestic arrangements at
some happy length – she lives as part of the household of an
adopted younger brother and his pregnant wife and their other
children, all of whom she enjoys. She concludes, 'an old maid
can enjoy all the pleasures of maternity without its pains and its
trials, and believe with me that Ellen Maitland in her old age is
as happy as the happiest of the schoolmates of Oakwood.'

This story shares with the first two stories and the next story
the structure of a story within a story. The narrative device is
common to much nineteenth-century fiction. In this case, the
device serves to unify the collection of short stories.

# MARY AND ELLEN GROSVENOR, OR THE TWO SISTERS

* * *

"There may be faithful friendships formed in after years, but where a sister is a sister's friend, there can be none so tender and none so true. It is in seasons of affliction that we prove the real value of the deep well-spring of a sister's love." MRS. ELLIS

A few years ago, when I was suffering from the effects of a severe spell of illness, my physician recommended a few weeks' residence at the Virginia Springs. I found on my arrival, the usual number of gay triflers who strangely delight in turning the resort of the sick and the dying into a scene of thoughtless frivolity and worldly amusements, and not meeting with any one with whom I cared to associate, I kept myself in the seclusion of my own room.

A week or two after I came there, as I was sitting by my window watching the alighting of some passengers who had just arrived in the stage, I saw two ladies among them whose countenances were familiar to me, but I could not recall the place where I had met them. For several mornings I saw these sisters, for such they appeared to be, taking their regular walks, for the benefit of the exercise and the fresh air. One seemed to be quite an invalid, and it was touching to see the devoted attentions paid to her by the other. No fond, anxious wife, or tender lover in the days of courtship, could evince a deeper sympathy or more untiring kindness. Fearful lest the invalid should task her strength too much, the sister would insist on her resting frequently beneath the shade of a tree, and as she reclined on the seat, the kind nurse would stand by and fan her, or wipe the moisture from her brow. Sometimes she would gather the sweet wild flowers that grew around, and bring them to refresh the sufferer. A melancholy smile and a look of deep affection rewarded these attentions, but an attachment like that of the one who tendered them, needed no other gratification than the feeling that drew them forth.

Sometimes the sisters would be accompanied by an old lady, who came with them to the Springs. She occupied the room next my own, and two or three trifling services I had an opportunity of rendering her, brought about an acquaintance. Upon inquiring from her the name of the two females in whom I had become so much interested. "They are," said she in reply, "the daughters of my old friend Mr. Grosvenor – one is a widow, the other is still unmarried." "Are their names Mary and Ellen?" I hastily inquired. She replied that they were. "Then," said I, "they must have been once schoolmates of mine, and I should gladly renew the acquaintance, if agreeable to them. Tell them, my dear Mrs. Merdaunt, that Ellen Maitland, a former pupil of the Oakwood school, is anxious to see them." The old lady soon returned to my room, with a kind invitation to visit them.

I found that they were indeed my old friends Mary and Ellen Grosvenor. We had a long and interesting conversation about Mrs. Norville and our old schoolmates, and we seemed mutually gratified to have met with companions with whom we could associate, in the crowd of strangers that thronged the place. Mary was but little altered in appearance, except by such changes as added years will bring, but Ellen's pale cheek and sad-thoughted countenance, bore traces of much sickness and sorrow. I felt anxious to know something of their history since we parted, and before I left the Springs, their old friend Mrs. Merdaunt made me acquainted with most of the particulars in the life and experience of the two sisters.

After Mary and Ellen left the Oakwood school, to accompany their parents upon their removal into another State, they continued to carry on a course of study at home. Fond of retirement and of literary pursuits, they divided their time between the domestic duties of their sex, and the refined pleasures of taste and intellect, and felt no desire to mingle in the gay scenes of fashion or worldly enjoyments. When asked by any of their acquaintance, when they intended to "come out," as it is termed, they would reply "never." "Then you must not expect to be married," said their gay friends, "it is necessary for every one who wishes to make a good match, to go out into society very frequently. The gentlemen, you know, will not take the trouble to seek out for wives, so that those who wish to become wives must come before their notice. As the mountain would not go to Mahomet, Mahomet must go to the mountain."

"If that be the alternative," said Mary, "I shall rest quite contented in my own place, without a wish to win or be won. I see nothing dreadful in the idea of remaining unmarried, or even in anticipating the title of 'old maid.' I have had dreams, and made fancy sketches like most of us do, but when I come down to sober reality, I think it doubtful whether I shall ever meet one who will satisfy my fastidious taste, and if I should, he would in all probability never take a fancy to me, so that I never give myself any uneasiness on the subject." Mary was the entire reverse of what is called "a susceptible young lady," and there was therefore no danger of her ever giving her heart where her reason disapproved. She possessed almost an intuitive perception of character, and a soundness of judgment which enabled her to form a true estimate of men and things. But Ellen, being more imaginative than Mary, viewed every one through the medium of her own fancy, and too often invested them with virtues not their own. It was this that led the gentle Ellen to yield up the rich treasures of her heart, to one who eventually proved unworthy of her. Edmund Bolton was a man of the world, and had studied the female character in all its phases. He knew how to accommodate himself to every taste, and to appear to every one all that they wished. He was captivated by Ellen's beauty, and knew also there was a prospect of her inheriting a large fortune at her father's death. These were the incentives that led him to use every means to win her for his own, and his endeavors at last proved successful.

Ellen knew nothing of the world. She loved Edmund Bolton with all the enthusiasm of woman's early love, and fondly imagined him all she thought him to be. But the illusion vanished before she was long a wife, for when once in possession of the prize he had sought, the husband thought it no longer necessary to maintain towards her the character he had assumed. He had no longer any motive for controlling his violent temper, or for repressing his impatience whenever she unconsciously excited it, for she was now irrevocably his own. Mary accompanied her sister to her new home, and remained some time with her, and soon discovered with an aching heart that Edmund Bolton was not the man to make her beloved sister a happy woman. The delicacy and refinement of their feelings, and the high sense of propriety in conduct and manners, which had always governed the society to which the sisters had been accustomed at home, rendered the contrast with the levity and freedom of Edmund and his companions, a striking and painful one. Ellen's love for her betrothed, was characterized by the blushing reserve and timid respect peculiar to a nature like hers, she loved to look up to him as a being superior to herself, and felt as if all should regard him with equal veneration. But when she found that he, whom she imagined to be all that was noble and dignified, could become the trifling, romping companion of giddy girls, the disappointment was as unexpected as it was painful. When she saw the husband, the pressure of whose lips was sacred to her as an evidence of his affection freely bestowing the same evidence on other females of his acquaintance, when she beheld the brow upon which she could not imprint a timid kiss, without bringing blushes to her cheeks, familiarly kissed by strangers, she was startled from her dream of happiness, and her confidence in his attachment became weakened. He saw the pain that it gave her, and being unable to appreciate the delicacy and refinement of her deep affection, he continued his flirtations, sneeringly smiling at the effects they produced in disturbing her peace. For his own amusement he recklessly trifled with her feelings, but the love of a devoted heart is not a thing to be trifled with. She could have borne with his impatient spirit, and his outbursts of temper, by learning to look on them as natural infirmities, which called for her compassion but when she saw him thus deliberately destroying her trust in his love, for the pretty gratification of the moment, a feeling of contempt for him came over her involuntarily and chilled the current of her affections to their utmost depths.

Edmund Bolton was intensely selfish. His own ease and his own gratification were all that he thought of, or cared for. He exacted the most slavish attention to his wants and caprices, and all that his wife did for him was received without acknowledgement or gratitude. And often the only return she met with, was bitter sarcasm, if her services happened to fall short of what he unreasonably required. Poor Ellen bore all this with the patience of a meek and quiet spirit – she did all that she could, but without the hope or expectation of pleasing him or satisfying his demands on her time and attention.

Mary's proud and independent spirit could scarcely brook the treatment of her sister in silence. It was difficult for her to refrain from reproof, but this she knew would only add to Ellen's unhappiness, and she prudently forebore all expression of her feelings towards him. When the period of her return to her parents had arrived, she could not bear the thought of leaving her beloved sister, and as she pressed her hand in bidding her farewell, the tears that started to Ellen's eyes spoke all that her tongue had refused to utter. It was her husband that caused her grief, and she had kept all that she suffered close within her own heart, not even breathing one word of complaint against him, to the beloved companion with whom she had been accustomed from infancy, to share every thought and every sorrow.

When Mary returned home, her grief at the loss of her sister's society was bitterly felt. It would have been so, had she been assured that Ellen had only exchanged one happy home for another; but oh, how much bitterness was added to her unhappiness, when she knew that the dearly beloved associate of her infancy and womanhood had been cruelly taken from kindred, whose tenderness and affection had made her life like a pleasant dream, to spend the remainder of her days with one who was incapable of loving or appreciating her as she deserved.

Several months after Mary had left Ellen, she received the following brief letter from her, whose handwriting bore painful evidence that it was penned in much weakness and exhaustion.

"I am sorry, my dear Mary, to ask you to come to me in this inclement season; but I am sick, very sick. I want some one near and dear as you are to nurse and attend to me – the servants do as well as they can, but they are inexperienced and unskillful. My husband has never been accustomed to a sick room, and, of course, I cannot expect him to be with me, as he knows not what to do for me. My physician said this morning that I must send for my mother or sister, as good nursing was necessary for my recovery. This must be my apology, dear Mary, for my selfishness in asking you to leave a comfortable fireside, and expose yourself to the unpleasant voyage across the bay at this season."

When Mary showed the letter to her parents, they at first refused to let her go, telling her it would be hazardous to attempt to reach her sister. But Mary's resolution was taken – her sister needed her assistance, and nothing was deemed a sufficient obstacle to deter her. Her father finding her determined to incur all risks, made inquiries for a suitable opportunity. He found a small vessel which was to sail on the following day, and as the captain thought he would be able to make a short and successful trip, Mr. Grosvenor at last consented that she should go.

It was upon a bright, cloudless day, in early winter, that Mary embarked in the vessel that was to bear her to her sister. The wind blew freshly from the shore, and the captain being anxious to take advantage of it, hurried the preparations for departure. As soon as all was in readiness, the word was given, and the boat started onward in its pathway through the waters, as if rejoicing in its freedom from the tether which had bound it. Mary felt all that exhilarating excitement which is peculiar to the sensation of sailing, and she sat upon the deck to enjoy the delightful emotion. The breeze flapped the white sails and whistled through the rigging with a wild, melancholy sound; sometimes with a shrill, screaming note, like the cry of a sea-bird, and then sinking into those low, mournful tones, such as the mysterious and many-voiced wind alone can bring forth. The light bark glided rapidly through the dashing waves, as if it were borne upon wings, and Mary gladly watched each swiftly receding point as they passed by, feeling that every moment brought her nearer and nearer to her beloved Ellen.

The wind increased and blew so strongly, that the captain was obliged to slacken his sails, – for fear of the safety of his little vessel. Night was drawing near, and he was still many miles from their destined port. The cold had become so intense since the morning, that he was unwilling to cast anchor, lest they might be locked in the ice which would rapidly form around them, as soon as the wind was lulled. He knew not whether to remain where they were, or to push forward to the nearest point of land; each alternative was a dangerous and doubtful one, but he decided in choosing the latter, as he was well acquainted with the coast, and hoped to reach it before night had set in. It was an exciting moment. At the hazard of engulfing his vessel in the roaring waters around him, he put on more sail, and as they flew onward, the rushing waves every now and then would dash over the deck, threatening to draw in the vessel after them as they receded. Dark clouds were gathering over the sky, adding to the shadows of approaching night, and the stout hearts of the captain and his men began to quail at the impending danger. Large masses of ice which had been loosened from the rivers by the mild weather of one or two previous days, were now seen by the dubious twilight, rapidly driving towards them by a sudden change in the wind, and they felt that all hope was lost. Mary sat in the cabin, conscious of her danger, yet calmly awaiting the result in all the unshrinking fortitude of woman, strengthened by the confiding trust of a Christian. A sudden shock, and a wild piercing shriek from the men told that death was before her. Mary was unconscious of all that followed, until she found herself on the shore, supported by the captain, beside a fire that was kindled on the beach. The sailors had wrapped her in the only blanket they could procure, and had even taken off their own coats to add to her comfort. As soon as she opened her eyes, the old captain exclaimed, "Thank God, the dear lady lives!" Mary's heart responded to the feeling, and her prayers of gratitude arose to Him who had thus miraculously preserved her.

It was a wild scene, — that midnight watch on the lonely shore! A wide waste of snow covered all the land, as far as the eye could reach, over which the full moon was pouring her silvery light. Tall trees stood here and there, whose leafless branches were whitened by the feathery flakes that rested on them; and these were interspersed with clumps of the dark pine and cedar, through whose fringed boughs the wind was wailing, in low mournful tones; while farther off, the gloomy waters were dashing on the frozen beach with a sullen roar, as if madly disappointed of the prey which had been so lately rescued from their power. Before her, was the bright fire, casting its crimson radiance upon the snow, with its flames curling round the fragments of the wreck, that had been cast on the shore; and ever and anon rising in renewed brilliancy by the addition of the scattered boughs that had been torn from the forest by the storm. The captain and his men were conversing round the blaze, enlivened by its grateful warmth, and exchanging their mutual congratulations on their unexpected deliverance from the dangers that surrounded them. And as Mary looked on them, she saw with thankfulness, that not one had been lost. As soon as the day dawned, the Captain sent one of his men to find the nearest dwelling, that Mary might have a shelter from the weather, until he could provide some means of conveying her to the place, where her sister resided. The sailor was successful in his search, and returned with an invitation to Mary from a hospitable farmer who lived several miles distant. After an hour's walk she was kindly received by the family, who provided every thing necessary to her comfort, and urged her to remain with them until she had entirely recovered from her fatigue and exposure. But when the worthy old Captain arrived with the welcome intelligence that he had procured a carriage, and was ready to accompany her as soon as she felt able to travel, her anxiety to see her dear Ellen would not admit of any longer delay.

After a long ride of forty miles, Mary had the happiness of embracing her dear Ellen, and of finding her better than she was, at the time the letter was written, – but yet she was altered, sadly, sadly altered by sickness and suffering. Her disease was one that required undisturbed quiet, and mental repose, – and for many, many days did Mary sit by the solitary bedside of her sister, and watch and wait on her with the keenest anxiety, and with alternate hope and fear; excited by the frequent changes that came over her. Edmund Bolton seldom came to see his wife, for he could not bear the solitude of a sick room. His evenings were spent abroad in scenes of merriment, and his much enduring wife was so accustomed to his neglect and desertion in her hours of health, that she thought it no strange thing, that he should absent himself from her, when sickness had rendered her incapable of ministering to him.

When Ellen had sufficiently recovered to receive the calls of her acquaintance, she frequently heard of her husband's gayety in society, and a giddy girl one day said to her, "Mr Bolton and I had quite a flirtation at the ball last night; he has engaged me for his second wife." "The opportunity of fulfilling your engagement," Ellen replied, with a sad smile, "may be nearer than either of you anticipate." There was a time when this evidence of the heartless levity of her husband, and his cold indifference to her sufferings, would have pierced her heart with sudden agony; but she had so long grown familiar with these things, that her feelings seemed to have become paralyzed to insensibility. She looked forward to the grave as a release from mental and physical suffering; and the fears expressed by her physician met with a willing credence on her part, which continued even when there was a hope that she might again be restored to health. The calmness with which Ellen referred to her own death, in her reply to her thoughtless visitor, startled Mary; and the indignation she felt against the giddy trifler, who could jest on such a subject, at such a time, could scarcely be repressed, – a bitter sarcasm struggled to find utterance, but she looked on her sister, and for her sake, kept silence.

Mary could not bear the idea that Ellen should remain an uncomplaining victim to the unkindness and injustice of Edmund Bolton. In her love for her sister, she forgot that Ellen was a wife, – but in all her trials, Ellen never ceased to remember that there were obligations still due to her husband, even if his were neglected. Mary wished her sister to return with her in the Spring, and often entreated her to do so, but Ellen steadily refused, – "No," said she, "my duty to my husband, requires that I should not leave him, even for a few weeks." "Talk not thus, dear Ellen," replied Mary, "your duties are cancelled by his conduct, and you are not called on to sacrifice yourself for one who is incapable of appreciating all you have done and suffered for him." "My Bible dear Mary does not tell me this," said Ellen, "I am his wife, and my course is prescribed both by reason and religion."

Mary knew that Edmund was wholly devoid of virtue in principle, or action; and she thought Ellen would be justified in leaving him. Although she refrained from upbraiding him in her sister's presence, yet she took the first opportunity, when she saw him alone, to reproach him keenly for her sister's unhappiness. "I have been persuading Ellen," said she to him, "to return to her old home, that she may be restored to herself in its atmosphere of peace and affection. You found her a beloved inmate of a happy home; and you took her to yourself, to make her a miserable woman." "She has my consent to go," he coldly replied, "for a sickly wife is a dull companion, and in my pleasures I am wholly independent of Mrs. Bolton's society." In saying this, he abruptly quitted the room. His utter heartlessness so unfeelingly expressed, struck like an arrow into Mary's soul, and in painful sympathy for her sister's fate, she wept long and bitterly.

She had the consolation of seeing Ellen restored to health before she left her, – but soon after her return home, a sudden bereavement made that home a scene of gloomy desolation. Her beloved father died after a short illness, leaving his widow and daughters overwhelmed by the unexpected stroke. The afflicted mother did not long survive his loss; and Mary was left an orphan in her solitary home. Recent losses in her father's commercial transactions had taken so much from his estate, that it was supposed there would be but a small portion left for the daughters. Edmund Bolton's disappointment was visited upon his wife; and he added to the grief she felt in having lost her beloved parents, by his own increased harshness. Ellen had given birth to two lovely twin daughters, a few weeks previous to the death of her parents, and these were the only earthly sources of consolation that was left her, – for her husband had denied her request to have Mary with her.

Edmund Bolton's health had been failing for some time, and the increased irritability of his temper caused his uncomplaining wife every variety of suffering he could inflict on her. At last he was taken ill of a dangerous fever, from which it was thought he could not recover, as his constitution had become so much weakened by his previous indisposition. Ellen watched by his bedside day and night, and nursed him with as much tenderness and devoted attention as she could have done, had he been to her all that he ought to have been. She tried gently and gradually to prepare him for the probable result of his disease, but apparently without any effect. When she offered to read to him, he refused to listen, and could not bear the slightest allusion to death. The only evidence of a better state of feeling toward Ellen, was the wish he expressed that she would send for Mary to relieve her, as he plainly saw that his wife was nearly exhausted by her unremitted attendance. Ellen gladly availed herself of this permission, and in a few days Mary was with her sister. As Edmund became weaker and weaker, under the slow fever which was destroying him, he felt all that his wife was to him; a feeling of remorse often came over him, – and at times, visions of his past life haunted his memory. He was too feeble to give expression to his feelings except in occasional broken accents, – but oh, how eagerly did his poor wife drink in these faltering words; earnestly ponder them over in her heart, and treasure them up for future consolation. He declined rapidly the week after Mary's arrival; and breathed his last, expressing penitence for the past; but no words of hope in futurity. Poor Ellen sought comfort in clinging to his broken expressions of remorse and conviction, and she confidently hoped for him, where others were afraid to hope, yet unwilling to doubt. All his sins against her were forgiven and forgotten, one or two kind words, – a slight pressure of his hand, as a token of gratitude for her devotion, – a few tears shed for the past, – these were treasured in her heart, to the exclusion of all his neglect and unkindness. She only thought of him as she once fondly imagined him, when he was the lover of her youth, – and mourned his loss as if he had realized her dearest expectations, and fulfilled all her brightest dreams.

After Ellen had become sufficiently calm, to examine into the state of her affairs, and to arrange plans for the future, she found that the portion left to her was too small for the maintenance of herself and her children. She roused herself from the effects of her grief, for she knew there was a necessity for exertion. She thought over several modes of supporting herself, and of providing for the future education of her daughters. When she suggested these to Mary for her judgment and counsel, Mary replied, "No, my dear Ellen, your health is too much shattered to make such attempts, you are not equal to these exertions, all that I have is yours, and if it be not sufficient for our support, I will open a school in our former happy home, and this will supply us with ample means. I am strong and healthy, and can endure confinement and fatigue, but you are wholly unfit for any of the plans you have proposed."

Soon after Mary had brought her widowed sister and her infant daughters to the home which was still her own, she commenced her proposed plan with all the energy of a determined and persevering spirit. She had the satisfaction of gaining the requisite number of pupils, and found that her annual income would be more than sufficient to supply all their wants, and would even allow them to keep up the refined elegancies of their youthful home. Ellen's health continued feeble for several years, and Mary had brought her sister to the Springs where I met them, in the hope of restoring her languid frame to its healthful energies. Ellen was much benefitted by her visit, but her anxiety to return to her beloved daughters, whom she had left in the charge of a faithful servant, hastened her return much earlier than Mary wished.

Before we parted, they made me promise to visit them before my return home, and I soon after availed myself of their pressing invitation. The place where they resided was beautifully situated near the suburbs of the city, on a lofty eminence which commanded a fine prospect of the bay, the river, and its wooded shores. The noble old oaks that shaded the lawn gave an air of rural seclusion, although the church spires and chimneys of the city were visible here and there through their aged trunks. The time for re-assembling Mary's pupils had not yet arrived, and I found the two sisters enjoying the sweets of leisure, and employing their hours in those refined and elegant pursuits which had made the happiness of their youthful days. It was delightful to see these devoted sisters again re-united in one home, after their painful separation. Ellen's twin daughters, Mary and Ellen, were two lovely, interesting children, and the affection with which they were treated by both, would have left a stranger in doubt as to which was the mother.

After a delightful visit, I bade farewell to these affectionate sisters and the dear children, with the hope of their fulfilling a promise of spending the next summer's vacation at Glenwood. Both Mary and Ellen are my frequent correspondents, and from the latter I have learned that Mary has had several offers of marriage, from men of high standing and moral worth, but she has refused them all, having determined to live only for Ellen and her children. Her devotion to her dear sister's happiness has met its reward in the consciousness of having fulfilled a sacred duty. She is beloved and respected by all with whom she associates, and one of the happiest women among my acquaintance, is the noble-minded and self-sacrificing Mary Grosvenor.

# AUNT MABLE'S LOVE STORY

*

## *Susan Pindar*

'*Aunt Mable's Love Story*' *was originally published in* Graham's Magazine *in 1848. Months of searching have turned up no information about Susan Pindar except for the titles of six books she wrote which all seem to be children's books. They are:* Fireside Fairies, or Christmas at Aunt Elsie's *(D. Appleton, New York, 1849, 1850, 1852, 1865);* Midsummer Fays, or The Holidays at Woodleigh *(D. Appleton, New York, 1850, 1851, 1852, 1865);* Legends of the Flowers *(D. Appleton, New York, 1852, 1865);* Storybook *(A Compilation) (D. Appleton, New York, 1853);* Poems *(J.A. Jenkins, 186?); and* The Wentworths: Their Home and Friends *(B. Lothrop & Co., Boston, 1876). It is not unusual to find a woman's name listed as author of one or two stories that seem promising in terms of literary potential, and then to find nothing more about or by her, as is the case with this writer. This story, which conforms down to the smallest detail to the paradigmatic early old maid vindication story, seems to have just that right touch of linguistic compression, that bit of wry authorial humor that bespeaks an urge to push just a little bit harder on the boundaries of the literary conventions, just to see what will happen.*

Graham's Magazine *grew from a merger between* Gentleman's Magazine *and a monthly called* Atkinson's Casket, *purchased by George Graham in 1841. The 28-year-old Philadelphian hired Charles Jacob Peterson, later to become the proprietor of* Peterson's Magazine, *to help with the preparation of the first issue. The next month Edgar Allen Poe joined the staff to handle the literary editorial duties, a post he held until April 1842, when he was replaced by Rufus Griswold, a man still famous for both his prose and poetry anthologies of*

*American writers and his malicious literary quarrels.*

*The mid and late 1840s were the beginning of the rise to dominance of the American literary scene by the periodicals.* Graham's *was, from its beginning, a successful publication because it paid the highest prices offered, attaining a very large circulation. Appleton's* Cyclopaedia of American Biography *(1880) called it 'the best periodical of its kind published in the United States.' It included among its contributors Edgar Allen Poe, William Cullen Bryant, Henry Wadsworth Longfellow, James Fenimore Cooper and Nathaniel Hawthorne.*

*There is no periodical publishing today in the United States that can boast a readership that represents such a large percentage of the population as could* Graham's, *which exerted great influence on its readers in that time of no radio, no telephones, no stereos, no televisions, no movies and no cars.*

# AUNT MABLE'S LOVE STORY*

*

"How heartily sick I am of these love stories!" exclaimed Kate Lee, as she impatiently threw aside the last magazine; "they are all flat, stale, and unprofitable; every one begins with a *soirée* and ends with a wedding. I'm sure there is not one word of truth in any of them."

"Rather a sweeping condemnation to be given by a girl of seventeen," answered Aunt Mable, looking up with a quiet smile; "when I was your age, Kate, no romance was too extravagant, no incident too improbable for my belief. Every young heart has its love dreams; and you too, my merry Kate, must sooner or later yield to such an influence."

"Why, Aunt Mable, who would have ever dreamed of your advocating love stories! You, so staid, so grave and kindly to all; your affections seem so universally diffused among us, that I never can imagine them to have been monopolized by one. Beside, I thought as you were never — " Kate paused, and Aunt Mable continued the sentence.

"I never married, you would say, Kate, and thus it follows that I never loved. Well, perhaps not; I may be, as you think, an exception; at least I am not going to trouble you with antiquated love passages, that, like old faded pictures, require a good deal of varnishing to be at all attractive. But, I confess, I like not to hear so young a girl ridiculing what is, despite the sickly sentiment that so often obscures it, the purest and noblest of our higher nature."

"Oh, you don't understand me, Aunt Mable! I laugh at the absurdity of the stories. Look at this, for instance, where a gentleman falls in love with a shadow. Now I see no substantial

*From *Graham's Magazine*, vol. 33, 1848.

*foundation* for such an extravagant passion as that. Here is another, who is equally smitten with a pair of French gaiters. Now I don't pretend to be over sensible, but I do not think such things at all natural, or likely to occur; and if they did, I should look upon the parties concerned as little less than simpletons. But a real, true-hearted love story, such as "Edith Pemberton," or Mrs. Hall's "Women's Trials," those I *do* like, and I sympathize so strongly with the heroines that I long to be assured the incidents are true. If I could only hear one *true* love story – something that I knew had really occurred – then it would serve as a kind of text for all the rest. Oh! how I long to hear a real heart-story of actual life."

Kate grew quite enthusiastic, and Aunt Mable, after pausing a few minutes, while a troubled smile crossed her face, said, "Well, Kate, *I* will tell you a love story of real life, the truth of which I can vouch for, since I knew the parties well. You will believe me, I know, Kate, without requiring actual name and date for every occurrence. There are no extravagant incidents in this 'owre true tale,' but it is a story of the heart, and such a one, I believe, you want to hear."

Kate's eyes beamed with pleasure, as kissing her aunt's brow, and gratefully ejaculating "dear, kind Aunt Mable!" she drew a low ottoman to her aunt's side, and seated herself with her head on her hand, and her blooming face upturned with an expression of anticipated enjoyment. I wish you could have seen Aunt Mable, as she sat in the soft twilight of that summer evening, smiling fondly on the young, bright girl at her side. You would have loved her, as did every one who came within the sphere of her gentle influence; and yet she did not possess the wondrous charm of lingering loveliness, that, like the fainting perfume of a withered flower, awakens mingled emotions of tenderness and regret. No, Aunt Mable could never have been beautiful; and yet, as she sat in her quiet, silver-gray silk gown, and kerchief of the sheerest muslin pinned neatly over the bosom, there was an air of graceful, ladylike ease about her, far removed from the primness of old-maidism. Her features were high, and finely cut, you would have called her proud and stern, with a tinge of sarcasm lurking upon the lip, but for her full, dark-gray eyes, so lustrous, so ineffably sweet in their deep, soul-beaming tenderness, that they seemed scarcely to belong to a face so worn and faded; indeed, they did not seem in keeping with the silver-threaded hair so smoothly parted from the low, broad brow, and put away so carefully beneath a small cap, whose delicate lace, and rich, white satin, were the only articles of dress in which Aunt Mable was a little fastidious. She kept her sewing in her hand as she commenced her story, and stitched away most industriously at first, but gradually as she proceeded the work fell upon her lap, and she seemed to be lost in abstracted recollections, speaking as though impelled by some uncontrollable impulse to recall the events long since passed away.

"Many years since," said Aunt Mable, in a calm, soft tone, without having at all the air of one about telling a story, "many years since, there lived in one of the smaller cities in our state, a lady named Lynn. She was a widow, and eked out a very small income by taking a few families to board. Mrs. Lynn had one only child, a daughter, who was her pride and treasure, the idol of her affections. As a child Jane Lynn was shy and timid, with little of the gayety and thoughtlessness of childhood. She disliked rude plays, and instinctively shrunk from the lively companions of her own age, to seek the society of those much older and graver than herself. Her schoolmates nicknamed her the "little old maid;" and as she grew older the title did not seem inappropriate. At school her superiority of intellect was manifest, and when she entered society the timid reserve of her manner was attributed to pride, while her acquaintance thought she considered them her inferiors.

This, however, was far from the truth. Jane felt that she was not popular in society; and it grieved her, yet she strove in vain to assimilate with those around her, to feel and act as they did, and to be like them, admired and loved. But the narrow circle in which she moved was not at all calculated to appreciate or draw forth her talent or character. With a heart filled with all womanly tenderness and gentle sympathies, a mind stored with romance, and full of restless longings for the beautiful and true, possessed of fine tastes that only waited cultivation to ripen into talent, Jane found herself thrown among those who neither understood nor sympathized with her. Her mother idolized her, but Jane felt that had she been far different from what she was, her mother's love had been the same; and though she returned her parent's affection with all the warmth of her nature, there was ever within her heart a restless yearning for something beyond. Immersed in a narrow routine of daily duties, compelled to practice the most rigid economy, and to lend her every thought and moment to the assistance of her mother, Jane had little time for the gratification of those tastes that formed her sole enjoyment. "It is the perpetual recurrence of the little that crushes the romance of life," says Bulwer; and the experience of every day justifies the truth of his remark. Jane felt herself, as year after year crept by, becoming grave and silent. She knew that in her circumstances it was best that the commonplaces of every-day life should be sufficient for her, but she grieved as each day she felt the bright hues of early enthusiasm fading out and giving place to the cold gray tint of reality.

With her pure sense of the beautiful, Jane felt acutely the lack of those personal charms that seem to win a way to every heart. By those who loved her, (and the few who knew her well did love her dearly,) she was called at times beautiful, but a casual observer would never dream of bestowing upon the slight, frail creature who timidly shrunk from notice, any more flattering epithet than "rather a pretty girl," while those who admired only the rosy beauty of physical perfection pronounced her decidedly plain.

Jane Lynn had entered her twenty-second summer when her mother's household was increased by the arrival of a new inmate. Everard Morris was a man of good fortune, gentlemanly, quiet, and a bachelor. Possessed of very tender feelings and ardent temperament, he had seen his thirty-seventh birthday, and was still free. He had known Jane slightly before his introduction to her home, and he soon evinced a deep and tender interest in her welfare. Her character was a new study for him, and he delighted in calling forth all the latent enthusiasm of her nature. He it was who awakened the slumbering fires of sentiment, and insisted on her cultivating tastes too lovely to be possessed in vain; and when she frankly told him that the refinement of taste created restless yearnings for pursuits to her unattainable, he spoke of a happier future, when her life should be spent amid the employments she loved. Ere many months had elapsed his feelings deepened into passionate tenderness, and he avowed himself a lover. Jane's emotions were mixed and tumultuous as she listened to his fervent expressions; she reproached herself with ingratitude in not returning his love. She felt toward him a grateful affection, for to him she owed all the real happiness her secluded life had known; but he did not realize her ideal, he admired and was proud of her talents, but he did not sympathize with her tastes.

Months sped away and seemed to bring to him an increase of passionate tenderness. Every word and action spoke his deep devotion. Jane could not remain insensible to such affection; the love she had sighed for was hers at last – and it is the happiness of a loving nature to know that it makes the happiness of another. Jane's esteem gradually deepened in tone and character until it became a faithful, trusting love. She felt no fear for the future, because she knew her affection had none of the romance that she had learned to mistrust, even while it enchanted her imagination. She saw failings and peculiarities in her lover, but with true womanly gentleness she forebore with and concealed them. She believed him when he said he would shield and guard her from every ill; and her grateful heart sought innumerable ways to express her appreciating tenderness.

Mrs. Lynn saw what was passing, and was happy, for Mr. Morris had been to her a friend and benefactor. And Jane was happy in the consciousness of being beloved, yet had she much to bear. Her want of beauty was, as I have said, a source of regret to her, and she was made unhappy by finding that Everard Morris was dissatisfied with her appearance. She thought, in the true spirit of romance, that the beloved were always lovely; but Mr. Morris frequently expressed his dissatisfaction that nature had not made her as beautiful as she was good. I will not pause to discuss the delicacy of this and many other observations that caused poor Jane many secret tears and sometimes roused even her gentle spirit to indignation; but affection always conquered her pride, as her lover still continued to give evidence of devotion.

And thus years passed on, the happy future promised to Jane seemed ever to recede; and slowly the conviction forced itself on her mind that he whom she had trusted so implicitly was selfish and vacilating, generous from impulse, selfish from calculation; but he still seemed to love her, and she clung to him because having been so long accustomed to his devotedness, she shrunk from being again alone. In the mean season Mrs. Lynn's health became impaired, and Jane's duties were more arduous than ever. Morris saw her cheek grow pale, and her step languid under the pressure of mental and bodily fatigue; he knew she suffered, and yet, while he assisted them in many ways, he forebore to make the only proposition that could have secured happiness to her he pretended to love. His conduct preyed upon the mind of Jane, for she saw that the novelty of his attachment was over. He had seen her daily for four years, and while she was really essential to his happiness, he imagined because the uncertainty of early passion was past, that his love was waning, and thought it would be unjust to offer her his hand without his whole heart, forgetting the protestations of former days, and regardless of her wasted feelings. This is unnatural and inconsistent you will say, but it is true.

Four years had passed since Everard Morris first became an inmate of Mrs. Lynn's, and Jane had learned to doubt his love. "Hope deferred maketh the heart sick;" and she felt that the only way to acquire peace was to crush the affection she had so carefully nourished when she was taught to believe it essential to his happiness. She could not turn to another; like the slender vine that has been tenderly trained about some sturdy plant, and whose tendrils cannot readily clasp another when its first support is removed, so her affections still longed for him who first awoke them, and to whom they had clung so long. But she never reproached him; her manner was gentle, but reserved; she neither sought nor avoided him; and he flattered himself that her affection, like his own passionate love, had nearly burnt itself out, yet he had by no means given her entirely up; he would look about awhile, and at some future day, perhaps, might make her his wife.

While affairs were in this state, business called Mr. Morris into a distant city; he corresponded with Jane occasionally, but his letters breathed none of the tenderness of former days; and Jane was glad they did not, for she felt he had wronged her, and she shrunk from avowals that she could no longer trust.

Everard Morris was gone six months; he returned, bringing with him a very young and beautiful bride. He brought his wife to call on his old friends, Mrs. Lynn and her daughter. Jane received them with composure and gentle politeness. Mrs. Morris was delighted with her kindness and lady-like manners. She declared they should be intimate friends; but when they were gone, and Mrs. Lynn, turning in surprise to her daughter, poured forth a torrent of indignant inquiries, Jane threw herself on her mother's bosom, and with a passionate burst of weeping, besought her never again to mention the past. And it never was alluded to again between them; but both Jane and her mother had to parry the inquiries of their acquaintance, all of whom believed Mr. Morris and Jane were engaged. This was the severest trial of all, but they bore up bravely, and none who looked on the quiet Jane ever dreamed of the bitter ashes of wasted affection that laid heavy on her heart.

Mr. and Mrs. Morris settled near the Lynns, and visited very frequently; the young wife professed an ardent attachment to Jane, and sought her society constantly, while Jane instinctively shrunk more and more within herself. She saw with painful regret that Morris seemed to find his happiness at their fireside rather than his own. He had been captivated by the freshness and beauty of his young wife, who, schooled by a designing mother, had flattered him by her evident preference; he had, to use an old and coarse adage, "married in haste to repent at leisure;" and now that the first novelty of his position had worn off, his feelings returned with renewed warmth to the earlier object of his attachment. Delicacy toward her daughter prevented Mrs. Lynn from treating him with the indignation she felt; and Jane, calm and self-possessed, seemed to have overcome every feeling of the past. The consciousness of right upheld her; she had not given her affection unsought; he had plead for it passionately, earnestly, else had she never lavished the hoarded tenderness of years on one so different from her own ideal; but that tenderness once poured forth, could never more return to her; the fountain of the heart was dried, henceforth she lived but in the past.

Mr. and Mrs. Morris were an ill-assorted couple; she, gay, volatile, possessing little affection for her husband, and, what was in his eyes even worse, no respect for his opinions, which he always considered as infallible. As their family increased, their differences augmented. The badly regulated household of a careless wife and mother was intolerable to the methodical habits of the bachelor husband; and while the wife sought for Jane to condole with her — though she neglected her advice — the husband found his greatest enjoyment at his old bachelor home, and once so far forgot himself as to express to Jane his regret at the step he had taken, and declared he deserved his punishment. Jane made no reply, but ever after avoided all opportunity for such expressions.

In the meantime Mrs. Lynn's health declined, and they retired to a smaller dwelling, where Jane devoted herself to her mother, and increased their small income by the arduous duties of daily governess. Her cheek paled, and her eye grew dim beneath the complicated trials of her situation; and there were moments when visions of the bright future once promised rose up as if in mockery of the dreary present; hope is the parent of disappointment, and the vista of happiness once opened to her view made the succeeding gloom still deeper. But she did not repine; upheld by her devotedness to her mother, she guarded her tenderly until her death, which occurred five years after the marriage of Mr. Morris.

It is needless to detail the circumstances which ended at length in a separation between Mr. Morris and his wife – the latter returned to her home, and the former went abroad, having placed his children at school, and besought Jane to watch over them. Eighteen months subsequent to the death of Mrs. Lynn, a distant and unknown relative died, bequeathing a handsome property to Mrs. Lynn, or her descendants. This event relieved Jane from the necessity of toil, but it came too late to minister to her happiness in the degree that once it might have done. She was care-worn and spirit-broken; the every-day trials of her life had cooled her enthusiasm and blunted her keen enjoyment of the beautiful; she had bent her mind to the minor duties that formed her routine of existence, until it could no longer soar toward the elevation it once desired to reach.

Three years from his departure Everard Morris returned home to die, and now he became fully conscious of the wrong he had done to her he once professed to love. His mind seemed to have expanded beneath the influence of travel, he was no longer the mere man of business with no real taste for the beautiful save in the physical development of animal life. He had thought of all the past, and the knowledge of what was, and might have been, filled his soul with bitterness. He died, and in a long and earnest appeal for forgiveness he besought Jane to be the guardian of his children – his wife he never named. In three months after Mrs. Morris married again, and went to the West, without a word of inquiry or affection to her children.

Need I say how willingly Jane Lynn accepted the charge bequeathed to her, and how she was at last blessed in the love of those who from infancy had regarded her as a more than mother."

There was a slight tremulousness in Aunt Mable's voice as she paused, and Kate, looking up with her eyes filled with tears, threw herself upon her aunt's bosom, exclaiming.

"Dearest, best Aunt Mable, you are loved truly, fondly by us all! Ah, I knew you were telling your own story, and – " but Aunt Mable gently placed her hand upon the young girl's lips, and while she pressed a kiss upon her brow, said, in her usual calm, soft tone,

"It is a true story, my love, be the actors who they may; there is no exaggerated incident in it to invest it with peculiar interest; but I want you to know that the subtle influences of affection are ever busy about us; and however tame and commonplace the routine of life may be, yet believe, Kate," added Aunt Mable, with a saddened smile, "each heart has its mystery, and who may reveal it."

# OLD MAIDISM VERSUS MARRIAGE

*

## Susan Petigru King

*Upon receiving and reading a copy of* Busy Moments of an Idle Woman *(D. Appleton and Co., New York, 1854) published under the pseudonym 'An Idle Woman,' James Louis Petigru, South Carolina lawyer, wrote to his daughter, Susan Petigru King (1824-75), 'You have burst upon me as an author almost as surprisingly as Miss Burney did on her unsuspicious parents. . . . I have no doubt you will receive a great deal of praise, for the dialogue is witty and sparkling, and the descriptions circumstantial and striking. I dare say that if you were to take to study, you might, in time, attain to the deliniation of the passions and rise to the walk in which Miss Austen is admired. But it is something to do as much, though in a lower style of art, and tho' your performance is indebted for its success to the initiation of temporary evanescent modes of behavior and can hardly be expected to survive the present fashion. . . . ' However, her literary output was quite small. She followed this collection of five stories with her only novel, the semi-autobiographical* Lily *(1855), a novella and two short stories published in one volume under the title* Sylvia's World, *and* Crimes Which the Law Does Not Reach *(1859), and ended her decade-long literary career with another novella,* Gerald Gray's Wife *(1864). Her work is remarkable for its realism in a period characterized by sentimentality. In a 1903 essay surveying fiction in his home state of South Carolina, Ludwig Lewisohn, despite a tendency on other occasions to judge women writers more harshly than men (if he bothers to acknowledge them at all), praises her as 'a woman of clear and vigorous spirit, eagerly ready amidst a somewhat narrow social life, to think for herself and not afraid to put her thoughts on record . . . she deserves praise.'*

*However, she has failed to receive either praise or notice. Her literary reputation seems to have been obscured by responses to latter activities that left her with no champions. She had been sent, at the age of 15, to a fashionable finishing school in Philadelphia. Soon after her return to Charleston, South Carolina she was married at the age of 19 to Henry C. King, a law student in her father's office and the son of his good friend. He was admitted to full partnership in the firm in 1851. Although her father, James L. Petigru, was opposed to secession, respect for him was so great in South Carolina that he and his family were safe in the heart of the Confederacy. Sue's husband Henry, however, joined the Confederate army and was killed in 1862, early in the war. One writer records that she left her marriage and went to Washington, DC, where she had gone to work in the Republican administration. There she met and married Christopher Columbus Bowen who represented South Carolina in Congress from 1868 to 1871 and is treated as a dishonest villain by all the historians of the Reconstruction period. When they married, he was still married to his first wife and he stood trial for bigamy. One historian reports that he was acquitted; another that he served time in prison after having been convicted. In all the varying descriptions of his political and legal machinations, it is clear that his wife supported him in every way that she could, including the publication of a weekly newspaper she wrote in which she exposed whatever skeletons she knew about in the closets of her husband's political enemies, thereby making of herself a figure wholly inimical to Charlestonian society.*

*There is passing mention of her in Mary Boykin Chesnut's* A Diary from Dixie *but the mention makes clear the ambivalence felt towards her by those in her social milieu.*

*However, despite her temperament and her politics and her marriages, she is a writer who deserves more attention than she has received. Her work seems to be informed by the bitter irony of a Cassandra who sees but cannot avert pain and danger. Her female characters view with an almost pitiless clarity the inequities and inadequacies of their circumstances and the limitations of choice available to them. They have the courage to speak of what and how they see, but they lack the ability to take the kinds of actions that might lead to change. They do not see any possibility of change. The author doesn't make clear whether her characters have too little imagination or too much. At any rate, their understanding of their own reality leaves them with few and painful choices between being vulnerable — and inevitably victimized — or heartless — and dead inside, between stifling, and potentially killing conformity or self-defeating isolating defiance. Because her writing is so startlingly realistic and therefore seems to be more contemporary than it is, the absence of a political vision is disappointing.*

# OLD MAIDISM VERSUS MARRIAGE

---*---

PART I

Seven fair girls! what a pretty sight! All young, all lovely, and all sufficiently clever to make their gay gossip entertaining.

It was a cold winter evening, – in fact, it was during the Christmas holidays, and the well warmed room with its huge crackling fire of great oak logs, its deep crimson curtains, its old-fashioned yet comfortable chairs, its luxurious sofas piled with cushions, and its general air of sturdy hospitality, would have formed a delicious contrast, to gladden any one hardy enough to venture out into the dismal, dark night, and then, shuddering, return to this cosy apartment. It was the dining-room of Mrs. Bloomfield, a rich widow, who, with her one son and only daughter, was "keeping Christmas" at her fine old estate, "Oak Forest."

Dinner was just over – the brilliant light of numerous candles in tall silver candelabra shone upon the relics of the dessert, where, *pêle-mêle*, were displayed walnuts, peccans, West India fruits, liqueurs, excellent old *Southern* Madeira, ground-nut paste, and other articles, foreign and indigenous, the whole richly served in beautiful glass, massive plate and gorgeous china, all of some fifty years' date or more. At the head of the table sat Caroline Bloomfield. She had taken the seat just quitted by her mother, and, with her fairy fingers, was stripping the thick yellow peel from a golden banana. Just eighteen, above the usual height, fully and gracefully formed, with raven hair and dark blue eyes, regular yet expressive features, and a manner by turns soft and winning, dignified and reserved, Caroline bade fair to long retain the reputation she had already acquired of an accomplished coquette, for there lurked a spark of diablerie in her bright eye, and yet she had a way of sweeping her cheek with the fringes of her white lids before she fairly raised them, that was infinitely startling to an unaccustomed observer. Then her complexion was pure and dazzlingly fair, and her black braided tresses, falling low upon either side of her oval face, were, at the back of her small head, gathered into a richer plait, that crowned her queenly brow with a natural tiara.

Next to Caroline sat her most intimate friend, Laura Stanley, a quiet grave woman of twenty, with no very great beauty of face or figure, but handsome nevertheless from her air of intelligence, fashion and elegance. She was exquisitely dressed, as usual; and, bending over a newspaper, she was the most silent of the party, only occasionally looking up with a smile when some lively sally from the group attracted her notice. Her younger sister Fanny, a giddy little sixteen years old pet, had left the table, and was lounging on a sofa, her golden ringlets tossed back upon the cushion that supported her head, her brilliant hazel eyes half closed, her red, pouting lips opening but to yawn, and with her tiny foot stretched out and buried in the long hair of Bruno – Caroline's Newfoundland dog, – her entire person wore an air of languor very seldom visible in this prettiest of pretty creatures. Adelaide Clifton was diligently shelling and eating nuts. She was the musician of the party, a fine-looking, handsome girl, more like a Northern belle than a Southern gracieuse; for she was slight, slender and active, with a bright color, fine teeth, talked rather loud, and was more striking than delicate in her appearance. A soft, gentle maiden, with great blue eyes, luxuriant fair hair, a lovely figure, a sweet, yielding smile, and rather sentimental and moonshiny altogether, was at Caroline Bloomfield's other side. Louise Merrington was a general favorite. Very slight, very fairy-like, with auburn hair and black eyes, snowy skin, and such a mischievous mouth, was Louise's cousin, Julia Merrington, who formed the sixth of this bevy of beauties. Seventh and last, but with the exception of their young hostess, the handsomest of all, was Annie Hamilton. She was a glorious brunette, and it would have been almost impossible at the first glance to find a fault in the perfect picture she presented of youth and beauty; but then a closer examination showed that, in a certain nameless grace, she must yield to Caroline. Such was the collection of Charleston's fairest daughters, who might have challenged criticism. But where were the cavaliers that should have been in attendance upon this bright phalanx? Let us listen to the youngest hostess.

"Well, really, I had no idea we would miss those men so much! Very tiresome of them to choose this evening to pay their visit to Colonel Hunscome. I told George, the Colonel had a dinner to-day, and would be sure to keep them till late to-night, but dine they would at two o'clock, and off to Briarly. So we must suffer the ennui of a 'ladies' party,' with nobody to tease and abuse."

"Worse than that, Garry," said Adelaide Clifton; "the night is growing so dark and dismal, that if they attempt to return, they may pitch into some of the swamps and we will be forced really to mourn. For my part, if harm comes to Willis Lawrence, I shall put on weeds, for I consider myself 'as good as engaged' to that gentle and genteel Adonis, don't I, Fanny?"

"I neither know nor care," said pretty Fanny, almost roused into a toss of her languid head, for her flirtation with Willie Lawrence had often been broken in upon by Adelaide's persistence in calling upon the handsome youth to attend to her and her musical affairs.

"Don't make Fanny wretched, pray," laughed Caroline, "can't you see the poor child is suffering now? She is thinking of Mary Hunscome's attractions, and shows her misery by going to sleep. Dear Fan, don't gape your head off, for though we have often heard Madame G. say 'cette enfant n'a pas de tête,' yet I think, on the whole, you would miss that little cocoanut you dignify with the name."

"Now, Caroline, don't you try to be as witty as Annie Hamilton, it's a signal failure; you neither move me, nor succeed in your effort at brilliancy – lie quiet, Bruno. Arn't these women too stupid?"

"Thanks, Fanny," joined in Annie Hamilton, "for the compliment to me, and, as I am bound, after that to subscribe to all your sentiments, I do say, I think we are very dull. Since Mrs. Bloomfield went off just now to read that long letter, we have done nothing but grumble, except Laura, who pores over that "Saturday Courier" as if it were the philosopher's stone of amusement. I, for one, will give my silver étui to any young lady of the present company, who will devise some entertainment for us to pass the time, till these recreant knights return to us and to their duty."

"What candid young souls we are! what amiable simplicity pervades our group!" said Julia Merrington. "How unblushingly we proclaim that we can't amuse ourselves for one evening without the 'Lords of Creation,' apropos, sing it, Addy, will that pass the time, and gain me the étui, hey, Annie?"

"No, I bar music," cried Annie; "Adelaide walks over us at all times, with her fingering, skill, execution, taste, voice, knowledge, &c., &c., and, besides, don't you see she has been devouring nuts for the first time these three weeks; she won't be able to sing decently, and, as there is no one to profit by our advantage this evening, we won't even have the pleasure of listening to her usually sweet notes, without huskiness. That won't gain you the prise, Julia."

"I am very glad there are no men to listen to your *doléances* and regrets," broke in the low voice of Louise Merrington; "our set of attendants are sufficiently conceited as it is – pray don't let them ever find out how we miss them."

"Pahaw, child, don't you suppose they know it?" at last spoke Laura Stanley, raising her fine gray eyes. "But I have a proposition, Annie, and this old newspaper which you sneer at, is my inspiration. I have just been reading the story of those young bachelors, who met on some jovial occasion, vowed a solemn vow to meet again in ten years' time in that very room (all those who remained single, that is), compare notes, and drink a bottle of vinegar as punishment for their neglect of the fair sex. They sealed up the bottle, and at the close of the two lustres, but one solitary individual – one wretched *old* bachelor – survived of the group, who sat down with the musty bottle, and was forced by his conscience to swallow the contents, while he read epistles from his fettered friends, detailing their matrimonial experience. Now, suppose we make a compact of the like nature? Deciding upon the number of years to wait, drawing up the papers, &c., will fully occupy us for an hour or so, and pass the time which you all appear to find so heavy."

"Agreed, agreed," cried every voice.

"But I propose an amendment," said Annie Hamilton. "Let it be 'cherry bounce' or 'maraschino,' not vinegar. I speak, openly I confess it, mesdemoiselles, from interested motives, for I dread that fate will cast this drink ultimately upon me, and I have a regard for my teeth and complexion."

"Stop, Annie, before you fly for desk, pen and paper; where is the étui? Hand over."

"What a screw you are, Laura; here it is, and now to business. Caroline, you who hold the pen of a professor of fine strokes and dark, rounds and turns, you who dot your i's and cross your ti's, let Laura dictate and you transcribe, we will all follow or copy."

Each busy girl seized a sheet of "Bath hot pressed," and, with quills or steel pens, as luck or fancy prompted, was prepared to do her part. Even Miss Fanny pushed away Bruno, rose to a sitting posture, and was wide awake in three minutes.

Thus ran the important document which was not decided upon without much discussion and dispute.

"OAK FOREST, *December 22d,* 1837

"We, the undersigned, all spinsters, more or less young, and all reasonably attractive, do hereby vow and declare, that on the 22d day of December, 1847, being ten years from this date, we will meet in this very spot and drink with much solemnity a certain bottle of 'Maraschino,' in token of our present friendship and good fellowship. Those who shall meanwhile have entered into the holy bonds of matrimony will be excluded, but hereby promise that, in lieu of themselves, they will send to the survivors in life and maidenhood, a letter describing their position as wives or widows. If one of these belowmentioned subscribers be tempted to forget her promise, and refuse to come, or refuse to betray the secrets of her prison-house, or write falsely, each of the subscribers who faithfully keeps hers, shall be entitled to claim from the defaulter a diamond ring. All this being fully settled and agreed to, we have hereunto set our hands and seals.

'CAROLINE MOORE BLOOMFIELD,
LAURA ELIZABETH STANLEY,
ADELAIDE R. CLIFTON,
BLANCHE LOUISE MERRINGTON,
JULIA MERRINGTON,
FANNY STANLEY,
ANNIE HAMILTON.'

ALL'S
WELL THAT
ENDS
WELL

"Well, I don't consider that a lawyer-like paper, I am sorry to say," said Laura, "but it is my best attempt, though I am a lawyer's daughter. Young ladies, are you satisfied?"

"Perfectly; we are easily pleased, glad young things as we are. Now for the maraschino. A glass around; in true club style, 'our noble selves.' Carry, give us a bottle to seal, and then we shall deposit it with dear Mrs. Bloomfield, with as many directions and cautions, as if it were the regalia of England. Fanny, who so grave?"

"I am thinking how old I shall be when we open that cordial. Twenty-six! Good heavens, shall I be worth speaking to then. That is what makes me grave, Annie."

"Not the speaking to, little Fan, but the looking at, is what afflicts your young mind. Courage, though, pretty pet; I, with spectacles on nose (for I shall be twenty-eight, and decrepid of course), shall have the pleasure of reading your letter, signed a happy wife, Fanny Lawrence, and indifferent to age.

"Pray, Miss Hamilton," Fanny was just beginning, when the sound of horses and horsemen approaching, the rapid roll of a swift-going buggy, the rattling of carriage wheels, many voices, and much laughter announced the approach of a large company, and startled our captivating busy group.

"Girls!" cried Mrs. Bloomfield, through the half-opened door, "the night has cleared a little, and George has brought all the Hunscome party with his own to finish the evening, so make haste, and of course you will have a dance. Mary Hunscome has with her Mrs. William Arnold, and a host of others. Pray smooth your ringlets, and join us as soon as possible. Carry, come to the drawing-room first, dear, and see if the ladies would not like to take a chance at your brushes and mirror, after their drive. Where are you carrying that bottle, child?"

"Lock it up, mamma, and I will give you the reason why in ten years, mamma," and, with laugh and jest, and merry musical voices, the pretty band flew to their rooms, to hasten their Abigails, as they bared white necks and round arms, and doffed boots, and donned French slippers. Some twined garlands of scarlet holly in their flowing curls. Annie Hamilton looked like a brilliant Bacchante, with her dark tresses bound with ivy leaves. Fanny Stanley placed a bouquet of *pensées* in her glittering hair, and Caroline Bloomfield shone, as usual, the brightest of all, with her unadorned braids and simple snowy dress.

## PART II

Ten years have rolled away. Ten long years to some – passing short to others, and it is now December, 1847.

It is the 4th of the month, however, and not the 22d, and the scene lies in Charleston, and in a ball room. Some chance guests – Englishmen – and a Northern *bel esprit*, with her husband, are the reasons given for this unusual occurrence, a large party – a regular February entertainment at the beginning of December, a time when our city is generally deserted.

The accomplished and witty Northern belle, of course, attracted the most attention, but, next to her, reigned the still lovely, and still enchanting heiress, Miss Bloomfield, of Oak Forest. Twenty-eight summers have passed over her radiant head, and she is in all the bloom of her beauty. She is much changed since I first introduced her at eighteen, it is true, but the change is not to her disadvantage. If the pure complexion has taken a creamy tint, while ten years ago its whiteness had only a rosy shadow, this *couleur mâte* shows out with more striking effect the light of her deep blue eyes, the blackness of her ever-luxuriant hair, and the vivid red of her beautifully formed mouth. Her figure has now reached perfection; it is amply developed – the shoulders broad yet falling, the bust exquisitely proportioned, and the arms gleam out, round and polished, as they rest upon her harp. She has been singing – this charming Caroline, and, as she strikes the last chords, and the melody of her voice dies away in one long, heart-thrilling note, a burst of thanks ensues from the whole company; but her expressive eyes and lips turn from them to seek the praise which falls quietly and earnestly upon her willing ear, while murmured by a person who bends over her with marked attention. He is not strictly handsome, but he is tall and well made, with a decided air of fashion, very small feet and hands, admirably dressed, short perfumed curls shading a brow of promise, and such eyes! Perhaps I dwell too much upon eyes, but they go a great way with me. I have a passion for eyes, and no fixed rules as regards my admiration. I have admired green eyes more than I ever shall black or blue ones, and small eyes, where great ones were defying me to find in them a fault. If you tire (my possible reader) of my prosing about these "mirrors of the soul," pray forgive me, but take up the study yourself in your leisure hours, and you will soon begin to watch all your acquaintances' visual orbs, as I do mine, not much to the satisfaction of some. But to resume. These eyes I was about to speak of were very saucy and very handsome, and said fifty different things in as many seconds, when they chose, but now they wished only to repeat the same thing fifty times, so they reiterated, "I adore you," to Carry Bloomfield, till she turned aside, and, busying herself with her music, tried to conceal the rising colour that spread over her face. "Ah! Caroline Bloomfield at her old tricks," said some kind and observant old lady; "well, she has her match in Edward Allingham – that is one comfort."

At this moment Caroline rose, and, pushing away her harp, took her companion's arm, and allowed him to lead her towards a recess where a small table, covered with books, prints and toys, gave excuse for a lounging flirtation, which two great arm-chairs helped on. Caroline began replacing her gloves, and, as she slid the soft kid over her dainty fingers, Edward Allingham made a petition. "Pray, dear Carry, let them stay off a moment longer. I always wish, when I am with you, that gloves were not; it is only when some one else appears, and some man looks at or takes your hand, that I rejoice in these otherwise odious coverings. Let me see your pretty fingers – what ring is that?" and bending over so that she was concealed from the company, he pressed the little hand to his lips, and tried to slip on her third finger a superb emerald hoop.

"*Halte là!*" cried Caroline, laughingly disengaging herself from his grasp; "I am not your *fiancée* yet, – and, seriously, Edward, you must wait, as I have told you, till the 23d of this month, for my answer."

"What folly!" said Edward, indignantly.

She bowed.

"I beg your pardon, Carry, but you know I love you, and I hope you love me, – what then is the meaning of this?"

"Simply because it depends upon six letters I shall receive on the 22d, whether I ever marry you or not. Listen to me, Edward – don't start off and look furious, – that avails you nothing; on the contrary, listen to me, and I will tell you a secret. Ten years ago, seven young maidens, of whom the eldest was barely twenty, were met together to keep a merry Christmas in an old Southern country-house. To beguile the weariness of a leisure hour, the giddy creatures drew up a written document, in which they promised to meet at the same spot ten years afterwards (all those who remained single, that is), and renew their friendship, and talk over their adventures in life, while those of the band who had married, should send, in their places, letters describing their experience of the wedded state. The ten years have passed, and of that gay and thoughtless group, I alone remain in 'single blessedness,' and, singular enough, I have never dreamed of marriage till just when I am on the point of receiving six faithful accounts of six *ménages*, and I have determined to let my decision abide by what I can gather and judge from this trial."

"Do you mean to say, that if any of these six women should happen to have made an unhappy match, you will thence conclude that all marriages are miserable, and keep yourself from the chances of such a fate?"

"I mean to say, that if the average of these marriages is unsatisfactory, such will be my decision, for, if half a dozen women, whom I know to have been all well-bred, amiable, agreeable, and lovable, – and, what is more, all remarkably pretty, should have failed to find contentment in these 'holy bands,' I cannot hope for a better destiny. But this is scarcely possible, dear Edward; so set your mind at ease, and on Thursday the 23d, you shall have my answer."

"Foolish woman," said her lover, quite confidently and admiringly, for a moment's reflection induced him to conclude that he ran no great risk, and he led her off to dance with as unclouded a brow as if he had already placed the rejected emerald upon the third finger of her right hand.

## PART III

The old dining-room at Oak Forest! Dear, charming spot! but how much gayer and brighter it shone, those ten years ago. Then, such a group of beauties graced its wide and hospitable table, and now, there was but our Caroline, alone and somewhat sad, her head pillowed upon her white hand, while she lay at full length upon the sofa, a lamp shedding its brilliancy just upon her bended brow; and glancing from it down to six voluminous letters, and a small dark bottle, scrupulously sealed. Such was the picture. There lay the six epistles, and there mused Carry. Some had come that day – one was a week old, – the rest had dropped in during the interval.

73

None had been opened. Caroline drew from the pocket of her cashmere dress (gros bleu à corsage montant et aux manches justes) a folded paper. It rustled as she smoothed it out, and a delicate perfume of Patchouli escaped from it. It was the contract. A soft smile broke the sadness of Carry's face, and lingered amid the dimples that graced her lips.

"Well, I shall read them, as they come upon the list. Let me see – 'Caroline Moore Bloomfield;' here's a striking illustration, – 'the first shall be last.' I, who head the train, am the only maiden to keep the agreement. 'Laura Elizabeth Stanley.' Dear Laura, – dear noble-minded Laura! What does she say of married happiness? Where is her testimony?" and Carry rose from her lounging attitude, settled the little standing collar that encircled her snowy throat, and while, with one hand, she arranged the heavy folds of her dress around her slight waist (with that pretty gesture so common to some women, and which has such an air *agaçant*), with the other, she searched out the letter which bore Laura's seal. "Now for it."

"MILLGROVE, *December 1st,* 1847

"I begin my letter to-day, my very dear Carry, because, as my quiet home is so far from you, and our mails so irregular, I must allow for all accidents, failures, and stoppages, and give my epistle full three weeks' start of the eventful 22d. Is it not strange that you, the handsomest and cleverest of us all, should be the only 'old maid' of the group? And yet it is not strange, for, of course, as the most superior, your claims and expectations were higher – are still; and you have a right to be very fastidious and difficult in your choice. How well I remember how you looked ten years ago – in fact, how we all looked, – when, with girlish frolic, we wrote the famous compact; and the gay dance that ended the evening! How dear Fanny flirted with Willy Lawrence, and how Annie Hamilton protested that Fanny was bent upon showing that she should not drink the maraschino at the appointed time. Poor dear Fanny; she has such a family now! I often ask her if she regrets those gay, *insouciants* days – but I must not tell her answer; that will fill her own letter. And now to begin my history. You know, dear Carry, that we are far from rich. Mr. Leslie has many debts, and we must live plainly and quietly. My two boys are sturdy fellows, and my little girl is a pattern of prettiness and sweetness. She is a great comfort to me. Ned and Harry are at school all the week, and only return home on Saturday. Mr. Leslie is kept much occupied in his fields, and, as I never visit Savannah, which is our nearest city, I see no one but my little Fanny. Mr. Leslie is kind and indulgent to me in all my whims, but he does not fancy books, so that I seldom read, as he prefers seeing me occupied in domestic concerns. My harp has long since been 'hung upon the willow,' — that is, I think, three years ago, it was banished to the barn, to make room in our very small parlor for Mr. Leslie's turning-lathe, which interests him very much; and, as he does not like music, it was no great sacrifice to me to give up my songs. I do a great deal of sewing; my boys are what is called 'hard upon their clothes,' and, therefore, keep me hard at work. I have not touched a pencil or paint brush for years, so you see I am quite a *bonne ménagère*, and have discarded such frivolous pursuits as accomplishments. In winter, I cannot take any exercise, there being no place to walk except the rice-banks, and Mr. Leslie thinks that women find more wholesome exercise in stirring about the house than in sauntering over rice-banks. During the summer, in the Pineland, I have a saddle-horse, but Mr. Leslie likes his gait so much, that he generally rides him himself, so Fan and I then take rousing walks, and lay in a supply of health and strength for the winter. You see I lead a very humdrum existence, dear Carry and I dare say you would vote such vegetation 'a horrid bore,' but I am quite satisfied and contented with it, and I have shown its sharpest edges and truest colors, so as to write with the candor that we promised each other. I long to see you. I think it is nine years since you were my bridesmaid, and I saw you last. Yes, my twin boys are eight years old, and you have never seen them. Fanny is six. I inclose you a curl of her golden hair. She has eyes as blue as yours, dearest; and such a white skin. Well, I must say good-bye; it is now six months since I wrote to you, and I shame to confess it, — two sweet letters of yours lie by me, unanswered till now; but what can I write to you about? What have I to interest such a dainty creature as 'Miss Bloomfield' — the fascinating 'Miss Bloomfield?' I read an account of your appearance at the Newport fancy ball this last August. One of my Pineland neighbors lent me the Herald. How charming you must have been. Dear Carry, love me always — don't forget your old friend,

LAURA LESLIE

75

"I drink with you in spirit the first glass of maraschino."

The letter dropped from Caroline's hand. "Poor, poor Laura! What a fate! Is that a life for any one to lead! and for Laura, so clever, so accomplished, so refined! No books, no music, no society; nothing but a hard, selfish husband. Can I recognize Robert Leslie in this picture — 'Far from rich;' — what folly! He is very well off; but he is close and grasping; and he ties Laura down, and they live poor and pinching that he may scrape together a huge fortune — for what? To double it; and yet Robert Leslie was thought a good match. I liked him very much; he seemed very much in love; gave her fine presents; and it was altogether very suitable — but now" — She read over the letter; it seemed sadder and more touching than before; tears dimmed her eyes; she sighed heavily, and turned with an effort toward Adelaide Clifton's flowing penmanship. But first the tiny bottle was unsealed and uncorked, and filling a glass, she murmured, "Better times to dear Laura," and touched with her lips the bright cordial.

"COLUMBIA",                                            *December 18th*, 1847

"Well, dear Carry, the 22d draws near, and your warning note tells me that I must prepare to fulfil my share of our little compact. I must give you my history. Lord! my dear Child, what can I say? I see you almost every winter, so that you know a good deal of my proceedings; and for one who lives such a dull life as I do, what news have I to transcribe. You are well acquainted with my liege lord, and know as well as I do all his whims and oddities. He is a very good kind of husband, as good as any, I believe; the only thing very difficult for me to get over is his dislike for music. I must own, it was very hard for me to give up my piano; and when I thought of all the time and money wasted upon it, I really mourned. But John has not the slightest ear, and he says, besides, that a woman becomes too much public property when she has people racing after her to listen to her playing and singing. My two children show very little musical taste, and their father rejoices in it. He says that a good housekeeper had better be in her kitchen than practising love ditties. Do you recognize John Gilmore and his gallantries beside my piano in all this? Ah, my dear Carry, men change very much after marriage. They say women do – but their husbands more.

"Another thing I find very hard to stand is, I have been married barely five years, and yet it is three since I have gone to a party. John hates balls (he who was such a dancer and flirter), and it is not the style in this place for married women to go much into company, so we mope at home, and have solemn tea-parties and grave visitings, and are dreadfully dull and proper; and, oh dear! it is all very tiresome when one comes to write it down, though life jogs on '*tant bien que mal*,' when one does not begin to analyze it. But as we were to write truth, I have written, and may you profit. Adieu, dear Carry; if you do marry, try and find out (if you can) what your husband's real tastes are before the knot is tied. I will be in town to spend Christmas with Aunt Elizabeth. Should you return from Oak Forest before the 5th January, you will see

"Your constant friend,

"ADDY GILMORE"

"A health to Addy," said Caroline, and then broke the seal of "Blanche Louise Merrington's" letter.

"RED RIVER                                    *November 23rd,* 1847

"Away from the far West comes this token, dear Carry, that I remember our agreement, and that I know you are the only spinster of us all. I will not begin with any usual compliments and questions, for as this will be one of six, you will not care to wade through many sheets, I hasten to give you, in as few lines as possible, my experience. You are aware, that through some unfortunate business transactions, we became straitened in our means, and Mr. Radnor determined to remove West. We had been married little more than a year (we have only been married now three and a half), and my baby was but a few months old, when we emigrated, and I found every thing very dismal and wretched. No neighbors; no society; a church ten miles off, and the nearest city fifty. Our house was small, dirty, unfurnished. I almost screamed when I saw it, but matters improved in that after a while, and now I am quite comfortable; but it is a dreary sort of life, and I long to return to civilization. I miss my summer trips to the North, and whenever mamma writes, telling me that she, and Gertrude, and Lizzie, are off for Newport, &c., I constantly ask Harry if he is worth all I gave up for him. Harry is a nice person, but he is not quite so energetic as I hoped to find him. You know I am not a stirring person myself, so I expect those I am with to stir for me; and Harry is so slow. We never would have lost so much had he exerted himself; and then his ideas are so *bornées*. Having lived always with those queer stuffy aunts, he expects every body to be like them, and therefore looks for old-fashioned ways and looks in me. He is wedded to his own notions: in short, if truth must out, he is dreadfully stubborn; horribly afraid of being ruled by his wife; so he is constantly kicking against imaginary obstacles, held up to his wrath by possible antagonists. Do you remember how amiable and yielding we used to think him. 'Harry Radnor will agree to it,' was always said! Ah, dearest Carry, it is very difficult to know people before you come to live with them. If ever you are tempted to choose a husband, bear this in mind. I never was successful at letter-writing, as you know, so I plunge right into the midst of the business, and having given you a slight picture of my marriage lines, I will close this. We are fast making money, in spite of Harry's slow ways; so if we don't lose it again, you may expect, some time or other, to embrace once more

"Yours ever affectionate

"LOUISE RADNOR

"How is dear Annie Hamilton, and all the others of our set? I only hear from Julia, poor thing."

"What has become of Lou's sweet temper! How querulous and dissatisfied is her tone – she who was once the mildest and gentlest of beings. Alas! alas! marriage makes strange changes. A health to Louise. And now for Julia."

"CHARLESTON,                                    *December 19th*, 1847

"I received your note yesterday, dear Carry with the pretty dress for your name child's Christmas gift and I join my thanks to hers for your kind remembrance. You recall to me that I owe you a letter, so that, seizing a leisure moment, I hasten to redeem my pledge, given ten years ago. A history of my married life! a true history! You know almost as much as I. Fanny Stanley and I were married within a week of each other, two years after our visit to Oak Forest. Both were love-matches — mine a most ill-advised one. I was headstrong and self-willed; chose my husband for his handsome person and endearing ways, without one doubt given to the warning voices that bade me recollect his flighty unstable principles. I loved Edward Calvert, and with the giddiness of barely eighteen, plunged headlong to my ruin. I love him still, dear Carry; and though his death, three years ago, has left me penniless and burthened with the care of two children, I still think he did his best. But he was a gay spendthrift; dissipated his own fortune and mine; took to 'evil courses;' and I am a widow, teaching for my daily bread, and difficult to be recognized as the haugty Julia Merrington, who thought this world an invention got together for her entertainment. I do not set you against marriage; far from it. They tell me that Edward Allingham is a suitor of yours. Is it so? Johnny and Caroline send you showers of kisses. Where are you reading this? In the dining-room? Ah, those past years! how they rush back upon one.

> "Sincerely and truly,
> "yours ever attached
> "J. M. CALVERT."

Silently and sadly Caroline laid aside this letter, and turned to Fanny's. As she broke the seal her clouded brow and anxious look seemed to say, "not one happy wife?"

"THE OAKS – SANTEE,                    *December 16th*, 1847

"In the midst of all my Christmas preparations, my dear Caroline, while I was turning over some old letters to find some waste-paper for the children, I fell upon a sealed manuscript, and behold, it was our foolish contract. How it made me laugh. Charley said, "Mamma, please give me the funny paper;" so I gave it to him, and no doubt he has made, if not "ducks and drakes," at least chickens and boats of it before this. As I do not relish your coming upon me for a diamond ring, I determined to sit down and write my letter. If there are any mistakes, attribute them to Helen, who is overturning my inkstand every five minutes, and pulling my hair between whiles. I do not know exactly what to write about. Am I to give a history of married life? It is just like other peoples'. I have six children, the youngest only four months old; but this you know quite well. Mr. Lawrence is very good, and makes a capital husband and planter. I have a good deal of my own way; we live a great deal in the country; we quarrel occasionally, but make it up again. My children give me most concern. Two of them are far from healthy and I am frequently confined to their room for weeks, as neither Mr. Lawrence nor I can leave them at all to the care of servants. I am now in all the agony of deciding whether I will have a governess for my eldest girls, or send them away from me to town, to school. This has been the important subject on my mind for months. I might ask your advice; but how can a girl decide for the mother of six children. Ah, Carry, perhaps you have chosen the wisest course in remaining single. I am very little my own mistress now, with so many claims upon my attention. I can hardly realize that I am only twenty-six. Why, you are twenty-eight, and as free as the air. Don't misunderstand me, though; I think a woman's surest happiness is found in marriage. The children are calling me, and baby is crying at the height of his voice; so in haste, adieu.

"Your affectionately,

"FANNY L."

" 'A woman's surest happiness;' humph," mused Caroline; "and this is the brightest picture yet. Five letters are over, and there only remains my own dear Annie's. Edward, I fear your chance is small." This was said gayly; but a bright spot burnt in each cheek, and there was a feverish impatience in her manner as she pushed aside the heap of letters, and opened Mrs. Atherton's. It was the longest of all, filling closely four sides of thin French paper.

"NEW YORK,                                                    *December 14*, 1847

"'Hail, hail, all hail,' thou wisest of Carolines! — the only one of seven who has steadfastly kept her much (ought to be) prized liberty — but stop; while I write, a thought comes across me, that perhaps this opening may stand against all future thoughts of matrimony on your part. Far be it from me to thus decide you; and besides, I have just been reading a little story of De Balzac's, which comes so *apropos* I must tell it to you; for,

of course, a '*jeune fille, une demoiselle bien née*,' does not read
De Balzac herself. There is a certain young countess, who has
married her cousin, a colonel under Napoleon; and being very
romantically given, when she discovers that after rubbing off
his glittering exterior, there nothing remains but a hearty,
coarse, good-tempered soldier, she falls into great distress, and
loses all her natural gayety. M. le Colonel is ordered to the
wars, and leaves Madame under the care of his aunt, a
marquise of *la vieille roche*, who begins to love very dearly her
new relative. One night, when the young countess had retired,
more than ever miserable she bethinks herself of a promise
made to an old schoolmate and bosom friend to describe to her
her new state – a promise long neglected. Seizing her pen, she
begins to write, and the picture was far from flattering to the
male sex in general, and to M. le Colonel in particular. In the
midst, enter la Marquise, who takes from Julie's passive hand
the treasonable epistle, and calmly reads it through. What says
the wise dowager? '*Ma petite, une femme mariée ne saurait
écrire ainsi à une jeune personne, sans manquer aux conven-
ances. Car, si à table un mets ne nous semble pas bon, il n'en
faut dégouter personne. Surtout mon enfant, lorsque, depuis
Eve jusqu'à nous le mariage a paru chose si excellente.*' Julie
throws her letter into the fire, and under the tuition of her
courtly aunt becomes – but that is the rest of the story, and
regards us no longer. What I have just written is the case in
point. You will, perhaps, wonder why I should really hesitate
to write to you (my dearest friend) with the openness and
candor we promised each other. But, though you may come
down upon me for the diamond *solitaire*, the price of forfeiture,
I am determined. A little bird has whispered in my ear that my
fascinating acquaintance, Ned Allingham, is caught at last; and
knowing you so well, I begin to fancy that you will not, with
your usual caution, let slip this capital opportunity to decide,
from others' experience, before you place the yoke upon your
own snowy and well-shaped shoulders. So I am silent, and the
next steamer will bring you a tiny package. Wear the ring for
my sake, and it may, perchance, prove a wedding gift. We are
so gay here just now! Can't you come on for a week or two
before Lent? I have just bought such a cloak of violet velvet,
with a pink bonnet to match – divine! and I should so fancy
your dear self in them! If you will come, I sha'nt wear them till
you get something quite as becoming. Mr. Atherton desires me

81

to add his entreaties to mine. We are a model *ménage* (this much I will say), and see each other so little, that we are as pleased to meet as if we were mere acquaintances. Adieu, dear Carry! Though I have already pressed you a great deal to come on this winter, don't hold out in your refusal, but be a good girl, and tell me I may hope to see you before New-Year's day. I must close in all haste, for the sun is shining a brilliant request that I should rush to bask in his rays. The horses are ready; my beautiful Zara is pawing up the paving stones at the door. Mr. Ledyard and John Leigh are patiently waiting till I seal my voluminous letter, so I must don my habit, and ho! for a merry canter to Bloomingdale, while you, puissant and unkind Miss Bloomfield, obstinately refuse to be one of the party. We will put it off till you come. Oh! for a telegraph to give your answer.

> "Now and ever, your
> "ANNIE"

Perplexed, tormented, saddened, uncertain what to do, now that she had finished reading the letters, which she had fondly hoped were to give so much comfort and decide her fate so easily, Caroline hid her eyes upon her open palms, and thought, and thought, till her brain whirled. "I was very, very foolish," she said, half aloud, "to tell Edward that these should form my answer. Surely they are not much in favor of matrimonial felicity, and yet" — yes, the truth must out; Caroline, like Mr. Allingham, had had no doubt but that the epistles would all tend to prove the bliss of wedded life, and she had demanded the test as a lingering touch of power, nothing more.

"Pshaw! I will consult with Dora. There is no use in telling mamma what a simpleton I am, but Dora is the very person." She rang the bell — "Ask Miss Dora to come here" — to the servant, and again she pored over the fatal letters.

"Well, Carry dearest," said a sweet, musical voice, "what do you wish? Here I am. You won't mind Jim, will you? I was playing with him, and brought him along. Lie there, my pet, and don't cry, but be a man, and do as much mischief as you can quietly." So saying, Mrs. George Bloomfield tossed her infant son upon a pile of cushions on the floor, flung him her embroidered handkerchief to tear to pieces, and turned to her fair sister-in-law for an explanation. Dora was a New Yorker, small and graceful as a fairy, and pretty as a dream, exquisitely dressed, with a certain set about her whole person and attire that spoke the admired belle.

"First, my dear Dora, read that," and Carry handed up the contract.

"Why, I never heard of this wisdom before. How comes this?"

"Oh, I never spoke of it, and had never thought of it till about a month ago; and then – then when – in short, Dora, you know Edward Allingham," and Carry told the whole story. How Dora laughed!

"And this is the delicate distress! Poor child! What a prospect! Though you have the united counsel of six wiser heads than mine, and though they all say, as plainly as veiled words can speak, 'Caroline, stay free; Caroline, stay free,' still you wish my tiny voice. Now there remains but one obstacle in my way. What would you like me to say?" And Dora's gayety again rang a merry peal.

"I vow, Dora," exclaimed Carry, "you are incorrigible. Be serious as you can be, and advise me."

"Serious, my sweet sister; – oh, Jim, in what a situation is your mamma placed! Don't look at me, young gentleman; if you are tired of my handkerchief, here comes something more;" and loosing a gorgeous bracelet from her wrist, it rolled over and over till it reached her baby's feet, who crowed with delight as he clutched the brilliant jewel in his chubby hands. "Profiting by Jim's lapidary tastes, and while he is gravely inspecting my 'Christmas,' I will be serious. To remain single, my dearest Carry, is all very well so long as, young and beautiful, you have shoals of admirers and crowds of friends; but in ten or fifteen years from now, with your circle scattered, yourself wearied of out-door amusements, your contemporaries grown old, and retiring, day by day, more into their own shells and houses, you will find yourself alone, and shut out from many privileges. No one depends upon you; no life, no happiness is twined closely with your own. There will be George and myself and our children, and 'Aunt Carry' will always be to us a 'personage;' but will Aunt Carry not consider herself as secondary when her feelings and her ambitions may wish a first part? You may do a deal of good; your life may be very useful, very cheerful, very full of pleasant duties; but still a mother will always rank you in actual necessity to those around her. Your nephews and nieces will love you dearly, but not with that clinging tenderness that belongs to a child's love, that heart-to-heart affection. Are you convinced? Say then you marry, now comes the rub. Make your choice well. By well, not well in looks or goods alone; never dream of matrimony till you find a man, tender, devoted, whose appearance, manners, rank, means, all please you. Judge if his conversation suits you, if your tastes assimilate, and prefer him to all the world before you say 'I am yours' in the face of heaven and earth. Then prepare to enter courageously upon your new life. For months be guarded. Do not let a hasty impression of many discomforts with regard to your husband or his family influence your future existence. Question yourself your own faults; dwell more on them than on his; – you will soon understand each other. In a word, there is no maxim like the old one, 'Bear and forbear.' But, at the same time, should you have been deceived in the man you love, – should it indeed be a nature of tarnishing brass, and not pure gold, – hold fast your woman rights; yield where you should, and where you should not, be firm. And hear me clearly: if he is unworthy, part, at once and for ever, were it in the honey-moon. Better a life of strict seclusion, a life of mourning and of sorrow, than a miserable double existence, dragged on in continual wretchedness, bringing children into the world to follow, possibly, in their parent's footsteps; or, worse still, have some horrible, disgraceful wind-up of an ill-assorted union. Such instances as these are rare, my dearest Carry; a man must be worthless indeed, who, properly managed, changes so much after marriage as some men have done. But their wives have acted foolishly. What was right they should have stuck to, and never have given up what they knew was their just due. As a conclusion, on earth there cannot be greater contentment than in a family where a man and wife truly love, and worthily endeavor to make each other's happiness. I am done."

"Ah! Dora, your marriage is fortunate. George is so good, so kind, you could not be otherwise. He spoils you."

"Spoils me! Nay, Carry, we have learned what I preach, 'bear and forbear;' 'yield and yield.' For instance, George wishes to spend a part of each winter at the South, and I wish to go this summer to Europe, we will do both – both yield. I wished to learn the polka, George wished me to give up riding 'Selima,' who was very frisky and dangerous. Selima, was sold, and I am a *polkeuse comme il y en a peu, – voilà!* Not that this should be viewed in the light of a *bargain*; but naturally, when we are gratified by a concession, we like to give one in return, and a system which begins in gratitude, ends in conviction. But do you know, I think we northern women make better wives than you southerners. Southern women are apt to be either slaves or tyrants; and themselves aid in making their husbands despots or Jerry Sneaks. They have such a trick of losing their own individuality in the imposing grandeur of the 'he' and 'him' who is the arbiter of their destiny. Prove that I am wrong, and show me what a real southern wife can do. Come, what answer will you send poor Edward? Your heart speaks for him. Reason speaks for him. Decide;" — and Mrs. George, with a playful gesture, put pen, ink, and paper before her sister, and paused for an answer.

Ere that answer came, the dining-room door was opened, and Mrs. Bloomfield entered; with her was George.

"A wandering knight claims the hospitality of these halls," said Mrs. Bloomfield. "I offer it freely, but he awaits your consent, my Carry."

"A consent to more than that, dear, dear Carry," whispered Edward Allingham, as he rushed past his friends to the sofa where sat his mistress.

Caroline drew herself up, hesitated, partly frowned. "Your own hand has penned the answer, my uncertain and doubting sister," said Dora, triumphantly; "while I was delivering my long peroration, your trembling fingers have first written on Annie Atherton's letter, 'Dearest Edward,' and then, 'Mrs. Edward Allingham.' I proclaim our blushing Caroline wooed and won."

Mrs. Bloomfield's arms were around her weeping yet happy daughter; Dora's hand rested on her husband's shoulder, who held his handsome Jim close to his heart; and the lover, "too blest for words," looked with glistening eyes at his priceless treasure.

So ends the tableau and this history.

# FRUITS OF SORROW,
# OR AN OLD MAID'S STORY

—————————— * ————————————

## Mary C. Vaughan

'Fruits of Sorrow, or An Old Maid's Story' was originally
published in Ladies' Wreath, a women's magazine edited by
Helen Irving, in March 1856. Mary C. Vaughan, the author,
has proved an almost completely elusive figure. Her earliest
published story in Ladies' Wreath was 'The Faithful Friend,'
published in Volume 12, one year earlier than 'Fruits of
Sorrow.' The earlier story, set on a southern plantation during
the Revolutionary War, depicts the heroic behavior of a dog
who saves his mistress and her household from the depreda-
tions of British soldiers. It is one of five stories published by
Vaughan in that volume. Among them is 'Duty; or Ada Lester's
Story,' another old maid story which, although longer and
somewhat more complex than 'Fruits of Sorrow,' tells a similar
tale of a life of renunciation and service. That story has
received some attention from a number of feminist historians,
but there is apparently no complete copy of the story extant.
The story included here was her only story for 1856. In the
following year, there was one. And then no more.

In 1867, Woman's Work in the Civil War: A Record of
Heroism, Patriotism and Patience was published under the joint
authorship of L.P. Brockett, MD, to whose further credit are
listed the titles of five earlier books, and Mrs. Mary C.
Vaughan. In his 'Preface' to the book, Dr Brockett tells us all
that we know of her beyond what might be surmised by the
'Mrs' that precedes her name:

> In the autumn of 1865, Mrs. Mary C. Vaughan, a skilful [sic]
> and practiced writer, whose tastes and sympathies led her to
> take an interest in the work, became associated with the
> writer in its preparation, and to her zeal in collecting, and

*skill in arranging the materials obtained, many of the interesting sketches of the volume are due. (pp. 6-7)*

When Ladies' Wreath *was first published in May 1846, Volume 1, number 1 included an introduction which set the tone maintained by the periodical during its sixteen years of publication:*

*In presenting to our beloved countrywomen, a new periodical, devoted to their interests . . . we should state briefly, the objects we have in view. . . . It is to be emphatically the* Voice of Woman: *giving utterance to truths in her behalf, whose value has never yet been adequately appreciated or understood. If we can succeed in awakening the wives, mothers, and daughters of the land, to a sense of their true dignity, and the important agency they are destined to exert in the moral and physical regeneration of the world, our utmost expectations will have been realized.*

\*　　　\*　　　\*

*A wife — a mother — magical words, comprising the sweetest and purest sources of earthly felicity. The empire of women is that of the affections, her reign, the reign of love, of beauty, of reason. The sternest and most impassive nature yields in some degree to the gentle influence of the wife, and the son continues to obey his mother longer after she has ceased to live. . . . On the character of mothers depends, under God, the regeneration of mankind.*

*Are then the claims we have made for our sex too exalted? Is it not rendering to mankind a valuable service, to impress on the mind of woman, the* fact *of this influence, and to enlighten her as to its nature, its extent, and the duties it imposes?*

*Such is the work, to which the magazine we propose to issue, is to be mainly devoted. As its mission will be chiefly confined to our own sex, so woman's character and destiny, her wants, her rights, but above all, her duties, will chiefly occupy its columns. The cause of the oppressed seamstresses of our cities, who are suffering from the grinding oppression of unprincipled employers, will be advocated . . . nor shall we turn a deaf ear to the cry of our sisters in bonds, because the Creator has given them a skin darker than our own. Wherever an evil is found, that experience has proved to be a source of general corruption, there will our efforts be directed to expose it fearlessly. . . .*

*To the MOTHER, as the source of moral influence, and the former of the moral atmosphere, on whose healthfulness so much depends, we shall speak of her solemn obligations, her precious privileges, and the blessed rewards of maternal faithfulness and care.*

*On the mind of the youthful female we shall seek to impress the thought, that 'women are not to live for themselves' – that their mission from cradle to grave is one of benevolence and love; and that only in proportion to their reception of this truth, is their beneficial action on society at large.*

*The claims of labor, not only to an adequate compensation, but to the respect of the community, and its perfect compatibility with true dignity of character and mental culture, will be constantly urged in these pages, which shall never, while under our control, be closed against any cause which seeks the removal of moral evil, or the alleviation of human misery.*

Here we have evidence of that melange of commitment to social change and the continued oppression of women through the application of ideas about her nature and purpose all neatly summarized by the ever-incanted theme, 'Women are not to live for themselves.' And yet, as if its meaning were not clearly contradictory to the purposes both implicit and explicit in the above statement of purpose, the same editor included under the heading 'Beautiful Thought' the following quotation from Elizabeth Barrett Browning's feminist novel-in-poetry, Aurora Leigh:

*I breathe large at home. I drop my cloak; unclasp my girdle, loose the band that ties my hair. Now could I but unloose my soul! We are sepulchred alive in this close world, and want more room.*

This, however, appeared sixteen years later.

# FRUITS OF SORROW,
# OR AN OLD MAID'S STORY

*

I was recovering from a long illness. Reclining upon my couch, with its carefully arranged pillows and snowy drapery, I enjoyed to the utmost the sensation of renewed life which, with increasing strength, thrilled through every vein. The sashes were raised, and through the closed blinds came the soft breath of a June morning, bearing on its invisible wings the mingled perfume of a thousand flowers. On a table within reach of my hand stood a vase filled with rare exotics, and by my side sat the dear friend who had brought this beautiful offering.

I never tire of gazing on flowers; but now something inexplicable attracted my attention to the countenance of Lucy Latimer — a countenance which, notwithstanding her thirty-five years, still wore a calm and mournful beauty. Upon her features beamed their usual sweet benevolent smile, yet at intervals a convulsive spasm distorted the small mouth or contracted the broad, fair brow, and I thought that, more than once, a bright tear glistened in her downcast eye.

For the first time the thought flashed across my mind that there might be "story" connected with the life of Lucy. I had known her from my childhood, and her course had been ever the same. She had few pleasures, but many duties. She had literally gone about doing good. A true sister of charity, wherever misfortune came in the extensive circle of her influence, she was seen binding up the broken heart, and pouring the oil of consolation upon the bruised spirit. For all ailings, mental or physical, she had a ready sympathy. From the couch of the sufferer, hurried by some devouring pestilence to the confines of eternity, she shrank not while life remained. She smoothed the pillow of the consumptive, and held the cooling draught to fever-parched lips; and, above all, her warnings and her prayers often led their object to exclaim, in true penitence and submission, "Not my will, O Lord, but Thine be done!"

Did a fond mother bend in agony over the form of her departed darling, Lucy's gentle soothings brought comfort to her sorrowing heart. Did some young wife see the husband of her heart's choice, the father of her little ones, stricken in his prime, and borne away to the silent tomb — the soft voice of Lucy awakened her to present duties, and reminded her of the loving care of Him who is the "Father of the fatherless, and the widow's God." In short, she who had been an only child, and was now an orphan, seemed never to feel the want of kindred; for she was the daughter, the sister, the beloved friend of all who suffered.

"Dear Lucy," said I suddenly, after a long silence, during which all these thoughts had passed in review before me, "you are very sad to-day, and I know by the dreamy look of your eyes, that it is some sorrowful memory of the past which thus disturbs you. Will you not tell me what it is? You have never spoken to me of your past life; yet I remember having heard my mother say, long ago, that your youth had been blighted by some fearful misfortune. If it is not too painful, will you tell me about it? I feel that I can sympathize with you, though, before this illness, I have hardly known sorrow or pain."

Lucy's face was turned from me as I spoke; but when I concluded, she arose and approaching the bed, stopped and kissed me. — Then, without saying a word, she buried her face in the pillow, and gave way to an uncontrollable burst of tears. Surprised and grieved that I should have caused such pain to that dear friend, who, under all previous circumstances had seemed calm and self-controlled, I mingled my tears with hers, beseeching her forgiveness, and endeavoring to soothe her by the gentlest words. But the repressed sorrows of years had found vent in tears which could not at once be checked. After a long time, however, her sobs ceased, and when, at length, she raised her face, nothing but the mournful expression of her moistened eye told of the conflict which, of late, had raged so fiercely in her soul.

"Forgive, my dear young friend," said she, "these tears which may have seemed to reproach your kindness. On this day, the anniversary of my bitter trials, a word recalls their memory; but believe me, your gentle expressions of sympathy alone could have unsealed the fountain of my grief. But I will tell you the story of my youth, and then you will cease to wonder at my occasional hours of sadness or even violent grief.

"When the month of June, 1832, was ushered in, I like you now, was young, and lived with my parents in a luxurious home; but, unlike you I had one great sorrow. I had been long engaged to Cecil Alleyne, a young clergyman, who had devoted his life to the work of a missionary. We were to have been married on the first of June, and to have gone out to India as missionaries. But Cecil was in declining health. A cold, taken during the previous winter, while in the exercise of parochial duties, had preyed upon a delicate constitution, and it was now feared that that scourge of northern climates, consumption, had marked him for its prey. At the time appointed for our marriage and embarkation, he was too ill to leave his room, and the ship sailed without us.

"You may well believe that it was a bitter trial to this noble young man, full of earnest enthusiasm in the cause he had espoused, to be thus cut short in a career which promised to be one of more than ordinary usefulness. But he bowed meekly to his Maker's will with scarcely a murmur at the blighting of all his hopes. But with little of his child-like confidence in our heavenly Father, I rose in fierce rebellion at this unexpected disappointment. Alas! how little did I dream of the sorrows yet in store for me! or how soon my proud heart would be humbled by repeated afflictions!

"Cecil's father lived at S—; six miles from my own home, and thither, at an early hour, I was summoned on the 16th of June. – Cecil was very ill, the old servant said. He had broken a blood vessel during the previous night, and believing that his hours were numbered he earnestly desired to see me.

"I had returned from S— but a few days before, and left him apparently better – so much so, that we had planned a quiet marriage as soon as he should be able to ride over to us. For this I was, if possible, more anxious than himself, that I might gain the sweet privilege of being his constant nurse. Thus when I saw Mr. Alleyne's carriage drive to the gate, I ran eagerly down the path, expecting to see dear Cecil alight from it. Judge then of my disappointment at the intelligence I received.

"Making my preparations with tearful haste, I was soon on my way, and anxiously urging greater speed. The journey seemed interminable, but we arrived, at last, and springing from the carriage, I soon stood by the bedside of my dying

Cecil. The bed, for freer circulation of air, was drawn to the centre of the apartment. Opposite to it was the vine-covered window which opened into the garden, from whence rose the perfume of countless flowers, the busy hum of bees from the quaint old apiary in its sunniest nook, and the song of birds from out the branches of the magnificent horse-chestnuts which, even in the sultriest noon, threw their cooling shadows upon the house. Without, all was life and joy – within, gloom and the shadow of death.

"There lay Cecil, but how changed! The pallid brow, the sunken eye, the labored breath – all told how swift were the strides which the destroyer was taking with his victim. But a holy calm sat on brow and lip, for to him death had no terror. A bright smile beamed on his pale face as he saw me, and he feebly raised his arms to clasp my neck as I knelt beside him and wept with grief that would not be controlled.

" 'Weep not, my beloved one,' he said, in feeble accents; 'mourn not, my Lucy, our parting will not be long, and we shall meet above. Gladly would I have lived to have passed the years with you here; but God wills otherwise, and let us not repine. Grieve not, Lucy, that he is so soon taking me from a world where poison lurks in every cup, where danger follows our footsteps in every path, and where the blight of sin is on all we hold most dear.'

"With a violent effort I controlled the manifestations of my sorrow. But it was his office to cheer me; the words of the dying infused courage into the heart that was so soon to be left alone. But few more words passed between us, for exhausted by the violent hemorrhage and long-suffering he desired sleep to refresh him for the farewells which soon must take place. I passed my arm beneath his head, and, after a glance of undying affection from those glorious eyes which had always beamed with love for me, he closed them in a soft slumber, peaceful as an infant's upon its mother's breast. His sleep was long, and when he awoke, the shadows of evening were falling, and the honeysuckle at the window had filled the apartment with the rich fragrance that twilight dews always win from its perfumed challices. It seemed the fitting incense to bear the pure soul to heaven.

"This slumber had been refreshing, and Cecil was able to converse with his parents and every member of the household. Never will aught connected with that evening fade from the memory of those who stood around that death-bed, and listened to his inspired words. His glorious intellect, almost cleared from the dull film of mortality, grappled with ideas seemingly too great for human utterance; and his words fell upon the ear solemnly, as 'oracles from beyond the grave.' Never had the lamp of his affections burned brighter. Dear, exceedingly, as the loved ones who now surrounded him had ever been, in this hour words failed to express his affection for them. And as his eye full of love, wandered over the circle, each felt that the bond which connected our spirits was one which should endure to all eternity. He spoke at intervals for several hours, but at length fell into a quiet slumber, and all, except his parents and myself, departed to seek repose. He awoke again at midnight, and with kind consideration, entreated his aged and grief-worn parents to seek the rest they so much needed.

" 'Lucy will remain with me,' he said, in answer to his mother's remonstrances, 'she is young, and will not feel the loss of sleep, while watching will make you ill, mother. And do not fear to leave me, for Lucy is the gentlest and kindest of nurses.'

"Left alone, hours of sweet communion ensued between myself and Cecil. He seemed much better. He felt, as he said, no pain, and at times his voice rang out full, clear, and harmonious, as in health. He spoke of our early love, hallowed as it was by many pleasant memories, and besought me not to allow the current of my affections, thus suddenly checked, to return and create bitterness at their source; but, rather, that I should permit it to flow out in widening channels, till it should embrace all who needed love or kindness, and till its blessed waters should create fresh fertility in desert hearts, and cause flowers to bloom by desolate firesides. His apparent ease lulled me into security, and I almost hoped his life would be prolonged. At any rate, his words gave me courage to live and perform my appointed work, and to await with patience our reunion in heaven.

"After a time, he was silent, and lay motionless and with closed eyes. Alarmed by his death-like stillness, I arose and knelt beside his pillow to listen to his breathing. He moved slightly as my lips touched his, and murmured, as I thought, a few incoherent words of prayer.

"I remember no more, till I awoke with a start an hour after, and found the grey light of early dawn struggling with the dying flame of the lamps in the apartment, and the morning breeze blowing chill through the open windows. But colder still was the cheek against which mine rested. I sprang to my feet and gazed earnestly at the pale, upturned face. Alas! it was the face of the dead!

"Oh, the agony of that moment! With a wild, thrilling shriek, the wail of a breaking heart, I sank fainting upon the floor.

"It was a long time before consciousness returned, and then my first thought went back to that dying scene. I attempted to rise, but still faint, I fell back upon pillow. But, after a time, strength returned, and I arose and returned to Cecil's room. A long, white object lay in the centre of the apartment, for hours had passed and his remains had been prepared for the grave. It was long before I could summon courage to look upon the face of the dead; but at length I raised the snowy linen that covered it, and all my wild, rebellious feelings were rebuked by the calm and placid smile which rested upon those features, to which even death could not impart rigidity. It told of peace and perfect joy, and, as I gazed, there grew in my soul a sweet calm and resignation.

"I sat many hours with the grief-striken parents, beside that shrouded form. Noon came and passed, and the day was waning to its close, when a messenger arrived from my home, and I was summoned from my mournful vigil to meet him in the hall. He was a stranger, but his face expressed sympathy.

" 'It grieves me much, Miss Latimer,' said he, 'to be the bearer of unpleasant tidings, more especially as I have just learned the sad event which has occurred here. But I am directed by Dr. S— to summon you to your parents, who are both attacked by the cholera, which, within the last twenty-four hours, has appeared in our city. My carriage is at the door, and I will return as soon as you are ready.'

"I listened like one entranced. Cecil dead, my parents perhaps dying! Yet I had left them in health but a day since. I must fly to them, yet could I leave the dear remains of Cecil? But I thought of his words of the preceding night, and they gave me courage. — With desperate calmness I ascended to the apartment of death, pressed my last kiss on Cecil's cold brow, bade farewell to the bereaved parents, and in a few moments found myself retracing the road I had travelled yesterday on a similar errand.

"Such was the wild tumult of my thoughts, that I scarcely

noted the lapse of time before I reached my home. The sun had set, and in the dim twilight, the house looked very desolate. There were no lights in the windows, no sounds from the open doors, for all had fled on the first alarm of the pestilence. In the hall I was met by Dr. S—. He was our family physician; I had known him from my childhood, and never before had he met me without a smile. But now he looked grave and very sad, and I knew that my fears had not exaggerated the reality. I would have rushed past him, but he detained me.'

" 'Tell me,' said I, 'if they live. Let me go to them at once. Do not detain me!'

"But the good doctor still held my hand.

" 'Summon all your fortitude, my dear child,' said he. 'Can you bear to hear that your father is no more?'

" 'My father!' I shrieked. 'Oh, do not tell me he is dead! And my mother! — let me go to them. Do not detain me! — I will be calm, indeed I will!' I continued, as I saw the look of hesitation on the good doctor's face.

"His strong arm aided me up the staircase, and in a moment more, I stood beside the corpse of my beloved father. Still cold and pale he lay, who but two days since I had left in perfect health. Could it be that his pious, loving smile would never rest on me more, or his kind voice greet my ear?

"But a moment I lingered there, for he was beyond my aid, and my mother's moans smote my ear reproachfully from the next apartment. In vain I sprung to her relief; in vain I called her by every endearing name; in vain were all my cares. An hour after I entered the house I was an orphan. During all the watches of that terrible night, I sat alone by the dead bodies of my parents — utterly alone, for even the good doctor had departed to the bedsides of fresh sufferers. In the early morning they were laid in the churchyard, and when I returned to my splendid, but now desolate home, I felt that no tie now bound me to my race.

"For days and weeks the dull apathy of despair rested upon my soul, and I wandered about my once cheerful home without aim or employment. During all this time, the disease which had made me an orphan was walking with fearful strides over the land. Our beautiful city had become one vast charnel-house. Day and night the death-carts with their fearful burden went on their mournful way to the burying-places. Happy firesides were fast becoming desolate, and, at length, the universal wail of sorrow pierced even the dull apathy which had fallen upon me. I roused myself, and went forth among the sick. I stood, day by day, by the bedside of the pestilence-stricken. I wiped the death-sweat from pallid brows; I bathed the convulsed limbs; I prepared the healing draught – and many an eye gazed upon me with gratitude in the hour of suffering. I found my reward springing up amidst my exertions, for, in ministering to the sufferings of others, my own were lessened. I blessed the dying words of Cecil, which had pointed me to an antidote to my own grief, so unselfish, and so complete.

"At length the summer of 1832 drew to its close, and the pestilence raged no more among us. But my attendance upon the sick had introduced to my notice many cases of want. My sphere of duty was ample, nor has it ever lessened, and I still find my happiness in contributing to that of others. My days and years glide calmly on, and I await in patience the time when I shall rejoin my loved ones in a world where there is neither sorrow nor parting."

She ceased; but her simple story had left its impression. I drew from it juster views of life and human responsibility. It has left me wiser, if not better, and so I trust it will leave my readers.

# AN OLD MAID'S STORY

*

## *Alice Cary*

'An Old Maid's Story' is taken from Pictures of Country Life,
1859, Alice Cary's fourth collection of stories and character
sketches drawn from the rural Hamilton County, Ohio area in
which she was born and spent her first thirty years. All
seventeen books – whether poetry, novel, or short stories –
published during her lifetime elicited good responses from both
contemporary critics and general readers. The reviewer for the
London Literary Gazette, a publication with a reputation for
being harsh on American writers, said of Pictures of Country
Life:

> Every tale in this book might be selected as evidence of some
> new beauty or unhackneyed grace. There is nothing feeble,
> nothing vulgar, and, above all, nothing unnatural or
> melodramatic. To the analytical subtlety and marvellous
> naturalness of the French school of romance she has added
> the purity and idealization of the home affections and home
> life belonging to the English; giving to both the American
> richness of color and vigor of outline, and her own
> individual power and loveliness.

A study of the life of Alice Cary (1820-71) would provide
insight into some of the most interesting elements of mid-
century literary life, women's independent social lives, and
women's rights activities. She was the fourth of nine children of
Elizabeth Jessup, an intelligent and artistically inclined woman
whose opportunities to develop her talents were quelled by the
toil of bringing up nine children on a farm near Cincinnati in
newly settled country. Her husband, Robert Cary, was a farmer
reputed to have had a poetic temperament. Alice wrote about

her mother, who died when she was about 15, that she 'was . . . a woman of superior intellect, and of a good, well-ordered life. In my memory, she stands apart from all others, – wiser, purer, doing more, and living better, than any other woman.'

Alice was especially close to two of her sisters, Phoebe, four years her junior, and Elmina, the youngest in the family. There are elements in their life together that are reminiscent of the Brontë family. Their father remarried soon after Elizabeth's death from tuberculosis. Their stepmother was so unsympathetic to the literary aspirations of the sisters that she refused to give them candles to write by in the evenings. They used a dish of lard with a rag for a wick for light.

When Alice Cary was 18 years old, her first poem was published in a Cincinnati newspaper. She wrote and published steadily for the next ten years, although she never earned any money for her work. Phoebe began to publish poetry as well, although she was not as prolific a writer as her older sister.

Elmina married, moved to Cincinnati, and shortly thereafter died from the tuberculosis that had killed their mother and that would eventually kill Alice and had earlier claimed the lives of two other sisters. Alice and Phoebe published a volume of their poetry in 1849 and the book was well received. The combination of Elmina's death, the stepmother's unpleasantness, and the literary success of their first book motivated the sisters to take the extremely daring and unusual step of leaving home. They moved to New York City, described by one of their many contemporary biographers, Horace Greeley, as the 'great emporium,' where they successfully established not only a home for themselves and a literary career for Alice which was to become the source of their income, but one of the first great literary salons in the United States. Among the notables who frequented their parlour were Greeley, John Greenleaf Whittier, whose poem 'The Singer' is written about Alice Cary, Elizabeth Cady Stanton, Anna E. Dickinson, Edgar Allan Poe, Bayard Taylor, Madame Le Vert, Mary E. Dodge, Jane C. Croly, the most prominent woman connected with journalism of the time, and Charlotte Beebee Wilbour, who, along with Croly, founded the first incorporated women's club in the United States, Sorosis, of which Alice Cary was the first president. The club was founded in response to the fact that women were not permitted to attend the New York Press Club *dinner given in honor of Charles Dickens.*

*The devotion to each other evinced by the two sisters has been seen as charming and virtuous by all their biographers who never speak of one of the sisters without frequent reference to the other. They do not, however, all interpret the sisters' relationship in the same way. Some say that Phoebe was the more burdened and sacrificial of the two, more or less abandoning her own literary work to assume the domestic responsibilities in their lives. Others say that Alice's was the more noble and sacrificial life because she assumed the economic burden of supporting them with her writing.*

*My impression is that neither sister lived a sacrificial existence and that neither saw love or devotion as demanding that; rather, each sister did most what she did best and liked best and did some of the other, too. Had they been a married couple, and Phoebe the wife, the relationship would not have been examined so diligently in terms of these issues. Various among their biographers have stressed, often with some sense of bewilderment, the fact that each of the sisters refused numerous marriage proposals. Perhaps the sisters' sensitivity to the changes in their life style that would be necessitated by conventional marriage as well as their devotion to each other had something to do with those refusals.*

*Rufus Griswold praised Alice Cary's writing in his* Female Poets of America *and a number of obituary summaries of her life indicate that her poetry was her best work and most likely to assure her a place in literary history. However, I have been unable to find any of her poetry included in any of the standard anthologies of American poetry published in this century. Recently, however, there has been renewed interest in her remarkably detailed and lively studies of life in what was, in her time, the western frontier – Ohio.*

*When she died, she left unfinished her final novel,* The Born Thrall. *The first seventeen instalments had been published in* The Revolution, *a woman's suffrage weekly edited by Susan B. Anthony. During her lifetime, her poems and stories appeared in all the variety of periodicals that flourished, from the* Universalist *and other Protestant papers, to the ladies' books and magazines, to the increasingly prestigious and important general and literary periodicals such as the* Atlantic Monthly, Harpers, *and* Putnam's Monthly.

# AN OLD MAID'S STORY*

✻

I was sitting one summer afternoon in the shadow of a grapevine and cherry tree – for the one running through the top of the other cast a shadow on the short, thick grass beneath, through which scarcely a sunbeam found way. I was sitting there with an open book on my knee, but I was not reading; on the contrary, two or three thicknesses of the cloth which I had been sewing at intervals lay on the open page, and on this rested my idle hands. I was not working, nor thinking of work. On the side of the hill, behind me, the mowers were wading through billows of red clover – they were not whistling nor singing that I remember of – they had no grape-vines nor cherry-tree limbs between their bent backs and the sun beams that fell straight and hot upon them – and yet, perhaps, they were happier than I with all my cool shadows, for we have to pay to the uttermost farthing for the enjoyments of this life. The water was nearly dried up in the run that went crookedly across the hollow, and the sober noise it made I could not hear. The grey, dry dust was an inch deep along the road, which was consequently almost as still as the meadows. Now and then a team went by, taking a little cloud with it; and now and then a young woman trotted along on the old mare, which at home did nothing but switch flies, and was evidently averse to any other employment. Two or three young women I remember to have seen go along with bundles on their saddle-horns, and a little cloud of dust, similar to that in which they moved, half a mile, perhaps, behind them, in which trotted the colt, after its mother. I had seen, without especially noticing them, and yet it

*From *Pictures of Country Life* by Alice Cary, 1859.

was an unusual thing that two, or three young women should ride along on the same afternoon.

Immediately above my head, and fronting me, there was a porch, level with the second floor of the house, and on this porch a young, rosy-cheeked girl was spinning wool. She was running up and down as gaily as if it were gold and not common wool she held in her hand, and her face was beaming as though the rumble of her wheel were pleasantest music. Her thoughts run little further than the thread she spun, good simple girl, and, therefore never became so tangled as to vex and puzzle her; and so it was easy to spin and smile, and smile and spin, all day. Once in a while the high well-sweep came down and down, and then went up and up – the iron hoops of the bucket rattled against the curb – some mower drank his fill, and with a deep breath of satisfaction went away, never wondering how or why half the clover along his path drew so bright a red from the black ground, and the other so sweet a white; and it was well he did not wonder, for had he done so ever so much all would have ended in the fact that there was red and white clover, and that the same ground produced both.

A little shower of dust blew over me and settled in the green grass and the white dying roses about me, and Surly, our dapple-nosed house-dog, dashed by me and gave noisy welcome to the visitor then about unlatching the gate. I hastened to conceal my book under the rosebush at hand, and to shake the dust from my work preparatory to using my needle, for to be found reading or idle would have been considered alike disgraceful in the estimation of our neighbors. When the visitor appeared, I recognized Miss Emeline Barker, and at the same time became aware that she was bent on holiday pleasure. She had been riding on horseback, but her white dress showed scarcely a wrinkle, so well had she managed it – a sash of pink ribbon depended from the waist, and the short sleeves were looped up with roses – her straw hat was trimmed with flowers and ribbon, and her boots were smoothly laced with tape instead of leather strings. But more than her dress, her face betrayed the joyous nature of the errand she was bent on. "Somebody is going to be married," was my first thought, "and Emeline has come to invite me to the wedding," and I was confirmed in this when she declined the seat I offered, with the assurance that she had not time to stay a moment. Expectation was on tiptoe, and when I said "how do they all at home?" I had no doubt she would tell me that Mary Ann, who was her elder sister, was to be married; but she answered simply that all were very well, and went on to tell about the harvest, the heat of the day, and other commonplaces, just as if she wore her every-day calico dress and not a white muslin one, looped up at the sleeves with roses.

Directly she bid me good bye without having said anything extraordinary at all, and then, as if suddenly recollecting it, she exclaimed, "Oh! I want to see Jane a moment." I pointed to the porch where Jane Whitehead was spinning, and with my heart drawing strangely into itself took the banished book from its place of concealment, quite careless of what Emeline Barker might think of me.

I felt dissatisfied and unhappy. I knew not why; the shadow of an unseen sorrow had fallen over me, and I could not escape it – in truth, I did not try. If I had taken a few steps I should have found the sunshine, but I did not, and the vague discomfort took a more definite shape.

I lifted the book to conceal my face, which it seemed to me must reflect my unhappy mind, but I did not read any more than before. Another book was opened which seemed to me the Book of Fate, and to be illustrated with one picture – that of an unloved old maid. We might be made wiser sometimes, perhaps, if it were permitted us to see ourselves as others see us, but we should rarely be made more comfortable.

There were whispers and laughter, and laughter and whispers, on the porch, but the rumble of the wheel so drowned the voices that for some time I heard not one word; but the first that reached me confirmed my feeling – myself was the subject of conversation.

"I should have thought they would have asked her," said Jane, half piteously, and turning her wheel slowly as she spoke, but not spinning any more. After a moment she continued, "suppose, Em, you take it upon yourself to invite her."

"Fie!" exclaimed Emeline, "if I were an old maid, I should not expect to be invited to young parties. Let old folks go with old folks, I say; and I am sure we would not be mad if all the old maids in the county should make a frolic and leave us out, would we, Jenny?"

"Why no," replied Jane; "but then this seems like another case, and I can't help liking Miss"—

"So do I like her well enough in her way," said Emeline,

"but I would not like her at a party of young folks. She must be as old as the hills, and the dear knows she has no beauty to recommend her."

"Oh, she is not so very old — past getting married to be sure, or being cared for in that way, but she could help sew, you know, and be amused by our fun in the evening. Suppose we ask her to go with us?"

"I tell you she would be in the way," persisted Emeline, "and I suppose if Mrs. Nichols had cared to have her she would have invited her."

"Perhaps she forgot it," insisted Jenny.

"No, she didn't," replied Emeline. "Didn't I hear her talking all about who she wanted and who she did not, and who she felt obliged to ask; and she said if she asked Miss— there were two or three others a good deal older and less desirable that would think themselves entitled to invitations, and she must stop somewhere, and on the whole might better not begin."

"Well, then, you tell her," pleaded Jane, evidently receiving, and sorry to receive, the stubborn facts.

When I became aware that I was the "old maid," so compassionated and dreaded, I was as one stunned by some dreadful blow. I felt it due to myself to remove from where I sat, but I had no strength to go; I seemed not to be myself. I saw myself by the new light whereby other people saw me. I began to count up my years. I was twenty-five the May past, but my life had been entirely confined to the old homestead, and no special, peculiarly interesting, or peculiarly sorrowful events had broken its monotony, so that I found it hard to realize the truth. I was young in knowledge — young in experience, and one year had been drawn into another without the visible separation of even a New Year's dinner. I had never thought of dividing myself from the younger people of the neighborhood, and till now I had never suspected that they desired to divide themselves from me. Directly Jenny sliped the bands, set by her wheel, and whispering and laughing the two girls came down and essayed to make some explanation which should not be wholly false, and yet soften the truth. Emeline was to remain a little while and assist Jenny, after which the two were to go together to Mrs. Nichols' to help with some sewing she was busy about.

So the old mare was led into the door-yard, Emeline hung her gay hat on a low limb of the cherry-tree, and tying on one

103

of Jenny's aprons the happy pair set busily to work.

My task was much harder than theirs, for I must keep close the misery that was in my heart, and not suffer one single pang to break the expression of quietude in my face. The hat swinging gaily in the wind – the laughter of the girls, smothered away from my participation, seemed like injuries to my insulted sorrow. I could have lifted myself above hatred. Against a false accusation I could have proudly defended myself, but my crime was simply that of being an old maid, whom nobody cared to see, and against that there was nothing I could interpose. For the first time in my life I felt a sort of solemn satisfaction in the white and dying roses, and in the yellow leaves that fell from the cherry-tree over my head and into my lap.

Sometimes, when the girls came near me, they would lift up their voices as if in continuance of a conversation previously going forward, but I understood very well that these cleartoned episodes were put in for the occasion.

When the heart is light the hands are nimble, and the work was soon done, and Jenny ready to make her toilet – a task for which a country girl, at the time and place I write of, would have been ashamed to require more than ten minutes. The shadow of the cherry-tree was stretching far to the east when the old mare, quite used to "carry double," was led to the fence-side, and Emeline and Jane mounted and rode away.

I put my hands before my face when they were gone, but I did not cry. It was a hard, withered feeling in my heart, that tears could not wash away. In all the world I could see no green and dewy ground. There was nothing I could do – nothing I could undo. There was no one I blamed, no special act for which I blamed myself, unless it were for having been born. The sun went down under a black bank of clouds, and the winds came up and began to tell the leaves about a coming storm.

Pattering fast through the dust a little boy passed the gate, climbed into the meadow, and was soon across the hollow, and over the hill. The men were very active now, pitching the mown hay into heaps, turning their heads now and then towards the blackening west, and talking earnestly and loud. The boy drew close to them and seemed to speak, for all the workmen stood silent, and the rake dropped from the hand of the foremost and his head sunk down almost to his bosom. Presently one of the men took up the rake, another brought the coat and hat of the foremost laborer, who had been working bareheaded, and assisted him to put them on, for he seemed as one half dead, and quite unable to help himself – then the little boy took his hand and led him away, and I noticed that he walked with staggering steps, and often passed his hand across his eyes as he went. The men left in the field resumed work directly, but though a deep silence fell with the first shadows I could not hear a word, so lowly they spoke to one another. Till long after dark they kept rolling and tumbling the hay into heaps, but at last I heard them gathering water pails and pitchers together, and soon after they crossed the meadow towards the house – not noiselessly, as they came generally, but speaking few words and the few in low and kindly tones. The black bank of clouds had widened up nearly half the sky, and a blinding flash of lightning showed me their faces as they drew near the well and paused – not so much because they wished to drink, as because they felt reluctant to separate and go their different ways. While one of the men lowered the bucket, another approached me, and wiping his sunburnt face with his red silk handkerchief, said – "One of our hands has had bad news this evening."

I felt what it was before he went on to say, "his youngest child died about five o'clock, and will be buried to-morrow morning, I suppose."

Poor, poor father – no wonder the rake had fallen from his hands, and that he had suffered himself to be led away like a little child. What anguish must be the mother's, thought I, when the sterner and stouter-hearted father so bows himself down, and forgets that there is anything in the world but the cold white clay that is to be buried to-morrow.

I forgot Mrs. Nichols and the gay people she had about her; forgot that I had been forgotten, and remembered only our common humanity and our common need.

The sky was black overhead and the lightning every few minutes illuminated the grey dust before me, that was beginning to be dotted with drops of rain, falling at intervals, as I hurried through the darkness to the humble home where last year a babe had been born, and where the last day it had died. Two or three living children were left, and yet it seemed as if all were gone, the room was so still and gloomy. The little mouth had never spoken, and the little hands had never worked for food or for clothing, yet how poor the parents felt, having the precious burden laid from off their bosoms.

Close by the window, where the morning-glories grew thick, dressed in white and as if quietly asleep, lay the little one, waking not when the flowers dropped on its face, nor when the mother called it by all the sweetest names that a mother's fondness can shape.

"You must not grieve – the baby is better off than we," said a tall woman, dressed in black, and she led the poor mother from the white bed where it lay. After some further words of admonition and reproof, she proceeded to light the candles and to arrange the table preparatory, as I supposed, for morning service.

The rain came plashing on the vines at the window, and the mother's grief burst out afresh as she thought of the grave it would fall upon in the morning. A step came softly along the rainy grass, and a face whose calm benignity seemed to dispel the darkness, drew my eyes from the sleeping baby to itself. But the voice – there was in it such sweetness and refinement – such a mingling of love and piety, that I was blessed, as I had never been blessed, in being permitted to listen to it.

I recognized the visitor for the village clergyman who had lately come among us, and whom I had only seen once, when he gave baptism to the little one that was now returned to dust.

I recognized not only the form and features, but I also recognized, or thought I did, a spiritual kindred – the desolation that had divided me from the world an hour past was gone – heaven came down near to me, so near that earth was filled with the reflection of its glory and happiness.

All the night we were together. There were few words spoken. There was nothing to do but to listen to the rain and the beating of my heart. There was nothing to see but the baby on its white bed, the dimly-burning candle and the calm soul-full eyes of the clergyman – now bent on the sacred page before him, now on the leaves that trembled in the rain, and now, as something told me, for I scarcely dared look up, upon myself.

I wished there were something I might do for him, but I could think of nothing except to offer the rocking-chair which had been given me on my coming, and which was all the luxury the poor man's house afforded. In my over-anxiety to serve, I forgot this most obvious service I could render, and when it occurred to me at last my unfortunate forgetfulness so much embarrassed me that I knew not how to speak or stir. If there had been any noise – if any one had been present but our two selves – if he would speak to me – but as it was, I could not for a long while find courage for that proffer of my simple courtesy. There he sat silent, as far from me as he could well be, and as more time went by, looking at me more and more earnestly, I thought. At last the steadfast gaze became so painful that I felt that any change would be relief, and mastering my embarrassment as I best could, I offered the rocking-chair to the clergyman, whose name was Wardwell, with the energetic haste with which one touches the lion he would tame.

"No, my child," he said, very calmly, "you have most need of it."

I know not what I said, but in some vehement way, which I afterwards feared expressed all I was most anxious to conceal, made my refusal.

He smiled and accepted the chair, I thought in pity of my confusion, and rather to place me at ease, than for the sake of his own comfort.

He asked me directly whether I had ever been far from the village – a natural question enough, and asked doubtless for the sake of relieving the tedium of silence – but I saw in it only the inference of my rusticity and want of knowledge, and replied with a proud humility that I was native to the village – had scarcely been out of sight of it, and had no knowledge beyond the common knowledge of its common people.

With a changed expression – I could not tell whether of pain or annoyance – Mr. Wardwell moved his position slightly nearer me, but the habitual smile returned presently, and he rocked quietly to and fro, saying only, "well, well."

There was nothing in the tone or the manner to give force to the words. They might indicate that it was as well to live in the village as any other place. They might indicate that he had no interest in the inquiry – and none in the answer – or it might be that they expressed the fixedness of a foregone conclusion. I chose to receive the last interpretation, and leaned my head on the hard sill of the open window to conceal the tears with which, in spite of myself, my eyes were slowly filling.

All the time the clergyman had remained silent I had longed with a sincere and childish simplicity to be noticed or spoken to, and now if I could have unsaid the few words he had directly addressed to me a tormenting weight would have been

107

lifted from my bosom.

The wet leaves shook almost in my face, and now and then some cold drops plashed on my head; but I would not manifest any inconvenience. I felt as if Mr. Wardwell were responsible for my discomfort, and I would be a patient martyr to whatever he might inflict.

"My child, you are courting danger," he said, at last; "the chill air of these rainy midnights is not to be tampered with by one of your susceptible organization."

Ah, thought I to myself, he is trying to pour oil on the wound he has made, but doubtless he thinks no amount of chill rain could injure me, for all of his soft speaking. So I affected to sleep, for I was ashamed to manifest the rudeness I felt, though my position was becoming seriously uncomfortable, to say nothing of its imprudence. My heart trembled, audibly, I feared, when Mr. Wardwell approached, and stooping over me, longer I thought than need were, softly let down the window. I would have thanked him, but to do so would have been to betray my ill-nature, which I was now repentant, and ashamed of. He passed his hand over my wet hair, and afterwards brought the cushion of the rocking-chair and placed it stealthily beneath my head. Soothed from my sorrow, and unused to watching, I was presently fast asleep. I dreamed I was at home, and that some one was walking across and across my chamber, and so close to my bedside that I felt a distinct fear. So strong was the impression I could not rid myself of it, even when, fully conscious, I unclosed my eyes and saw the still baby before me, and the clergyman apparently dozing in his chair. Was it he who had been walking so near me, in forgetfulness of me and simply to relieve the monotony of the time? Yes, said probability, even before my eyes fell upon a handkerchief of white cambric, lying almost at my feet, and which I was quite sure was not there when I took my seat at the window.

I took it up, partly from curiosity, partly for the want of other occupation, examined the flowers in the border, and read and re-read the initial letters, worked in black in one corner – C. D. W. I fancied the letters had been wrought by a female hand, and with a feeling strangely akin to jealousy, and which I should have blushed to own, tossed the handkerchief on the table and took my own from my pocket, more aware of its coarseness and plainness than I had ever been till then. It was as white as snow, neatly folded, and smelling of rose-leaves;

but for all that I felt keenly how badly it contrasted with that of the clergyman.

I wished he would wake, if he were indeed asleep – move ever so slightly, look up, or speak one word, no matter what; but for all my wishing he sat there just the same – his eyes closed, and his placid face turned more to the wall than to me.

From the roost near by, and from across the neighboring hills, sounded the lusty crowing – it might be midnight or daybreak; I could not tell which, for the night had been to me unlike any other night. I arose softly, and taking the candle which burned dimly now, held it before the white face of the skeleton of a clock, to tell the hour, but the clock had been forgotten and was "run down."

I crossed the room on tiptoe and reseated myself without noise, but had scarcely done so when Mr. Wardwell, evidently aware of my movements and wishes, took from his vest an elegant watch and named the time, which was but half an hour after midnight. I sighed, for I felt as if the morning would never come.

"The time is heavy to you, my dear child," he replied, as if in answer to my sigh, and replacing the cushion, he offered me the easy-chair, blaming himself for having deprived me of it so selfishly and so long – and professing to be quite refreshed by the sleep which I suspected he had not taken.

I tried to decline, for in my heart I wished him to have the best chair, but when he took my hand with what I felt to be rather gallantry than paternal solicitude, I could no longer refuse, and in affectation of a quietude I did not feel, took up the hymn-book which lay at hand, and bent my eyes on the words I did not read.

"Will you read the poem that interests you?" asked Mr. Wardwell, coming near, and turning his bright, blessed face full upon me.

I trembled, for it seemed to me that my heart was open before my companion, and even if it were not I knew my cheek was playing the tell-tale, but in some way I stammered an answer to the most obvious sense of the words, and replied that it was the hymn-book I held.

"I know it," replied my pleasing tormentor; "but it is a *poem* you are reading for all that."

I said there were some hymns which were also most ennobling and beautiful poetry, and I went on to instance a few which I regarded as such. He seemed not to hear my words, but said, rather as if musing aloud than speaking to me, –

"Yes, yes, my dear child," – (he said *dear* child now, and not child as at first) – "at your time of life there are many sweet poems for the heart to read, which it does read without the aid of books."

He looked on me as he spoke with a sort of sorrowful compassion, I thought, and yet there was something tenderer and deeper than compassion, which I could not define.

He was greatly my senior, but it was not a filial feeling that caused me to say, I was past the time when frivolous fancy most readily turns evanescent things to poetry, and I mentioned myself as twenty-six the May coming, and not twenty-five the May past, as most women would have done.

"To me that seems very young!" replied my companion, solemnly, "I am" – he hesitated, and went on hurriedly and confusedly I thought, "I am much older than you are."

He went away from me as he spoke, and passed his hand along his deeply-lined forehead and whitening hair, as if in contemplation of them.

I could not bear the solemn gladness that came like a soft shadow over the dewier glow that had lighted his face awhile past, and hastened to say, though I had never thought of it before, that the best experience and the truest poetry of life should come to us in the full ripeness of years. He shook his head doubtfully, smiled the old benignant smile, as he replied:

"It is quite natural, my dear child, that you should think so."

I had no courage to say more, especially as his thoughts seemed to return to their more habitual channels; but oh, how much I wished he could feel this life as richly worth living as I did.

He raised the sash, and leaned his head close to the wet vines, though he had reproved me for doing the same thing, and before I could find courage to remind him of it, or to say anything, he was fast asleep.

I recalled every word I had spoken, and conscious of an awakening interest that I had never before experienced for man or woman, I thought I had betrayed it, and the betrayal had produced the sleepy indifference, which, in spite of myself, mortified me to the quick. I read the hymn-book till I was weary of hymns; and afterwards thought till I was weary of thinking, then read again, and at last, to keep the place which I had no interest in keeping, I placed my handkerchief between the leaves of the book, and so turning my face as to see just that part of the wall which Mr. Wardwell had looked at an hour previously, I forgot him and myself and all things.

It was not the noise of the rain that woke me — nor the crowing of the morning cocks, nor the sun's yellow light that struggled through the room, nor yet the mother calling in her renewed anguish to the baby that smiled not for all her calling, nor lifted its little hands to the bosom that bent above it in such loving and terrible despair — it seemed to me it was none of these, but a torturous premonition of solitude and desolation.

Mr. Wardwell was gone, and the night was gone — but there was a pleasant voice in my ear, and a serene smile, kindling now and then in transient enthusiasm, whichever way I turned. O night of solemn joy, O humble room, made sacred by the presence of death — O dream, whose sweet beginning promised so beautiful a close, how often have I gone back to you, and hewed out cisterns that I knew must break!

Surely in the mysterious providences that wrap themselves around us and which to our weak apprehensions seem so dark and so hard, there are true and good meanings, if we could but find them out.

Help us to be patient, oh, our Father, and give us the trusting hearts of little children, and the faith that mounts higher and brighter than the fire.

In the southern suburb of the village, and in sight of my own chamber window, is a low, gloomy stone church, which stood there before I was born, and which had scarcely changed any within my remembrance. All the long summer afternoons I used to sit at this window, looking up often from my sewing or my book, and always in one direction — that of the dark little church. I could see the oak trees that grew in different parts of the churchyard, and made deep shadows over the green mounds below, and it pleased me not a little to think Mr. Wardwell might be looking on them at the same moment with myself, for the parsonage, or "preacher's house," as it was called, stood in the same inclosure with the church building.

I could not see the parsonage itself, but I could see the smoke drifting from its chimneys, and know when a fire was being made, and could guess at the probable work that was going on indoors — whether dinner or tea, or whether it were the day for scrubbing or for baking, for I took the liveliest interest in such faint and far-away observations of Mr. Wardwell's household affairs, as I was able to make. Sometimes I would see a white fluttering among the trees, and know it had been washing day at the preacher's house, and then I would imagine the discomfort that had reigned in the kitchen all day, and the scouring of the ash floor, and the brightening of the hearth, that came afterward. I never made my seat under the grape-covered cherry tree, after the day that solemnized my destiny with the appellation of "old maid," and the evening that saw our first hand led away.

The night that followed had opened a new page in my life – a page where I saw my future reflected in colors brighter than my spring flowers, that were all dead now. I did not regret them. Often came Emeline and talked and laughed with Jenny as she spun on the porch, and I praised the pink and blue dresses she wore, and the roses that trimmed her hat, and said I was too old for pink dresses and roses, without a sigh on my lips, or a pang in my heart. I lived in a world of my own now; on Sunday eve we went to church together, and yet not to the same church – we sat in the same pew, but the face of the preacher turned not to the faces of my companions as it sometimes turned to mine, and for me there were meanings in his words which they could not see nor feel.

When he spoke of the great hereafter, when our souls that had crossed their mates, perhaps, and perhaps left them behind or gone unconsciously before them – dissatisfied and longing and faltering all the time, and of the deep of joy they would enter into, on recognizing fully and freely the other self, which, in this world, had been so poorly and vaguely comprehended, if at all – what delicious tremor, half fear and half fervor, thrilled all my being, and made me feel that the dust of time and the barriers of circumstance – the dreary pain of a life spearated from all others – death itself – all were nothing but shadows passing between me and the eternal sunshine of love. I could afford to wait – I could afford to be patient under my burdens and to go straight forward through all hard fates and fortunes, assured that I should know and be known at last, love and be loved in the fullness of a blessedness, which, even here, mixed with bitterness as it is, is the sweetest of all. What was it to me that my hair was black, and my step firm, while his hair to whom I listened so reverentially was white, and his step slow, if not feeble. What was it that he had more wisdom, and more experience than I, and what was it that he never said, "you are faintly recognized, and I see a germ close-folded, which in the mysterious processes of God's providence may unfold a great white flower." We had but crossed each other in the long journey, and I was satisfied, for I felt that in our traversing up the ages, we should meet again.

How sweet the singing of the evening and the morning service used to be. Our voices met and mingled then, and in the same breath and to the same tune we praised the Lord, for his mercy, which endureth forever.

One afternoon Emeline and Jenny teased me to join them on the porch – they pitied me, perhaps, shut up in the dim old chamber, as we often pity those who are most to be envied, and finding they would not leave me to my own thoughts, I allowed myself to be drawn from my favorite position.

Emeline was cutting some handkerchiefs from a piece of linen, and she asked me for one of mine as a measure. I opened a drawer where my nicest things were, sprinkled over with dried rose-leaves, and took up a white apron with a ruffled border, which I had worn the most memorable night of my life, and folded away just as I wore it – I took it up, thinking of the night, drew a handkerchief from the pocket and laid it across the lap of Emeline.

What laughter and clapping of hands and accusations of blushes followed, and true enough, the blushes made red confusion in my face when Emeline held up, not my own coarse, plain handkerchief, but a fine one with a deep purple border, and marked with the initial letters of Mr. Wardwell's name.

In vain I denied all knowledge of how I came by it; they were merrily incredulous, and asserted that if I knew nothing of the handkerchief I of course cared nothing for it – they would keep it and return it to the owner, who had no doubt dropped it by accident – just as I had taken it up.

I said it must be so, and spoke of the watch we had kept together, which gave the utmost probability to their suggestion, and which involved me in a serious dilemma. In the early twilight, they said we would walk together to the preacher's house – return him the lost handkerchief, and in return for our good office receive some of the red pears that grew at his door.

I could not bear that Mr. Wardwell should be mentioned in the same sentence with red pears – just as I would have mentioned any other person, and yet for the world I would not have had them see him as I saw him. I could not bear the thought of parting with my treasure which I had unconsciously possessed so long; I would speedily have folded it just as I found it and as he had folded it, and replacing it in the pocket of my apron, have kept it forever shut in the drawer among the rose-leaves.

But how to evade the plan of my young friends without betraying my own secret I could not discover. Having forced myself to comply for they insisted that they would go without me if not with me, I tried to reconcile myself by the light of judgment and the cold probabilities of the case. Between dreaming and walking I must have taken up the handkerchief instead of my own. But convinced against my will, I was of the same opinion still. I remembered very distinctly placing the handkerchief on the table before me, and of seeing it there when I placed my own between the leaves of my hymn-book – and I remembered too, right well, that Mr. Wardwell was gone when I awoke – how then could the accident have occurred? And yet, if not by accident, how came I by the handkerchief? I could not tell, but one thing I was forced to do, to give it back. If it must be done, it should not be the hand of Emeline or of Jenny that did it, but my own. When it was time to go I folded my treasure neatly, and hid it under my shawl and next my heart. It was autumn now and there were no flowers but the few deep red ones that were left on the rose of Sharon that grew by my window. I gathered a green spray that held two bright ones, and hiding my heart as carefully as I did my treasure, I seemed to listen to what my young friends said as we went along.

A little way from the door, in a rustic seat, beneath the boughs of an apple-tree Mr. Wardwell sat reading – as he looked up, the expression of a young and happy heart passed across his face, and gave way to a more sober and paternal one. He laid the book he had been reading in the rustic chair and came forward to meet and welcome us. He called me dear child again and laid his hand upon my head with a solemn and tender pressure, that seemed to me at once a promise and a benediction.

I said why we were come, and in my confusion offered the handkerchief with the hand that held the flowers. He smiled sadly as we sometimes do when we are misunderstood, and pointing my friends to the pears that were lying red on the ground, he took the handkerchief, the flowers and the hand that held them in both his own, and for a moment pressed them close to his bosom. When my hand was restored to me the handkerchief was in it, but not the flowers.

"I want the roses," he said, "and will buy them with the handkerchief, for we must pay for our pleasures whether we will or no."

I knew not how to understand him, and was yet holding my treasure timidly forth, when, seeing my friends approach, he put my hand softly back, and I hastened to conceal it as before – next my heart. The youthful expression, that dewy-rose-look of summer and sunshine, came out in his face again – my heart had spoken to his heart, and we felt that we were assuredly bound to the same haven.

The aprons of my young friends were full of red pears, and their faces beaming with pleasure, and I, whom they compassionated as an old maid, hid my sacred joy deep in my bosom, and turned aside that their frivolous and frolicsome mirth might not mar it. Involuntarily I turned towards the rustic chair, and with an interest which I felt in everything belonging to Mr. Wardwell, opened the book he had left there. It was the well-remembered hymn-book, and my handkerchief was keeping the place of the hymn I had read so often on the most memorable of the nights of my life. How happy I was, and what dreams I dreamed after that. The blessed handkerchief is shut up with rose-leaves in my drawer, but the giver I never spoke with but once again.

It was years after I had learned that my treasure was not an accident, and when Jenny and Emeline were each the happy mother of more than one pretty baby – still liking me a little, and pitying me a great deal because I was an old maid, when one snowy night, the old woman, who kept house at the parsonage, came for me. I must make haste, she said, for good Mr. Wardwell had been that day seized with a fit, and seemed to be slowly dying. It was true, as she said, he seemed but to wait for me. The Bible and hymn-book were by his bedside; the plain linen handkerchief was between the leaves of the latter, and placing his hand on it, he whispered –

"Put this over my face when I am dead and the flowers" –

"He could not say more, but I understood him and softly placing my hand on the heart where the life-tide was ebbing, I bent my face down close and kissed the cheek that was already moistening with death-dew. All the face brightened with that sweet, sweet expression that was manhood and angelhood at once – then came the terrible shadow, and the eyes that had known me, knew me no more – the lips gave up their color, but the habitual smile fixed itself in more than mortal beauty. As I unfolded the handkerchief two roses fell from it, which we buried with him.

His grave is at the south of the old church, and a rose-tree, grown from the slip of the one at my window, blooms at his head. Nothing now would tempt me away from the hills I was born among – from the old grey church, and the grave near which I hope to be buried.

"Come see my treasure;" and Abbie Morrison (for that was the story-teller's name) unlocked the drawer, where folded among rose leaves, almost scentless now, was the handkerchief with dark border, and marked with the initials, C. D. W.

To her neighbors Abbie Morrison is only an old maid in whose praise there is not much to be said. If any one is sick she is sent for, but in seasons of joy nobody has a thought of her. What does she know of pleasure? they say, or what does she care for anything but singing in the church and cutting the weeds from the graveyard?

The children love her sweet voice, and stop on the way to school if she chances to sing in the garden, and, as she gives them flowers, wonder why their sisters call her old and ugly. It may be that angels wonder too.

# THE TWO OFFERS

*

## *Frances Ellen Watkins Harper*

'The Two Offers' first appeared in the September 1859 issue of the first black literary magazine in the United States, The Anglo-African Magazine, founded in that year by Thomas Hamilton. In many ways, it is the most interesting story in this collection. It is the first story published in the United States by an Afro-American. When, very occasionally, it is included in a collection of American black documents, black literature, or black 'firsts', it always seems to be accompanied by editorial hesitancy. Perhaps the regret stems from the fact that the story is by a woman; perhaps from the fact that the story deals only peripherally with racial issues; perhaps because the story is apparently about white women. But what is important about the story is that it is about women. White abolitionists and feminists had frequently drawn the analogy between the condition of blacks under slavery and women under patriarchal marriage, but there seems to have been some embarrassment when a black woman reversed the analogy.

The story is important in the many levels on which it speaks to us. It tells white women that they can and must be willing to be instructed in how to live and what choices to make in their women's lives by a black woman. It tells all women that independence is preferable to the marriages of most women who choose to marry carelessly because they haven't the courage not to at that period in life when most of their peers marry. There may also be a message to black men about the kinds of women black women aspire to be in freedom, the freedom they are together, men and women, working to achieve. Black men ought not to want to do to and with black women what white men, in their freedom, do to and with white women.

*Frances Ellen Watkins Harper (1825-1911) was born of free parents in Baltimore. When her mother died, Harper, only 3 years old, went to live with her aunt and uncle, whose school for free Negro children she attended until she was 13 when she left to earn her own living. Her uncle, the Rev. William Watkins, a hard worker and an abolitionist, early on introduced her to his friends among whom were included William Lloyd Garrison and Benjamin Lundy. She supported herself with domestic labor in the household of a bookseller where she was able to continue her education by herself. In 1845 she published her first book of poetry and prose writings,* Forest Leaves. *She taught sewing after that in Columbus, Ohio, and Little York, Pennsylvania, until she began her career as a public speaker in the cause of abolition in 1854 with her first public address on 'Education and the Elevation of the Colored Race.' Her success led to a two-year tour in Maine for the state Anti-Slavery Society and was followed during the next four years by speaking engagements in most of the northern states. She frequently read from her second volume of poetry,* Poems on Miscellaneous Subjects *(1854) and became the most well-known black poet since Phillis Wheatley. She was married for four years to a widower, Fenton Harper, who died in 1864, leaving her with a daughter to raise alone.*

*She resumed her career as a lecturer after the Civil War, touring the South, speaking against white racism, for more and better education for Negroes, temperance, and against a double standard of morality.*

*She published* Moses, A Story of the Nile, *a versification of the Biblical story, in 1869; collections of poetry in 1871 and 1900; a collection of sketches of reconstruction life drawn from her extensive travels in the South,* Sketches of Southern Life *in 1872 and an enlarged edition in 1896; and the novel,* Iola Leroy, or Shadows Uplifted *in 1892. An 1894 collection of poetry,* The Martyre of Alabama and Other Poems *was inspired by the lynching of a Negro boy.*

*Phebe A. Hanaford wrote of her in* Daughters of America *(1882) that she*

> *is one of the most eloquent women lecturers in the country. As one listens to her clear, plaintive, melodious voice, and follows the flow of her musical speech in her logical presentation of truth, he can but be charmed with her*

*oratory and rhetoric. . . . She is one of the colored women of whom white women may be proud, and to whom abolitionists can point and declare that a race which can hold such women ought never to have been held in bondage.*

*The texts of several of her lectures survive. A reading of any of them leaves one with a clear impression of her eloquence and power as a speaker.*

# THE TWO OFFERS

*

"What is the matter with you, Laura, this morning? I have been watching you this hour, and in that time you have commenced a half-dozen letters and torn them all up. What matter of such grave moment is puzzling your dear little head, that you do not know how to decide?"

"Well, it is an important matter: I have two offers for marriage, and I do not know which to choose."

"I should accept neither, or to say the least, not at present."

"Why not?"

"Because I think a woman who is undecided between two offers has not love enough for either to make a choice; and in that very hesitation, indecision, she has a reason to pause and seriously reflect, lest her marriage, instead of being an affinity of souls or a union of hearts, should only be a mere matter of bargain and sale, or an affair of convenience and selfish interest."

"But I consider them both very good offers, just such as many a girl would gladly receive. But to tell you the truth, I do not think that I regard either as a woman should the man she chooses for her husband. But then if I refuse, there is the risk of being an old maid, and that is not to be thought of."

"Well, suppose there is? Is that the most dreadful fate that can befall a woman? Is there not more intense wretchedness in an ill-assorted marriage, more utter loneliness in a loveless home, than in the lot of the old maid who accepts her earthly mission as a gift from God and strives to walk the path of life with earnest and unfaltering steps?"

"Oh! what a little preacher you are. I really believe that you were cut out for an old maid – that when nature formed you she put in a double portion of intellect to make up for a deficiency of love; and yet you are kind and affectionate. But I do not think that you know anything of the grand, overmastering passion, or the deep necessity of woman's heart for loving."

"Do you think so?" resumed the first speaker, and bending over her work she quietly applied herself to the knitting that had lain neglected by her side during this brief conversation. But as she did so, a shadow flitted over her pale and intellectual brow, a mist gathered in her eyes, and a slight quivering of the lips revealed a depth of feeling to which her companion was a stranger.

But before I proceed with my story, let me give you a slight history of the speakers. They were cousins who had met life under different auspices. Laura Lagrange was the only daughter of rich and indulgent parents who had spared no pains to make her an accomplished lady. Her cousin, Janette Alston, was the child of parents rich only in goodness and affection. Her father had been unfortunate in business and, dying before he could retrieve his fortunes, left his business in an embarrassed state. His widow was unacquainted with his business affairs, and when the estate was settled, hungry creditors had brought their claims and the lawyers had received their fees, she found herself homeless and almost penniless, and she, who had been sheltered in the warm clasp of loving arms, found them too powerless to shield her from the pitiless pelting storms of adversity. Year after year she struggled with poverty and wrestled with want, till her toilworn hands became too feeble to hold the shattered chords of existence, and her tear-dimmed eyes grew heavy with the slumber of death.

Her daughter had watched over her with untiring devotion, had closed her eyes in death and gone out into the busy, restless world, missing a precious tone from the voices of earth, a beloved step from the paths of life. Too self-reliant to depend on the charity of relations, she endeavored to support herself by her own exertions, and she had succeeded. Her path for a while was marked with struggle and trial, but instead of uselessly repining she met them bravely, and her life became not a thing of ease and indulgence, but of conquest, victory and accomplishments.

At the time when this conversation took place, the deep trials of her life had passed away. The achievements of her genius had won her a position in the literary world, where she shone as one of its bright particular stars. And with her fame came a competence of worldly means, which gave her leisure for improvement and the riper development of her rare talents. And she, that pale, intellectual woman, whose genius gave life and vivacity to the social circle and whose presence threw a halo of beauty and grace around the charmed atmosphere in which she moved, had at one period of her life known the mystic and solemn strength of an all-absorbing love. Years faded into the misty past had seen the kindling of her eye, the quick flushing of her cheek and the wild throbbing of her heart at tones of a voice long since hushed to the stillness of death. Deeply, wildly, passionately, she had loved. . . . This love quickened her talents, inspired her genius and threw over her life a tender and spiritual earnestness.

And then came a fearful shock, a mournful waking from that "dream of beauty and delight." A shadow fell around her path; it came between her and the object of her heart's worship. First a few cold words, estrangement, and then a painful separation: the old story of woman's pride. . . . And thus faded out from that young heart her bright, brief and saddened dream of life. Faint and spirit-broken, she turned from the scenes associated with the memory of the loved and lost. She tried to break the chain of sad associations that bound her to the mournful past; and so . . . her genius gathered strength from suffering, and wondrous power and brilliancy from the agony she hid within the desolate chambers of her soul . . . and turning, with an earnest and shattered spirit to life's duties and trials, she found a calmness and strength that she had only imagined in her dreams of poetry and song.

We will now pass over a period of ten years, and the cousins have met again. In that calm and lovely woman, in whose eyes is a depth of tenderness tempering the flashes of her genius, whose looks and tones are full of sympathy and love, we recognize the once smitten and stricken Janette Alston. The bloom of her girlhood had given way to a higher type of spiritual beauty, as if some unseen hand had been polishing and refining the temple in which her lovely spirit found its habitation. . . .

Never in the early flush of womanhood, when an absorbing love had lit up her eyes and glowed in her life, had she appeared so interesting as when, with a countenance which seemed overshadowed with a spiritual light, she bent over the deathbed of a young woman just lingering at the shadowy gates of the unseen land.

"Has he come?" faintly but eagerly exclaimed the dying woman. "Oh! how I have longed for his coming, and even in death he forgets me."

"Oh, do not say so, dear Laura. Some accident may have detained him," said Janette to her cousin; for on that bed, from whence she will never rise, lies the once beautiful and light-hearted Laura Lagrange, the brightness of whose eyes had long since been dimmed with tears, and whose voice had become like a harp whose every chord is tuned to sadness — whose faintest thrill and loudest vibrations are but the variations of agony. A heavy hand was laid upon her once warm and bounding heart, and a voice came whispering through her soul that she must die. But to her the tidings was a message of deliverance — a voice hushing her wild sorrows to the calmness of resignation and hope.

Life had grown so weary upon her head — the future looked so hopeless — she had no wish to tread again the track where thorns had pierced her feet and clouds overcast her sky, and she hailed the coming of death's angel as the footsteps of a welcome friend, and yet, earth had one object so very dear to her weary heart. It was her absent and recreant husband; for, since that conversation [ten years earlier], she had accepted one of her offers and become a wife. But before she married she learned that great lesson of human experience and woman's life — to love the man who bowed at her shrine, a willing worshipper.

He had a pleasing address, raven hair, flashing eyes, a voice of thrilling sweetness and lips of persuasive eloquence; and being well versed in the ways of the world, he won his way to her heart and she became his bride, and he was proud of his prize. Vain and superficial in his character, he looked upon marriage not as a divine sacrament for the soul's development and human progression, but as the title deed that gave him possession of the woman he thought he loved. But alas for her, the laxity of his principles had rendered him unworthy of the deep and undying devotion of a pure-hearted woman. But, for a while, he hid from her his true character, and she blindly loved him, and for a short period was happy in the consciousness of being beloved. Though sometimes a vague unrest would fill her soul, when, overflowing with a sense of

123

the good, the beautiful and the true, she would turn to him but find no response to the deep yearnings of her soul – no appreciation of life's highest realities, its solemn grandeur and significant importance. Their souls never met, and soon she found a void in her bosom that his earthborn love could not fill. He did not satisfy the wants of her mental and moral nature: between him and her there was no affinity of minds, no intercommunion of souls.

Talk as you will of woman's deep capacity for loving – of the strength of her affectional nature. I do not deny it. But will the mere possession of any human love fully satisfy all the demands of her whole being? You may paint her in poetry or fiction as a frail vine, clinging to her brother man for support and dying when deprived of it, and all this may sound well enough to please the imaginations of schoolgirls, or lovelorn maidens. But woman – the true woman – if you would render her happy, it needs more than the mere development of her affectional nature. Her conscience should be enlightened, her faith in the true and right established, and scope given to her heaven-endowed and God-given faculties. The true aim of female education should be, not a development of one or two, but all the faculties of the 'human soul, because no perfect womanhood is developed by imperfect culture. Intense love is often akin to intense suffering, and to trust the whole wealth of woman's nature on the frail bark of human love may often be like trusting a cargo of gold and precious gems to a bark that has never battled with the storm or buffeted the waves. Is it any wonder, then, that so many life-barks . . . are stranded on the shoals of existence, mournful beacons and solemn warnings for the thoughtless, to whom marriage is a careless and hasty rushing together of the affections? Alas, that an institution so fraught with good for humanity should be so perverted, and that state of life which should be filled with happiness become so replete with misery. And this was the fate of Laura Lagrange.

For a brief period after her marriage her life seemed like a bright and beautiful dream, full of hope and radiant with joy. And then there came a change: he found other attractions that lay beyond the pale of home influences. The gambling saloon had power to win him from her side; he had lived in an element of unhealthy and unhallowed excitements, and the society of a loving wife, the pleasures of a well-regulated home, were enjoyments too tame for one who had vitiated his tastes by the pleasures of sin. There were charmed houses of vice, built upon dead men's loves, where, amid a flow of song, laughter, wine and careless mirth, he would spend hour after hour, forgetting the cheek that was paling through his neglect, heedless of the tear-dimmed eyes peering anxiously into the darkness, waiting or watching his return.

The influence of old associations was upon him. In early life, home had been to him a place of ceilings and walls, not a true home built upon goodness, love and truth. It was a place where velvet carpets hushed his tread, where images of loveliness and beauty, invoked into being by painter's art and sculptor's skill, pleased the eye and gratified the taste, where magnificence surrounded his way and costly clothing adorned his person; but it was not the place for the true culture and right development of his soul. His father had been too much engrossed in making money and his mother in spending it, in striving to maintain a fashionable position in society and shining in the eyes of the world, to give the proper direction to the character of their wayward and impulsive son. His mother put beautiful robes upon his body but left ugly scars upon his soul; she pampered his appetite but starved his spirit. . . .

That parental authority which should have been preserved as a string of precious pearls, unbroken and unscattered, was simply the administration of chance. At one time obedience was enforced by authority, at another time by flattery and promises, and just as often it was not enforced. . . . His early associations were formed as chance directed, and from his want of home training, his character received a bias, his life a shade, which ran through every avenue of his existence and darkened all his future hours. . . .

Before a year of his married life had waned, his young wife had learned to wait and mourn his frequent and uncalled-for absence. More than once had she seen him come home from his midnight haunts, the bright intelligence of his eye displaced by the drunkard's stare, and his manly gait changed to the inebriate's stagger; and she was beginning to know the bitter agony that is compressed in the mournful words

"drunkard's wife."

And then there came a bright but brief episode in her experience. The angel of life gave to her existence a deeper meaning and loftier significance: she sheltered in the warm clasp of her loving arms a dear babe, a precious child whose love filled every chamber of her heart. . . . How many lonely hours were beguiled by its winsome ways, its answering smiles and fond caresses! How exquisite and solemn was the feeling that thrilled her heart when she clasped the tiny hands together and taught her dear child to call God "Our Father"!

What a blessing was that child! The father paused in his headlong career, awed by the strange beauty and precocious intellect of his child; and the mother's life had a better expression through her ministrations of love. And then there came hours of bitter anguish, shading the sunlight of her home and hushing the music of her heart. The angel of death bent over the couch of her child and beckoned it away. Closer and closer the mother strained her child to her wildly heaving breast and struggled with the heavy hand that lay upon its heart. Love and agony contended with death. . . .

But death was stronger than love and mightier than agony, and won the child for the land of crystal founts and deathless flowers, and the poor stricken mother sat down beneath the shadow of her mighty grief, feeling as if a great light had gone out from her soul and that the sunshine had suddenly faded around her path. She turned in her deep anguish to the father of her child, the loved and cherished dead. For a while his words were kind and tender, his heart seemed subdued and his tenderness fell upon her worn and weary heart like rain on perishing flowers, or cooling waters to lips all parched with thirst and scorched with fever. But the change was evanescent; the influence of unhallowed associations and evil habits had vitiated and poisoned the springs of his existence. They had bound him in their meshes, and he lacked the moral strength to break his fetters and stand erect in all the strength and dignity of a true manhood, making life's highest excellence his ideal and striving to gain it.

And yet moments of deep contrition would sweep over him, when he would resolve to abandon the wine cup forever, when he was ready to forswear the handling of another card, and he would try to break away from the associations that he felt were working his ruin. But when the hour of temptation came his strength was weakness, his earnest purposes were cobwebs, his well-meant resolutions ropes of sand – and thus passed year after year of the married life of Laura Lagrange. She tried to hide her agony from the public gaze, to smile when her heart was almost breaking. But year after year her voice grew fainter and sadder, her once light and bounding step grew slower and faltering.

Year after year she wrestled with agony and strove with despair, till the quick eyes of her brother read, in the paling of her cheek and the dimming eye, the secret anguish of her worn and weary spirit. On that wan, sad face he saw the death tokens, and he knew the dark wing of the mystic angel swept coldly around her path.

"Laura," said her brother to her one day, "you are not well, and I think you need our mother's tender care and nursing. You are daily losing strength, and if you will go I will accompany you."

At first she hesitated; she shrank almost instinctively from presenting that pale, sad face to the loved ones at home.... But then a deep yearning for home sympathy woke within her a passionate longing for love's kind words, for tenderness and heart support, and she resolved to seek the home of her childhood and lay her weary head upon her mother's bosom, to be folded again in her loving arms, to lay that poor, bruised and aching heart where it might beat and throb closely to the loved ones at home.

A kind welcome awaited her. All that love and tenderness could devise was done to bring the bloom to her cheek and the light to her eye. But it was all in vain; hers was a disease that no medicine could cure, no earthly balm would heal. It was a slow wasting of the vital forces, the sickness of the soul. The unkindness and neglect of her husband lay like a leaden weight upon her heart....

And where was he that had won her love and then cast it aside as a useless thing, who rifled her heart of its wealth and spread bitter ashes upon its broken altars? He was lingering away from her when the death damps were gathering on her brow, when his name was trembling on her lips! Lingering away! when she was watching his coming, though the death films were gathering before her eyes and earthly things were fading from her vision.

"I think I hear him now," said the dying woman, "surely that is his step," but the sound died away in the distance.

Again she started from an uneasy slumber: "That is his voice! I am so glad he has come."

Tears gathered in the eyes of the sad watchers by that dying bed, for they knew that she was deceived. He had not returned. For her sake they wished his coming. Slowly the hours waned away, and then came the sad, soul-sickening thought that she was forgotten, forgotten in the last hour of human need, forgotten when the spirit, about to be dissolved, paused for the last time on the threshold of existence, a weary watcher at the gates of death.

"He has forgotten me," again she faintly murmured, and the last tears she would ever shed on earth sprung to her mournful eyes, and . . . a few broken sentences issued from her pale and quivering lips. They were prayers for strength, and earnest pleading for him who had desolated her young life by turning its sunshine to shadows, its smiles to tears.

"He has forgotten me," she murmured again, "but I can bear it; the bitterness of death is passed, and soon I hope to exchange the shadows of death for the brightness of eternity, the rugged paths of life for the golden streets of glory, and the care and turmoils of earth for the peace and rest of heaven."

Her voice grew fainter and fainter; they saw the shadows that never deceive flit over her pale and faded face and knew that the death angel waited to soothe their weary one to rest, to calm the throbbing of her bosom and cool the fever of her brain. And amid the silent hush of their grief the freed spirit, refined through suffering and brought into divine harmony through the spirit of the living Christ, passed over the dark waters of death as on a bridge of light, over whose radiant arches hovering angels bent. They parted the dark locks from her marble brow, closed the waxen lids over the once bright and laughing eye and left her to the dreamless slumber of the grave.

Her cousin turned from that deathbed a sadder and wiser woman. She resolved more earnestly than ever to make the world better by her example, gladder by her presence, and to kindle the fires of her genius on the altars of universal love and truth. She had a higher and better object in all her writings than the mere acquisition of gold or acquirement of fame. She felt that she had a high and holy mission on the battlefield of existence – that life was not given her to be frittered away in nonsense or wasted away in trifling pursuits. She would willingly espouse an unpopular cause, but not an unrighteous one.

In her the downtrodden slave found an earnest advocate; the

flying fugitive remembered her kindness as he stepped cautiously through our Republic to gain his freedom in a monarchial land, having broken the chains on which the rust of centuries had gathered. Little children learned to name her with affection; the poor called her blessed as she broke her bread to the pale lips of hunger.

Her life was like a beautiful story, only it was clothed with the dignity of reality and invested with the sublimity of truth. True, she was an old maid; no husband brightened her life with his love or shaded it with his neglect. No children nestling lovingly in her arms called her mother. No one appended Mrs. to her name.

She was indeed an old maid, not vainly striving to keep up an appearance of girlishness when "departed" was written on her youth, not vainly pining at her loneliness and isolation. The world was full of warm, loving hearts, and her own beat in unison with them. Neither was she always sentimentally sighing for something to love; objects of affection were all around her, and the world was not so wealthy in love that it had no use for hers. In blessing others she made a life and benediction, and as old age descended peacefully and gently upon her, she had learned one of life's most precious lessons: that true happiness consists not so much in the fruition of our wishes as in the regulation of desires and the full development and right culture of our whole natures.

# NUMBER 13

✳

## *Elizabeth Stuart Phelps*

'*Number 13*' *was first published in* Harper's New Monthly
Magazine *in March, 1876, and later included in Elizabeth
Stuart Phelps's short story collection,* Sealed Orders, *published
in 1879. This story is only one of many written by Phelps in
which the central character is an unmarried woman who is
financially and emotionally self-supporting. It was written
when its author (1844-1911) was, at 32 and still single, already
a famous and successful writer whose first novel,* The Gates
Ajar *(1868), the first of a utopian trilogy, had become a
bestseller on two continents and changed her life. Much of
Phelps's other fiction focuses on normal middle-class white
married life from the perspective of the woman for whom it
becomes a form of destructive servitude.*

*Her mother, Elizabeth Wooster Stuart Phelps (1815-52),
whose death in her daughter's eighth year left permanent scars,
a sense of almost unbearable loss, and resentment of her
father's role in her mother's too-early death, had also been a
writer. Upon her mother's death, the daughter, who had been
christened Mary Gray, took her mother's name. The daughter
wrote many years later of her mother, 'Genius was in her and
would out. She wrote because she could not help it . . . a wife, a
mother, a housekeeper, a hostess, in delicate health, on an
academic salary, undertakes a deadly load when she starts on a
literary career . . . she fell beneath it.'*

*Her father, Austin Phelps, a Congregational minister and
Andover, Massachusetts Theological Seminary teacher, married
his dead wife's tubercular sister less than two years later.
Elizabeth witnessed another dying within eighteen months. Her
father married a third time in 1858 and the new stepmother*

*quickly bore two more sons to add to the two the first Mrs Phelps had left behind at her death.*

*Here we see another instance where a young girl watches a beloved mother die from causes only too clear to her and then witnesses the amazing alacrity with which nineteenth-century widowers tended to remarry. It is a familiar tale by now, and one too often unacknowledged. Women become what they become, achieve something valuable, on the basis of our understandings of who our mothers were and what their lives were like. The perceptions are intimate and have too often remained private. But it is surely no accident that the daughter of such a mother wrote stories in which women who chose never to marry were championed.*

*Miss Phelps became ill after the publication of her most brilliant and moving novel,* The Story of Avis, *published in 1877. Avis is the story of a young woman who, inspired by her reading, at the age of 16, of Elizabeth Barrett Browning's novel in blank verse,* Aurora Leigh, *vows to dedicate her life to art. She becomes a much praised painter of whom much is expected but succumbing to the urgent pleas of a suitor who promises that their marriage will only enhance her work, she marries. Her life as an artist is destroyed by the incursions of domesticity, childbirth and child rearing, illness and her husband's endless needs.*

*Phelps's illness was both physical and emotional. After her health failed, she began to lose confidence in her independent life. In 1888, at the age of 44 she married a man seventeen years younger than herself. The marriage was a disaster. Herbert Dickinson Ward had apparently expected to use her literary reputation and connections to establish his own. However, his career as an author languished, and, despite her increasing ill-health, he abandoned the marriage in all ways except legally. She died alone.*

*'Number 13' is a rather remarkable story. It contains a strong assertion of female values in a social world controlled by rules that support the values of the patriarchy. Although the tone of the story is one that is appropriate for the apparently modest narrator, the events in the story make clear the author's evaluation of the boarder in number 13 as an heroic figure. The heroine 'wins'; she carves out her own survival, independently, in a world full of strangers whom she transforms into a caring community. She discovers amidst her perceptions of her own*

*financial hardships that she has abundance; she identifies what she gives away as 'more than she needs.' More than one needs is luxury. She is an economic success because she has discovered her own surplus. At the end of the story she is rewarded for her good works in a way that upsets the traditional pattern of marriage to a handsome prince with more power, wealth and status than a woman alone could achieve. She is rewarded by reunion with her long-lost baby brother, returned from the sea. Because this is a woman's story the heroine is not rewarded by being robbed of her independence, her opportunity for adventure and the taking of risks, and scope for her talents.*

# NUMBER 13*

*

My dear, it's my opinion that if all folks that thought of getting married were compelled by state law to spend six months with some respectable family, under the same roof, before they did it, there wouldn't be more than one wedding sift through that sieve to where there's twenty now.

Since you *asked* me why I never got married, that's why. Bless you, no! I don't say you put it in so many words, but that's what you've been a-saying, every look and motion and tone of you, since you sat here, turning your pretty eyes about my room and over me, my dear, quite gentle and uninquisitive, but full of a kind of wonder and a kind of sadness too. I've seen that look in young folks' eyes times and times. But it isn't often Number 13 sees such eyes as yours, my dear, though there's been enough that was kind, and enough that was sorrowful in it, for that matter, too. I took a fancy to the look of you, I tell you plainly, the first day you come – three weeks ago come Thursday – with those half dozen lawn petticoats for a fine tuck, you remember, and the insertin that was wore to be taken out from above. I'm set in my fancies, as I am in my ways. It isn't everybody one feels a drawin' to. You know you feel a drawin' in you sometimes to folks, when all the folds of your heart seem gathered up toward them like fine gathers – so close you'd hardly see to stroke 'em down. There's folks I've cut and basted this dozen year, and those I've done for by the fortnight, and even those I've made and finished, that I couldn't set and talk to as I'm going on to you, my dear – not for a steady engagement on their trussows or

*From *Sealed Orders* by Elizabeth Stuart Phelps, 1879. Originally published in *Harper's New Monthly Magazine*, no. 52, pp. 580-9, March 1876.

their mournin' for a year to come; and if you thought it was because you made it a dollar a day when I was askin' only eight-five, I should be sorry; and you did it such a pretty way, how could I help it? And when I heard how Miss Jabez Smithson run on about you for settin' me up to ask more than your neighbors was able to pay me, I'd have — I'd have asked her one thirty-seven and a half, my dear, if I could have got it.

Stand a mite this way, if you will, my dear, nigher to the glass. There! Will you have the walnut silk cut bias for the shirr? I cut one on the square for Miss Colonel Adams's navy blue repellant. I'll pin it up a scrap, and let you see it for yourself — so!

You see, my dear, he was my cousin, and he come to our house the winter mother was failin' — when we lived down East in Franklin — to help do for us, father being dead and the boys gone. There was two boys, Ned and 'Li'kim. Ned was the one that died. I never did know what of. Our old doctor said he had wind in his brain. My little brother 'Li'kim — there! I needn't keep you standin' any longer in the blazin' light — I always said that 'Li'kim meant well, my dear, and I always, always will, and I'd rather not talk about it just now; but he got into bad company, poor little chap! and after father died he — ran — away. One night I come home from the sewin' circle, and I found his common close and his little skates and things he'd left in a heap, and a little note atop to mother. And mother she just threw up her arms and ran to meet me, screechin' through the entry; and, my dear, it left her ravin' wild from that hour till she died. For she'd had a fever, and been a scrap weakly in her head since father's funeral.

But that doesn't matter now, only it will explain some things to you, and how my cousin Peter Doggett come to live with us. And that doesn't matter, only that when I got through with that job, I didn't want him for a husband, nor no man else. The ways they have with their boots, my dear, and the smell of blacking, I don't like; and the pipes, and laying them against your clean mantel-piece after you have dusted, and the bein' so particular about the pudden sauce when you're wore with watching sick folks all the night, and the sitting still and seeing you bring kindlen and draw water, and the getting used to you, my dear, and snapping of you up. And then the way of speaking to your mother!

My dear, when it all began, I was that fond of Peter

Doggett I'd have carried kindlen, or bore with pipes, or fussed with pudden sauces, or run my feet off for him to all eternity, and thought myself well off. And when it all was over, I wouldn't have lifted a winker, much less an eyelash for him, come what might. For when we come to set down day by day and meal by meal and worry by worry together, then all the temper and all the selfishness and all the meanness there was in us come up. I don't know what he thought of *mine*, my dear. Temper enough, the Lord knows, but I *couldn't* have snapped him up, my dear, as he did me; and if I'd spoke to his mother as he spoke one afternoon to mine – she very troublesome in the head that day, poor old lady, and requirin' all the patient love of son and daughter both to keep her strong and still – if I had, I'd have looked to be turned into a pillow of salt, like Lot's poor wife, my dear, and kept a-standin' in the settin'-room for a shame to the family forever after. So after that I says to him, "Peter Doggett, we're never fitted to make each other happy as married folks if we can't get along as common folks." And so that was the end of *that*. And mother died the next week, and Peter went home after the funeral; and so I was left to myself, my dear, for my aunt Hannah, Peter's mother, was offended, very natural, and there was no other of my blood in all the world. I wouldn't have thought that meant much once. Young folks don't understand such things. You've no more idea, my pretty, setting there with your great eyes, what the drawin' of kith and kin is like, when you're left to shift without it, than an unhatched boblink, and please God you never, never may! Nor I'd no more idea till after the house was sold to pay off old mortgages of father's, and I come to this place, my dear, on the recommendation of a friend of mine, to take in, or go out if desired, but much preferring to take in, and only advertising to begin with, for plain sewing, on account of a little weakness in my eyes. Her name was Susannah Greenwich, and the first month I rented Number 13 she was a comfort to me, my dear; for she had the second rear, and ran a Wheeler and Wilson, with a dreadful backache, and I used to make a drop of tea for her of evenings, and I got a new teapot big enough for two on purpose; and that was a pleasure you'd never guess, my dear, unless you'd drunk out of the smallest size a while, and cried into it a good deal of stormy nights alone. But Susannah Greenwich she got married. She married the first floor, that I cured of the toothache; and it was coming up after the drops that he took the notion to her, when I'd got her fixed comfortable with a Scotch plaid blanket shawl across the chair, and that red cricket to her feet, and the mug a-steaming in her hand; for I hadn't any tea-cups at that time, and the wash-stand mug has more comfort in it than you'd think, my dear, when tea-cups are out of the question for lack of steady work.

Now I'll tell you that this minute I never told Susannah nor a living soul. He asked me first, the first floor did. His name was Thrasher. But I wouldn't have a man named Thrasher if he was first cousin to the Angel Gabriel. And he took it very kind indeed, and made up to Susannah that day come a fortnight, for he was in a taking for a home as ever I saw; and she moved her Wheeler and Wilson away, and they went across the river to live, for he kept a lard factory, and it was more convenient for the hogs.

It wasn't till Susannah'd gone that it all came over me, my dear. Long as you have a cup of tea to make or a toothache to cure for folks, it ain't so bad, but when you've settled down in a big houseful of those that you haven't the right to lift a finger for, nor one of them the heart to do for you, and all going their own ways, and living their own lives, and sorrowin' their own sorrows, and lockin' their souls against each other as they do their drawers and trunks, and if you was to die in your bed of some lonesome night, my dear, not a soul of 'em would know nor care until the landlady noticed, maybe, by next evening that you didn't make a noise about your room, and sent up the Loon to see. I call her the Loon, my dear, for she's the chamber-maid and nigh as crazy; besides, the color of her eyes the same, if you noticed it upon the stairs. I've lost my collection of ideas, my dear, but I was going to say, it is a way of living that folks can't dream nor guess at till they've lived it. It seems to me, as I set and think it over, as if we had to live such large whiles in this world, my dear, to understand the least, least little things!

Hard? Yes, my dear, I thought so then. When first I knuckled to it down in Number 13 I thought it was a little hard. But, bless you! that was before I knew what hardness was, or where the comfort of it was coming in. It's like the soft side of a pine board, boardin' is. There! I didn't *mean* that for a conundrum, but it's a pretty good one; don't you think so?

Turn a scrap this way, while I pin the gore against the loop.
Yes.

Comfort? I've had enough of comfort in this scrimpy little
wee worn room, my dear, to warm a cold heart through for
forty harder lives than mine. No, I don't know as I could tell
you *how* it comes. Comfort is like sunshine of an afternoon:
you can't reason how it comes, but only know the blessed
comin', and set and curl up in it a-warmin' through and
through, my dear. And it ain't so much then as it is afterward
that you know how warm you are. I've taken a surprising deal
of pleasure in the course of my experience in thinking how
well off I was once, after it was over. Some folks can't, I
know. Eggs ain't speckled all alike, nor there don't no two
kittens in a batch run after their tails with just the same degree
of sperit. I've seen cats that would do it in a melancholy
manner, as if they were doing you a personal favor, and cats
that would do it in a superior manner, as if they'd show the
other cats how much it was beneath 'em. There's cats and cats.

If you'd rather set and wait for me to baste the bilt platin'
together, I'll try and tell you something about it; but it's a
scrimpy story, like the room, my dear, and wee and worn too,
like the room. Everything's been scrimpy in my life, my
pretty, but the comfort.

After Susannah, it all began with Miss Major Cracklejaw,
upon the same floor front. I'd seen her going in and out – a
little creetur with big eyes and stylish hair; but I'd never taken
notice to speak to most the folks, for the third floor rear, with
one window and a gas stove and do for yourself, ain't just
abreast of the full soots or front parlors and board besides,
you see. So, after Susannah Thrasher went, I fought mostly
shy of 'em, unless it was a little plain sewing, and once or
twice the week's mendin' for Miss M'Henry Dumps (as true as
you stand in your bustle, that was her blessed name!) – the
first floor she was, with three babies and a nurse with neuralgy
twice a week in the frouziest head I ever saw, that dropped the
baby down the steps if you'll believe it, twice that winter.

And so, because I kept so mostly to myself, and because
Number 13 *was* cold, my dear, when the gas was contrary and
I hadn't that chair in there made out of the barrel, with the
patchwork cover – poor Miss Flynn and Tommy Harkness,
they gave me that chair, but I haven't come to them yet – nor
the Turkey-red valance on the curtain, my dear: and you can't

guess the comfort there is in a mite of Turkey red, nor how my poor dear Helen Goldenough looked blushing in the day she knocked and said, Might she give herself a *great* comfort by putting of it up? And I hadn't got the tea-set then, nor that little shelf old Mr. Hopkinson put up to hold the cups I bought next quarter, nor the pretty shade across the gas, for your poor eyes, or the lace and paper with the maple leaves between, sent by the attic rear, my dear, with the sweetest poor face, and, oh! *she* got into such a trouble! nor the little book-case either from Miss Cracklejaw herself, one Christmas-eve, with John G. Whittier's poems a-standing all alone and looking such a comfort! Nor I hadn't got this blessed stove in then that I save a year to run the pipe through, and to get the landlady quite willing; for anybody's temper would be wore a little thin, my dear, with folks that didn't pay, to say nothing of the Loon. And make the best you might, my dear, there is *no* comfort in the Loon.

So I was setting all alone, my dear, one night without a light, and shivering over the gas stove, and moping by myself, for I was out of work; and, setting there, I began to think. All at once I began to seem to be setting in the keeping-room at home with my little brother 'Li'kim. What I said about the drawin' that you feel for folks, you know, and you know how some drawin's is as much tighter than other drawin's as is the difference between the sunlight and the moonlight, or between the fire and the freeze! I don't know how it was – I can't talk much about it even, after all – but in all my life I never had such a drawin' of all that in you that makes you love and live for folks, and be blessed when they're by you, and be wretched when they ain't, and most of all that feelin' that makes you glad to do and suffer for 'em and spare'em pain, and shelter of 'em up as hens brood over their poor chicks, or like young mothers cuddlin' their first babies, as the feelin's that I had for my little brother 'Li'kim. What I thought of Peter Doggett before he come to live with us come nighest to it; but it never, never was the same.

'Li'kim was a pretty boy, my dear, and his hair curled. I used to curl it across my fingers for him every morning; and he brought his little lessons to me, and he always liked to get by me, and he'd rather I'd go up to hear his prayers. And oh, my dear, from the night he left us till – till long afterward – till this very living night – I'll own to you, when I've kneeled to say my own, there's never, never been a night, not one, that I haven't said over "Now I lay me" through for *him*, my dear, fearin' he'd grown too wild and wayward to say it for himself.

But I've wandered far from Miss Cracklejaw; you must excuse me. I haven't often spoke of 'Li'kim — not for many years. He was the light of my eyes, my dear — poor boy! — just the living light of my young eyes. I used to tell him so sometimes when we sat alone; but *then* I didn't even know what I was a-saying when I was a-saying that.

But when I was setting there that evening it all come back, and all I could think of was that little fellow; and the strange old mystery of kith or kin, and how I was left battlin' without it, come over me; and how dreary the room looked, and how cold it was, and I without a friend in all that big drear house, and the tea-pot only lukewarm upon the stove! And I seemed to see my life go stretching out, out, like an awful seam to which there is no end, and me sitting taking stitches to shorten of it up, just so, pent up alone with my tea-pot in that little room, and never a face to kiss nor a hand to get hold of when your head aches like to split, my dear, and never a voice to speak nor to talk back to, and in all the wide, old world no speck of comfort to your name, my dear.

Then all at once within the little lonely room I seemed to see my little brother 'Li'kim kneeling down to say his prayers; and I put down my tea-cup — for it was dark, and my eyes never very strong, and I often saw queer things — and I kneeled down where I seemed to see him and went through "Now I lay me" by myself, till the tea was cold. But I felt better for it, somehow, that I did, my dear, and before I was off my knees, Miss Cracklejaw knocked sudden, and I jumped as if I'd been struck in a heap to let her in.

She wanted a little sewin' done, she said, and would I just step into her room and see if I could do it for her? So I went in with her, and we set down and began to talk about the work. They was little things, my dear, a little blanket, and a little shirt, and what not, and she'd given out on finishing 'em off, for she wasn't very well; and I was sorry for her as we set and talked, for now and then the tears come and trickled down, and she in a sadder way, my dear, than she'd ought to be, till I knew there was a trouble on her mind; and at last, while we were talking, it come over me, with a great stirring in my heart, to find out what it was that wore on her, and be a comfort if I could. So, though I *was* the third rear and a gas stove, I up and says: —

"Miss Cracklejaw, something worries you. I'm a poor woman, but your neighbor, and if ever I can do for you, just let me know, and there I am; for it's lonesome boardin' with your worries, as I know, my dear."

Well, she thanked me pretty enough — very prettily for a woman with such a stylish head of hair, and cried again, and said she'd see, and said there *was* a worry, and it broke her heart.

Now it was that very night, my dear, I sittin' in my dressin'-gownd to read my chapter, that I heard the noise outside my door, a stumblin', scrapin' noise, and then a bangin' like the last trumpet up against my door, and I went to see, for it was half after eleven o'clock, and the hours in the house are half past ten, excepting latch-keys to gentlemen of good habits at eleven, and there, my dear, I come plump on Major Cracklejaw, drunk as drunk.

His poor wife come out as I come out, in a pretty white wrapper, with shirred pink merino up the front, you know, and her hair all streaming and her face as white! And we helped him into bed together, he never knowin', and neither of us spoke a word till it was done. Then says I, "I know your worry now, Miss Cracklejaw, and Heaven help you!"

And she says: "Oh, what shall I do? what shall I *do?* It was so last week and the week before, and twice last month, and some other times. And I've let him in quite quiet, nobody knowin' his disgrace; for he's a young man, my husband is, and never was like this before, and promised me he never, never would. But he's got into a bad set," she says, and "he's troubled in his business" — we had to excuse so much in men, she said, on account of business — and now, when she was taken ill, oh! who would let him in at nights, and save the house from knowin' of the shame? she says. And she was in such a taking as you never saw. So of course I said I'd let him in, my dear, and so I did. And I let him in with a vengeance, I tell you; for when it happened twice, I gave him such a talkin' to, she lying weak and miser'ble up-stairs, poor creetur, that, for very shame, it was a fortnight before he dared to try it again, my dear. And I talked when he was sober, and I talked when he was drunk, and I set up always till that man was in, as if he'd been a boy a dozen years old; and after the baby was born he got ashamed of it, or else I made it too much trouble, and he pulled through and come out all right, my dear; and such a grateful creetur, when I sat of evenings now and then to help about the baby! for she was a long time getting up. And never a soul but them two and myself knew of his disgrace, my dear, for I never let on a word of it; and if they hadn't been unknownst to you, and gone to California besides, I wouldn't let on now. I don't know why she took on so about it, as if I'd done her some tremenjous favor. Any woman would have done it she'd seen fit to let.

Now when I saw that young thing well and spry, and him as well-behaved as need be, and the baby with the whooping-cough, and him so tender to it, and home of evenings, I got such comfort in it as you'd never guess. It was 'most as good as having a husband and baby of your own, without the bother or the blacking. And there was that in the way them two looked at me, and the tones of their voice when they spoke to me, my dear, forever after, that made my scrimpy little room a sort of home to me — if you can understand the feelin' — even when I set alone.

And oh! the tones, my dear, and oh! the voices and the looks these walls have seen. I don't know why! And the folks that have made this house a comfort to me, I don't know how! I think I got the most out of poor Miss Flynn and Tommy Harkness for a while, though why they ever should have come to *me!* You see, it had been going on a long while: she very young and pretty, and her mother dead, and working in a dollar store all day; and Tommy Harkness, he was young and thoughtless, and he had the second opposite, but he was in the retail grocery; and I don't suppose they thought of marrying. But she was lonesome, and the boy was good-natured, and this had been goin' on for nigh two years, till, my dear, she was the talk of the house.

One evening, up comes Miss Barker — she's the landlady, you know — and says she, "I can't have this any longer," says she; "there's such goin's-on, and in her room at reasonable and onreasonable hours, and caught a kissin' of her a Tuesday last! All my folks are talkin' about it. Maggie Flynn must suit herself with a less respectable house," says Miss Barker.

Now, my dear, I was in that distress I couldn't bear myself for a half an hour, for I liked Miss Flynn, though very imprudent; but I'd as soon think evil of myself, my dear, as of

141

that child. And in she comes while I was turning of it over, all her hair tumbled, and her eyes as red as the Loon's herself, and wringing of her hands and wringing of her hands. Oh! what would ever become of her? What had she done? What should she do? And she clings to me, and begs me to save her from such a shameful, awful thing. In all the house, she said, I was the only friend she had to tell. I don't know why, for more than taking in a hot brick or so when she had an influenza, and watching for a word, and wishing she'd confide in me about the boy — for I'd felt uneasy — I'd never done.

I think, my dear, that was the hardest three days' work I ever did, for it took three days to straighten of it out. And such a time! Miss Cracklejaw did most of that, though set against the girl to start with. But we talked it over, and we had Miss Barker up, and Miss Flynn, all red and crying, and Tommy too; and Miss Cracklejaw she said if we could carry it out, she'd invite me down to supper on Christmas evening — for it was Christmas time. She'd invited me before, my dear; but when it's only a dried herring and a cup of tea *and* a gas stove you can ask back to, you feel a delicacy. So Miss Cracklejaw invited me to supper, and Miss Barker, we prevailed upon her to say she'd abide by the decision of the house if it was laid before the house. So then I goes to Tommy Harkness, and I says, "Thomas, you and Maggie Flynn must be engaged to be married before six o'clock to-night. And then, Thomas, you'll have to go across to old Miss Phipps's to board, and call on Maggie in the parlor."

Says Thomas, groaning out between his hands, "Oh, is it so bad as that? Oh, I wish she'd never seen me! I wouldn't have had this happen, not for the worth of State Street," say Tommy Harkness; for he was fond of Maggie, and never meant to harm her. Then he holds up his head, with his cheeks hot. "Maggie's a lady!" says he, fast and mad. "She's been a lady to me. It's I that wasn't the gentleman," says he, "for I ought to have thought of her. Maggie is a good girl," says Tommy, mighty proud. Then he melted down quite piteous, and cries, "I didn't think! I didn't think! And we haven't any thing to marry on, and how *could* a fellow get engaged?"

So I made quick work of Tommy Harkness, but it was three blessed days before Miss Flynn would show her poor face to any soul but me, or barely eat a morsel, and crying her eyes out, my dear, till she was almost blind. But when the Christmas come, I told Miss Cracklejaw I'd accept her invitation to supper, seeing it would run on forever if I didn't take a step decided; and I took her just as she was, all pale and blinded with the tears, one hand in mine, and Tommy Harkness with the other on his arm. My! how that boy did tremble! And Miss Cracklejaw she was very polite and pretty, and so I took my first tea, my dear, at Miss Barker's table.

All the house was there, and the room as bright as bright. And you never saw how the silver seemed to me to shine, or the pleasant look about the cake-basket, my dear. And I stood up before them all, and I says, for I knew them mostly by that time.

"My friends," I says, "I've come to ask you to congratulate these two young people for being promised to each other to be man and wife." I says it very solemn, 'most like a marriage service, and the people's faces, though black enough, my dear, took on a solemn look. "They're very young," I further says, "without father or mother to guide them or advise them – very young," I says; and when I felt her poor hand shake in mine, there come that trembling in my voice I hardly could get out the words. "And I think," says I, "that you'll all agree with me as it's easier in this world to do foolish things than prudent ones, and sweeter to think well of folks than ill of folks, and nobler to remember that we none of us ain't sure till we are in our graves that the time mayn't come we'll need folks to believe in us too against appearances, and to forgive us too the little follies we may commit despite ourselves. My friends," says I, "it's my belief no man nor no woman of us will ever grow so old as to be sure we mightn't make a blunder and be sorry for it, and yet have hearts as innocent as two young hearts I've looked into and know all about. And so, because it's the blessed Christmas time, in which we all love to think kindly and believe much in one another, I'm sure you'll join with me in the little supper of congratulation I've come down to take with you and my two dear young friends to-night."

And, my dear, they did – yes, they did. Even Miss Barker she cleared up, and they helped Miss Flynn six times to marmalade among'em, and wished her merry Christmas, and talked politics most beautiful, when she began to cry afresh, to change the subject. And when that supper was over, first I knew that whole tableful of folks, they rose up, and Major Cracklejaw says he: –

143

"A hundred merry Christmases and three cheers for her that has the Christmas soul among us!" says Major Cracklejaw. And so, as I sat looking round, quite pleased and happy, and wondering who it was of whom the Major thought that pretty thought, my dear, would you believe it? All those folks they got up and they cheered *me!* ME!

My dear, I like to have fell through the floor, not so much because the Loon dropped the preserved ginger down my neck that minute, as she truly did, and very cold I found it for so hot a tasting thing, and my best alpaca too – but you can't scold a creetur with no more gumption than that creetur has – but because of the fright of it and the surprise. But afterwards, when I come to think it over, there come such a comfort to it I could hardly close my eyes that blessed night.

Ah, my dear, and so it's been this thing and been that; but I wish you'd seen my poor Miss Goldenough before the small-pox winter. Not so very pretty, but gentle and well-looking, though I never can abide loops brought round behind and puffed across the bustle. And when she was taken down up there in that attic, and not a relative nigher than Kentucky, when she come on to sing in the Beatoven chorus, there was I, with a full week on Miss Jabez Smithson, for she was going to New York to make a little visit; and when Miss Barker come up all of a zeal about sending of the poor creetur to the hospital, I says, "What shall I do?" Indeed I did! But then I thought of being down with small-pox in that attic, and no kith nor kin to stand by you, and of the terror that she had about the hospital, for she'd often told me, and it was something of a cousin that was neglected in one once, and died most horrible. And I says, my dear, what has Heaven left me without own folks for, if it ain't to be own folks to those that are similar? and I says: –

"Miss Barker, let the poor thing stay, and shut us up together in the attic, and the Loon will bring the meals and my good-by to all the house," says I, "and tell no one to come nigh us."

And so she did it, for she's a grateful creetur; and ever after not scolding her about the ginger, she was most willing *for* a Loon: a little used to sharp words, I guess, for most things.

So I stayed three weeks in that attic, and the doctor and the Loon come every day – at least the tips of her fingers with the dishes – and I never saw her eyes so blazin' red before nor since. And we did the best we could; but one night, Tuesday three week, as I was dropping into a scrappy nap upon the comfortables I'd laid upon the floor, Helen Goldenough she called me in a ringing voice.

I spring, and am by her in a minute, and there she sits, bolt-upright and awful, in the bed. Says she: —

"Why, mother!" says she — "why, mother, how good of you to come!"

My dear, she took me for her mother; and when I saw the change upon her, I can't tell you the solemn feelings of my heart to hear that word.

But they weren't as solemn as the feelings that I had a minute after, when that poor thing did what she did. My dear, upon my living word, she rose upon her knees and folded of her hands and begun to say her prayers to me. I'm 'most afraid to tell you what she said. Says she: —

"*Our mother who art in heaven!*" that's what she says — "*our mother who art in heaven, hallowed be thy name!*" says Helen Goldenough. And then, whether she took me for mother on earth or mother in heaven I can't say, not knowin', but she puts her poor hands about my neck, for I wouldn't have deceived her not to move an eyelash if I'd died for it that minute; and, my dear, I was so much own folks to her, and whether those of earth or heaven doesn't matter as I know, that she fell into my arms, all dreadful as she was, and there she died.

Her mother did come on two days after, and I told her how it was. I don't think, if I'd live to the next Centennial and the ballots, I'd forget that woman's look nor the words she said to me. I can't tell them to you, my dear, for they were far, far above my best deserving; and she gave the Loon a dollar bill, and slept with me and cried upon my neck till she went home.

No, I never had it, after all; only three days' touch of varyloid, that the Loon brought the meals to, and Miss Cracklejaw she sent up grapes; and after you have found out it isn't it, my dear, it ain't so bad to be alone. First two days I didn't know, and I thought a great deal about my little brother 'Li'kim, and of bein' glad I had no own folks, after all, to take into mortal danger for my sake, till there fairly was a comfort in it, don't you see?

And now, my dear, if I had time to tell you about Mr. Hopkinson and his broken arm, or about Miss M'Henry

Dumps's baby, or about that matter in the first floor rear, or about Miss Barker herself and the invitation down to dinner, or a thousand thousand things that took place to bless me! but I see you're getting tired, and if I'm going to tell a story all about myself, I must tell it I suppose, and you'll excuse me for the impoliteness, and I'll make it short as possible.

But, oh! I wish you'd seen the attic rear poor thing of which I spoke. Mercy Maynard was her name, and saleswoman in a fancy store, and a little wild and fond of dress, but a modest woman, in spite of him, my dear; for he owned the store, and he kept the wages down on purpose. And she used to come of evenings, and set on that cricket at my feet, and tell me; and it was a cursed story, that it was, my dear – may I be forgiven for a little swearing when I think of him! – and often and often it happens in this town to them poor girls. And there was a time I thought I'd lost, her, for I'd talked till I was wore out, and she got as wild as wild with desperation, not knowing any place to go to; and poor girls must earn their bread, my dear, in spite of cursed men. And it wasn't much to do, I'm sure, but all I could; so I persuaded her and I begged her till she came. Says I: "Just quit, and stop with me a while and help me at my work, till you find more, two in a room being nigh half as much a week, and two to a tea-pot nothing more to speak of, and twice the comfort," as was true, my dear. And so she come and stayed till Mr. M'Henry Dumps he found her something in a corset store that a woman owned it, and only peace and women all around her. I was a little short of work just then, it's true; but, bless you! somehow we seemed to get along. I've often thought of a thing she said one night, and stroking of my hair in a little way she had. "You poor old dear!" says she. "You love your boardin'-house neighbor as yourself." says she. I'm just so mean, my dear, I suppose I did for her twice as happily for hearing that. It's the very Alderney cream of comfort when folks think kinder of you than you deserve.

But it was about this time there come slowly growin' on me that trouble and that terror that drove all other folks' troubles half out my crazy, selfish heart.

It come slowly, and yet it come sudden too. I'll put it in few words now if I can, for there's nothing in it worth the telling to make a fuss about.

It was about my eyes, my dear – never very strong, and sewing so constant, and perhaps a little with watching with

Miss Barker when she had the fever; but, first I knew, the black work had to lay by till morning; and then it couldn't be black work at all; and then I noticed that the sewing in the evening had to slip; and sudden, one afternoon, as I sat hurrying to get the narrow velvet on Miss M'Henry Dumps's polonaise, there come to me a dreadful thing.

My dear, I couldn't thread my needle.

Thinkin' to mercy it might be a headache, I let it go till next day, and the next; and when it got no different, I put my bonnet on and went out, sayin' nothing to nobody, and asked the doctor.

My dear, I think I know how folks feel when they jump into rivers in their night-gownds, and swallow poison (which must be a most unpleasant manner to select), and even a pistol or a razor – any dreadful, desperate, wild, mad way that you can think of of getting rid of the life the Lord has laid upon your breaking shoulders. When he told me it was cataract, and very doubtful, but they would try it at the hospital if I could get in, I never even said a Thank you, Sir. I tied on my bonnet and come home, and I crawled up stairs to my little room – my precious little room, my dear, where it wasn't the dyin' light that made things look so dim and strange to me – and down I sat and locked the door, and there I stayed.

I can't tell you how long it was – maybe till next evening, maybe days and more; I never could exactly tell. Folks come and come. I sent them all away. They knocked and questioned, but I turned 'em off. I had to turn it over in my mind alone.

I turned it over in a curious way. I seemed to see myself a-setting there, much as I'd seen 'Li'kim on his knees beside the bed, distinct – a miserable woman, half dazed and crazed. I seemed to set and talk about myself as if I'd been one of the poor creeturs in some other room I'd gone to do for. And as I set, I talked like this: –

"Dependent on her needle. Poor. A woman. Living by herself. Beginning to grow old. No home. No folks. And growing blind. Oh, poor thing!"

Then I'd have it over a little different: –

"Growing blind. No home. No folks. Poor. Living all alone. A woman. Takes in sewing for a living. How sorry I am for her!"

Then I'd try it once again: –

"An old woman. Took in sewing for a living. Long gone

147

blind. No home. No folks. Sent her to the poor-house. There she sits. Stone-blind. May live to be eighty. Poor thing! What can I do for her? Oh, what can I do?"

It was when this had been going on a while that, sudden, as I sat there, Helen Goldenough, that was dead and buried, come walking up across the room to my poor eyes that saw all thing so queer. And she took me by the hand, and down she pushed me gently on my knees. And I saw her kneel beside me, and seem to take my hands and lift 'em up – so! And I saw her talking – so! And, my dear, she says: –

"Our mother who art in heaven" – and seems to wait for me to say it after. And after thinkin' of it a little while, I says: –

"Our Father and mother who art in heaven," and then I stopped. I felt easier, my dear – I truly did. I *sensed* it, as we used to say to home, that there was another kith and kin than that I hadn't got, and lovin'er own folks than the own folks I had lost, and I felt ashamed, my dear – I was ashamed to have forgot it, for I was brought up religious always, though never quite settled in my mind on justification by faith and the election doctrine, with a leanin' to immersion, I will confess.

So when I'd said those words, and Helen Goldenough she'd seemed to go, I let in Maggie Flynn, most uneasy and crying at the door, and told her all about it.

My dear, it was just three days since the people in the house had known, and I never, never was deservin' of it, when up it come! I sitting all forlorn and at my wits' end in the dark, and the Loon one mortal grin – I don't, indeed, believe no other creetur could, *unless* the bird itself. And in she brought the round robin on a stone-china plate, with a red doyley and two apples. Miss Barker's compliments and the house's love, she says; and they begs you to accept, she says.

I'll get you the paper, my dear, and let you read it for yourself. Rather not? Well, I will try; but it always makes my voice a little shaky, and Mr. Hopkinson, I think it must have been, that drew it, for he's a school-teacher, my dear; and never was there a mortal thing but helping when the arm was set, and now and then a stockin' or so; he'd got no women-folks to do for him.

"Miss Barker's boarders" – (it begins) – "Miss Barker's boarders beg leave to send their profound sympathy and sorrow to Number 13, in the unexpected trial that has falled on that room. And in token of their grateful remembrance of unnumbered large and little kindnesses" — (my dear, those are the very words, though blush I do to say it) — "of unnumbered large and little kindnesses that they, Miss Barker's boarders, have received from the occupant of that room in this and other times, and in memory of her endeavors to bring the spirit of a home among so many homeless people, and of their great indebtedness to her for much neighborly, unselfish service, offered in a sweet and modest manner peculiar to herself, Miss Barker's boarders hereby request her to favor them by accepting the inclosed trifle, hoping it may help to defray the expenses of that affliction which it has pleased Heaven mysteriously to send upon her, and wishing it might testify one half of both the sadness and the hope that is felt throughout this house for her.

"(*Signed*): M'Henry Dumps, Althea Dumps, E. G. Hopkinson, Maggie Flynn, T. Harkness, John Cracklejaw, May Cracklejaw, O. L. Smith, P. Jones, Susannah G. Thrasher, Caleb Thrasher, Mercy Maynard, E. P. Green, Sarah Barker, Elizabeth Tudor, Mary Ann Shamway."

And, my dear, it was eighty-five dollars and forty-two cents.

But I never would have thought the forty-two cents of them two girls; and Mary Ann Shamway's neuralgy, I never could help her much, poor thing, do or not do; and before I could get it into my head that Elizabeth Tudor was the Loon! To say nothing of Miss Barker's receipt for three months' rent, my dear. And those strange gentlemen, that more than a civil "Pleasant morning, sir!" never did I have the pleasure.

And so I went to the hospital, my pretty, quite happy. And a paid bed *is* a comfort, my dear, if go you must. And for all the courage and all the happiness that bore me through, like wings, I have to thank their generous way of saying so. For, oh! there's no tonic and no ether to bear pain and weakness on like joy, my dear; and the feeling that you're cared for and thought kindly of, comes nighest to the name of joy of any that I know.

So I left my little room, my dear, saying good-by to all the things, to wonder if I'd ever see them more; the Turkey-red valance, and the tea-pot, and the cricket in especial, and Mercy Maynard's ivy growing in the bottle over there. Eyes looked out of them plain and scrimpy things, my dear, to my eyes, and voices spoke from them to answer me, and grace and blessin's seemed to stand in 'em and reach to me, and seem to say: —

"Goin' to the hospital. Goin' to be cured. Pretty well off. Hosts of friends. And a round robin. Needn't worry. Coming back to us. Not so much a happy woman as a quiet. Plenty of folks. Our Father and our mother who art" —

And then I shut the door, my dear, and, as I told you, went and bore it through.

Well! well! well! it was, oh! the loveliest spring night, my dear, when I come home. And, oh! so much beyond my grumpiness and deserving when first they told me all was going well. Never did I half believe nor understand it till the very night they drove me home. It was of an April evening, and the grass was springing greenish here and there in spots upon the Common, and pleasant to the eyes, if weak, my dear, in driving by. And the same I thought with the dyin' light, a pink and gentle one, and many thin, high clouds. So many little boys a-whistling in the street, and standin' on their heads to scare the wits of you, I never saw. And I counted twenty little girls a-laughing, happy as the angels, between that hospital and home. And warm, too; and so mild! One of the hospital doctors he come with me, for they were kind as kind, and him and the driver they got me out the carriage as if I'd been the Queen.

My dear, for all the fits of blues and undeserving may I hope to be forgiven! But I was kind of hustled into the parlors, and in a sort of soft, low light, and very thoughtful of my eyes in 'em, all smilin' to their eyebrows, there stood the house — the whole of 'em, all in a row, my dear, to greet me home, they said. And up they come, and like to been the end of me, and Susannah Greenwich too. Some they shook my hands and some they kissed me, but they were women, only poor old Mr. Hopkinson, that you must excuse; and some they cried and some they laughed, and Miss Barker in the middle, with a tea-table spread out, and a little speech, with ice-cream that the Loon she tripped and stuck her elbow through; but if you didn't happen to see it, it tasted just as well.

But there was a strange gentleman among 'em that I'd never seen, and he didn't come to shake hands quite natural with the rest, not ever having had the pleasure; but he stood apart, a little sober; and Mary Ann Shamway, with her poor head tied up, she said it was his way, and there about a fortnight, and a little sickly, when I went to kiss the Dumpses' baby. I'm a little bashful with strange gentlemen, and though he kinder looked at me, I didn't trouble with him not to notice him particular; and the doctor said too much excitement and the pleasure wouldn't do, for he stayed to the ice-cream, as Miss Barker invited him most prettily; and I thought the Loon would be the death of him, in spite of tryin' to be most polite and handin' Mercy Maynard out.

So by and by I creep up softly to my own old little room, not to disturb their pleasure, and unbeknownst to most.

There it was, my dear, And the pretty shade against the gas, and a pink geranium in the window, with Mercy Maynard's love, and the towel rack from Maggie Flynn; and never did know who put the English breakfast tea into the tea-caddy, but, by the spillin' round, I knew it was the Loon that tried to set the tea-pot boilin' ready. And as for that chromio upon the wall, I *suspect* Miss Cracklejaw, but never did I know; nor the five roses and smilax, with a bit of heliotrope, upon the table, and the little vase.

It wasn't till next mornin' that I found the note upon the bureau from Aunt Hannah, sayin' how she'd but just heard of my condition, and that Peter he had married Sarah Amelia Bolingbroke – her that was Miss Patterson before her first – an excellent woman, but fully equal to it if there was any snappin' of you up, and havin' had her hand in once besides. And she said would I come on and make a visit, by-gones bein' by-gones, and her health but poorly?

That wasn't till next mornin', as I tell you. And, oh! my dear, as I set down alone, so grateful and so happy, no cur that runs is meaner than was I to take exception to my lot. But after all their kindness, they *wasn't* own folks, was they? And across my feelings there ran a littly chilly longing, something as if your soul had taken cold. I couldn't get my little brother 'Li'kim out of my head, do what I could. And all his little ways come up to me, and the feel of his fingers, don't you know, and wonderin' what it would be like if he had grown like other folks' brothers, faithful and considerate, and been by me through any troubles, and been there to set down in your pretty room and call you by your Christian name you'd most forgotten, being mostly Miss in that great house.

And as I set, I seemed to see him, though fainter than it was before the operation, kneeling by the bed. But the most peculiar prayer, my dear! Like this: –

"Cured. Come home. Every body glad to see her. Better

151

blessed than she deserves. Grumblin' over what she hasn't got. Ought to be ashamed. Got a cataract upon her heart. Ought to have it operated on. Hopeless case."

It was then, my dear, that there come a knock upon the door, and up I jumps to wipe the mean, ungrateful tears and let it in.

My dear, it was a gentleman — the strange gentleman I saw lookin' at me now and then down-stairs.

Says I, "Sir, most happy, if I had the honor, but the wrong room, perhaps," says I.

Says he, "No; the right room — the right room, I am sure, thank God!" says he.

For something in his voice, I don't know what, I began to tremble very sudden; and for something in his way, I can't explain, I thought I should have lost my wits. And there was that drawin' drew me to that unknown man — I can't begin to tell you — till up he steps and shuts the door. And, oh! my pretty, I see it in your eyes — you understand it all!

He never was a boy of many words, my dear, and all he says was this: —

"If your little brother 'Li'kim come back, sick and sorry, would you care to live with him?" says he. "I can go away again," says he, "if you think you'd rather not."

And, oh, the way the stars shone through the window hours and hours! And the people laughing down below as if all the world had got its own folks back, my dear! And the tea-pot that the Loon had spilled, it bubbled up and bubbled up, and the flowers on the table, and all the dear old things set looking on. And like a little child that hears a fairy tale I set and heard 'em say: —

"Happy woman! No cataract. Cured! cured! cured! *The light of her eyes has come back!* Oh, happy, undeservin', blessed woman! Cured! cured! cured!"

And if you think I asked him many questions to pry into his poor past life, my dear, you're wrong, that's all. And if folks tell you how he's ailing and works irregular and a burden, never do you listen to 'em — not a word of *that* my dear, for the tenderest and the lovin'est there never was a brother more so.

And up the Loon comes, when the people wondered, and Miss Barker red and white, for there sat I in his lap a sight to see.

"If it had been a physician," says Miss Barker, "at such hours, or even a clergyman, if in spiritual need. But even if it was — and he told me he was flour and grain — *such* a state of things is most unnecessary, and I never would have though it of you if I died!" says Miss Barker, mad as mad.

So when I tell her, like to die of laughing, down we go. And all the house is there, and Mercy Maynard in pink ribbons, and the gas as bright! And away at the other end I could see the Loon a-singein' her hair against it while I spoke. And I went in upon his arm, and says, for Miss Barker'd let a whisper of it round: —

"Dear friends, you've come to wish me joy on my great happiness to-night, and I thank you kindly. There are eyes of the body," says I, "and eyes of the soul, and there's blindness comes to both, and cures sometimes. And the light of the eyes of my body and the light of the eyes of my soul have come back both at once: and may yours be as bright forever, and bless you all!" says I.

# ONE OLD MAID

*

## *Marion Harland*

'One Old Maid' is taken from the collection of stories called Handicapped by Marion Harland (a pseudonym for Mary Virginia Hawes), published by Scribner's in 1881.

Mary Virginia Hawes won a fifty-dollar prize when she was 23 years old for the best serial on the subject of temperance offered by the Southern Era, a literary weekly, in 1853. Encouraged by this first success, she rewrote a novel she had begun earlier. When she couldn't find a publisher for Alone, her father arranged to have it privately printed in 1854. In those days, self-publishing did not automatically preclude a book from being reviewed. Enthusiastic reviews brought the book to the attention of a New York publisher, J. C. Derby, who brought the book out again in 1856. Sales of more than one hundred thousand copies encouraged Derby to bring out her second novel, The Hidden Path, two years later. In that same year, as an established and successful novelist, the 25-year-old author married Presbyterian minister Edward Payson Terhune. She continued to write until by 1873 she had published seventeen novels, given birth to six children, and successfully carried out domestic and parish duties that in themselves were enough for two full-time careers. In addition to a lifetime output of twenty-five novels and three volumes of short stories, she wrote more than a dozen books of travel, biography and colonial history, as well as an additional twenty-five volumes of domestic guidance. She lived from 1830 till her death in 1922 of old age. All three of her surviving children became authors.

It is perhaps to her remarkable health and vitality that we must look for an explanation of her failure to support feminist demands. She was, through a combination of a strong constitution and good luck, a superwoman.

*Her short stories are more interesting than her novels. She has long been dismissed as an unimportant writer, partly because of her phenomenal output (I think many critics assume that such quantity can't be of high quality) and partly because of the fact that those who cherish the ideals she advocated do not ordinarily go looking for forgotten women writers.*

*Nevertheless, 'One Old Maid' is a masterpiece of tragic irony. The ironic effect is achieved subtly, by playing out the tragedy in light of two comments made early in the story. The author uses one of the classic settings for introducing a major theme: the dinner table. The topic of the conversation is heroism, as exemplified by ancients and moderns. The cynic says ' "Live and let live" is a decent and sensible motto. To die that others may live and have a jolly time is to my perception simply and barbarously unreasonable.' His sister and her fiancé assert in answer that 'Self-abnegation is a glorious thing. There is a spring in every man's heart that stirs at such stories. . . .'*

*The tragic situation faced by Corrine Boyle is one that has still not been solved in our society, one hundred years later. Co faces the destiny dictated by the choice she feels morally obligated to make with dignity and courage, but her heroic stature stirs the springs in the hearts of none of those who observe her life. Because she is perceived by them through the haze of the stereotype of Old Maid that dehumanizes the unmarried women for those enslaved by its perjorative connotations, they simply don't notice that she exemplifies heroism as they define it. The artistry of the author is that she presents us her heroine through the eyes of those who view her with contempt and yet we cannot help but see her heroic dimension. We are not deceived. And insofar as we are undeceived by the distortions of the stereotype in this one instance, we will be less likely to be deceived by the distortions of the stereotype in other instances.*

# ONE OLD MAID*

The Scribas were dining *en famille* on the afternoon of the last day of the year. Mr. Scriba, gentlemanly and quiet – one of the solid men of the town, who, if he found solidity a serious matter, was yet amiably disposed toward the world that had bestowed the distinction upon him – discussed the contents of his plate as he did most subjects, with deliberate care, the slight plait between his brows becoming a shrewd and solid man. Mrs. Scriba had been passably pretty in her youth, and being plump and well-dressed was even more comely in the autumn of her matronhood. Complacent in her house, the dinner, her toilet and her children; satisfied with her husband, and content for the time with her servants, she listened with beaming face to the merry rattle of the young people, answered indulgently and judiciously the various appeals to her judgment and memory.

There were four of her children at the table – John, Jr., aged twenty-five; Emma, twenty-two; Effie, eighteen, and Harry, thirteen. They were all goodly to look upon, pleasant of temper, well-educated and stylish. I do not like the word, but through much use it has come to express what I mean – a certain air of high-bred fashion and ease that is not put on and off with one's clothes. The equally well-looking young gentleman who sat at Emma's right was Mr. Edwin Rowland, her betrothed, and therefore entitled to a place in the family circle even upon not-at-home days, and such is New-Year's Eve generally in households that expect to be overrun by emulous friends on the morrow. Only nobodies paid visits on this day, and the Scribas were too near the top of the tree to trouble

*From *Handicapped* by Marion Harland, (Mary Virginia Terhune), Charles Scribner's Sons, New York, 1881.

themselves about that class of their fellow-creatures. Sitting there under their own frescoes and chandeliers, they suffered no thought of possible intruders to make them afraid, and enjoyed the goods of fortune with open hearts and happy faces.

Until the conversation struck something projected into the frothy current by John, that diverted it from its course. Effie, a giddy tease, had accused him of a lack of philanthropy in remaining single to the ripe age of twenty five, "when so many worthy women were sinking into elderliness and melancholy without the husbands to which their merits entitled them."

"I am not a philanthropist!" asserted her brother boldly. "I have no patience with the stock cant about doing good to one's kind, self-immolation for the elevation of others and the like heroic humbug. I don't want to serve my age one-tenth as much as I want to serve myself; to make such use of my time, talents and money as will make me wisest and happiest. Providence has put me into John Scriba's keeping and he means to take excellent care of the consignment."

"But it is surely nobler to live for others?" ventured Emma, with a slight blush.

John laughed. "Put it in the singular, Em, and I grant you it must be a nice thing – so very comfortable as to come within the range of my philosophy of self-improvement. What I inveigh against is separation, not identification of interests; this making one man's meat to be another's bane. When it comes to that, I respectfully decline the bane. 'Live and let live' is a decent and sensible motto. To die that other people may live and have a jolly time is to my perception simply and barbarously unreasonable."

"That is a terrible blow at heroism, as exemplified by ancients and moderns," said young Rowland. "What would become of the poet-historians if you class Curtius, Lycurgus, Arnold Winkelried and a host of other stand-bys among the world's chief simpletons, instead of worthies? No, Emma is right. Self-abnegation is a glorious thing. There is a spring in every man's heart that stirs at such stories as these; that chokes and blinds him when he hears, in our day, of conduct like Herndon's, the commanding officer of the *Central America*. You remember it, Mr. Scriba? And so should you, John. When the vessel was foundering, he kept the men on board at bay by force of exhortation, command and threat, until all the women and children were in the boats, then suffered the remaining

157

places to be filled by other passengers. There were still many on the sinking steamer for whom no room could be made. Herndon put his favorite servant in the seat reserved for himself, took off his watch and sent it by the man with a parting message to his wife. 'As for me, I shall stay by the ship, and with *these!*' he said, pointing to the doomed band. These were the last words the survivors ever heard him speak."

"That was grand! sublime!" cried Emma, twinkling back the tears that applauded the story and her lover's rhetoric. "Is it possible, John, that you can see no beauty in such conduct?"

"Beauty! do you call it? I name it arrant folly, the rankest kind of absurdity, since he threw away his life for an idea. The sacrifice did not save the meanest creature in what you term 'the doomed band.' They died as surely as if he had not widowed his wife and perhaps beggared his children. You can extract no grains of romance out of my composition, Em. Even in my boyhood I saw the fatuity of that undersized, overrated prig, Casabianca, the boy of burning deck notoriety."

"I thought his name was Pat Malloy," interrupted Harry. "The song says so. What are you all laughing at?" hotly, as the merriment heightened.

> " 'The boy stood on the burning deck,
> His baggage checked for Troy' " –

"Miss Boyle!" announced the footman, throwing wide the dining-room door.

A tall, meagre lady entered wrapped in a thick plaid shawl, simpering and blinking as the blaze of the gas-lights struck her eyes.

"I am afraid I have called at an inopportune moment, but I get out so seldom, and I could not deny myself, to-morrow being New-Year's, and I was at your very door as I may say" –

"Miss Boyle, allow me to present Mr. Rowland," said the stately host, checking her in mid-career.

"Happy to make your acquaintance, Mr. Rowland." Miss Boyle bowed stiffly, yet low, until Effie afterwards declared she was afraid she would break in the middle, backing away as she did so from the gentleman who had arisen to be introduced. "I have often heard of you from our mutual friends – cannot meet you as a stranger, as indeed I know you are not in this house," another simper. "Fine winter weather this, Mr. Rowland;

bracing to the entire system. I enjoy walking – pedestrian exercise – in cold weather much more than I should riding – although the street cars *are* a great convenience – it imparts a fine glow to the whole frame. No thank you, my dear girls, positively nothing for me! It is near my tea-hour, as you are aware; I cannot think of tasting a morsel."

"Sit down, Co. Coffee will be brought up directly," said Mrs. Scriba, in the tone of good-humored patronage people near the top use to those at the foot of the allegorical tree aforesaid. "You will feel better for eating and drinking something warm. James, take Miss Boyle's hat and shawl."

"I won't trouble James – thank you, Juliana! Since you are so urgent, I will just loosen my shawl but not remove my bonnet. Thank you!" to the waiter who set a chair for her next Mrs. Scriba's. "I am absolutely ashamed to put you all to such trouble. I only said to myself in passing – I will just peep in for half an instant to see how they all are and to wish them 'Happy New Year.' It has been such an age since I saw you, and I get out so seldom, and to-morrow of course no lady can show herself in the street. No, my dear Harry, no oyster *pâté* for me, thank you! I rarely touch such rich dainties. No wine, *thank you*, John! Or, if you insist, just the wee-est drop – enough, thank you! Dear me! and *I* keeping the table waiting?"

"There is no haste," remarked Mr. Scriba, politely, while Effie said she was glad there was somebody to keep her in countenance, "since she was not half through her dinner, having talked while the others ate."

Miss Boyle would not be put at her ease. She felt that she ought to make herself agreeable, especially to her new acquaintance; but the walk in the frosty air had sharpened her appetite; the dinner, so much more savory than she was wont to see on her own board, appealed irresistibly to her senses. She was keeping everybody waiting, she could see, despite the well-bred feint of occupation kept up by most of the party; her bonnet-strings got into her plate; the wine titillated her palate until she *had* to cough behind her napkin, vulgar as she deemed the action; the trained waiter's attention embarrassed her, especially as she turned her head to thank him every time he offered a dish, and she was unused to eating in the presence of so many people. The sweat – she would have said perspiration – oozed in minute specks to the surface of her sallow skin by the time she laid down her knife and fork, her hunger but half-appeased. She remembered, just in season to mention it in justification of her ravenousness, how little dinner she had eaten at noon.

"I had just taken my seat at the table when I was interrupted, and when quiet was restored — I would say a degree of comfort — that is, when I could resume my meal, I found the zest had departed. Indeed I do not think dining alone is conducive to appetite at any time. I consider sociability the very sauce of — ahem! gastronomical refreshment. Do not you agree with me, Mr. Rowland?"

Emma thanked her lover in her heart that his smile was polite, not one of amusement.

"I do, madam, entirely. I think fasting is preferable to taking one's meals in solitary wretchedness. Cheerful society and conversation upon pleasant topics — even such accessories as the tasteful arrangement of the dishes — a clear, soft light, flowers and fair faces surrounding the board, undoubtedly promote not only appetite but digestion; and the reverse likewise holds true. We study these things too little as a nation and as individuals" —

"A very just observation," Miss Boyle interposed hastily. "Very neatly put. My dear Juliana, how well you are looking; and Mr. Scriba, also. You are actually renewing your youth. It is a gleam of genuine sunshine, the glimpse at this festive scene. This ice cream is truly delicious; and what luscious grapes."

Nevertheless Mr. Rowland noticed that she plucked but a single berry from the cluster, leaving the rest upon her plate.

"What noble oranges!" she exclaimed when they were passed to her, and selected one which was laid beside the grapes.

The gentlemen quitted the dining-room with the young ladies, leaving Miss Boyle alone with the hostess. Mr. Rowland sat opposite the open door of the parlor, fifteen minutes afterwards, when the lean figure tip-toed through the hall, still with the air of being in the house upon sufferance. She was accompanied by Mrs. Scriba and Harry, and the latter had a covered basket in his hand. The visitor's apologies, uttered in a wheezing undertone, were quite audible to the young lover, while she halted to put on her overshoes and tie a thick veil over her best bonnet.

"It is a downright imposition, Harry, dear, to make you play porter, but your mamma most generously pressed the hamper upon me. Say 'Good-night' to the girls for me. I hear the piano, so won't disturb them. If I were not pressed for time – for I have not outlived my love of music – I should be tempted to linger. I think one never outlives a real, honest love for anything. Good-night, Juliana! I have had a charming visit – *char*ming."

"Harry, be sure you put your aunt on the right car," was Mrs. Scriba's parting injunction.

"Aunt!" Emma's betrothed believed he had not heard aright. He had supposed the gaunt spinster who had made herself so uncomfortable as his *vis-à-vis* at table to be an old school friend, or at the nearest, a far-off poor relation of his plump mother-in-law-expectant. Yet he now recollected that Mrs. Scriba's maiden name was Boyle. This was then her own sister whom he had never seen, who had never been named in his presence. It was odd. The duet was finished and Effie flitted back to him from the piano.

"I hope your abstraction is born of our music, and not of a sudden passion for our fascinating aunt," she said saucily. "Em, Mr. Rowland is congratulating himself upon your resemblance to Aunt Co. It is so nice to think that you will look just like her when you are – Mamma!" as Mrs. Scriba entered, "*how* old is Aunt Co? Forty? fifty? seventy-five? a hundred?"

"She looks older than she really is, and her secluded life has made her old-fashioned in dress – stiff in manner," responded Mrs. Scriba, with gentle seriousness. "Don't laugh at elderly people, dear, or papa and I will come in for our share."

"Now, mamma, as if I could. But why must old maids be" –

"Old maids!" supplied John. "Don't struggle for an expressive adjective. I have covered the whole ground. Celibacy in man or woman is an offence against natural laws, and the offender bears the stamp for all time. Nobody, for example, could mistake our excellent aunt for anything but an elderly maiden of increasingly uncertain age."

"She *is* an excellent woman," said Mrs. Scriba, yet more gravely. "And although you may not credit it, Miss Effie, she was really handsome in her youth, besides being very vivacious and pleasing in conversation. Young people are incredulous and uncharitable as regards the ravages of time and care."

"They needn't make one finical and artificial," murmured Effie to her sister, somewhat sobered by her mother's manner. "What is it, James?" to the servant who appeared at the door with a card in his hand.

"A gentleman to see Mr. Scriba, ma'am."

Mrs. Scriba took the card, and her face lighted up instantly. "He's in the sitting-room, James. Take this to him when you have showed the gentleman in here." She advanced a step nearer the door, and the irrepressible Effie made time for her query.

"Who is he, mamma?"

"Mr. Lloyd — Aleck Lloyd we used to call him; an old friend whom I have not seen since John there was a baby."

The stranger was on the threshold as she said it. He was tall and sinewy, erect in figure, quick of eye and motion although his hair and beard were grizzled. The spectators noted without interpreting it the searching glance that swept the room ere his hand met Mrs. Scriba's in a long, hearty grasp.

"I cannot tell you how great this unexpected pleasure is," said the lady, cordially.

"What must it be, then, to me, who have not looked upon my former home and friends for almost a quarter of a century?" said a deep voice, so round and pleasant as to prepossess his youthful auditors at once in his favor. "And to meet you so becomingly surrounded enhances the enjoyment. Are these all yours?"

"Almost."

The visitor caught the meaning of her smile.

"More congratulations?" asked he, returning it brightly. "There is no need to tell me which are already and quite yours. I see father and mother in each face."

Effie was the prettier of the two, as the wicked witch well knew, and she was puzzled to understand why he looked oftener and more earnestly at Emma during the half hour that he stayed.

"He's the most delightful old gentleman I have seen this century," she grumbled aside to John. "And I always had a fancy for being an 'auld man's darling.' "

Mr. Lloyd had lived in Mississippi since his removal from his native city, the Scribas learned in the course of their familiar chat. He had married there, had three sons born to him, and was now a widower. Effie imagined that her mother looked more serious at this announcement than was required by decorous regret, his wife having died three years before.

"I wonder if she suspects in him a possible aspirant for my

162

hand!" she meditated, maliciously. "But won't I tease her for that when he's gone!"

The seriousness deepened into sadness when he contrived to talk aside with the lady of the house for a few minutes just before he took his leave. Effie was near enough to catch the drift of the conference.

"Your sisters are well, I hope? Do they live near you?"

"Mrs. Rawdon resides in Hartford, but I see her frequently. She has a fine family and a beautiful home. My youngest sister" – there was no mistaking the mutual embarrassment that prevented them from meeting one another's eyes – "still lives at the old homestead. It was left to her, you know. Her health is very good. She was here this evening a little while before you came."

A second's pause, in which his mien questioned – the bent head and waiting eyes – and his lips were mute.

"She is still single," Mrs. Scriba added, unable to resist the silent interrogation. "The reason – or what she construed long ago into a reason for not changing her condition – exists still."

"I shall try to see her to-morrow," and he turned to his host to ask some question about local politics.

"Mamma," whispered Effie, crazed by curiosity, yet half awed by the magnitude of her discovery, dancing up to her mother's side by the time the guest passed from the parlor, "was he an old beau of Aunt Co's? Did she really ever have one?"

"Yes, and threw him away for a whim," ejaculated Mrs. Scriba, petulantly, also *sotto voce*.

"You don't say so! But it seems so queer. Why, he's splendid! and she – isn't!"

"Hush child! I will tell you all about it by and by. Some things are not suitable subjects for parlor talk."

To her husband, when they went together to their own sitting-room, she said: "What a wreck that obstinate girl has made of her life. But for her overstrained notions of duty and persistency in her mad scheme she might marry Aleck Lloyd even now. He cannot name her yet without emotion. He is going to see her to-morrow."

"She would do a good thing for herself in marrying him," observed Mr. Scriba, in a matter-of-fact way. "But it is not at all likely that he will be inclined to renew his suit when he sees her. He is rich and a live man, full of energy and enterprise. He has kept up with his generation; she has fallen far behind it. You will see that nothing will come of the visit."

Meanwhile Miss Boyle was making her way by car and on foot to a quiet street quite on the other side of the city. The night was clear and cold; but the pavements were damp from recent heavy rains, and the stiffening mud at the crossings was mixed with half-melted snow. Aunt Co's feet sank into it several times above her rubbers, and more than once she clutched the basket tightly and threw out the other hand to balance herself upon the slippery flagging. It was a disagreeable thing – this going out on winter evenings alone. Yet it was nobody's business to look after her. Her nephews were kind and respectful when they met. Harry had stopped a car for her and seen her safely into it, getting on himself for a moment to put her basket in after her and to pay her fare, as she discovered when the conductor came through. His mother had given him his orders probably. His aunt could not have expected, indeed would not have allowed the lad to accompany her all the way – a full mile at least. Still less could she suppose that John would put himself to such inconvenience. She could get along safely enough; was accustomed to dispense with the service of an escort, as they all knew. Only there was a tremendous distance between her sister's home and hers on this New Year's Eve; between the two who for twenty years had lived in the same house, known the same joys and griefs. Juliana's life had been growing deeper, richer, brighter every year, and month, and day; hers narrowing and glooming in like ratio.

"Not that I would complain," she thought, deprecatingly, as was her wont to think and to speak, and she drew both ankles out of a very sloshy gutter. "Of course I know it is the Lord's will, but I do get sore and tired sometimes. I have learned not to mind many things that used to seem unbearable; but there are others that will get at the quick, do what I will to ward them off. I suppose it is with the sensibilities as it is with my feet," helped to the simile by another mud-hole; "the rubber doesn't go all the way up."

She was at home – a plain but spacious house, with what had been in its day a handsome flight of stone steps leading to the front door. It was a dingy quarter, from which fashion had long since fled, although it remained perfectly respectable. Miss Boyle let herself in with a latch-key and went along a dimly-lighted entry to a back room, whence issued an odd sound, like the plaining of a cross child, uttered in a coarse masculine voice. Shriller tones made response as Aunt Co's hand touched the lock.

"Hush up that noise! You'd ought to be well shaken, you had ought! It ain't my fault she isn't here to give you your supper. If I'd my way you would go to bed without it. Be quiet, or she shan't ever come home!"

Amid the burst of lamentations aroused by this threat Miss Boyle entered. Something sat on the floor in the middle of the room, whimpering and rubbing one eye with a big fist – a woman as tall as Miss Boyle herself, and obese to unsightliness: with a thick hanging jaw and small eyes set very far apart, low forehead, beetling brows, long upper lip and a mane of coarse gray hair hanging over her shoulders – a creature from which sane humanity turned, sick at the caricature of itself. The face was wet with tears and smeared with dirt from her soiled hands, but she stopped crying at sight of her sister. Springing up, clumsy and eager, she ran to her, caught hold of her dress and babbled in furious gibberish illustrating her meaning by angry gestures toward the other occupant of the apartment. This was a shrewish little woman in cap and spectacles, who without noticing the pantomime stooped to lift a tea-pot from the hearth to a round table set on one side of the fire.

"Yes, my baby; sister knows," responded the guardian, patting the fat cheek, and smiling fondly. "Sister didn't mean to leave her so long. Now Lulu will be good and she shall have something nice for her supper. Has she been very troublesome, Mattie?" to the sharp little maid.

" 'Bout's usual. She's always ugly as sin. She throwed a new handkerchief of yours into the fire, and would 'a sent your work-box after it if I hadn't ketched it as 'twas goin'. You was out later'n common, and she worried awful 'bout that. She knows when time's up well as you do."

"It is wonderful how smart she is!" commented Miss Boyle, in plaintive admiration. "I didn't mean to be away so long – I just ran in for a minute to see Juliana."

She was washing the idiot's face with a wet cloth, and panted out the broken bits of sentences in a frightened way that seemed to be habitual to her.

"Hold still, my precious child! You see I hadn't seen her for an age – and they were just at dinner – such an elegant affair it was, too – I wish you had seen it, Mattie – and Emma's betrothed was there, a very handsome, agreeable young man he is – and they would make me sit down, although I told them I hadn't time – and I ran away the minute I was through eating. That is," with conscientious accuracy, "the instant Juliana had this basket ready. Yes, there is something in it for Lulu," the idiot was tugging at the cover; "but she must eat her bread and milk first, like a nice girl, and not slop it over the table or pull the cloth off as she did at dinner-time."

Lulu began to cry again; then stopping suddenly laughed yet more disagreeably, and pointed to a large grease-spot on the carpet.

"The carpet will have to come up before that can be cleaned," snapped Mattie. "I've been at work scouring it, off and on, the whole afternoon. If she'd been mine I'd a boxed her ears for that job. She knowed better."

Lulu spit at her spitefully, and Miss Boyle stepped between them.

"Here, Mattie, that is for you," she whispered, covertly conveying an immense bunch of black Hamburg grapes into her hand – the cluster had been saved from her own dessert. Juliana had sent some to Lulu; but these were honestly her own, and she threw them as a sop to the household Cerberus. "Lulu doesn't mean to be naughty, but it is natural for Mattie to get a little, just a little out of patience with her sometimes when she is very mischievous. Mattie is very good and kind, and Lulu mustn't be cross to her."

"She'd behave herself more like folks, if somebody else wasn't so partial with her," growled the sharp one. "It ain't the right way to manage 'em, as I've told you a thousand times. If she was in a 'sylum, she'd be taught after a different style, I can tell you."

Miss Boyle's face twitched. "Don't speak of it, Mattie. Haven't I thought of all that? I can't be hard upon her. I haven't the heart to do it even if I hadn't promised my mother. The Scotch call them 'innocents.' I remember mother told me that when I was a little child. It has helped me often and often when I remembered it."

They were twins – these two – and the fond mother, who had just finished Madame de Staël's popular romance, had them christened respectively Corinne and Lucile. Corinne grew up shapely in body and intellect; Lucile had never spoken an articulate word, never passed in mind the first year of babyhood. It was a sore affliction to the father, and, as they came to the understanding of it, a trial and mortification to the brothers and elder sisters. But to the mother and Corinne, Lulu was the most interesting member of the household. Her bursts of temper, her crying fits, the demon of wanton mischief that continually possessed her, the helplessness that demanded the constant services of one or the other of her devoted nurses, could not weaken their attachment. When the father, secretly urged by the other children, spoke of hiding what he was disposed to regard as a family disgrace in the safe seclusion of an asylum, Mrs. Boyle's terror and indignation were like the rage of a bereaved lioness. The subject was never broached again while she lived. She survived her husband but a year; and dying bequeathed the unfortunate girl – a sacred legacy – to her twin-sister's keeping, exacting from her a promise that she would never be overpersuaded to abandon her to the care of hirelings; that while Corinne lived her household should be Lucile's also. Corinne gave the pledge without visible hesitation. She was alone with the sick woman. There was no one by to remind the parent of the blight she was laying upon her child's life, to remonstrate against a sacrifice so disproportioned to the end to be gained, or to mark how deadly white grew the girl's face as she made the vow. For Aleck Lloyd and she were troth-plight even then, and the mother knew it. In the death-hour she remembered it, perhaps with futile misgivings, for her eyes turned wistfully to the faithful daughter nearest her pillow.

"About Lulu," she whispered. "If there were any other way, if Aleck should not like it – but if he really loves you he will not mind! You will watch over her, will you not? Nobody else cares for the poor darling."

"My home shall be hers while she and I live," repeated Corinne, steadily. She had sworn to her own hurt, but she changed not at the united expostulations of brothers, sisters and friends; went not back from her word when her betrothed husband besought her to lift the shadow from his path and hers, to delegate to others the heavier duties involved by her acceptance of the trust. Without violation of her pledge to her mother she might engage a keeper – a trustworthy person, who could be with the imbecile night and day – and her asylum be his house.

"*Ours*, dearest, for in the sight of heaven you are my wife.

Have mercy upon me! Be just to yourself! Is it right to bind down your free, full life to such a service? To crucify your heart that an idiot girl who cannot appreciate your devotion may not be subjected to the trifling pain of being tended by a stranger?"

"I see now more plainly than I ever did before that she would be a curse in any home but mine," was the sadly-patient rejoinder. "I will not take her into yours, Aleck; I love you too truly for that."

Within a month after the mother's death the twins were left to themselves in the old house. Mrs. Boyle had willed it to them with a sufficient sum for their support. The other daughters were married; the brothers settled elsewhere. Aleck Lloyd went "out West." The words were a synonym for "lost" at the date when the Boyle homestead was in a fashionable locality. It was out of the world now, and so were the inmates. For twenty-four years the twain had lived there together without other companionship than such servants as could be hired to assist in the work of an establishment to which there was such an objectional appendage as the mischievous, mindless "Lulu." Mattie had, as she put it, "stuck it out" for ten years as "help," not servant. She liked to rule; and in consideration of her privileges in this respect she stayed on from month to month, always grumbling, and making herself at once indispensable and terrible to the nominal mistress.

Twenty-four years! Aunt Co thought them over when the tea-tray had been removed and she had put Lulu to bed and waited to see her sound asleep. Her time was at her own disposal for some hours. The fire burned brightly in the sitting-room. Sharp Mattie was as neat as her mistress, and the old-fashioned furniture was in irreproachable condition, dustless and shining. The curtains were dropped, the reading-lamp was on a table in front of the grate, and a rocking-chair beside it. Miss Boyle understood the practice of many small economics. She was not as rich as when her mother left her this house and the rent of certain others. Her property had depreciated in value until her income just met the necessary expenses of the small family. She never complained; and her wealthier kinspeople spoke approvingly of her modest wants and thrify management, and made her New-Year's presents of hot-house fruit and sweetmeats. She made over these to Mattie and Lulu. But she did like to read. A new book was a Lethean spring, in sipping which she forgot time and care. One lay on the stand now — a gift from Effie, who "found it too solemn for her taste," and amiably handed it over to her novel-reading aunt. The title was "Waiting for the Verdict," and a little silver paper-cutter Aleck had given her was laid between the leaves against a spirited wood-cut of a kneeling woman; her arms crossed on the sill of an open window, her head embraced by them. Her hair floated wide, and the tense clasp of the locked hands told the intensity of her supplication. Underneath was written, "THOU *knowest I have need of these things!*"

Aunt Co adjusted her eye-glass and scanned the print long and fixedly. The book sank gradually to her knee; the eye-glass fell into the place of the silver marker. No need of that to read the record of the four-and-twenty years stretching in monotonous dreariness between her and all she could rightly term life. Youth was gone forever, and all of beauty and grace and sprightliness she had ever possessed. It was as if a butterfly had folded its wings tightly and been fastened again into the chrysalis. Whims and habits — little "old-maidisms" — learned in her straight and eventless existence — clung to her like barnacles to a becalmed ship. The petty, oftentimes annoying, oftener ludicrous peculiarities that incrust the characters of so many single women, are not always the offspring of selfishness. They seem to me more like dead shoots that would have been noble, beneficent growth, had not circumstances stifled them in their birth.

"I *am* different from most people," said the dreamer to herself, drawing a deep breath. "Different from what I once was. Most different from what I might have been had the Lord appointed to me the lot I would have chosen for myself. It's past my finding out. He knows I have needs, too," glancing at the book. "Somehow I feel them more than usual to-night. I suppose it was seeing them all so happy at Juliana's — and Emma and Mr. Rowland — Bless me!" aloud. "That is the door-bell! Somebody wanting to inquire the way to somebody else's house, probably."

But after the front door opened a man's footsteps came along the hall. Getting up in a flutter, she shook out the skirt of her black alpaca and adjusted her head-piece of brown ribbon. Announcements were a refinement of etiquette unknown to Mattie. She merely pushed back the door, said huskily, "There she be," and returned to the kitchen fire.

"Is this Miss Corinne Boyle?"

She saw nothing but the hand, half-extended, after she heard the unforgotten voice that hailed her ear, and, it seemed, her soul also.

"I don't wonder you ask, Aleck," faltered the poor lady, standing stock still by the chair from which she had arisen; "but I should have known you anywhere."

Then – she was ashamed of it even while the excitement of the meeting was fresh upon her – she put her handkerchief to her eyes and cried heartily. The softhearted Westerner came down at once from the stilts of comparative strangerhood. He made her sit down, helped himself to a chair and begged her to compose herself.

"I should not have come in upon you unexpectedly," he said, and went on to tell how, being in town for a day or two, he could not resist the temptation of calling to see a few of his oldest friends; and how he had just missed her at Mr. Scriba's. "I had a delightful visit here. What a charming family your sister has! Emma reminded me of you," he added.

By this time it was safe to lower the handkerchief and apologize for her nervousness. They talked for an hour after that; of old acquaintances and old times, and the changes that had come into their lives – especially his – since they parted. Talked as elderly friends – nothing more. This was not the woman whose image Aleck Lloyd had kept locked away in the far-in chamber of heart and memory for the twenty years in which another woman had called him husband; which he had brought forth to the light, and studied of late until he had obeyed the ardent impulse that urged him to seek and woo her if she was still single. He had come to her from the gladness and beauty of her sister's home, the treasured picture the fairer and more distinct after seeing pretty, modest Emma, saying to himself as he hurried along, "We were made for each other, I will make her believe this."

He was met by a prim, neutral-tinted spinster, who towered up lankly and bonily for an instant, then dropped into a chair, without touching the back, and cried into a starched handkerchief until her prominent nose was red. The shock killed love, and romance fled affrighted out of sight. He could not squeeze the hand half covered with a black silk mitt. It would have been absurd to put his arm around the flat perpendicular of her waist. Cured were the passion and the pain of expectancy; gone like a mist was the dream of reunion and constant companionship. Something besides duty put and held them asunder now. What a fool! what a sentimental simpleton he had been to forget that a woman must fade fast in a life like hers! fade, and shrivel, and dry into hardness! He was very kind with all this going on within him; so sorry for her in her isolation that some sweet drops of comfort dropped through his talk into the starving heart.

"I may not see you again soon," he said, rising at half-past nine. "Perhaps never again in this world, for our ways lie far apart."

"Far, indeed," echoed his heart drearily over the crumbled image.

"But I wish you would let me help you feel that I had been of some use to you before we part."

A silvery tinkle on the marble-topped table diverted his eye from the face that was very gray and wan in the lamp-light, and strange, with the bunches of curls he had thought a bewitching setting for it when it was young and rosy, which were wiry corkscrews now. The book-marker had fallen off a pile of books where Miss Boyle had laid it. He took it up; looked at it intently as it lay in his palm.

"You have kept it all this while, Corinne?"

She did not speak. Knowing that he was going from her again – and why – how could she?

"It was a happy time," mused the disenchanted lover to himself, not to her, although he spoke aloud. "So fair, it grieves one to think it is dead with so many other dear and beautiful things. Yours is a sad lot, dear old friend. I wish I could comfort you in some way; do something to lessen your privations, or give you pleasure."

"I do not complain. I have fallen into the Lord's hand, not that of man," Miss Boyle said meekly, looking up at him. "I have tried to do my duty in a humble sphere, but still it was duty. I know my best friends have blamed me – do blame me. It has troubled me sometimes that they didn't see things as I do, but I have this great cause for thankfulness: The Lord has never let me doubt for a moment that I was bearing the cross He meant for me and for nobody else. It would have been a great deal harder had I ever imagined that I had gotten hold of the wrong one. And there are compensations. The poor child is very fond of me. It keeps up one's heart to know that one is absolutely necessary to some living creature. She couldn't get

171

along without me."

"This is all the comfort she has. This persuasion is all the fruit of her twenty-four years of bondage," thought Aleck Lloyd, as he tramped back to his hotel with a great void in his heart. "Heaven help her!"

Miss Boyle turned out the light, looked at the grate to see that the fire was safe, at the windows to be sure they were fastened, and went slowly up-stairs. The gates of Paradise had opened a very little way, and in swinging to had dashed her to the ground. The cross was heavy and sharp, and the thongs that bound it upon her very tight and cruel. Her face was grayer and more drawn as she made the arrangements for the night in her chamber, omitting none of her old-maidish precautions and "notions." When she knelt to pray the faded lips parted for the first time since she had said "Good-by" to Aleck.

"THOU knowest I have need of these things,'" she groaned. "THOU knowest! THOU *knowest!*"

It was the drowning wretch's death-clutch at the rock. She felt it beneath her – a sure foundation – when, far into the night that had been for her sleepless, the mindless creature who had not slept away from her side in all these years stirred and cried out in a distressing nightmare.

"Yes, my baby," as her hand was caught fast by the dreamer. "Sister knows."

The words came involuntarily to her lips, but they broke the spell of the dumb anguish. Slowly through the thick darkness the light of the better knowledge dawned.

"Sister knows!" She said it a hundred times a day. It meant protection, strength, sympathy, whatever was loving and reassuring. The imbecile did not grasp the full import of it; understood neither the extent of her will nor her power to serve her, but the mere sound quieted her.

"She trusts me as I ought to trust my Heavenly Father. I am in His sight as ignorant and helpless as she is in mine. As she gropes for me in the darkness, help me, LORD, to feel after THEE; and when I have found THEE, to hold!"

My story has preached its sermon. Sad – is it, dear and patient readers? I grant it; sad and yet so true that my heart has ached in the writing as it did in the hearing of the simple tale of the heroism of a lowly heart in one of life's by-places. In my short-sightedness I would – had this been a fancy sketch – have given Corinne's history a happier ending. And yet when she has passed through the mire and frost (for she still lives upon the earth), when no longer tired and sore, she finds all the goods of which she had need here with greater and more abundant riches in the light and warmth and companionships of the "other side," she may think that the tenderest love could have awarded her no more blessed portion even in this life than to "touch and hold."

# AN IGNOBLE MARTYR

*

## *Rebecca Harding Davis*

'An Ignoble Martyr' *was originally published in* Harper's Magazine *in March 1890. Two years later it was reprinted in a collection of stories by Rebecca Harding Davis (1831-1910) called* Silhouettes of American Life. *Every single story in this collection is alive and deserving of attention.*

*At the present time, she is best known for her 1861 story, 'Life in the Iron Mills' which was reprinted by the Feminist Press and includes a brilliant and deeply moving biographical interpretation of Davis's life by Tillie Olsen. This story, published when she was 20, represented the real beginnings of her literary career. The following year her first book was published by Ticknor & Fields, the book publishing arm of the* Atlantic Monthly, *in which* Margret Howth *had originally been published serially as 'A Story of To-day.' In 1862, the year of her book's publication, she made a trip to Boston from her home in Wheeling, Virginia (later West Virginia) where, through the generous and renowned hospitality of the* Atlantic's *editor and his wife, James and Annie Adams Fields, she met and became friends with many of the writers whose work she had long admired. On her way home, she stopped in Philadelphia to meet Lemuel Clarke Davis, a young lawyer three years her junior, who had written admiringly to her after reading 'Life in the Iron Mills.' They were married the following year and thirteen months later their first son was born. A second son followed two years later and their only daughter was born in 1872.*

*Although she continued to write during all the years of childrearing and domestic labor, critics generally agree that her work during these years, written hastily, often while exhausted, to help with family expenses, is of greatly inferior quality to her early work. However, by the time she wrote the stories included in* Silhouettes of American Life, *her children were grown.*

'An Ignoble Martyr' *is remarkable for the naturalistic detail with which Davis paints her picture of unremitting poverty of pocket and soul and the sudden lush images she juxtaposes to the barren life of the Pettit family. The sexual implications of the natural southern images surprise our senses. The ironic tone of the story, captured in the very title, makes something both grimmer and more ennobling than traditional tragedy the life Prue chooses when she is given a choice. Once more it is impressed upon us that the patterns in women's stories are different from the patterns in men's stories, because our myths are different. Our myths are about endurance and growth and experience accumulating and being transformed. The element of competition with fate, of conflict, is eliminated. What we read about are the enduring fruitions of enduring.*

*When her mother says to her, 'For a fool, give me an old maid!' only we, the readers, know the full extent of her foolishness, and see that what her mother attacks as foolishness is urged upon her by everyone else in her life as wisdom.*

# AN IGNOBLE MARTYR*

Old Aaron Pettit, who had tried to live for ten years with half of his body dead from paralysis, had given up at last. He was altogether dead now, and laid away out of sight in the three-cornered lot where the Pettits had been buried since colonial days. The graveyard was a triangle cut out of the wheat field by a certain Osee Pettit in 1695. Many a time had Aaron, while ploughing, stopped to lean over the fence and calculate how many bushels of grain the land thus given up to the dead men would have yielded.

"They can keep it. I'll not plough it up," he would mumble to himself with conscious virtue. "But land was to be held for the fencin' then, evidently, or no Pettit would have wasted it on corpses that might as well have lain in the churchyard."

Now, Aaron himself was in the wasted triangle, and as his daughter Priscilla saw his coffin lowered into it she felt a wrench of pity for him, because he never again could see the wheat grow in the lot around him, nor count how many dollars profit it would yield that year to pay the interest on the mortgage. It was natural that she should feel that he was really dead in just that way, for the wheat lot was the only property owned by the Pettits, and that mortgage their only active interest in life.

When the funeral was over, the neighbors, as is the custom in North Leedom, came back to the house, and sat in silence for half an hour in the little parlor. The undertaker had given the silver plate from the coffin lid to Prue, as the oldest child,

*Originally published in *Harper's Magazine*, vol. 80, March 1890. Reprinted in *Silhouettes of American Life*, Charles Scribner's Sons, New York, 1892.

and she hung it up now with a sad pride over the mantel-shelf. There were six other coffin plates there, the only decorations on the parlor wall.

Her younger brother, who had left "the mourners" and was in the kitchen, called her out impatiently. "Are you going to put that horrible thing up there, Prissy?" he said.

"Horrible!" said Prue, aghast. "It is very handsome, Bowles. It cost three dollars and sixty-three cents. And why should I show disrespect to father?"

"Oh, if it is counted disrespect! — Prue, can't we give these people a cup of tea? There are the Waces, they have come ten miles, and they have to go back without any dinner. And the Fords. Some tea and doughnuts?" He looked anxiously into her face.

The heat rose into Prue's cheeks, and her eyes shone. There was something delightful to her in this bold proposal, for she had, unknown to herself, a hospitable soul. She had never seen a stranger break bread under their roof. But on such an occasion as this —

"What would mother say?" she whispered. "Oh, no, no, Bowles! I can't do it. There are ten of them" — peering into the parlor — "ten. It would take a quarter of a pound of tea; and then the sugar. Oh no, we couldn't afford it!" and she went back and sat down again with the mourners, comforting herself that nobody would expect to be fed. In North Leedom the folks did not eat in each others' houses. It would have been thought a wicked waste to "treat to victuals," as, it was reported, was the common custom in larger towns.

This was no time, Prue felt, for her to appear eccentric or extravagant; and it would have been extravagant. Tea and cakes for ten would have made a big break in the money to be saved for the fall payment on the mortgage.

The Pettits during the next week took up the thread of their daily life unbroken. The little four-bedroomed house had, of course, a thorough cleaning. Undertakers and neighbors had left dust behind them. Mrs. Pettit had grace to help her bear the pains which death had left; but dirt she would not put up with. The furniture was all taken out into the yard to be sunned; the stair carpet, with its hundred neat patches, was washed, dried, and tacked down again. The furniture in the house was of the cheapest kind, but it had belonged to Mrs. Pettit's grand-mother, and had always been cared for with a tender reverence, not because of its associations, but for its money value. Indeed, so much of the lives of the Pettit women for generations had gone into the care of the speckless chairs and tables that one might suspect a likeness between the condition of their souls and that of the filthy Fijian who worships the string of bones which he polishes incessantly.

Bowles despised the tables and chairs. But the mortgage! That was another thing – a thing so serious that it seemed to overshadow, to choke his whole life. John Pettit, his grandfather, in some great emergency, had put the house under a mortgage, had worked for twenty years to clear it off, and died, leaving the task to Aaron. Aaron had accepted it as a sacred trust; every penny he could save had gone to it. Now he was dead, and there was still a thousand dollars due on it.

Mrs. Pettit was too nearly blind to work. Prue sewed on men's seersucker coats for a factory in Boston. She was paid sixty cents a dozen for them. This paid the taxes and bought their clothes.

Bowles knew that his mother and sister and all of the village expected him to take up the payment of this mortgage as the work of his life.

The minister, old Mr. Himms, had said as much to him after the funeral.

"It is a noble ambition, my boy," he said, "for a man to own the home of his fathers free of debt. In our New England towns there are thousands of men and women struggling in dire poverty all their lives with this aim before them."

This aim! What aim?

Bowles, sitting one evening under the old elm-tree as the sun was going down, looked at the ugly, bare little house and hated it. Had life nothing more for him than – *that?*

He looked about him. North Leedom was made up of just such ugly, clean, bare houses. There were no trees on the sidewalks, no flowers in the yards. The people had been poor for generations, and they had reduced the economy of their Puritan ancestors to an art so hard and cruel that it dominated them now in body and soul. To save was no longer a disagreeable necessity for them; it had become the highest of duties.

The Pettits had always crept along in the same rut with their neighbors. They would not buy sufficient food to satisfy their craving stomachs. With each generation they grew leaner and weaker; the sallow skin clung more tightly to their bones; the men became victims of dyspepsia, the women of nervous prostration.

Each generation, too, carried the niggardly economy a little farther. They "could not afford time" for flowers nor for music; they could not afford to buy books nor newspapers. They came at last in their fierce zeal for saving to begrudge smiles and welcomes to each other or kisses and hugs to their children.

They stripped their lives of all the little kindly amenities, the generosities of feeling and word which make life elsewhere cheerful and tender. If their starved hearts, sometimes, like their bodies, gave signs of hunger, they were only mortified at their own lack of self-control. Their history was that of countless families in New England villages.

Bowles Pettit, thinking over the lives of his neighbors and family, tried to judge fairly of his own. But he was ashamed to find that he could scarcely think at all, he was so hungry. He was a big, raw-boned, growing boy; the nervous strain of the last week had been severe on him. He needed food, and he knew he would not have enough to-day. He could not remember the day when he had had enough. He knew how it would be. Presently the cracked tea bell would ring, and he would go in to eat a small slice of cold, soggy pie, washed down with a glass of cold water. To-morrow morning for breakfast more cold pie and a doughnut. For dinner, potatoes and cold milk only. On Mondays, when Prue had to make a fire for the washing, two pounds of cheap meat were boiled, which furnished dinner for three days.

Bowles had no trade. He was what was called in North Leedom "a helper." He could do a bit of carpenter or mason work, or paint a door, or plough a field when called upon, for which he received a few pennies. There was no opening in the dead village for any regular business. It was out of these occasional few pennies that he must support the family and save the thousand dollars for the mortgage.

There was a slight quiver on the boy's cleft chin as he sat staring at the mortgaged house. He had the eager brain and fine instincts of the New Englander. It was not a dull beast of burden on whom this yoke for life was to be laid, but a nervous, high-bred animal, fit for the race-course.

"Ah-ha, Bowles, my son!" a subdued voice whispered over the fence.

179

He started up. It was Mr. Rameaux, an agent for some orange planters in Mississippi, who had found boarding for his little daughter in North Leedom that summer, while he travelled about the country. He was so short and stout that his fat smiling face barely reached to the top of the fence. He thrust his chubby ringed fingers through the rails and wrung the lad's hands.

"My dear boy, I came down from Boston this afternoon, and Lola met me with this terrible news. What can 'I say? Your worthy father! *Il est chez le bon Dieu!* But you – poor child! It is thirty years since my own father left me, and still – I – " He choked, and real tears stood in the twinkling black eyes.

Bowles pulled him through the gate. The boy said nothing. He had not shed a tear when his father died. He had never learned how to talk or to shed tears. But this little man's volubility, his gestures, his juicy rich voice, with its kindly and sweet inflections, affected Bowles as the sudden sight of tropical plants might a half-frozen Laplander. He had hung about Rameaux all summer whenever he was in the village.

"I came to make my condolences to madame *votre mère.* And Lola – she also" – dragging after him a child in a white gown and huge red sash, of the age when girls are principally made up of eyes, legs, and curiosity.

Together they entered the kitchen, where Mrs. Pettit and Prue sat knitting, one on either side of the cold black stove. The little man poured forth his "condolences" to the widow. Aaron's virtues, her own grief, the joys of heaven, the love of *le bon Dieu*, were all jumbled *en masse*, and hurled at her with affectionate zeal. Prue dropped her knitting in her lap; a red heat rose in her thin cheeks as she listened. But Mrs. Pettit's large gray eyes scanned the pursy little agent with cold disapproval. What did the man mean? None of Aaron's neighbors, not she herself, had wept for him, nor talked much of his virtues, or his entrance into heaven. Why should this play-acting fellow be sorry for her? She resented his affectionate tone, his fat body, his red necktie, the unnecessary width of brim of his felt hat. It was all unnecessary, redundant – a waste.

She waited until he stopped for breath, then nodded without a word, and taking up her knitting, began to count the stitches. Rameaux, shocked and discomfited, stood pulling at his moustache and shuffling uneasily from one foot to the other.

Lola, in the mean time, had crept to Prue's side, and put her arm around her waist.

The Rameaux were not of good caste in Mississippi; they were by no means well-bred people. The agent's oaths and jokes, when alone with men, were not always of the cleanest. But they came from a community where men carried the kindness and pity of their hearts ready for constant use in their eyes and lips. Even the ungainly child now was giving to Prue eager caresses such as she had never in her whole life received from father or mother.

"Your father is dead," Lola whispered. "My mamma died two – two years – " and then she burst into sobs, and dropped her head on the woman's lap. Prue, with a scared glance at her mother, patted her gently.

"Poor lonely little thing!" she thought. Then she noticed that the child's gaudy sash was spotted with grease, and that the holes in her black stockings were drawn up with white thread. "Tut! tut! poor *dear* child!" she whispered, a motherly throb rising in her own flat breast.

Mr. Rameaux, bewildered at his rebuff, was turning to the door, but Bowles stopped him.

"You promised to speak to her," he whispered, excitedly.

"Not now, my boy."

"Yes, now! Now!"

The little man dropped into a chair, fanning himself with his ridiculous hat. He too was excited. He spoke to Mrs. Pettit, but his eyes wandered to Prue. "Madam, there is a subject – Your son, Mr. Bowles here, and I have talked of it. If I may intrude upon your grief – But I must first tell you something of my home."

"Indeed? Your home, Mr. Rammy," said Mrs. Pettit, in her dry, shrill tone, "is the least of my concerns." Then she turned her back on him. "Light the candle, Priscilla."

Rameaux rose, red and angry.

"Mother," said Bowles, sharply, "I wish you to listen to this man."

There was a meaning in his voice new to her. She stared at him, and at the agent, who, after a moment's hesitation, went on, growing fluent as an auctioneer as he proceeded.

"There was a reason for speaking of Lamonte to you, madam. It is a village near the gulf. That is a rich country – the ground, fat black; the trees, giants; the woods full of birds, and the waters of fish. A man has but to set his traps and drop his lines and lie down to sleep, and nature feeds him. And the air – so warm and sweet!" He took a step nearer to Prue, who was listening. His eyes were on hers. They were kind eyes, he thought – mother's eyes. Miss Prue had a soft voice too. Her cheeks were lean, but there was a pretty color coming and going in them, and the lips were red and kissable. He and Lola had a lonely life of it. "The air," he repeated, awkward and bewildered, "is sweet with flowers. You would like my house, Miss Prue, on the beach. At night the wind in the magnolias and the waves plashing on the shore make a very pleasant sound – a – very pleasant sound." He quite broke down here, but his little black eyes held hers, and it seemed to her that he was still talking rapidly, passionately saying something that she never had listened to before.

"You told me about the place before, Mr. Rammy," she stammered. "You said that the flowers – "

"Hola! chut! I had forgotten!" he exclaimed, tugging at his pocket. "I sent for these. They came to-day. You said you never had seen any." He pulled out a small paper box. When she opened it, a strange and wonderful fragrance startled the chill New England air.

"Orange blossoms!" explained Rameaux, with a significant chuckle.

Prue said nothing. She took her box to the window. The blood grew cold in all of her gaunt body. What did it mean?

She had scarcely ever thought of love. She had known but two women of her age in the village who had been courted and married. The others had all grown into old maids like herself. She never had thought that *she* – He had paid thirty cents postage on that box! And for her!

That wonderful life down there – little work, and plenty to eat! – the warm, sweet air! the plashing waves! In the mean time, the strange, creamy flowers, with their heavy fragrance, seemed actually to talk to her of this life and this man.

What was that he was saying? Urging her mother to sell the house and go to Lamonte, where there was a fine chance for Bowles!

"There is no opening for the boy here, madam," he persisted. "I speak as a business man. Lamonte is a live place. I go to start a cypress-wood mill, a cotton-seed-oil factory. It is a boom. A young man with Northern energy shall make money fast. Or, if you will not sell the homestead, why not rent it? Bowles, once settled in Lamonte, in two years – in two months perhaps, if this boom lasted – could clear off the mortgage." Rameaux spoke as he did when driving a bargain – clearly, and to the point. "I will give you this to consider," he said. "I will state the matter now to Miss Prue from another point of the view." He strode quickly across to her, and led her authoritatively out of the kitchen.

"Mother, do you understand?" said Bowles, in a high, sharp tone. "I can make money there hand over hand. I will clear off the mortgage dretful fast. I won't have to drudge here like a nigger slave till I'm as old as father."

The face which Mrs. Pettit turned on him was set and strained as it had not been when she looked at her husband dead.

"You want to – *go?*" she said.

"Yes, I want to go. I must get out of here. I want enough to do; I want enough to eat!"

She looked at the hunger-bitten face and starving eyes of the boy, a tragic sight enough if she had understood it. But she was simply bewildered. Most of the people in North Leedom had that clayey color and restless look which result from an ill fed body and a strong brain condemned for life to work upon trifles. But they did not know what ailed them. Nor did Mrs. Pettit.

"Want to leave North Leedom?" she repeated, with a contemptuous laugh. "Sech fancies! You always was ridickelous, Bowles, but I didn't think you was quite sech a fool. Draw some water, child. It's high time we was lockin' up an' makin' ready for bed," looking at Lola, who was coiled up on a chair, her big black eyes curiously turning from one to the other.

The door into the yard opened, and Prue came hurrying in. Her mother stared at her. She had never seen her face burn nor her eyes shine in that way, except when she had the typhoid fever twelve years ago.

"Lola," she said, going up to the girl and catching her by the shoulders – "Lola!"

"Yes," said Lola, standing up.

Miss Prue pulled the child toward her as if to kiss her. Her thin face worked; she panted for breath. She caught sight of her mother's amazed face, and pushed Lola away.

"Your – your papa wants you, dear," she said, in a low

whisper, every tone of which was a caress. "I'll take you to him."

"You stop right here, Priscilla. Bowles can take his daater to the play-actor," snapped Mrs. Pettit.

Priscilla dared not disobey. She was thirty, but she was as submissive and timid as when she was six. But she did follow Lola out on to the porch. The girl stopped her there peremptorily, and stretching up on her tiptoes, threw her arms around her neck.

"You're coming home with us? Papa said so. Yes? Oh, goody! You'll come?"

"Hush-h!"

Priscilla dropped on her knees in the dark, and strained the child tight to her breast. The blood burned hotly through her whole body as she pressed a light shamed kiss upon her lips, and then springing up, ran back into the kitchen.

Bowles walked sulkily with Lola down to the road where her father was waiting. She thrust her arm in his and hung on it; she rolled her beautiful eyes coquettishly; she spoke to him with profound awe and timidity. Lola, like many Southern girls of her class, had given much of her short life to thought of "the boys," and of how to manage them. She managed Bowles now completely. Her homage thrilled him with triumph and self-conceit, which her father's eager talk increased. His mother treated him as a child. These people appreciated him, recognized him as the shrewd Northern man who would make money hand over hand in the South. He laughed loudly with Rameaux, even tried to joke a little.

His sister, through the kitchen window, saw them standing by the gate. The moon had risen, Lola leaned sleepily against the fence. Rameaux's sultry black eyes, while he talked to Bowles, searched every window in the house.

"*For me?*"

Priscilla's knees shook under her. She hurried to her mother, who was beginning to grope her way up the stairs, and took the candle from her, trembling so that she could scarcely speak. It seemed as if she must cry and laugh out loud.

"Mr. Rameaux tells me that his house is all on one floor. You will have no stairs to climb if you go there, mother," she said.

Mrs. Pettit stared at her. "*I* go? Bowles's brain is addled enough, but he's not so mad as that."

She had reached her room by this time. Prue hurried in after her.

"Mother, it's not Bowles; it's me. If there was a chance for me to go down yonder and give you a comfortable providin', would you go?"

Mrs. Pettit paid no attention to her. She was unbuttoning her shoes, and had found a thin place in one of them. She rubbed it with alarm, held it close to her purblind eyes, set it down with a groan. "It ought to hev lasted two year more," she muttered.

"Would you go?" said Prue, stooping over her with a breathless gasp. "You should have as many shoes as you chose, and the hot air even in winter, and full and plenty to eat and wear."

Mrs. Pettit turned her dull calm face on her. "Why, Priscilla Pettit! You've been listenin' to that Rammy's crazy talk too! For a fool, give me an old maid!" She took up the worn shoe anxiously again. "Think of *me* goin' outside of North Leedom!" she said, with a hoarse, rasping laugh.

Priscilla, as she looked at her, could not think of it. It was an impossibility; as impossible as to make the dead alive.

"Tut! tut! It's worn near through to the counter."

"Give it to me. I'll mend it," said Miss Prue.

"Your hands are like ice," said her mother, as she took the shoe. "You'd better get to bed. There's that lot of coats to begin on in the morning. You'll have to be up by four."

"Yes," said Prue. She carried the shoe down stairs. The coats lay in heaps in the corner, tied together by twine. Their raw edges stuck out. Prue thought they would not have been so hateful if it had not been for those raw edges.

Bowles was waiting for her. His eyes shone; he looked bigger and stouter than before; the very down on his lip seemed coarser and browner.

"You are going too," he said. "Rameaux told me. Lord! such luck to come to us!"

"Mother will never go, Bowles."

"Then leave her. Other sons and daughters marry and go away. Cousin Sarah can take care of her. We'll pay the mortgage, and pay Sarah for tendin' her. Mother's rugged. She may live twenty year yet. 'Tisn't fair you should slave forever."

He said much more, but Prue scarcely heard him. She sat in the kitchen without moving long after he had gone to bed.

Somehow the raw-edged seersucker coats seemed to fill up her mind, and to bulk down, down, through her whole life. Rameaux had pointed to them angrily last night, and said, "Send that trash back to-morrow."

He wanted her to marry him to-morrow; to pack up their things, and start for Lamonte next Monday. He would stop in New York to buy her some gowns to please his own taste. "A red silk gown and a black-plumed hat."

"Think of me in red silk and plumes!" thought Priscilla, tears of sheer delight standing in her eyes.

Her mother coughed hard, and called to her several times, while she sat there, to bring her medicine. She always needed care in the night. Cousin Sarah was a high-tempered woman and slept heavily.

When Bowles came down in the morning, he found his slice of leaden pie and greasy doughnut, as usual, on a plate on the bare table. Prue was at the machine, a heap of finished seersucker coats beside her.

"I guess you were at work all night?" he said.

"I couldn't sleep," she answered.

"Are you goin' to finish all them things?"

She nodded, turning her wheel faster.

He looked at her face for a minute or two, and then, for some reason, walked behind her, where he could not see it. "Prue," he said, "are you always goin' on makin' coats?"

The wheel stopped, the thread broke. Bowles waited, silent.

"Yes," she said, in a low voice. Then she threaded her needle again.

"What else should she do?" said Mrs. Pettit, coming into the kitchen.

Neither of her children answered her; but presently Prue got up suddenly, and going to her, gave her a fond hug and kiss.

Mrs. Pettit started, amazed. It was a new thing in her life; but, on the whole, she liked it.

Ten days later Bowles left North Leedom for Mississippi. His hopes were more than answered there. Lamonte did have the promised boom, and he made money fast. In a few years he married Lola. But long before that time he paid off the mortgage. He did it for Prue's sake. Had not his life been successful, while hers was a miserable failure? His heart ached with pity for her.

186

But we are not sure that her life was at all miserable. From that night in which she made her choice, a singular change came over her. For thirty years she had done her dull duty faithfully, because, in fact, there was nothing else to do.

Then, as it seemed to her, the gates were opened, the kingdoms of the world were laid at her feet.

Of her own will she had given them up.

God only knew what the sacrifice cost her, but after it she was a different and a live creature. She was like a woman who has given birth to a child. She had struck her note in life, and it was not a mean one. She now looked out on the world with authoritative, understanding eyes; even her step became firm and decided.

When one climbs a height, the pure air expands the lungs ever after. We always carry with us down in the valley the wide outlook which we have seen but once.

Prue had now a life quite outside of North Leedom and the raw-edged coats. When the pain and soreness had passed, her struggle began to exert pleasant and tender influences on her. Stout, jolly Rameaux, with his twinkling black eyes and black moustache, began to take on the graces and charms of all the heroes of romance. When she read in the magazines a poem or love story, her eyes would fill with a tender light, and she would whisper, "I, too; I, too!"

When she saw mothers caress their children, she fancied she felt Lola's head again on her breast, and her heart throbbed with happiness.

After her mother died, she tried to bring into her life some of the things of which Bowles had told her of his home in Lamonte. She planted roses in the yard; she covered her table with a white cloth; and sometimes a bit of savory meat found its way to it. She visited her neighbors; she read novels; she joked in a scared way.

On the occasion of her one visit to New Bedford she went alone to a retail shop, and, blushing, asked to be shown some crimson silk and black-plumed hats. She fingered them wistfully.

"Are they for a young lady?" asked the shopman.

"Yes — for a young lady," said Prue, in a low voice. She held them a moment longer, and then, with a sigh, went out.

Soon after this, Bowles, who was a bad correspondent, suddenly appeared one day, bringing one of his girls, Prissy, with him. "Yes, she looks peaked," he said that night as they sat on the porch, after Prue had lovingly put the child to sleep in her own bed. "The doctor said she ought to have bracing air for a year or two. I told him I'd bring her to you. We've got four, and she's your namesake. She does not look like the Pettits, though."

"Her eyes are like Lola's father's," said Prue, hesitating. "Is Mr. Rameaux well?"

"God bless me! Didn't I tell you the old gentleman was gone? Died in Cuba last spring."

"Died – last spring?"

Bowles, who was about to add that too much bad whiskey had hastened his end, caught sight of her face, and with a sudden remembrance stopped short, and softly whistled to himself.

"Yes, in Cuba," he said, awkwardly. "Well, Prue, I was all right in bringing Prissy to you? You'll take care of the chick?"

"As if she were my own," she said. "I thank you, Bowles."

Soon afterward she went to her own room, and kneeling by the bed, kissed the child's face and hands passionately.

"She is very like him," she thought, opening, as she did every night, a little box in which were some yellow flowers. She fancied there was still a faint fragrance breathing from them. "We will know each other in heaven," she said, with a sigh, as she closed the box.

But it may be as well, perhaps, that in this too she will be disappointed.

# LOUISA

*

## *Mary Eleanor Wilkins*

'Louisa' is taken from A New England Nun and Other Stories
by Mary Eleanor Wilkins (1852-1930), published by Harper &
Brothers in 1891. Louisa is independent, courageous, stubborn,
and, in the eyes of her mother and the small community in
which she lives, another fool, like Prue Pettit in the previous
story. Wilkins's characters are frequently at odds with their
communities whose members urge on them choices that seem
better than they really are. She defies the conventional wisdom
for her own reasons but in the end it is borne out that her
choice was the right one in terms of the values of the
community she has defied. She is better off, after all, living in
harmony with her inner light. That pattern, repeated in many
of the stories in this collection although in situations that
resemble each other very little, might be taken as a metaphor
for Wilkins's treatment of the old maid theme.

And it might be applied to her own life, too. She lived with
her family until her parents both died and then she moved in
with the family of her lifelong close friend, Mary Wales. She
lived most of her domestic life in a world of women and her
literary success gave her the financial independence to travel
when she got restless. Her first success came with the
acceptance in 1883 by Harper's Bazaar of her story 'Two Old
Lovers' when she was 31 years old. In 1887 there were enough
stories published in that periodical and Harper's New Monthly
to make a collection; A Humble Romance was published. It
was followed four years later with A New England Nun. There
were many novels, more volumes of stories, and an historical
tragedy. Her life seemed full.

But in the 1890s she met Charles M. Freeman and entered
into an on-again-off-again romance that seems to have ended

*with their marriage in 1902. She continued to publish until 1923 although their marriage was painful and disrupted by his alcoholism and associated illnesses.*

# LOUISA*

❋

"I don't see what kind of ideas you've got in your head for my part." Mrs. Britton looked sharply at her daughter Louisa, but she got no response.

Louisa sat in one of the kitchen chairs close to the door. She had dropped into it when she first entered. Her hands were all brown and grimy with garden-mould; it clung to the bottom of her old dress and her coarse shoes.

Mrs. Britton, sitting opposite by the window, waited, looking at her. Suddenly Louisa's silence seemed to strike her mother's will with an electric shock; she recoiled, with an angry jerk of her head. "You don't know nothin' about it. You'd like him well enough after you was married to him," said she, as if in answer to an argument.

Louisa's face looked fairly dull; her obstinacy seemed to cast a film over it. Her eyelids were cast down; she leaned her head back against the wall.

"Sit there like a stick if you want to!" cried her mother.

Louisa got up. As she stirred, a faint earthly odor diffused itself through the room. It was like a breath from a ploughed field.

Mrs. Britton's little sallow face contracted more forcibly. "I s'pose now you're goin' back to your potater patch," said she. "Plantin' potaters out there jest like a man, for all the neighbors to see. Pretty sight, I call it."

"If they don't like it, they needn't look," returned Louisa. She spoke quite evenly. Her young back was stiff with bending

*From *A New England Nun and Other Stories* by Mary E. Wilkins, Harper & Brothers Publishers, New York and London, 1891.

over the potatoes, but she straightened it rigorously. She pulled her old hat farther over her eyes.

There was a shuffling sound outside the door and a fumble at the latch. It opened, and an old man came in, scraping his feet heavily over the threshold. He carried an old basket.

"What you got in that basket, father?" asked Mrs. Britton.

The old man looked at her. His old face had the round outlines and naive grin of a child.

"Father, what you got in that basket?"

Louisa peered apprehensively into the basket. "Where did you get those potatoes, grandfather?" said she.

"Digged 'em." The old man's grin deepened. He chuckled hoarsely.

"Well, I'll give up if he ain't been an' dug up all them potaters you've been plantin'!" said Mrs. Britton.

"Yes, he has," said Louisa. "Oh, grandfather, didn't you know I'd jest planted those potatoes?"

The old man fastened his bleared blue eyes on her face, and still grinned.

"Didn't you know better, grandfather?" she asked again.

But the old man only chuckled. He was so old that he had come back into the mystery of childhood. His motives were hidden and inscrutable; his amalgamation with the human race was so much weaker.

"Land sakes! don't waste no more time talkin' to him," said Mrs. Britton. "You can't make out whether he knows what he's doin' or not. I've give it up. Father, you jest set them pertaters down, an' you come over an' set down in the rockin'-chair; you've done about 'nough work to-day."

The old man shook his head with slow mutiny.

"Come right over here."

Louisa pulled at the basket of potatoes. "Let me have 'em, grandfather," said she. "I've got to have 'em."

The old man resisted. His grin disappeared, and he set his mouth. Mrs. Britton got up, with a determined air, and went over to him. She was a sickly, frail-looking woman, but the voice came firm, with deep bass tones, from her little lean throat.

"Now, father," said she, "you jest give her that basket, an' you walk across the room, and you set down in that rockin'-chair."

The old man looked down into her little, pale, wedge-shaped

face. His grasp on the basket weakened. Louisa pulled it away, and pushed past out of the door, and the old man followed his daughter sullenly across the room to the rocking-chair.

The Brittons did not have a large potato field; they had only an acre of land in all. Louisa had planted two thirds of her potatoes; now she had to plant them all over again. She had gone to the house for a drink of water; her mother had detained her, and in the meantime the old man had undone her work. She began putting the cut potatoes back in the ground. She was careful and laborious about it. A strong wind, full of moisture, was blowing from the east. The smell of the sea was in it, although this was some miles inland. Louisa's brown calico skirt blew out in it like a sail. It beat her in the face when she raised her head.

"I've got to get these in to-day somehow," she muttered. "It'll rain to-morrow."

She worked as fast as she could, and the afternoon wore on. About five o'clock she happened to glance at the road – the potato field lay beside it – and she saw Jonathan Nye driving past with his gray horse and buggy. She turned her back to the road quickly, and listened until the rattle of the wheels died away. At six o'clock her mother looked out of the kitchen window and called her to supper.

"I'm comin' in a minute," Louisa shouted back. Then she worked faster than ever. At half-past six she went into the house, and the potatoes were all in the ground.

"Why didn't you come when I called you?" asked her mother.

"I had to get the potatoes in."

"I guess you wa'n't bound to get 'em all in to-night. It's kind of discouragin' when you work, an' get supper all ready, to have it stan' an hour, I call it. An' you've worked 'bout long enough for one day out in this damp wind, I should say."

Louisa washed her hands and face at the kitchen sink, and smoothed her hair at the little glass over it. She had wet her hair too, and made it look darker: it was quite a light brown. She brushed it in smooth straight lines back from her temples. Her whole face had a clear bright look from being exposed to the moist wind. She noticed it herself, and gave her head a little conscious turn.

When she sat down to the table her mother looked at her with admiration, which she veiled with disapproval.

"Jest look at your face," said she; "red as a beet. You'll be a pretty-lookin' sight before the summer's out, at this rate."

Louisa thought to herself that the light was not very strong, and the glass must have flattered her. She could not look as well as she had imagined. She spread some butter on her bread very sparsely. There was nothing for supper but some bread and butter and weak tea, though the old man had his dish of Indian-meal porridge. He could not eat much solid food. The porridge was covered with milk and molasses. He bent low over it, and ate large spoonfuls with loud noises. His daughter had tied a towel around his neck as she would have tied a pinafore on a child. She had also spread a towel over the tablecloth in front of him, and she watched him sharply lest he should spill his food.

"I wish I could have somethin' to eat that I could relish the way he does that porridge and molasses," said she. She had scarcely tasted anything. She sipped her weak tea laboriously.

Louisa looked across at her mother's meagre little figure in its neat old dress, at her poor small head bending over the tea-cup, showing the wide parting in the thin hair.

"Why don't you toast your bread, mother?" said she. "I'll toast it for you."

"No, I don't want it. I'd jest as soon have it this way as any. I don't want no bread, nohow. I want somethin' to relish — a herrin', or a little mite of cold meat, or somethin'. I s'pose I could eat as well as anybody if I had as much as some folks have. Mis' Mitchell was sayin' the other day that she didn't believe but what they had butcher's meat up to Mis' Nye's every day in the week. She said Jonathan he went to Wolfsborough and brought home great pieces in a market-basket every week. I guess they have everything."

Louisa was not eating much herself, but now she took another slice of bread with a resolute air. "I guess some folks would be thankful to get this," said she.

"Yes, I s'pose we'd ought to be thankful for enough to keep us alive, anybody takes so much comfort livin'," returned her mother, with a tragic bitterness that sat oddly upon her, as she was so small and feeble. Her face worked and strained under the stress of emotion; her eyes were full of tears; she sipped her tea fiercely.

"There's some sugar," said Louisa. "We might have had a little cake."

The old man caught the word. "Cake?" he mumbled, with pleased inquiry, looking up, and extending his grasping old hand.

"I guess we ain't got no sugar to waste in cake," returned Mrs Britton. "Eat your porridge, father an' stop teasin'. There ain't no cake."

After supper Louisa cleared away the dishes; then she put on her shawl and hat.

"Where you goin'?" asked her mother.

"Down to the store."

"What for?"

"The oil's out. There wasn't enough to fill the lamps this mornin'. I ain't had a chance to get it before."

It was nearly dark. The mist was so heavy it was almost rain. Louisa went swiftly down the road with the oil-can. It was a half-mile to the store where the few staples were kept that sufficed the simple folk in this little settlement. She was gone a half-hour. When she returned, she had besides the oil-can a package under her arm. She went into the kitchen and set them down. The old man was asleep in the rocking-chair. She heard voices in the adjoining room. She frowned, and stood still, listening.

"Louisa!" called her mother. Her voice was sweet, and higher pitched than usual. She sounded the *i* in Louisa long.

"What say?"

"Come in here after you've taken your things off."

Louisa knew that Jonathan Nye was in the sitting-room. She flung off her hat and shawl. Her old dress was damp, and had still some earth stains on it; her hair was roughened by the wind, but she would not look again in the glass; she went into the sitting-room just as she was.

"It's Mr. Nye, Louisa," said her mother, with effusion.

"Good-evenin', Mr. Nye," said Louisa.

Jonathan Nye half arose and extended his hand, but she did not notice it. She sat down peremptorily in a chair at the other side of the room. Jonathan had the one rocking-chair; Mrs. Britton's frail little body was poised anxiously on the hard rounded top of the carpet-covered lounge. She looked at Louisa's dress and hair, and her eyes were stony with disapproval, but her lips still smirked, and she kept her voice sweet. She pointed to a glass dish on the table.

"See what Mr. Nye has brought us over, Louisa," said she.

Louisa looked indifferently at the dish.

"It's honey," said her mother; "some of his own bees made it. Don't you want to get a dish an' taste of it? One of them little glass sauce dishes."

"No, I guess not," replied Louisa. "I never cared much about honey. Grandfather'll like it."

The smile vanished momentarily from Mrs. Britton's lips, but she recovered herself. She arose and went across the room to the china closet. Her set of china dishes was on the top shelves, the lower were filled with books and papers. "I've got somethin' to show you, Mr. Nye," said she.

This was scarcely more than a hamlet, but it was incorporated, and had its town books. She brought forth a pile of them and laid them on the table beside Jonathan Nye. "There," said she, "I thought mebbe you'd like to look at these." She opened one and pointed to the school report. This mother could not display her daughter's accomplishments to attract a suitor, for she had none. Louisa did not own a piano or organ; she could not paint; but she had taught school acceptably for eight years – ever since she was sixteen – and in every one of the town books was testimonial to that effect, intermixed with glowing eulogy. Jonathan Nye looked soberly through the books; he was a slow reader. He was a few years older than Louisa, tall and clumsy, long-featured and long-necked. His face was a deep red with embarrassment, and it contrasted oddly with his stiff dignity of demeanor.

Mrs. Britton drew a chair close to him while he read. "You see, Louisa taught that school for eight years," said she; "an' she'd be techin' it now if Mr. Mosely's daughter hadn't grown up an' wanted somethin' to do, an' he put her in. He was committee, you know. I dun' know as I'd ought to say so, an' I wouldn't want you to repeat it, but they do say Ida Mosely don't give very good satisfaction, an' I guess she won't have no reports like these in the town books unless her father writes 'em. See this one."

Jonathan Nye pondered over the fulsome testimony to Louisa's capability, general worth, and amiability, while she sat in sulky silence at the farther corner of the room. Once in a while her mother, after a furtive glance at Jonathan, engrossed in a town book, would look at her and gesticulate fiercely for her to come over, but she did not stir. Her eyes were dull and quiet, her mouth closely shut; she looked homely. Louisa was very pretty when pleased and animated, at other times she had a look like a closed flower. One could see no prettiness in her.

Jonathan Nye read all the school reports; then he arose heavily. "They're real good," said he. He glanced at Louisa and tried to smile; his blushes deepened.

"Now don't be in a hurry," said Mrs. Britton.

"I guess I'd better be goin'; mother's alone."

"She won't be afraid; it's jest on the edge of the evenin'."

"I don't know as she will. But I guess I'd better be goin'." He looked hesitatingly at Louisa.

She arose and stood with an indifferent air.

"You'd better set down again," said Mrs. Britton.

"No; I guess I'd better be goin'." Jonathan turned towards Louisa. "Good-evenin'," said he.

"Good-evenin'."

Mrs. Britton followed him to the door. She looked back and beckoned imperiously to Louisa, but she stood still. "Now come again, do," Mrs. Britton said to the departing caller. "Run in any time; we're real lonesome evenin's. Father he sets an'sleeps in his chair, an' Louisa an' me often wish somebody'd drop in; folks round here ain't none too neighborly. Come in any time you happen to feel like it, an' we'll both of us be glad to see you. Tell your mother I'll send home that dish to-morrer, an' we shall have a real feast off that beautiful honey."

When Mrs. Britton had fairly shut the outer door upon Jonathan Nye, she came back into the sitting-room as if her anger had a propelling power like steam upon her body.

"Now, Louisa Britton," said she, "you'd ought to be ashamed of yourself — ashamed of yourself! You've treated him like a — hog!"

"I couldn't help it."

"Couldn't help it! I guess you could treat anybody decent if you tried. I never saw such actions! I guess you needn't be afraid of him. I guess he ain't so set on you that he means to ketch you up an' run off. There's other girls in town full as good as you an' better-lookin'. Why didn't you go an' put on your other dress? Comin' into the room with that old thing on, an' your hair all in a frowse! I guess he won't want to come again."

"I hope he won't," said Louisa, under her breath. She was trembling all over.

"What say?"

"Nothin'."

"I shouldn't think you'd want to say anything, treatin' him that way, when he came over and brought all that beautiful honey! He was all dressed up, too. He had on a real nice coat — cloth jest as fine as it could be, an' it was kinder damp when he come in. Then he dressed all up to come over here this rainy night an' bring this honey." Mrs. Britton snatched the dish of honey and scudded into the kitchen with it. "Sayin' you didn't like honey after he took all that pains to bring it over!" said she. "I'd said I liked it if I'd lied up hill and down." She set the dish in the pantry. "What in creation smells so kinder stron an' smoky in here?" said she, sharply.

"I guess it's the herrin'. I got two or three down to the store."

"I'd like to know what you got herrin' for?"

"I thought maybe you'd relish 'em."

"I don't want no herrin's, now we've got this honey. But I don't know that you've got money to throw away." She shook the old man by the stove into partial wakefulness, and steered him into his little bedroom off the kitchen. She herself slept in one off the sitting-rooms; Louisa's room was up-stairs.

Louisa lighted her candle and went to bed, her mother's scolding voice pursuing her like a wrathful spirit. She cried when she was in bed in the dark, but she soon went to sleep. She was too healthfully tired with her out-door work not to. All her young bones ached with the strain of manual labor as they had ached many a time this last year since she had lost her school.

The Brittons had been and were in sore straits. All they had in the world was this little house with the acre of land. Louisa's meagre school money had bought their food and clothing since her father died. Now it was almost starvation for them. Louisa was struggling to wrest a little sustenance from their stony acre of land, toiling like a European peasant woman, sacrificing her New England dignity. Lately she had herself split up a cord of wood which she had bought of a neighbor, paying for it in instalments with work for his wife.

"Think of a school-teacher goin' into Mis' Mitchell's house to help clean!" said her mother.

She, although she had been of poor, hard-working people all her life, with the humblest surroundings, was a born aristocrat, with that fiercest and most bigoted aristocracy which sometimes arises from independent poverty. She had the feeling of a queen for a princess of the blood about her school-teacher daughter; her working in a neighbor's kitchen was as galling and terrible to her. The projected marriage with Jonathan Nye was like a royal alliance for the good of the state. Jonathan Nye was the only eligible young man in the place; he was the largest land-owner; he had the best house. There were only himself and his mother; after her death the property would all be his. Mrs. Nye was an older woman than Mrs. Britton, who forgot her own frailty in calculating their chances of life.

"Mis' Nye is considerable over seventy," she said often to herself; "an' then Jonathan will have it all."

She saw herself installed in that large white house as reigning dowager. All the obstacle was Louisa's obstinacy, which her mother could not understand. She could see no fault in Jonathan Nye. So far as absolute approval went, she herself was in love with him. There was no more sense, to her mind, in Louisa's refusing him than there would have been in a princess refusing the fairy prince and spoiling the story.

"I'd like to know what you've got against him," she said often to Louisa.

"I ain't got anything against him."

"Why don't you treat him different, then, I want to know?"

"I don't like him." Louisa said "like" shamefacedly, for she meant love, and dared not say it.

"*Like!* Well, I don't know nothin' about such likin's as some pretend to, an' I don't want to. If I see anybody is good an' worthy, I like 'em, an' that's all there is about it."

"I don't — believe that's the way you felt about — father," said Louisa, softly, her young face flushed red.

"Yes, it was. I had some common-sense about it."

And Mrs. Britton believed it. Many hard middle-aged years lay between her and her own love-time, and nothing is so changed by distance as the realities of youth. She believed herself to have been actuated by the same calm reason in marrying young John Britton, who had had fair prospects, which she thought should actuate her daugter in marrying Jonathan Nye.

Louisa got no sympathy from her, but she persisted in her refusal. She worked harder and harder. She did not spare herself in doors or out. As the summer wore on her face grew as sunburnt as a boy's, her hands were hard and brown. When she put on her white dress to go to meeting on a Sunday there was a white ring around her neck where the sun had not touched it. Above it her face and neck showed browner. Her sleeves were rather short, and there were also white rings above her brown wrists.

"You look as if you were turnin' Injun by inches," said her mother.

Louisa, when she sat in the meeting-house, tried slyly to pull her sleeves down to the brown on her wrists; she gave a little twitch to the ruffle around her neck. Then she glanced across, and Jonathan Nye was looking at her. She thrust her hands, in their short-wristed, loose cotton gloves, as far out of the sleeves as she could; her brown wrists showed conspicuously on her white lap. She had never heard of the princess who destroyed her beauty that she might not be forced to wed the man whom she did not love, but she had something of the same feeling, although she did not have it for the sake of any tangible lover. Louisa had never seen anybody whom she would have preferred to Jonathan Nye. There was no other marriageable young man in the place. She had only her dreams, which she had in common with other girls.

That Sunday evening before she went to meeting her mother took some old wide lace out of her bureau drawer. "There," said she, "I'm goin' to sew this in your neck an' sleeves before you put your dress on. It'll cover up a little; it's wider than the ruffle."

"I don't want it in," said Louisa.

"I'd like to know why not? You look like a fright. I was ashamed of you this mornin'."

Louisa thrust her arms into the white dress sleeves peremptorily. Her mother did not speak to her all the way to meeting. After meeting, Jonathan Nye walked home with them, and Louisa kept on the other side of her mother. He went into the house and stayed an hour. Mrs. Britton entertained him, while Louisa sat silent. When he had gone, she looked at her daughter as if she could have used bodily force, but she said nothing. She shot the bolt of the kitchen door noisily. Louisa lighted her candle. The old man's loud breathing sounded from his room; he had been put to bed for safety before they went to meeting; through the open windows sounded the loud murmur of the summer night, as if that, too, slept heavily.

"Good-night, mother," said Louisa, as she went up-stairs;

but her mother did not answer.

The next day was very warm. This was an exceptionally hot summer. Louisa went out early; her mother would not ask her where she was going. She did not come home until noon. Her face was burning; her wet dress clung to her arms and shoulders.

"Where have you been?" asked her mother.

"Oh, I've been out in the field."

"What field?"

"Mr. Mitchell's."

"What have you been doin' out there?"

"Rakin' hay."

"Rakin' hay with the men?"

"There wasn't anybody but Mr. Mitchell and Johnny. Don't, mother!"

Mrs. Britton had turned white. She sank into a chair. "I can't stan' it nohow," she moaned. "All the daughter I've got."

"Don't mother! I ain't done any harm. What harm is it? Why can't I rake hay as well as a man? Lots of women do such things, if nobody round here does. He's goin' to pay me right off, and we need the money. Don't, mother!" Louisa got a tumbler of water. "Here, mother, drink this."

Mrs. Britton pushed it away. Louisa stood looking anxiously at her. Lately her mother had grown thinner than ever; she looked scarcely bigger than a child. Presently she got up and went to the stove.

"Don't try to do anything, mother; let me finish getting dinner," pleaded Louisa. She tried to take the pan of biscuits out of her mother's hands, but she jerked it away.

The old man was sitting on the door-step, huddled up loosely in the sun, like an old dog.

"Come, father," Mrs. Britton called, in a dry voice, "dinner's ready — what there is of it!"

The old man shuffled in, smiling.

There was nothing for dinner but the hot biscuits and tea. The fare was daily becoming more meagre. All Louisa's little hoard of school money was gone, and her earnings were very uncertain and slender. Their chief dependence for food through the summer was their garden, but that had failed them in some respects.

One day the old man had come in radiant, with his shaking hands full of potato blossoms; his old eyes twinkled over them like a mischievous child's. Reproaches were useless; the little potato crop was sadly damaged. Lately, in spite of close watching, he had picked the squash blossoms, piling them in a yellow mass beside the kitchen door. Still, it was nearly time for the pease and beans and beets; they would keep them from starvation while they lasted.

But when they came, and Louisa could pick plenty of green food every morning, there was still a difficulty: Mrs. Britton's appetite and digestion were poor; she could not live upon a green-vegetable diet; and the old man missed his porridge, for the meal was all gone.

One morning in August he cried at the breakfast-table like a baby, because he wanted his porridge, and Mrs. Britton pushed away her own plate with a despairing gesture.

"There ain't no use," said she. "I can't eat no more garden-sauce nohow. I don't blame poor father a mite. You ain't got no feelin' at all."

"I don't know what I can do; I've worked as hard as I can," said Louisa, miserably.

"I know what you can do, and so do you."

"No, I don't, mother," returned Louisa, with alacrity. "He ain't been here for two weeks now, and I saw him with my own eyes yesterday carryin' a dish into the Moselys', and I knew 'twas honey. I think he's after Ida."

"Carryin' honey into the Moselys'? I don't believe it."

"He was; I saw him."

"Well, I don't care if he was. If you're a mind to act decent now, you can bring him round again. He was dead set on you, an' I don't believe he's changed round to that Mosely girl as quick as this."

"You don't want me to ask him to come back here, do you?"

"I want you to act decent. You can go to meetin' tonight, if you're a mind to – I sha'n't go; I ain't got strength 'nough – an' 'twouldn't hurt you none to hang back a little after meetin', and kind of edge round his way. 'Twouldn't take more'n a look."

"Mother!"

"Well, I don't care. 'Twouldn't hurt you none. It's the way more'n one girl does, whether you believe it or not. Men don't do all the courtin' – not by a long shot. 'Twon't hurt you none. You needn't look so scart."

Mrs. Britton's own face was a burning red. She looked angrily away from her daughter's honest, indignant eyes.

"I wouldn't do such a thing as that for a man I liked," said Louisa; "and I certainly sha'n't for a man I don't like."

"Then me an' your grandfather 'll starve" said her mother; "that's all there is about it. We can't neither of us stan' it much longer."

"We could — "

"Could what?"

"Put a — little mortgage on the house."

Mrs. Britton faced her daughter. She trembled in every inch of her weak frame. "Put a mortgage on this house, an' by-an'-by not have a roof to cover us! Are you crazy? I tell you what 'tis, Louisa Britton, we may starve, your grandfather an' me, an' you can follow us to the graveyard over there, but there's only one way I'll ever put a mortgage on this house. If you have Jonathan Nye, I'll ask him to take a little one to tide us along an' get your weddin' things."

"Mother, I'll tell you what I'm goin' to do."

"What?"

"I am goin' to ask Uncle Solomon."

"I guess when Solomon Mears does anythin' for us you'll know it. He never forgave your father about that wood lot, an' he's hated the whole of us ever since. When I went to his wife's funeral he never answered when I spoke to him. I guess if you go to him you'll take it out in goin'."

Louisa said nothing more. She began clearing away the breakfast dishes and setting the house to rights. Her mother was actually so weak that she could scarcely stand, and she recognized it. She had settled into the rocking-chair, and leaned her head back. Her face looked pale and sharp against the dark calico cover.

When the house was in order, Louisa stole up-stairs to her own chamber. She put on her clean old blue muslin and her hat, then she went slyly down and out the front way.

It was seven miles to her uncle Solomon Mears's, and she had made up her mind to walk them. She walked quite swiftly until the house windows were out of sight, then she slackened her pace a little. It was one of the fiercest dog-days. A damp heat settled heavily down upon the earth; the sun scalded.

At the foot of the hill Louisa passed a house where one of her girl acquaintances lived. She was going in the gate with a pan of early apples. "Hullo, Louisa," she called.

"Hullo, Vinnie."

"Where you goin?"

"Oh, I'm goin' a little way."

"Ain't it awful hot? Say, Louisa, do you know Ida Mosely's cuttin' you out?"

"She's welcome."

The other girl, who was larger and stouter than Louisa, with a sallow, unhealthy face, looked at her curiously. "I don't see why you wouldn't have him," said she. "I should have thought you'd jumped at the chance."

"Should you if you didn't like him, I'd like to know?"

"I'd like him if he had such a nice house and as much money as Jonathan Nye," returned the other girl.

She offered Louisa some apples, and she went along the road eating them. She herself had scarcely tasted food that day.

It was about nine o'clock; she had risen early. She calculated how many hours it would take her to walk the seven miles. She walked as fast as she could to hold out. The heat seemed to increase as the sun stood higher. She had walked about three miles when she heard wheels behind her. Presently a team stopped at her side.

"Good-mornin'," said an embarrassed voice.

She looked around. It was Jonathan Nye, with his gray horse and light wagon.

"Good-mornin'," said she.

"Goin' far?"

"A little ways."

"Won't you – ride?"

"No thank you. I guess I'd rather walk."

Jonathan Nye nodded, made an inarticulate noise in his throat and drove on. Louisa watched the wagon bowling lightly along. The dust flew back. She took out her handkerchief and wiped her dripping face.

It was about noon when she came in sight of her uncle Solomon Mears's house in Wolfsborough. It stood far back from the road, behind a green expanse of untrodden yard. The blinds on the great square front were all closed; it looked as if everybody were away. Louisa went around to the side door. It stood wide open. There was a thin blue cloud of tobacco smoke issuing from it. Solomon Mears sat there in the large old kitchen smoking his pipe. On the table near him was an empty bowl; he had just eaten his dinner of bread and milk. He got his own dinner, for he had lived alone since his wife died. He looked at Louisa. Evidently he did not recognize her.

"How do you do, Uncle Solomon?" said Louisa.

"Oh, it's John Britton's daughter! How d'ye do?"

He took his pipe out of his mouth long enough to speak, then replaced it. His eyes, sharp under their shaggy brows, were fixed on Louisa; his broad bristling face had a look of stolid rebuff like an ox; his stout figure, in his soiled farmer dress, surged over his chair. He sat full in the doorway. Louisa standing before him, the perspiration trickling over her burning face, set forth her case with a certain dignity. This old man was her mother's nearest relative. He had property and to spare. Should she survive him, it would be hers, unless willed away. She, with her unsophisticated sense of justice, had a feeling that he ought to help her.

The old man listened. When she stopped speaking he took the pipe out of his mouth slowly, and stared gloomily past her at his hay field, where the grass was now a green stubble.

"I ain't got no money I can spare jest now," said he. "I s'pose you know your father cheated me out of consider'ble once?"

"We don't care so much about money, if you have got something you could spare to – eat. We ain't got anything but garden-stuff."

Solomon Mears still frowned past her at the hay field. Presently he arose slowly and went across the kitchen. Louisa sat down on the door-step and waited. Her uncle was gone quite a while. She, too, stared over at the field, which seemed to undulate like a lake in the hot light.

"Here's some things you can take, if you want 'em," said her uncle, at her back.

She got up quickly. He pointed grimly to the kitchen table. He was a deacon, an orthodox believer; he recognized the claims of the poor, but he gave alms as a soldier might yield up his sword. Benevolence was the result of warfare with his own conscience.

On the table lay a ham, a bag of meal, one of flour, and a basket of eggs.

"I'm afraid I can't carry 'em all," said Louisa.

"Leave what you can't then." Solomon caught up his hat and went out. He muttered something about not spending any more time as he went.

Louisa stood looking at the packages. It was utterly impossible for her to carry them all at once. She heard her uncle shout to some oxen he was turning out of the barn. She took up the bag of meal and the basket of eggs and carried them out to the gate; then she returned, got the flour and ham, and went with them to a point beyond. Then she returned for the meal and eggs, and carried them past the others. In that way she traversed the seven miles home. The heat increased. She had eaten nothing since morning but the apples that her friend had given her. Her head was swimming, but she kept on. Her resolution was as immovable under the power of the sun as a rock. Once in a while she rested for a moment under a tree, but she soon arose and went on. It was like a pilgrimage, and the Mecca at the end of the burning, desert-like road was her own maiden independence.

It was after eight o'clock when she reached home. Her mother stood in the doorway watching for her, straining her eyes in the dusk.

"For goodness sake, Louisa Britton! where have you been?" she began; but Louisa laid the meal and eggs down on the step.

"I've got to go back a little way," she panted.

When she returned with the flour and ham, she could hardly get into the house. She laid them on the kitchen table, where her mother had put the other parcels, and sank into a chair.

"Is this the way you've brought all these things home?" asked her mother.

Louisa nodded.

"All the way from Uncle Solomon's?"

"Yes."

Her mother went to her and took her hat off. "It's a mercy if you ain't got a sunstroke," said she, with a sharp tenderness. "I've got somethin' to tell you. What do you s'pose has happened? Mr. Mosely has been here, an' he wants you to take the school again when it opens next week. He says Ida ain't very well, but I guess that ain't it. They think she's goin' to get somebody. Mis' Mitchell says so. She's been in. She says he's carryin' things over there the whole time, but she don't b'lieve there's anything settled yet. She says they feel so sure of it they're goin' to have Ida give the school up. I told her I thought Ida would make him a good wife, an' she was easier suited than some girls. What do you s'pose Mis' Mitchell says? She says old

Mis' Nye told her that there was one thing about it: if Jonathan had you, he wa'n't goin' to have me an' father hitched on to him; he'd look out for that. I told mis' Mitchell that I guess there wa'n't none of us willin' to hitch, you nor anybody else. I hope she'll tell Mis' Nye. Now I'm a-goin' to turn you out a tumbler of milk — Mis' Mitchell she brought over a whole pitcherful; says she's got more'n they can use — they ain't got no pig now — an' then you go an' lay down on the sittin'-room lounge, an' cool off; an' I'll stir up some porridge for supper, an' boil some eggs. Father'll be tickled to death. Go right in there. I'm dreadful afraid you'll be sick. I never heard of anybody doin' such a thing as you have."

Louisa drank the milk and crept into the sitting-room. It was warm and close there, so she opened the front door and sat down on the step. The twilight was deep, but there was a clear yellow glow in the west. One great star had come out in the midst of it. A dewy coolness was spreading over everything. The air was full of bird calls and children's voices. Now and then there was a shout of laughter. Louisa leaned her head against the door-post.

The house was quite near the road. Some one passed — a man carrying a basket. Louisa glanced at him, and recognized Jonathan Nye by his gait. He kept on down the road toward the Moselys', and Louisa turned again from him to her sweet, mysterious, girlish dreams.

# HOW CELIA CHANGED HER MIND

*❋*

## *Rose Terry Cooke*

*'How Celia Changed Her Mind' is taken from Rose Terry Cooke's last collection of short stories,* Huckleberries: Gathered from New England Hills, *published in 1891. Huckleberries are smaller, have a thicker skin, and are more acid than blueberries; they mostly grow wild. When cultivated or domesticated they become something else; they become blueberries. Many of the characters in the stories of this important local colorist are like huckleberries.*

*Celia Barnes is defined at the beginning of this story through her relationship to another old maid who appeared in many and starred in some of Rose Terry Cooke's stories: Polly Mariner, the tailoress. Polly, too, had to have a thick skin and an acid tongue, but she nurtured Celia until she was a woman, and Celia grew up competent and independent.*

*But sometimes even the most self-sufficient women haven't skins thick enough to withstand the constant assault on self-esteem of the epithet 'old maid.' As Celia did, they then become unhappy with their lot as unmarried women. Such women often wish for a husband, believing that a husband, or rather the possession of a husband, or rather the public image of being themselves finally the possessions of husbands, will cure the unhappiness of their lives as old maids. But, as this story makes clear, a husband is not always or even often the right answer. The answer is a change in self-perception along with a change in social perceptions of unmarried women, a relaxing of the social rigidities and an elimination of the limiting stereotype.*

*However, there is one issue that appears again and again to create self-doubt in the minds of unmarried women about the blessedness of their condition. Every story of a woman, whether she has children or not, is the story of a person who*

208

has dealt with the issue of parenting and childbearing, and the uses of the human body available to us to choose among. We see this concern in Celia's story. Celia's response to insults by a married man for being a person deemed of no consequence because she is unmarried is to enter into a conspiracy with his daughter to get the daughter married. Marriage kills the daughter. It is as if Celia is flinging into her enemy's face her own idea of marriage: it is something that uses women up and kills them, that makes them subservient to the judgment and will of someone who might be their inferior. Celia is not satisfied by her revenge because she, too, loved the girl. Because she does not recognize her reasons for her dissatisfaction, she seeks further opportunities to get revenge. She, too, marries. She is the only old maid who does. And she regrets it almost instantly.

That was perhaps Rose Terry's response to her own marriage at the age of 46, a year after her own mother's death, to Rollin H. Cooke, sixteen years her junior, a widower with two daughters. From the time of her marriage until her death, Mrs Cooke (1827-92) suffered from financial problems and all the attendant pressures — work too rushed to satisfy, body too stressed to stay healthy.

Like many short stories written for the popular fiction market during the nineteenth century, this story appears to have been an occasional story — one written to commemorate an occasion surrounded by public and private ritual. This is a Thanksgiving story — but perhaps one of the most unusual and least sentimental ever written.

It is interesting to note that Rose Terry's first published story, sold when she was only 18 years old, appeared in Graham's Magazine in 1845, three years before 'Aunt Mable's Love Story', while Rufus Griswold, the sometime literary mentor of Alice Cary, was still editing the magazine.

# HOW CELIA CHANGED HER MIND*

———————————— ✳ ————————————

"If there's anything on the face of the earth I *do* hate, it's an old maid!"

Mrs. Stearns looked up from her sewing in astonishment.

"Why, Miss Celia!"

"Oh, yes! I know it. I'm one myself, but all the same, I hate 'em worse than p'ison. They ain't nothing nor nobody; they're cumberers of the ground." And Celia Barnes laid down her scissors with a bang, as if she might be Atropos herself, ready to cut the thread of life for all the despised class of which she was a notable member.

The minister's wife was genuinely surprised at this outburst; she herself had been well along in life before she married, and though she had been fairly happy in the uncertain relationship to which she had attained, she was, on the whole, inclined to agree with St. Paul, that the woman who did not marry "doeth better." "I don't agree with you, Miss Celia," she said gently. "Many, indeed, most of my best friends are maiden ladies, and I respect and love them just as much as if they were married women."

"Well, I don't. A woman that's married is somebody; she's got a place in the world; she ain't everybody's tag; folks don't say, 'Oh, it's nobody but that old maid Celye Barnes;' it's 'Mis' Price,' and 'Mis' Simms,' or 'Thomas Smith's wife,' as though you was somebody. I don't know how't is elsewheres, but here in Basset you might as well be a dog as an old maid. I allow it might be better if they all had means or eddication: money's 'a dreadful good thing to have in the house,' as I see in a book once, and learning is sort of comp'ny to you if you're

*From *Huckleberries: Gathered from New England Hills*, Houghton, Mifflin & Co., Boston and New York, 1891.

lonesome; but then lonesome you be, and you've got to be, if you're an old maid, and it can't be helped noway."

Mrs. Stearns smiled a little sadly, thinking that even married life had its own loneliness when your husband was shut up in his study, or gone off on a long drive to see some sick parishioner or conduct a neighborhood prayer-meeting, or even when he was the other side of the fireplace absorbed in a religious paper or a New York daily, or meditating on his next sermon, while the silent wife sat unnoticed at her mending or knitting. "But married women have more troubles and responsibilities than the unmarried, Miss Celia," she said. "You have no children to bring up and be anxious about, no daily dread of not doing your duty by the family whom you preside over, and no fear of the supplies giving out that are really needed. Nobody but your own self to look out for."

"That's jest it," snapped Celia, laying down the boy's coat she was sewing with a vicious jerk of her thread. "There't is! Nobody to home to care if you live or die; nobody to peek out of the winder to see if you're comin', or to make a mess of gruel or a cup of tea for you, or to throw ye a feelin' word if you're sick nigh unto death. And old maids is just as li'ble to up and die as them that's married. And as to responsibility, I ain't afraid to tackle that. Never! I don't hold with them that cringe and crawl and are skeert at a shadder, and won't do a living thing that they had ought to do because they're 'afraid to take the responsibility.' Why, there's Mrs. Deacon Trimble, she durstn't so much as set up a prayer-meetin' for missions or the temp'rance cause, because't was 'sech a responsibility to take the lead in them matters.' I suppose it's somethin' of a responsible chore to preach the gospel to the heathen, or grab a drinkin' feller by the scruff of his neck and haul him out of the horrible pit anyway, but if it's dooty it's got to be done, whether or no; and I ain't afraid of pitchin' into anything the Lord sets me to do!"

"Except being an old maid", said Mrs. Stearns.

Celia darted a sharp glance at her over her silver-rimmed spectacles, and pulled her needle through and through the seams of Willy's jacket with fresh vigor, while a thoughtful shadow came across her fine old face. Celia was a candid woman, for all her prejudices, a combination peculiarly characteristic of New England, for she was a typical Yankee. Presently she said abruptly, "I hadn't thought on't in that light." But then the minister opened the door, and the conversation stopped.

Parsons Stearns was tired and hungry and cross, and his wife knew all that as soon as she saw his face. She had learned long ago that ministers, however good they may be, are still men; so to-day she had kept her husband's dinner warm in the underoven, and had the kettle boiling to make him a cup of tea on the spot to assuage his irritation in the shortest and surest way; but though the odor of a savory stew and the cheerful warmth of the cooking-stove greeted him as he preceded her through the door into the kitchen, he snapped out, sharply enough for Celia to hear him through the half-closed door. "What do you have that old maid here for so often?"

"There!" said Celia to herself, — "there't is! *He* don't look upon't as a dispensation, if she doos. Men-folks run the world, and they know it. There ain't one of the hull caboodle but what despises an onmarried woman! Well,'t ain't altogether my fault. I wouldn't marry them that I could; I couldn't — not and be honest; and them that I would hev had didn't ask me. I don't know as I'm to blame, after all, when you look into't."

And she went on sewing Willy's jacket, contrived with pains and skill out of an old coat of his father's, while Mrs. Stearns poured out her husband's tea in the kitchen, replenished his plate with stew, and cut for him more than one segment of the crisp, fresh apple-pie, and urged upon him the squares of new cheeses that legitimately accompany this deleterious viand of the race and country, the sempiternal, insistent, flagrant, and alas! also fragrant pie.

Celia Barnes was the tailoress of the little scattered country town of Bassett. Early left an orphan, without near relatives or money, she had received the scantiest measure of education that our town authorities deal to the pauper children of such organizations. She was ten years old when her mother, a widow for almost all those ten years, left her to the tender mercies of the selectmen of Bassett. The selectmen of our country towns are almost irresponsible governors of their petty spheres, and gratify the instinct of oligarchy peculiar to, and conservative of, the human race. Men must be governed and tyrannized over, — it is an inborn necessity of their nature; and while a republic is a beautiful theory, eminently fitted for a race who are "non Angil, sed Angeli," it has in practice the effect of producing more than Russian tyranny, but on smaller scales and in far and scattered localities. Nowhere are there more despots than among village selectmen in New England. Those who have wrestled with their absolute monarchism in behalf of some charity that might abstract a few of the almighty dollars made out of poverty and distress from their official pockets know how positive and dogmatic is their use of power – *experto crede*. The Bassett "first selectman" promptly bound out little Celia Barnes to a hard, imperious woman, who made a white slave of the child, and only dealt out to her the smallest measure of schooling demanded by law, because the good old minister, Father Perkins, interfered in the child's behalf.

As she was strong and hardy and resolute, Celia lived through her bondage, and at the "free" age of eighteen apprenticed herself to old Miss Polly Mariner, the Bassett tailoress, and being deft with her fingers and quick of brain, soon outran her teacher, and when Polly died, succeeded to her business.

She was a bright girl, not particularly noticeable among others, for she had none of that delicate flower-like New England beauty which is so peculiar, so charming, and so evanescent; her features were tolerably regular, her forehead broad and calm, her gray eyes keen and perceptive, and she had abundant hair of an uncertain brown; but forty other girls in Bassett might have been described in the same way; Celia's face was one to improve with age; its strong sense, capacity for humor, fine outlines of a rugged sort, were always more the style of fifty than fifteen, and what she said of herself was true.

She had been asked to marry an old farmer with five uproarious boys, a man notorious in East Bassett for his stinginess and bad temper, and she had promptly declined the offer. Once more fate had given her a chance. A young fellow of no character, poor, "shiftless," and given to cider as a beverage, had considered it a good idea to marry some one who would make a home for him and earn his living. Looking about him for a proper person to fill this pleasant situation, he pounced on Celia – and she returned the attention!

"Marry *you*? I wonder you've got the sass to ask any decent girl to marry ye, Alfred Hatch! What be you good for, anyway? I don't know what under the canopy the Lord spares you for, – only He doos let the tares grow amongst the wheat, Scripter says, and I'm free to suppose He knows why, but I don't. No, *sir!* Ef you was the last man in the livin' universe I wouldn't

213

tech ye with the tongs. If you'd got a speck of grit into you, you'd be ashamed to ask a woman to take ye in and support ye, for that's what it comes to. You go 'long! I can make my hands save my head so long as I hev the use of 'em, and I haven't no call to set up a private poor-house!"

So Alfred Hatch sneaked off, much like a cur that has sought to share the kennel of a mastiff, and been shortly and sharply convinced of his presumption.

Here ended Celia's "chances," as she phrased it. Young men were few in Bassett; the West had drawn them away with its subtle attraction of unknown possibilities, just as it does to-day, and Celia grew old in the service of those established matrons who always want clothes cut over for their children, carpet rags sewed, quilts quilted, and comfortables tacked. She was industrious and frugal, and in time laid up some money in the Dartford Savings' Bank; but she did not, like many spinsters, invest her hard-earned dollars in a small house. Often she was urged to do so, but her reasons were good for refusing.

"I should be so independent? Well, I'm as independent now as the law allows. I've got two good rooms to myself, south winders, stairs of my own and outside door, and some privileges. If I had a house there'd be taxes, and insurance, and cleanin' off snow come winter-time, and hoein' paths; and likely enough I should be so fur left to myself that I should set up a garden, and make my succotash cost a dollar a pint a-hirin' of a man to dig it up and hoe it down. Like enough, too, I should be gettin' flower seeds and things; I'm kinder fond of blows in the time of 'em. My old fish-geran'um is a sight of comfort to me as't is, and there would be a bill of expense again. Then you can't noway build a house with only two rooms in't, it would be all outside; and you might as well try to heat the universe with a cookin'-stove as such a house. Besides, how lonesome I should be! It's forlorn enough to be an old maid anyway, but to have it sort of ground into you, as you may say, by livin' all alone in a hull house, that ain't necessary nor agreeable. Now, if I'm sick or sorry, I can just step downstairs and have aunt Nabby to help or hearten me. Deacon Everts he did set to work one time to persuade me to buy a house; he said't was a good thing to be able to give somebody shelter't was poorer'n I was. Says I, 'Deacon, I've worked for my livin' ever sence I remember, and I know there's no use in anybody bein' poorer than I be. I haven't no call to take any sech in and do for 'em. I give what I can to missions, – home ones, – and I'm willin', cheerfully willin', to do a day's work now and again for somebody that is strivin' with too heavy burdens; but as for keepin' free lodgin' and board, I sha'n't do it.' 'Well, well, well,' says he, kinder as if I was a fractious young one, and a-sawin' his fat hand up and down in the air till I wanted to slap him, 'just as you'd ruther, Celye, – just as you'd ruther. I don't mean to drive ye a mite, only, as Scripter says, "Provoke one another to love and good works."'

"That did rile me! Says I: 'Well, you've provoked me full enough, though I don't know as you've done it in the Scripter sense; and mabbe I shouldn't have got so fur provoked if I hadn't have known that little red house your grandsir' lived and died in was throwed back on your hands just now, and advertised for sellin'. I see the "Mounting County Herald", Deacon Everts.' He shut up, I tell ye. But I sha'n't never buy no house so long as aunt Nabby lets me have her two south chambers, and use the back stairway and the north door continual."

So Miss Celia had kept on in her way till now she was fifty, and to-day making over old clothes at the minister's. The minister's wife had, as we have seen, little romance or wild happiness in her life; it is not often the portion of country ministers' wives; and, moreover, she had two step-daughters who were girls of sixteen and twelve when she married their father. Katy was married herself now, this ten years, and doing her hard duty by an annual baby and a struggling parish in Dakota; but Rosabel, whose fine name had been the only legacy her dying mother left the day-old child she had scarce had time to kiss and christen before she went to take her own "new name" above, was now a girl of twenty-two, pretty, headstrong, and rebellious. Nature had endowed her with keen dark eyes, crisp dark curls, a long chin, and a very obstinate mouth, which only her red lips and white even teeth redeemed from ugliness; her bright color and her sense of fun made her attractive to young men wherever she encountered one of that rare species. Just now she was engaged in a serious flirtation with the station-master at Bassett Centre, – an impecunious youth of no special interest to other people and quite unable to maintain a wife. But out of the "strong necessity of loving," as it is called, and the want of young society or settled occupation, Rosa Stearns chose to fall in love with Amos Barker, and her father considered it a "fall" indeed. So, with the natural clumsiness of a man and a father, Parson Stearns set himself to prevent the matter, and began by forbidding Rosabel to see or speak or write to the youth in question, and thereby inspired in her mind a burning desire to do all three. Up to this time she had rather languidly amused herself by mild and gentle flirtations with him, such as looking at him sidewise in church on Sunday, meeting him accidentally on his way to and from the station, for she spent at least half her time at her aunt's in Bassett Centre, and had even taught the small school there during the last six months. She had also sent him her tintype, and his own was secreted in her bureau drawer. He had invited her to go with him to two sleigh-rides and one sugaring-off, and always came home with her from prayer-meeting and singing-school; but like a wise youth he had never yet proposed to marry her in due form, not so much because he was wise as because he was thoughtless and lazy; and while he enjoyed the society of a bright girl, and liked to dangle after the prettiest one in Bassett, and the minister's daughter too, he did not love work well enough to shoulder the responsibility of providing for another those material but necessary supplies that imply labor of an incessant sort.

Rosabel, in her first inconsiderate anger at her father's command, sat down and wrote a note to Amos, eminently calculated to call out his sympathy with her own wrath, and promptly mailed it as soon as it was written. It ran as follows:

DEAR FRIEND, — Pa has forbidden me to speak to you any more, or to correspond with you. I suppose I must submit so far; but he did not say I must return your picture [the parson had not an idea that she possessed that precious thing], so I shall keep it to remind me of the pleasant hours we have passed together.

> "Fare thee well, and if forever,
> Still forever fare thee well!"

Your true friend,                           ROSABEL STEARNS
P.S. — I think pa is *horrid!*

So did Amos as he read this heart-rending missive, in which the postscript, according to the established sneer at woman's postscripts, carried the whole force of the epistle.

Now Amos had made a friend of Miss Celia by once telegraphing for her trunk, which she had lost on her way home from the only journey of her life, a trip to Boston, whither she had gone, on the strength of the one share of B. & A. R. R. stock she held, to spend the allotted three days granted to stockholders on their annual excursions, presumably to attend the annual meeting. Amos had put himself to the immense trouble of sending two messages for Miss Celia, and asked her nothing for the civility, so that ever after, in the fashion of solitary women, she held herself deeply in his debt. He knew that she was at work for Mrs. Stearns when he received Rosa's epistle, for he had just been over to Bassett on the train — there was but a mile to traverse — to get her to repair his Sunday coat, and not found her at home, but had no time to look her up at the parson's, as he must walk back to his station. Now he resolved to take his answer to Rosa to Miss Celia in the evening, and so be sure that his abused sweetheart received it, for he had read too many dime novels to doubt that her tyrannic father would intercept their letters, and drive them both to madness and despair. That well-meaning but rather dull divine never would have thought of such a thing; he was a puffy, absent-minded, fat little man, with a weak, squeaky voice, and a sudden temper that blazed up like a bunch of dry weeds at a passing spark, and went out at once in flattest ashes. It had been Mrs. Stearns's step-motherly interference that drove him into his harshness to Rosa. She meant well and he meant well, but we all know what good intentions with no further sequel of act are good for, and nobody did more of that "paving" than these two excellent but futile people.

Miss Celia was ready to do anything for Amos Barker, and she considered it little less than a mortal sin to stand in the way of any marriage that was really desired by two parties. That Amos was poor did not daunt her at all; she had the curious faith that possesses some women, that any man can be prosperous if he has the will so to be; and she had a high opinion of this youth, based on his civility to her. It may be said of men, as of elephants, that it is lucky they do not know their own power; for how many more women would become their worshipers and slaves than are so to-day if they knew the abject gratitude the average woman feels for the least attention, the smallest kindness, the faintest expression of affection or good will. We are all, like the Syrophenician woman, glad and ready to eat of the crumbs which fall from the children's table, so great is our faith – in men.

Miss Celia took the note in her big basket over to the minister's the very next day after that on which we introduced her to our readers. She was perhaps more rejoiced to contravene that reverend gentleman's orders than if she had not heard his querulous and contemptuous remark about her through the crack of the door on the previous afternoon; and it was with a sense of joy that, after all, an old maid could do something, that she slipped the envelope into Rosa's hands, and told her to put it quickly into her pocket, the very first moment she found herself alone with that young woman.

Many a hasty word had Parson Stearns spoken in the suddenness of his petulant temper, but never one that bore direr fruit than that when he called Celia Barnes "that old maid."

For of course Amos and Rosabel found in her an ardent friend. They had the instinct of distressed lovers to cajole her with all their confidences, caresses, and eager gratitude, and for once she felt herself dear and of importance. Amos consulted her on his plans for the future, which of course pointed westward, where he had a brother editing and owning a newspaper. This brother had before offered him a place in his office, but Amos had liked better the easy work of a station-master in a tiny village. Now his ambition was aroused, for the time at least. He wanted to make a home for Rosabel, but, alack! he had not one cent to pay their united expenses to Peoria, and a lion stood in the way. Here again Celia stepped in: she had some money laid up; she would lend it to them.

I do not say that at this stage she had no misgivings, but even these were set at rest by a conversation she had with Mrs. Stearns some six weeks after the day on which Celia had so fully expressed her scorn of spinsters. She was there again to tack a comfortable for Rosabel's bed, and bethought herself that it was a good time to feel her way a little concerning Mrs. Stearns's opinion of things.

"They do say," she remarked, stopping to snip off her thread and twist the end of it through her needle's eye, "that your Rosy don't go with Amos Barker no more. Is that so?"

"Yes," said Mrs. Stearns, with a half sigh. "Husband was rather prompt about it; he don't think Amos Barker ever'll amount to much, and he thinks his people are not just what they should be. You know his father never was very much of a man, and his grandfather is a real old reprobate. Husband says he never knew anything but crows come out of a crow's nest, and so he told Rosa to break acquaintance with him."

"Who doe he like to hev come to see her?" asked Celia, with a grim set of her lips, stabbing her needle fiercely through the unoffending calico.

Mrs. Stearns laughed rather feebly. "I don't think he has anybody on his mind, Miss Celia. I don't think there are any young men in Bassett. I dare say Rosa will never marry. I wish she would, for she isn't happy here, and I can't do much to help it, with all my cares."

"And you can't feel for her as though she was your own, if you try every so," confidently asserted Celia.

"No, I suppose not. I try to do my duty by her, and I am sorry for her; but I know all the time an own mother would understand her better and make it easier for her. Mr. Stearns is peculiar, and men don't know just how to manage girls."

It was a cautious admission, but Miss Celia had sharp eyes, and knew very well that Rosabel neither loved nor respected her father, and that they were now on terms of real if unavowed hostility.

"Well," said she, "I don know but you will have to have one of them onpleasant creturs, an old maid, in your fam'ly. I declare for't, I'd hold a Thanksgiving Day all to myself ef I'd escaped that marcy."

"You may not always think so, Celia."

"I don't know what'll change me. 'Twill be something I don't look forrard to now," answered Celia obstinately.

Mrs. Stearns sighed. "I hope Rosa will do nothing worse than to live unmarried," she said; but she could not help wishing silently that some worthy man would carry the perverse and annoying girl out of the parsonage for good.

After this Celia felt a certain freedom to help Rosabel; she encouraged the lovers to meet at her house, helped plan their elopement, scwed for the girl, and at last went with them as far as Brimfield when they stole away one evening, saw them safely married at the Methodist parsonage there, and bidding them good-speed, returned to Bassett Centre on the midnight train, and walked over to her own dwelling in the full moonshine of the October night, quite fearless and entirely exultant.

But she was not to come off unscathed. There was a scene of

219

wild commotion at the parsonage next day, when Rosa's letter, modeled on that of the last novel heroine she had become acquainted with, was found on her bureau, as per novel aforesaid.

With her natural thoughtlessness she assured her parents that she "fled not uncompanioned," that her "kind and all but maternal friend, Miss Celia Barnes, would accompany her to the altar, and give her support and her countenance to the solemn ceremony that should make Rosabel Stearns the blessed wife of Amos Barker!"

It was all the minister could do not to swear as he read this astounding letter. His flabby face grew purple; his fat, sallow hands shook with rage; he dared not speak, he only sputtered, for he knew that profane and unbecoming words would surely leap from his tongue if he set it free; but he must – he really must – do or say something! So he clapped on his old hat, and with coat tails flying in the breeze, and rage in every step, set out to find Celia Barnes; and find her he did.

It would be unpleasant, and it is needless, to depict this encounter; language both unjust and unsavory smote the air and reverberated along the highway, for he met the spinster on her road to an engagement at Deacon Stiles's. Suffice it to say that both freed their minds with great enlargement of opinion, and the parson wound up with, –

"And I never want to see you again inside of my house, you confounded old maid!"

"There! that's it!" retorted Celia. "Ef I was n't an old maid, you wouldn't no more have darst to 'a' talked to me this way than nothin'. Ef I'd had a man to stand up to ye you'd have been dumber'n Balaam's ass a great sight, – afore it seen the angel, I mean. I swow to man, I b'elieve I'd marry a hitchin'-post if 'twas big enough to trounce ye. You great lummox, if I could knock ye over you wouldn't peep nor mutter agin, if I be a woman!"

And with a burst of furious tears that asserted her womanhood Miss Celia went her way. Her hands were clinched under her blanket-shawl, her eyes red with angry rain, and as she walked on she soliloquized aloud: –

"I declare for't, I b'elieve I'd marry the Old Boy himself if he'd ask me. I'm sicker'n ever of bein' an old maid!"

"Be ye?" queried a voice at her elbow. "P'r'aps, then, you might hear to me if I was to speak my mind, Celye."

Celia jumped. As she said afterward, "I vum I thought 'twas the Enemy, for certain; and to think 'twas only Deacon Everts!"

"Mercy me!" she said now; "is't you, deacon?"

"Yes, it's me; and I think 'tis a real providence I come up behind ye just in the nick of time. I've sold my farm only last week, and I've come to live on the street in that old red house of grandsir's, that you mistrusted once I wanted you to buy. I'm real lonesome sence I lost my partner" (he meant his wife), "and I've been a-hangin' on by the edges the past two years; hired help is worse than nothing onto a farm, and hard to get at that; so I sold out, and I'm a-movin' yet, but the old house looks forlorn enough, and I was intendin' to look about for a second; so if you'll have me, Celye, here I be."

Celia looked at him sharply; he was an apple-faced little man, with shrewd, twinkling eyes, a hard, dull red still lingering on his round cheeks in spite of the deep wrinkles about his pursed-up lips and around his eyelids; his mouth gave him a consequential and self-important air, to which the short stubbly hair, brushed up "like a blaze" above his forehead, added; and his old blue coat with brass buttons, his homespun trousers, the old-fashioned aspect of his unbleached cotton shirt, all attested his frugality. Indeed, everybody knew that Deacon Everts was "near", and also that he had plenty of money, that is to say, far more than he could spend. He had no children, no near relations; his first wife had died two years since, after long invalidism, and all her relations had moved far west. All this Celia knew and now recalled; her wrath against Parson Stearns was yet fresh and vivid; she remembered that Simeon Everts was senior deacon of the church, and had it in his power to make the minister extremely uncomfortable if he chose. I have never said Celia was a very good woman; her religion was of the dormant type not uncommon nowadays; she kept up its observances properly, and said her prayers every day, bestowed a part of her savings on each church collection, and was rated as a church-member "in good and regular standing;" but the vital transforming power of that Christianity which means to "love the Lord thy God with all thy heart, and mind, and soul, and strength, and thy neighbor as thyself," had no more entered into her soul than it had into Deacon Everts's; and while she would have honestly admitted that revenge was a very wrong sentiment, and entirely improper for any other

221

person to cherish, she felt that she did well to be angry with Parson Stearns, and had a perfect right to "pay him off" in any way she could.

Now here was her opportunity. If she said "Yes" to Deacon Everts, he would no doubt take her part. Her objections to housekeeping were set aside by the fact that the house-owner himself would have to do those heavy labors about the house which she must otherwise have hired a man to do; and the cooking and the indoor work for two people could not be so hard as to sew from house to house for her daily bread. In short, her mind was slowly turning favorably toward this sudden project, but she did not want this wooer to be too sure; so she said: "W-e-ll, 'tis a life sentence, as you may say, deacon, and I want to think on 'ta spell. Let's see, – to-day's Tuesday; I'll let ye know Thursday night, after prayer-meetin'."

"Well," answered the deacon.

Blessed Yankee monosyllable that means so much and so little; that has such shades of phrase and intention in its myriad inflections; that is "yes," or "no," or "perhaps," just as you accent it; that is at once preface and peroration, evasion and definition! What would all New England speech be without "well"? Even as salt without any savor, or pepper with no pungency.

Now it meant to Miss Celia assent to her proposition; and in accordance the deacon escorted her home from meeting Thursday night, and received for reward a consenting answer. This was no love affair, but a matter of mere business. Deacon Everts needed a housekeeper, and did not want to pay out wages for one; and Miss Celia's position she expressed herself as she put out her tallow candle on that memorable night, and breathed out on the darkness the audible aspiration, "Thank goodness, I sha'n't hev to die an old maid!"

There was no touch of sanctifying love or consoling affection, or even friendly comradeship, in this arrangement; it was as truly a *marriage de convenance* as was ever contracted in Paris itself, and when the wedding day came, a short month afterward, the sourest aspect of November skies threatening a drenching pour, the dead and sodden leaves that strewed the earth, the wailing northeast wind, even the draggled and bony old horse behind which they jogged over to Bassett Centre, seemed fit accompaniments to the degraded ceremony performed by a justice of the peace, who concluded this merely

222

legal compact, for Miss Celia stoutly refused to be married by Parson Stearns; she would not be accessory to putting one dollar in his pocket, even as her own wedding fee. So she went home to the little red house on Bassett Street, and begun her married life by scrubbing the dust and dirt of years from the kitchen table, making biscuit for tea, washing up the dishes, and at last falling asleep during the deacon's long nasal prayer, wherein he wandered to the ends of the earth, and prayed fervently for the heathen, piteously unconscious that he was little better than a heathen himself.

It did not take many weeks to discover to Celia what is meant by "the curse of a granted prayer." She could not at first accept the situation at all; she was accustomed to enough food, if it was plain and simple, when she herself provided it; but now it was hard to get such viands as would satisfy a healthy appetite.

"You've used a sight of pork, Celye," the deacon would remonstrate. "My first never cooked half what you do. We shall come to want certain, if you're so free-handed."

"Well, Mr. Everts, there wasn't a mite left to set by. We eat it all, and I didn't have no more'n I wanted, if you did."

"We must mortify the flesh, Celye. It's hullsome to get up from your victuals hungry. Ye know what Scripter says, 'Jeshurun waxed fat an' kicked.' "

"Well, I ain't Jeshurun, but I expect I shall be more likely to kick if I don't have enough to eat, when it's only pork 'n' potatoes."

"My first used to say them was the best, for steady victuals, of anything, and she never used but two codfish and two quarts of m'lasses the year round; and as for butter, she was real sparin'; she'd fry our bread along with the salt pork, and 'twas just as good."

"Look here!" snapped Celia. "I don't want to hear no more about your 'first.' I'm ready to say I wish't she'd ha' been your last too."

"Well, well, well! this is onseemly contention, Celye," sputtered the alarmed deacon. "Le''s dwell together in unity so fur as we can, Mis' Everts. I haven't no intention to starve ye, none whatever. I only want to be keerful, so as we sha'n't have to fetch up in the poor-us."

"No need to have a poor-house to home," muttered Celia. But this is only a mild specimen of poor Celia's life as a married woman. She did not find the honor and glory of "Mrs." before her name a compensation for the thousand evils that she "knew not of" when she fled to them as a desirable change from her single blessedness. Deacon Everts entirely refused to enter into any of her devices against Parson Stearns; he did not care a penny about Celia's wrongs, and he knew very well that no other man than dreamy, unpractical Mr. Stearns, who eked out his minute pittance by writing school-books of a primary sort, would put up with four hundred dollars a year from his parish; yet that was all Bassett people would pay. If they must have the gospel, they must have it at the lowest living rates, and everybody would not assent to that.

So Celia found her revenge no more feasible after her marriage than before, and, gradually absorbed in her own wrongs and sufferings, her desire to reward Mr. Stearns in kind for his treatment of her vanished; she thought less of his futile wrath and more of her present distresses every day.

For Celia, like everybody who profanes the sacrament of marriage, was beginning to suffer the consequences of her misstep. As her husband's mean, querulous, loveless character unveiled itself in the terrible intimacy of constant and inevitable companionship, she began to look woefully back to the freedom and peace of her maiden days. She learned that a husband is by no means his wife's defender always, not even against reviling tongues. It did not suit Deacon Everts to quarrel with any one, whatever they said to him, or of him and his; he "didn't want no enemies," and Celia bitterly felt that she must fight her own battles; she had not even an ally in her husband. She became not only defiant, but also depressed; the consciousness of a vital and life-long mistake is not productive of cheer or content; and now, admitted into the freemasonry of married women, she discovered how few among them were more than household drudges, the servant of their families, worked to the verge of exhaustion, and neither thanked nor rewarded for their pains. She saw here a woman whose children were careless of, and ungrateful to her, and her husband coldly indifferent; there was one on whom the man she had married wreaked all his fiendish temper in daily small injuries, little vexatious acts, petty tyrannies, a "street-angel, house-devil" of a man, of all sorts the most hateful. There were many whose lives had no other outlook than hard work until the end should come, who rose up to labor and lay down in sleepless exhaustion, and some whose days were a constant terror to them from the intemperate brutes to whom they had intrusted their happiness, and indeed their whole existence.

It was no worse with Celia than with most of her sex in Bassett; here and there, there were of course exceptions, but so rare as to be shining examples and objects of envy. Then, too, after two years, there came forlorn accounts of poor Rosabel's situation at the west. Amos Barker had done his best at first to make his wife comfortable, but change of place or new motives do not at once, if ever, transform an indolent man into an active and efficient one. He found work in his brother's office, but it was the hard work of collecting bills all about the country; the roads were bad, the weather as fluctuating as weather always is, the climate did not agree with him, and he got woefully tired of driving about from dawn till after dark, to dun unwilling debtors. Rosa had chills and fever and babies with persistent alacrity; she had indeed enough to eat, with no appetite, and a house, with no strength to keep it. She grew untidy, listless, hysterical; and her father, getting worried by her despondent and infrequent letters, actually so far roused himself as to sell his horse, and with this sacrificial money betook himself to Mound Village, where he found Rosabel with two babies in her arms, dust an inch deep on all her possessions, nothing but pork, potatoes, and corn bread in the pantry, and a slatternly negress washing some clothes in a kitchen that made the parson shudder.

The little man's heart was bigger than his soul. He put his arms about Rosa and the dingy babies, and forgave her all; but he had to say, even while he held them closely and fondly to his breast, "Oh, Rosy, I told you what would happen if you married that fellow."

Of course Rosa resented the speech, for, after all, she had loved Amos; perhaps could love him still if the poverty and malaria and babies could have all been eliminated from her daily life.

Fortunately the parson's horse had sold well, for it was strong and young, and the rack of venerable bones with which he replaced it was bought very cheap at a farmer's auction, so he had money enough to carry Rosa and the two children home to Bassett, where two months after she added another feeble, howling cipher to the miserable sum of humanity.

Miss – no, Mrs. – Celia's conscience stung her to the quick

when she encountered this ghastly wreck of pretty Rosabel Stearns, now called Mrs. Barker. She remembered with deep regret how she had given aid and comfort to the girl who had defied and disobeyed parental counsel and authority, and so brought on herself all this misery. She fancied that Parson Stearns glared at her with eyes of bitter accusation and reproach, and not improbably he did, for beside his pity and affection for his daughter, it was no slight burden to take into his house a feeble woman with two children helpless as babies, and to look forward to the expense and anxiety of another soon to come. And Mrs. Stearns had never loved Rosa well enough to be complacent at this addition to her family cares. She gave the parson no sympathy. It would have been her way to let Rosabel lie on the bed she had made, and die there if need be. But the poor worn-out creature died at home, after all, and the third baby lay on its mother's breast in her coffin: they had gone together.

Celia felt almost like a murderess when she heard that Rosabel Barker was dead. She did not reflect that in all human probability the girl would have married Amos if she, Celia, had refused to help or encourage her. It began to be an importunate question in our friend's mind whether she herself had not made a mistake too; whether the phrase "single blessedness" was not an expression of a vital truth rather than a scoff. Celia was changing her mind no doubt, surely if slowly.

Meantime Deacon Everts did not find all the satisfaction with his "second" that he had anticipated. Celia had a will of her own, quite undisciplined, and it was too often asserted to suit her lord and master. Secretly he planned devices to circumvent her purposes, and sometimes succeeded. In prayer-meeting and in Sunday-school the idea haunted him; his malice lay down and rose up with him. Even when he propounded to his Bible class the important question, "How fur be the heathen *ree*-sponsible for what they dun know?" and asked them "to ponder on't through the comin' week," he chuckled inwardly at the thought that Celia could not evade *her* responsibility; she knew enough, and would be judged accordingly: the deacon was not a merciful man.

At last he hit upon that great legal engine whereby men do inflict the last deadly kick upon their wives: he would remodel his will. Yes, he would leave those gathered thousands to foreign missions; he would leave behind him the indisputable testimony and taunt that he considered the wife of his bosom less than the savages and heathen afar off. He forgot conveniently that the man "who provideth not for his own household hath denied the faith, and is worse than an infidel." And in his delight of revenge he also forgot that the law of the land provides for a man's wife and children in spite of his wicked will. Nor did he remember that his life-insurance policy for five thousand dollars was made out in his wife's name, simply as his wife, her own name not being specified. He had paid the premium always from his "first's" small annual income, and agreed that it should be written for her benefit, but he supposed that at her death it had reverted to him. He forgot that he still had a wife when he mentioned that policy in his assets recorded in the will, and to save money he drew that evil document up himself, and had it signed down at "the store" by three witnesses.

Celia had borne her self-imposed yoke for four years, when it was suddenly broken. A late crop of grass was to be mowed in mid-July on the meadow which appertained to the old house, and the deacon, now some seventy years old, to save hiring help, determined to do it by himself. The grass was heavy and over-ripe, the day extremely hot and breathless, and the grim Mower of Man trod side by side with Simeon Everts, and laid him too, all along by the rough heads of timothy and the purpled feather-tops of the blue-grass. He did not come home at noon or at night, and when Celia went down to the lot to call him he heard no summons of hers; he had answered a call far more imperative and final.

After the funeral Celia found his will pushed back in the deep drawer of an old secretary, where he kept his one quill pen, a bottle of dried ink, a lump of chalk, some rat-poison, and various other odds and ends.

She was indignant enough at its tenor; but it was easily broken, and she not only had her "thirds," but the life policy reverted to her also, as it was made out to Simeon Everts's wife, and surely she had occupied that position for four wretched years. Then, also, she had a right to her support for one year out of the estate, and the use of the house for that time.

Oh, how sweet was her freedom! With her characteristic honesty she refused to put on mourning, and even went to the funeral in her usual gray Sunday gown and bonnet. "I won't lie, anyhow!" she answered to Mrs. Stiles's remonstrance. "I

227

ain't a mite sorry nor mournful. I could ha' wished he'd had time to repent of his sins, but sence the Lord saw fit to cut him short, I don't feel to rebel ag'inst it. I wish't I'd never married him, that's all!"

"But, Celye, you got a good livin'."

"I earned it."

"And he's left ye with means too."

"He done his best not to. I don't owe him nothing for that; and I earned that too, – the hull on't. It's poor pay for what I've lived through; and I'm a'most a mind to call it the wages of sin, for I done wrong; ondeniably wrong, in marryin' of him; but the Lord knows I've repented, and said my lesson, if I did get it by the hardest."

Yet all Bassett opened eyes and mouth both when on the next Thanksgiving Day Celia invited every old maid in town – seven all told – to take dinner with her. Never before had she celebrated this old New England day of solemn revel. A woman living in two small rooms could not "keep the feast," and rarely had she been asked to any family conclave. We Yankees are conservative at Thanksgiving if nowhere else, and like to gather our own people only about the family hearth; so Celia had but once or twice shared the turkeys of her more fortunate neighbors.

Now she called in Nabby Hyde and Sarah Gillet, Ann Smith, Celestia Potter, Delia Hills, Sophronia Ann Jenkins and her sister Adelia Ann, ancient twins, who lived together on next to nothing, and were happy.

Celia bloomed at the head of the board, not with beauty, but with gratification. "Well," she said, as soon as they were seated, "I sent for ye all to come because I wanted to have a good time, for one thing, and because it seems as though I'd ought to take back all the sassy and disagreeable things I used to be forever flingin' at old maids. 'I spoke in my haste,' as Scripter says, and also in my ignorance, I'm free to confess. I feel as though I could keep Thanksgivin' to-day with my hull soul. I'm so thankful to be an old maid ag'in!"

"I thought you was a widder," snapped Sally Gilett.

Celia flung a glance of wrath at her, scorned to reply.

"And I'm thankful too that I'm spared to help ondo somethin' done in that ignorance. I've got means, and, as I've said before, I earned 'em. I don't feel noway obleeged to him for 'em; he didn't mean it. But now I can I'm goin' to adopt

Rosy Barker's two children, and fetch 'em up to be dyed-in-the-wool old maids; and every year, so long as I live, I'm goin' to keep an old maids' Thanksgivin' for a kind of a burnt-offering, sech as the Bible tells about, for I've changed my mind clear down to the bottom, and I go the hull figure with the 'postle Paul when he speaks about the onmarried, 'It is better if she so abide.' Now let's go to work at the victuals."

# AFTERWORD

---
*
---

What these stories represent are the collective creation of an image. They are a representative selection of individual efforts in the common literary effort to create a new image for the woman who did not marry. The old image was one these women rejected. But it was not enough for them to declare that 'old maid' was not to be tolerated as a pejorative dismissal of a group of women who did not marry. Another image had to be built to replace the old one. And one does not build a new image overnight. In this case the collective creation continues to this day for these stories made possible the literary evolution of what came to be designated 'the new woman,' the woman whose life was lived independently, on her own terms, in accordance with the light she herself perceived rather than that she received. Such a woman today is called a 'woman-identified woman.'

That such a literary tradition exists might be a surprise for many. In the novels that have come down to us as part of the American literary canon, that 'new woman' is frequently portrayed as a woman who fails, who is punished, who dies by the end of the book. But what must be recognized is that at the same time as this canonized literature was being written, literature now forgotten and ignored was being written as well. In this 'other literature' the 'new woman' was increasingly carefully defined as autonomous, fulfilled by her choices, vigorous, and admirable. And this collection of stories traces the development of that new image, that literary invention become convention. Reading from the first story to the last we can trace the growth over a period of almost sixty years of an idea, a wistful wish, a hope, an angry demand, a staunch declaration of what-ought-to-be, watching it become what is.

Thus we can follow in this progression of stories the development of a woman-created cultural image.

These women writers recognized the power of language in our lives and sought to use language to empower women, to create new heroines whom we admire not for what they abdicate but for what they govern of their own lives; whom we love not for their selflessness but for their self-determination. These stories, then, trace the transformation of a literary image from one that belittled and constrained women to a literary image that frees and empowers women.

Today there are unmarried women living alone or with other women, women who have never married, women who support themselves, who have rich, full, active lives, and who do not think of themselves as old maids. They are the recipients of the empowerment of women towards which these stories progress. These women are free to think of themselves in any way they wish; they do not have to think of themselves as old maids. Naming ourselves, defining the perimeters of our own identities along axes we choose: that is the gift of these stories.

# UNWEDDED

Behold her there in the evening sun,
  That kindles the Indian Summer trees
To a separate burning bush, one by one,
  Wherein the Glory Divine she sees!

Mate and nestlings she never had:
  Kith and kindred have passed away;
Yet the sunset is not more gently glad,
  That follows her shadow, and fain would stay.

For out of her life goes a breath of bliss,
  And a sunlike charm from her cheerful eye,
That the cloud and the loitering breeze would miss;
  A balm that refreshes the passer-by.

'Did she choose it, this single life?' —
  Gossip, she saith not, and who can tell?
But many a mother, and many a wife,
  Draws a lot more lonely, we all know well.

Doubtless she had her romantic dream,
  Like other maidens, in May-time sweet,
That flushes the air with a lingering gleam,
  And goldens the grass beneath her feet: —

A dream unmoulded to visible form,
  That keeps the world rosy with mists of youth,
And holds her in loyalty close and warm,
  To her grand ideal of manly truth.

'But is she happy, a woman, alone?' —
  Gossip, alone in this crowded earth,
With a voice to quiet its hourly moan,
  And a smile to heighten its rarer mirth?

There are ends more worthy than happiness:
  Who seeks it, is digging joy's grave, we know.
The blessed are they who but live to bless;
  She found out that mystery, long ago.

To her motherly, sheltering atmosphere,
  The children hasten from icy homes:
The outcast is welcome to share her cheer;
  And the saint with a fervent benison comes.

For the heart of woman is large as man's;
  God gave her His orphaned world to hold,
And whispered through her His deeper plans
  To save it alive from the outer cold.

And here is a woman who understood
  Herself, her work, and God's will with her,
To gather and scatter His sheaves of good,
  And was meekly thankful, though men demur.

Would she have walked more nobly, think,
  With a man beside her, to point the way,
Hand joining hand in the marriage-link?
  Possibly, Yes; it is likelier, Nay.

For all men have not wisdom and might:
  Love's eyes are tender, and blur the map;
And a wife will follow by faith, not sight,
  In the chosen footprint, at any hap.

Having the whole, she covets no part:
  Hers is the bliss of all blessed things.
The tears that unto her eyelids start,
  Are those which a generous pity brings;

Or the sympathy of heroic faith
  With a holy purpose, achieved or lost.

To stifle the truth is to stop her breath,
   For she rates a lie at its deadly cost.

Her friends are good women and faithful men,
   Who seek for the True, and uphold the Right;
And who shall proclaim her the weaker, when
   Her very presence puts sin to flight?

'And dreads she never the coming years?' —
   Gossip, what are the years to her?
All winds are fair, and the harbor nears,
   And every breeze a delight will stir.

Transfigured under the sunset trees,
   That wreathe her with shadowy gold and red,
She looks away to the purple seas,
   Whereon her shallop will soon be sped.

She reads the hereafter by the here:
   A beautiful Now, and a better To Be:
In life is all sweetness, in death no fear: —
   You waste your pity on such as she.

*Lucy Larcom*

(Source: *The Poetical Works of Lucy Larcom*, Boston, Houghton, Mifflin & Co., 1884, pp. 26-7.)

# SUGGESTIONS FOR FURTHER READING

❋

## WOMEN'S HISTORY

1 *The American Jewish Woman, 1654-1980* and *The American Jewish Woman: A Documentary History* by Jacob Rader Marcus, respectively KTAV Publishing House, New York and American Jewish Archives, Cincinnati, 1981.

Special attention is paid to the circumstances of the unmarried woman during each period examined because, in part, of the significant number of Jewish women who chose to remain single rather than intermarry. Especially interesting on single women in business and in social welfare activities.

2 *Black Women in White America: A Documentary History* edited by Gerda Lerner, Vintage Books (Random House), New York, 1973.

Good source for beginning a study of Frances Ellen Watkins Harper.

3 *The Bonds of Womanhood, 'Woman's Sphere' in New England, 1780-1835* by Nancy F. Cott, Yale University Press, New Haven and London, 1977.

Using public records and private letters and diaries, this well-written historical study details carefully the relationships between private life and social change.

4 'The Cult of True Womanhood' by Barbara Welter originally appeared in *American Quarterly*, 1966; reprinted in *Dimity Convictions: The American Woman in the Nineteenth Century* by Barbara Welter, Ohio University Press, Athens, 1976.

5 *A Heritage of Her Own: Toward a New Social History of*

*American Women* edited and with an Introduction by Nancy F. Cott and Elizabeth H. Pleck, a Touchstone Book published by Simon & Schuster, New York, 1979.

6 *The Home: Its Work and Influence* by Charlotte Perkins Gilman, a reprint of the 1903 edition with an Introduction by William L. O'Neill, University of Illinois Press, Urbana, 1972. See especially Chapter XIII, 'The Girl at Home.'

7 *Liberty, A Better Husband: The Single Woman in Early Nineteenth Century America* by Lee Chambers-Schiller, forthcoming.

8 *The Remembered Gate: Origins of American Feminism, the Woman and the City, 1800-1860* by Barbara J. Berg, Oxford University Press, 1978. See especially Chapter 6, 'For Relief of the Body, Reconstruction of the Mind.'

9 *Woman's Share in Social Culture* by Anna Garlin Spencer, originally published by Mitchell Kennerley, New York and London, 1912; reprinted by Arno Press, New York, 1972. See especially Chapter IV, 'The Day of the Spinster.'

10 *Women's Diaries of the Westward Journey* by Lillian Schissel, Preface by Carl N. Degler, Gerda Lerner, Supervising Editor, Schocken Books, New York, 1982.

Interesting information on two women who made the westward trek as single women.

## LITERARY HISTORY

1 *The Development of the American Short Story: An Historical Survey* by Fred Lewis Pattee, Harper & Brothers, New York, 1923; reprinted by permission of Harper & Row, by Biblio & Tannen Booksellers and Publishers, New York, 1966.

2 *The Lowell Offering: Writings by New England Mill Women (1840-1845)*, edited and with an Introduction and Commentary by Benita Eisler, Harper Colophon Books (Harper & Row), New York, 1977.

3 *The Stereotype of the Single Woman in American Novels: A Social Study with Implications for the Education of Women* by Dorothy Yost Deegan, Octagon Books, Farrar, Straus & Giroux 1951, 1969.

# CONTEMPORARY CONSIDERATIONS OF THE SINGLE WOMAN

1 *Our Lives for Ourselves*: *Women Who Have Never Married* by Nancy L. Peterson, G. P. Putnam's Sons, New York, 1981. This interview-study of single women is especially interesting for the ways in which the themes from the nineteenth-century short stories are developed in the lives of these twentieth-century women.

2 *Solo*: *Women on Woman Alone* edited by Linda and Leo Hamalian, a Laurel Edition, Dell Publishing Co., New York, 1977. This is an international collection of twentieth-century short stories written by women about women — single, divorced, widowed — who are alone.

3 'Working at Single Bliss,' by Mary Helen Washington, *Ms. Magazine*, October 1982, pp. 55-8.

# PANDORA PRESS

an imprint of Routledge and Kegan Paul

For further information about Pandora Press books, please write to the Mailing List Dept at Pandora Press, 39 Store Street, London WC1E 7DD; or in the USA at 9, Park Street, Boston, Mass. 02108; or in Australia at 464 St. Kilda Road, Melbourne, Victoria 3004, Australia.

Some Pandora titles you may enjoy:

WOMEN'S HISTORY IN SHORT STORIES

the companion volume to Old Maids

## DARING TO DREAM

Utopian stories by United States women: 1836-1919

*Carol Farley Kessler*

Carol Farley Kessler has unearthed an extraordinary assortment of visionary writing, writings which encapsulate all the yearnings of a vanished generation for a future which has still to be made. Some women write with irony, describing journeys through time and space to parallel but inverted worlds where sober-suited women run commerce and affairs of state while men either prink and preen in beribboned breeches, or are weakened by the burden of unending housework. Other writers lay out complicated blueprints for a non-sexist society. One woman dreams, touchingly, of a fantastic future where men get up in the night to comfort crying children. The stories demonstrate that even in the early nineteenth century women were arguing that male and female 'character traits' were the product of their roles, not of their biology; and they make apparent the hidden roots of the discontent, longing and anger which was later to erupt in the great movements of women for change.

0-86358-013-0 Fiction/Social History 256pp 198 × 129 mm paperback

## ELIZABETH GASKELL : FOUR SHORT STORIES

The Three Eras of Libbie Marsh · Lizzie Leigh · The Well of Pen-Morfa · The Manchester Marriage

In her unaffected, direct description of the lives of working class women as lived out between the mean streets and the cotton mills of nineteenth century England, Elizabeth Gaskell chose to break with the literary conventions of Victorian ladies' fiction (which demanded genteel romances) and give her readers, instead, the harsh realities, the defiance and courage those lives entailed. Far from being delicate drawing room flowers, the characters in these four stories (collected here for the first time) are women who live unsupported by men, who labour and love and scheme and survive in strangely modern tales shot through with Gaskell's integrity of observation and deep compassion. The stories are prefaced by a long appreciation of Gaskell's life and work by Anna Walters.

'Mrs Gaskell draws the distinction between male and female values quietly, but forcefully' *School Librarian*

0-86358-001-7 Fiction/Criticism 122pp 198 × 129 mm introduced by Anna Walters paperback.


## DISCOVERING WOMEN'S HISTORY

a practical manual

*Deirdre Beddoe*

Rainy Sunday afternoons, long winter evenings: why not set yourself a research project, either on your own or in a group or classroom? This is the message from Deirdre Beddoe, an historian who tears away the mystique of her own profession in this step-by-step guide to researching the lives of ordinary women in Britain from 1800 to 1945. *Discovering Women's History* tells you how to get started on the detective trail of history and how to stalk your quarry through attics and art galleries, museums and old newspapers, church archives and the Public Records Office – and how to publish your findings once you have completed your project.

'an invaluable and fascinating guide to the raw material for anyone approaching this unexplored territory' *The Sunday Times*

'Thrilling and rewarding and jolly good fun' *South Wales Argus*

0-86358-008-4 Hobbies/Social History 232pp 198 × 129 mm illustrated

## ALL THE BRAVE PROMISES

Memories of Aircraftwomen 2nd Class 2146391

*Mary Lee Settle*

Mary Lee Settle was a young American woman living a comfortable life in Washington D.C. when the Second World War broke out. In 1942 she boarded a train, carrying 'a last bottle of champagne and an armful of roses', and left for England to join the WAAF. She witnessed the horror of war – the bombing raids, the planes lost in fog, the children evacuated, a blacked-out Britain of austerity and strain. She also witnessed the women, her fellow recruits, as they struggled to adapt to their new identities and new lives at the bottom of the uniformed pile. Dedicated 'to the wartime other ranks of the Women's Auxiliary Air Force – below the rank of Sergeant', this rare book captures women's wartime experience; a remarkable and important story by one of America's prizewinning novelists.

'One of the most moving accounts of war experience ever encountered' *Library Journal*

0-86358-033-5 General/Autobiography 160pp 198 × 129 mm paperback
*not for sale in the U.S.A. or Canada*


## MY COUNTRY IS THE WHOLE WORLD

an anthology of women's work on peace and war

*Cambridge Women's Peace Collective* (eds)

Women's struggle for peace is no recent phenomenon. In this book, the work of women for peace from 600 BC to the present is documented in a unique collection of extracts from songs, poems, diaries, letters, petitions, pictures, photographs and pamphlets through the ages. A book to give as a gift, to read aloud from, to research from, to teach from, *My Country is the Whole World* is both a resource and an inspiration for all who work for peace today.

'an historic document . . . readers will be amazed at the extent of the collection' *Labour Herald*

'a beautifully presented and illustrated book which makes for accessible and enlightening reading' *Morning Star*

0-86358-004-1 Social Questions/History 306pp A5 illustrated throughout paperback